MUST LOVE

Plague

A SISTERS OF THE APOCALYPSE NOVEL

SHELLY CHALMERS

For Matt and my girls. Thank you for your support, your love, and the many times you've not only talked me out of quitting, but in to reaching for my own success. I couldn't do this without you, and nor would I want to. You and the girls make me strong enough to reach for my dreams. You are my very own HEA.

This book is also for all the stubborn dreamers. Never give up. Don't keep waiting for someone to give you a HEA – make one for yourself. I know you can do it.

ACKNOWLEDGMENTS

This book wouldn't exist without the contributions of so many others, so you'll have to forgive me for the really long acknowledgments section.

Thank you to my 2014 Dreamweaver sisters, without whom this book probably wouldn't exist. Your experience, knowledge, and support helps keep me writing. You are all an inspiration.

A big thanks to my editor, Tera Cuskaden, for helping me shape this book into something worth reading—all errors are definitely my own. Thank you to Christa Holland with Paper & Sage for the beautiful cover and your artistic vision.

This book was very loosely inspired by the wonderful small town I live near—which is so much more beautiful, welcoming, and charming than I could hope for. All the bad things about Beckwell are strictly a work of my imagination. Thank you for being a place I'm proud to raise my children.

To my critique partner extraordinaire, Shelly Alexander: you continue to help me become a better writer through your wisdom, patience, and sense of humor. Thank you for answering my many questions, putting up with me...and for going through all the incarnations this book has experienced.

To my dearest friend, Neelam: thank you for being my number one fan for years...but never letting me get away with anything. You make me a better writer, and a better person. I'm forever grateful.

Last, but never least, thank you to my family and friends, for your support and belief in me. You keep me going. And if you want to skip a few chapters or scenes, I'm totally cool with that. It doesn't make you any less wonderful or supportive.   SC

CHAPTER 1

Normal was highly underrated. Especially if your entire childhood had been as distinctly *para*normal as Piper Bane's. It wasn't as though a kindergartner enjoyed the scrutiny, the whispers about how she might end the world.

Piper tightened damp hands on the steering wheel of her rental SUV. The dark shadowy blotch of the town sign would be visible soon, welcoming her home to Beckwell, Alberta.

Rock music pulsed through the speakers, at odds with the idyllic old clapboard homestead on the right. Slate October skies roiled uneasily and brightened the soaring yellow and orange stands of trees that segregated acres of rolling fields. This late in the season, the fields all had a military brush cut, hedged in on all sides by barbed wire.

Piper swallowed her nausea. She could do this. She might have to toss her cookies first, but she could come home for her best friend's wedding this weekend, and get out, never to return. Never to have anything to do with all the expectations, the weirdness associated with her hometown.

The SUV whizzed past the green sign marking the closest neighboring town of Buttercreek. Piper swallowed. Maybe ten minutes out now. Beckwell wasn't on any maps, to protect all of the paranormal folks who lived there…and to protect any Normals from accidentally ending up there. Lucky buggers.

Oh, Ginny. Why couldn't you have gotten married somewhere—anywhere—else? Antarctica is nice this time of year, isn't it?

She blew out an unsteady breath. Coming home had seemed less insane six thousand kilometers ago, back in that lonely hotel room in Edinburgh. There was only so long you could live out of a suitcase before the hotel rooms all started to look the same, one town blurring with the next.

The tree-lined highway and the fields looked unchanged in the ten years since she'd stepped foot in Beckwell. Ten years since she'd seen the place where she grew up, where her three closest friends still lived. Ten years since Piper Bane, Pestilence clan, had anything to do with the world she'd been born into. A world where myths held some grain of truth, magic was real, her family was part of the horsemen dynasty, and unicorns could fly. Okay, that last part wasn't true and probably wishful thinking, but the rest?

Yep, she was related to those four horsemen of the apocalypse: Death, War, Famine, and Pestilence. Who, when they weren't off causing disaster, had apparently gotten it on with every surviving female they met, creating clans that were now large and spread worldwide. Kind of like royal family lines, where some members were rich and powerful—in both human and non-human ways. The more powerful stood the best chance of becoming the true embodiment of their clan, to ride into the apocalypse as a true horseman and carry forth destruction.

The radio station turned to static. Piper shuddered. Definitely getting close now. She pushed the button and shut the static off, leaving only the collected ghosts of memory filling the car. Her stomach hardened.

What a nightmare. She'd held out hope that someone else would gain the powers of Pestilence, because when they did, they absorbed all the powers of their clan. Poof. Piper would finally be normal. You know…for that little while before the world ended. But she'd be *normal.* Life would be easier if she were normal. Average. Those people got to fall in love, have kids, have happy lives.

So far, though, no one had taken a ride on that damned horse, which left her in limbo.

Even with a tiny amount of ability—her family was more along the trailer-park trash level of the Pestilence family tree—she was still like asbestos. The longer you were around her, the more likely you were to get sick. And she'd sworn ten years ago she would never make anyone sick, ever again.

She tucked her pale hair behind an ear, a faint tremble in her fingertips and a small frown tightening her lips. Living out of a suitcase wasn't so bad. No, she could never spend more than a month in any one place. But unless she wanted to settle in a paranormal sanctuary like Beckwell, where people knew what the name "Bane" connoted, it was the closest to normal she could get.

Even if it was sometimes a bit lonely.

She fiddled with the radio controls on the steering wheel. Even cowboy music would be better than the silence, but there was only static, like jeers and hisses. In Beckwell, mystical powers ran through the ancient bloodlines of all the residents, and the nastier the family tree, the better. Having horns or being the descendant of some mythic creature no one ever liked was a *good* thing. Part of the town had always wanted her to be a full-fledged horsemen, willing to spread disease with a touch of a fingertip. Seriously, who wanted the powers of Pestilence anyway? Spreading disease and plague wasn't all it was cracked up to be.

Yet, the other part of the town—the ones with families and a somewhat-normal existence—they'd feared her and her friends from the start. If only they'd known Piper didn't want an apocalypse any more than they did.

She gave up on the radio, tried to relax the tightness in her neck.

Here she was. Less than eight minutes out from Beckwell. Gulp.

Ten years ago, she'd left here running. Heartbroken after she'd ended her engagement to the only man she'd ever loved with every cell of her being. Daniel Quilan.

Believing she was over him was a lot easier with both time and distance between them.

The wooden town sign hunkered in the shade of gold and yellow poplar trees and hazelnut bushes, like a gloomy shadow. Someone repainted it every year, but somehow it reverted back to peeling and foreboding. Too far away to read, she knew it said "Beckwell" in white. Her stomach churned. Could she really handle a few days with her family, possibly seeing Daniel, all the mess that was Beckwell?

Piper's foot lifted slightly from the gas pedal.

Just beyond the sign and to the left squatted the huge Cow Palace barn, a faded fuchsia glory in the middle of the town agricultural grounds, stacks of bleachers pushed together in the off-season. To the right was Sal's Autobody. Rows of cars gleamed through the surrounding brush.

What wasn't visible was the town barrier that made Beckwell the sanctuary it was and protected those with latent magic in their blood. It also protected the outside world from those magicals, and all the things normal people didn't really want to know about. The barrier sensed ability in the blood, and made Normals feel like pissing themselves. So far, worked like a charm. It usually killed their cars before they could pass through, leaving plenty of business for Sal to tow away.

Piper scrunched down in the seat and tried to imagine exactly where the border was. It creeped her out. Always had, always would. How was it not creepy—magic touching her all over, reading her blood?

Secretly, she'd always wondered if one of these days it would figure out she'd never really belonged in Beckwell, and wouldn't let her in.

After all her travels, she'd started to wonder if there was anywhere she *did* belong.

She sucked in a shuddering breath that didn't quell the nausea. The girls were waiting for her at the bar, and—glancing at the dash clock—she was already late. Ginny was her best friend. She couldn't skip her best friend's wedding. Besides, if she didn't make peace with Beckwell and her past, she'd always keep looking over her shoulder, waiting for it to catch up.

Piper hit the gas. The quicker she got through the barrier, the better.

The SUV chewed up pavement. The Beckwell sign grew larger.

The engine sputtered and went silent. The dash lights went black. Piper pumped the gas, then tried to move her foot to the brake. The spike of her kitten heel stuck in the floor mat. The wheel wouldn't turn.

She whimpered, frozen wheel clenched between her fingers, unable to look away from the rapidly approaching sign.

A large, fat toad plopped onto her windshield. Piper flinched. It turned and met her gaze, eyes huge and black, before giving an annoyed croak that sent a chill down her back.

Icy pinpricks settled over her skin. The air thickened around her, smothering her in sticky coldness like she'd been doused in wet cement. All she and the toad could do was watch the Beckwell sign and the huge old tree grow ever closer until the crunch of impact.

CHAPTER 2

Someone in town was planning an apocalypse. And where there was mischief, even the world-ending kind, five-to-one odds said his twin brother was in on it.

Daniel combed his fingers through his dark hair and rolled broad shoulders, weighed down after a long day of medical calls. His old truck grumbled along the road toward downtown Beckwell. The asphalt cut through thick boreal forest that concealed most of Beckwell's small population on farms and acreages that spread out from the town center like a disjointed spider web. "Downtown Beckwell" itself was a misnomer, seeing as it consisted of the four-way stop and small assortment of businesses clustered around it. Beckwell was many things, but big it was not. You'd miss it if you blinked. There wasn't even a traffic light to slow you down.

He still had to stop by the Senior Center and finish some paperwork. It'd been the only place in town with facilities to set up his practice and office. This last call had been out to the Ares place for chest pains. Lucky for

Old Man Ares it'd been nothing more than a second helping of Mrs. Ares's extra-spicy chili. But at least they'd called him. He'd been practicing medicine in Beckwell going on four years, but only recently had people to adjusted to the idea of asking a Fomorian for help. Usually after an encounter with a Fomorian, you *needed* help. Maybe even traction, or a visit to Intensive Care.

Gods, but he'd rather have been any other species. Anything other than like Dad. The bullies of the paranormal world, Fomorians were hard-living warriors with a knack for chaos, drinking and fighting. Large and muscular, sometimes even with wings, horns or tails, Dad always used to say they were made for the three "Fs": fighting, fury, and fornicating—though Dad preferred a different "F" word.

Fortunately, Daniel was the family black sheep. He'd gone into medicine. Helped people. Healed people. Did everything to prove that just because he had Dad's Fomorian genes, it didn't mean he had to turn out the same.

His brother, Mal, on the other hand, had always made the family proud.

Daniel's truck rumbled toward the stop sign. Sheila Dryad was filling up at the gas station to his right, shouting at two of her satyr sons chasing each other around the car on hooved feet, while her daughter slouched in the backseat of the minivan. Beautiful but harried, Sheila waved when she saw Daniel. A nymph happily married to a satyr, her family was one of many in Beckwell by necessity.

Unlike some of the other creatures who could blend into human society, Beckwell residents like the Dryads couldn't live elsewhere. They couldn't blend. Even if they wanted to. Beckwell was their haven, one of a few magical sanctuaries in this part of the world, and be darned if Daniel would let anyone—including his brother—take that away from them. He might only be the town doctor, but for better or for worse, this was his home and these were his people.

Sheila shouted at the boys again as a slick BMW pulled into the parking lot and stopped beside the bar next door. Ginny Lack climbed out from the driver's seat, her copper hair glinting in the afternoon sun. She didn't notice Daniel. Maybe she was distracted by her upcoming wedding. Instead, her cheeks flushed, arms waving, she spoke animatedly to her passenger.

Diminutive and black-clad Nia Amort stepped out from the other side of the car, and the two women entered the bar. Once, the two women had been his friends. Once, he would have rolled down the window and called hello. Maybe joined them for a beer. Congratulated Ginny in person on her engagement.

Not anymore.

Not since Piper Bane had left, taking his heart with her. But, despite his estrangement from Ginny and the other women, he'd still been invited to the wedding along with everyone else in town, and Ginny had sent a hand-written invite to the engagement party. And as of now, he hadn't come up with a viable excuse not to go. To avoid seeing Piper in the flesh.

The image of clear amber eyes and hair so blonde it was almost white flashed through his mind. The woman's hair blew across her face as her coral pink lips turned up in a seductive smile.

He shook the image out of his head and pulled up to the four-way stop. Blinked. Then leaned forward over the wheel. Was that his brother walking down the highway up ahead?

A faded 1965 custom Dodge silver convertible rolled into the grocery/gas station/bar parking lot to his right and honked, breaking his focus. The iron-haired lady who climbed out from behind the wheel was Ms. Boniface. School principal, she also seemed to feel it was her duty to direct the goings-on in town, too. She signaled for Daniel to roll down his window, approaching his truck.

He pasted on his best don't-make-the-lady-mad smile and cranked down the window. "Good afternoon, Ms. Boniface."

"Daniel. Any word yet when we can expect your brother to actually start performing the duties he was hired for? It's been six months. And I haven't seen one instance of Malcolm performing any policing duties. Instead, he seems content to get in drunken brawls with those cousins of yours and anyone else who happens to get in his way."

Daniel rubbed the back of his neck and felt the beginnings of a headache. "I'm sorry to hear that, Ms. Boniface," he said wearily. As though he wasn't more than aware of what Mal had been up to. The drinking and fighting were some of the less concerning behaviors. "I'll talk to him." Again. Because the first five times had been so productive.

He'd convinced the town council to hire his brother as the sole peace officer. The position had been vacant four years now. It'd seemed like a good idea at the time: give Mal purpose again, and a reason to stay in Beckwell. And out of trouble.

Hadn't worked out so well.

"Well. See that you do. With the Lack wedding on Saturday, there will be visitors from out of town who might bring who knows what trouble. Never mind the inevitable drunkenness and shenanigans that typically accompany events of this nature."

Trust Ms. Boniface to see a wedding as a disruption.

"Yes, ma'am. And until then, you can depend on

me to help out in my brother's place." Because there was always plenty of spare time for policing while also running the town's sole medical practice. He needed to find some kind of twelve-step-program to learn to stop volunteering.

"Excellent. There's a town council meeting tomorrow." She turned to stride back to her car in the parking lot, then turned back with a frown. "And please, could you secure that sign pointing out the Lack residence? I understand the fiancé still hasn't arrived, and we don't need him or any out-of-towners wandering willy-nilly all over the place." She offered a tight smile and marched off toward the bar, Lou's Place, without even waiting for an answer.

Daniel glanced at the signpost to his left and reluctantly noted that the arrow for Ginny's wedding did indeed look loose. For Ginny, he pulled over, and went around back to rummage in his toolbox for a hammer and a couple of nails before he headed for the post.

Said signpost was a big old clunker that pointed out all of Beckwell's chief attractions with crooked arrows. Like the library and school. The emergency station off to his right. The Cow Palace and agricultural grounds farther down the highway.

And one crooked, faded arrow labeled "Loki." Seeing as Loki, the reclusive town founder, was not standing at the end of the arrow, Daniel assumed it pointed in the direction of Loki's residence. The only person Daniel knew with the cajones—and gall—to follow the sign was his brother, Mal. He'd never told Daniel what he found on the other end.

Thinking of Mal brought Daniel's brows together, and he gently pried the foam-core arrow reading "Lack-Derth Wedding" off the post and held it as high as he could before stabbing it with a nail. One advantage to being Fomorian was nearly six and a half feet in height.

If only Mal didn't have to relish all the other parts about being Fomorian. Not the wings and horns—none of those, thank gods, but all the rest.

Daniel missed the nail and almost hit his thumb.

Mal hadn't been the same since he'd left the Royal Canadian Mounted Police. Which was why the policing job here in town had seemed like a good idea. Give him focus again. Mal had always had a natural affinity for the dark—and his dark side—but he'd become even more self-destructive and reckless. When he was around, bad things were more likely to happen. Even if he hadn't initiated the trouble.

Daniel hit the nail too hard and it bent. He grumbled and set about straightening it enough to hang the darned sign.

He didn't have Mal's charisma or fondness for mischief. At best, he was like a super-charged lucky rabbit's foot. And he was strong—never a sick day since grade two, and that had been to stay home and take care of Mom.

But, he was the oldest by two minutes, which made it his responsibility to look out for Mal.

He pounded the nail flat and headed back to the truck. Either it was a Fomorian thing or a twin thing, but he and Mal also shared strong emotions through a mental link. And Mal had been feeling disturbingly pleased with himself these past few days, in a darkly cynical fashion.

Which probably meant he was getting into trouble. Possibly involved with this latest Beckwellian plot to start the apocalypse.

He put the truck in Drive. Beckwell was a town of outsiders and rebels. The gods and more powerful beings had ignored and taunted their unpopular Beckwell-cousins too often, which led to a surplus of apocalypse plots. This time was more dangerous because the plot was rumored to involve the horsewomen. With Piper headed to Beckwell for the wedding, that meant all four of them were back in town.

If those four friends decided to end the world, there wasn't an earthly force that could stop them. Ten years ago, he never would have believed Piper or her three friends would consider using that deadly power. But a lot changed in ten years. People changed.

Light glinted off a car ahead on the highway. His gaze snapped up in time to see a silver SUV speed down the highway ahead and plunge into the trees.

Not again.

CHAPTER 3

Daniel hit the gas and made the old blue pickup grumble and rattle in protest. With the faded fuchsia Cow Palace barn to his right, he jerked the truck into Park, grabbed his med bag from the passenger seat, and jumped out, leaving the door open.

The barrier caught the occasional tourist every now and then. Usually it just killed the car. Sometimes, it killed the tourist.

Hopefully someone at emergency response had seen the crash, too, but they were mostly volunteer and he couldn't slow now. He was the best emergency medical care available to the driver out here.

Steam rose from the SUV's crumpled hood where it had bent around a large poplar tree, and somehow, miraculously, missed the Beckwell town sign. The engine was quiet, no visible spills, and the smell of gasoline was faint. The white billow of the air bag filled the driver's seat and began to deflate as he ran up to the car.

He had to put his shoulder into it, but the door opened with a groan, just in time for the airbag to settle around the driver like a perverted stage curtain. The sight of that pale blonde hair, the petite body, hit him like a two-by-four to the gut.

There she lay. Peaceful and beautiful. Still as death.

His hand clenched on the doorframe for a millisecond before he jerked back to action and checked for a pulse. It was hell to try and ignore her silken skin and focus on being a doctor, not just a man. He closed his eyes a moment and bowed his head a moment when he found a pulse.

Forcing his eyes open, he gently felt her neck for potential damage. His fingers shook as silky strands of hair slid over his hand.

"Piper, can you hear me? You've been in an accident. I'm here to help," he said loudly, firmly. His throat thickened. "It's Daniel."

Her pulse was steady. She was breathing well. It didn't look like she was bleeding. Heck, she had only a light dusting of powder from the airbag and it didn't look like it had even broken her nose. Sleeping Beauty, waiting for her Prince's kiss.

A large brown toad croaked at him before it hopped off the hood and disappeared into the underbrush.

Piper frowned and groaned. Her pale eyelashes tinted dark with mascara fluttered open. Her gaze zeroed in on him, and she licked her lips.

An electrical jolt of awareness shook through Daniel as their gazes met, those amber eyes just as he remembered them. Decades melted away, and he was staring down into her eyes as he rose above her body, her lips parting when she came.

Confusion filled that amber gaze now, coupled with wariness and recognition. She lifted a hand to her plump, moist lips before she slid it down the slim, pale length of her throat. Toward the low cut of her blouse, the silk artfully folding over her breasts. He tried to shake off his distraction, pushing himself through a medical checklist. Pupils even. No visible lumps or swelling. No blood. No liquid discharge from the ears.

Eyes gold like an angel's. Hair against his fingers like silken threads. Skin still smooth and lush.

"Did you…" Her voice cracked. She licked dry lips and tried again. "Did you see the toad?" Her voice was still simultaneously husky and sweet.

Yeah, and she'd just been in a car accident. He gently took her chin in his hand and checked her pupils again. Still even. "I saw it. Do you feel any pain or pressure anywhere? Can you wiggle your fingers and toes?"

Ignoring him, she raised a hand to her temple and rubbed her forehead, fingers trembling. "That stupid barrier killed my car and sent me into a tree." She dropped her hand and surveyed the car before she made a face. "Argh. I'm going to owe the rental company some cash. Just what I needed."

She started to turn her head. What if he'd missed an injury? Where the heck was emergency response?

"Piper, don't—"

She waved him off. "I'm fine. See? My head didn't fall off." She pressed the release on her seatbelt and turned toward him. Then held up her hands and waggled all ten fingers. Not a one of them had a ring. "Nothing hurts other than my rental agreement and bank account." She sighed. "Do you think I could sue Beckwell for damages? It's their barrier."

"Uh…no?" Yep, definitely a genius response. Daniel straightened and tried to ignore her familiar scent, but the fragrance of lilacs, summer thunderstorms, and hot, damp nights, curled around him, made him want to forget ten years had passed. Forget she'd dumped him in a move that would have hurt less if she'd dug out his heart with a plastic spoon.

He switched to his "I'm the doctor and I know what's best" voice. "Piper, you've been in a serious accident. We should get you to the Senior Center, maybe even to the city, to get you checked out."

"I'm fine, really. And I just got here. I'm not going all the way back to the city." She rolled her eyes, leaned over to grab a purse from the passenger seat before she straightened and tried to push him aside.

Her hand paused against his chest, fingers tangling in his shirt. She flushed and her gaze snapped to his.

He stood as immobile as the tree she'd hit, which had fared better than the SUV. "Piper, you could be more seriously injured than you know." His voice was thick and rough. And other parts of his anatomy were responding the same way. He tried to clear his throat, remember he was a doctor and she was in his care. "You could be in shock and not feeling the pain. You just hit a tree—"

She swung her legs around and slid out of the car. Which, unfortunately, meant she slid against him. Every inch of her petite frame aligned with his. His every nerve-ending went on high alert. She stared up at him, her fingers clenching the front of his shirt. Her lips parted. Delicious, lush lips. Her mouth was the perfect height for his if she came up on tiptoe and he bent over her.

He was keenly aware of how thin her skinny jeans were. Her warm thighs pressed against him, still slim, but rounder with maturity. Her breasts thrust against his chest, her silk blouse providing little barrier to the soft warmth against him, the memory of their weight in his palms, the way her nipples hardened in his hands.

Crud. He was in big trouble.

She'd just been in a car accident. He shouldn't have

let her out of the car, let alone be thinking about how good she felt against him while she could be suffering some kind of head injury.

But she was Piper Bane, who'd always reduced him to a pile of hormones, lust, and need with just a smile. Never mind how she spiked his protective instincts.

Yep. *Big* trouble.

"Daniel, I need you to step out of my way," she said, a slight breathlessness in her voice. She stared up at him, the vulnerability in her amber gaze doing him in the way it always had. She'd looked that way when she'd handed back the ring box, making him feel like he should make *her* feel better even though she'd served up his heart on a platter.

"You might be hurt," he offered lamely.

"Do I look hurt?"

"Well, no." She looked vibrant. Delicious. Tempting.

Her lips turned up in something that should have been a smile, but wasn't. She dropped her hand from his chest, and broke eye contact. "Besides, you're Daniel Quilan. Nothing bad ever happens when you're around, so I guess I should count myself lucky you were the first one I met when I got back, huh?"

"Yeah, sure." Them meeting the second she hit town was anything *but* lucky. He'd spent two days dreaming up ways he might avoid running into her as soon as he'd heard she planned to attend the wedding.

He had too much he had to take care of now. Namely, figuring out what trouble Mal was into this time and getting him out of it. Before it stirred up something worse. In Beckwell, trouble didn't mean teens causing a nuisance or the occasional act of vandalism. It meant apocalyptic troubles that had worldwide consequences. He couldn't afford to be distracted by Piper, by her scent, or by the way her breasts felt against him. He couldn't be distracted by the longing she stirred in him, the way that he'd always known exactly where he belonged when she was in his arms.

"Um, Daniel? Can you let me go?" Piper interrupted.

He should have let her and everything about their relationship go years ago. How was he supposed to ignore her? She was seductive temptation on two legs. Her and that sexy low-cut blouse, which from this angle displayed the most delicious enticement…He bit back a groan. A hint of purple lace against pale flesh he wanted to explore with his mouth and his tongue. Definitely tongue.

Piper cleared her throat, color creeping up her cheekbones.

He ran another quick visual assessment over her, even though he was really covering his return to horny teenager by pretending to be a doctor.

Unlike Mal, good things happened when Daniel was around. People survived accidents, medical crises, and the underdog won.

Although Piper appealed to the darker side of his nature, too. He wanted her. He'd dated through medical school and before he came back to Beckwell, but he'd always kept it safe and casual. It helped that no one affected him the way Piper had. After all these years, after all the ways he'd thought he'd changed, moved past her, he still craved her. She made him feel powerful, masculine, and like a flipping prince in shining armor.

Which was exactly why he had to stay as far away from her as he could. She *did* make him powerful. He and his brother grew stronger at a proportionate rate. Which meant Piper also made Mal powerful. And more dangerous. She called to the Fomorian in him, who wanted to conquer and enjoy every delectable inch of her.

He stepped aside and shoved a hand through his hair, trying to settle his body down from the ten-alarm blaze that roared through him at the briefest of contact with Piper. He hadn't felt that way with anyone before or since.

She went around to the back of the SUV, her little heels and slick clothing poorly suited to Beckwell.

He glanced down at his own khaki slacks and blue, button-up short-sleeve shirt. He probably looked like a country hick to her. Not as cosmopolitan as she'd become.

Piper's annoyed muttering jarred him out of his thoughts. She came around from the back of the SUV with a large pink, cheetah-print, hard-sided suitcase. She hauled it over the grass and scrub, her heels digging into the soft ground.

"For Pete's sake, Piper, let me take that." He leaped to her side. Crud. She'd just been in an accident, and here he was mooning about the past and coincidences. *Definitely proving yourself a great doc today, buddy.*

Piper shook her head. "I'm good." A small, tight smile. "I'm used to taking care of myself." She fought with the ridiculous suitcase. The wheels caught in the gravel, and her purse flopped against her thigh as she hauled it onto the pavement.

All while he stood there like an idiot. He stepped forward again. "I know you can take care of yourself. I just want to help."

She jumped away from him like he was dangerous and shoved her purse up onto her shoulder. Her face flushed, and her gaze flicked quickly away from his. "No. Thank you. I'm good." She paused a moment. "You don't have to take care of me anymore, Daniel," she said softly.

Yes, but I want to.

Almost as though she'd heard him, her gaze fell,

and she turned, headed off at a brisk pace down the highway toward town. "I'm not your responsibility anymore. Haven't been for some time."

The suitcase bounced along behind her, catching in every dip in the road. Her heels click-clicked along the asphalt, and a breeze shushed through the poplar trees lining the highway.

He clenched his hands a minute, watching after her. Geezus. Piper Bane. Every inch as breathtaking as she'd been when she'd left. Five-feet-six inches of pure temptation.

And no longer mine.

He shook his head, then scooped up his med bag and half-jogged back to his truck in front of the driveway to the Cow Palace. The engine still idled and grumbled away, the driver's side door wide open. He shut the truck off, slammed the door, and looked up.

He had seen Mal before. And now there went his brother, headed into the Cow Palace—which was closed for the season.

The click-click of Piper's heels was getting farther away. Daniel rubbed his ear. He and Mal had to talk later anyway. He'd ask about the Cow Palace then.

Daniel grabbed the keys and turned to jog after Piper. Everyone recognized the rusty, pockmarked truck, and the road was never busy.

He slowed a few feet behind her. "I know you're not my responsibility. But you were just in an accident. And you're a guest here in Beckwell. I was just being polite," he called. *You were supposed to avoid her. To focus on Mal. And on the threat to Beckwell. And a thousand other things other than the girl—woman—who broke your heart.*

Piper paused. Waited for him to catch up before she shot him a sideways look. She looked fresh, sweet, and sexy, a grown-up version of the spontaneous, passionate girl he'd known who dreamed big. Nothing like the cool persona she portrayed online, the woman who dated rock-stars and traveled the world, sharing her adventures on her blog.

Which he didn't read.

More than once a week.

He might have been better off if she'd been more like that woman and less like the girl he'd loved.

"I know you take your responsibilities and the protection of Beckwell seriously, but are you sure that's all it is?" She gave him a long look and cocked up a brow. A look that said she might have known he'd been staring at her butt. And noticed the purple bra.

His palms grew damp. "Of course."

"Oh. Good." She gave him a distant smile, the kind you gave to strangers. "Well, thank you for your help. Have a nice life, Daniel." She turned and continued marching.

He should have left it at that. He should have let her walk away. Again. Instead, he strode easily at her side, one of his long steps equal to two or three of her short, agitated steps. "You should probably stop by the office. Just so I can make sure you don't have a concussion, no lasting effects from the accident."

She frowned. "I don't think that's a good idea."

Of course, it wasn't a good idea.

Mal, remember? Group causing trouble. Your practice. The five-billion other things you should be thinking about rather than how Piper Bane's lips used to taste?

He cleared his throat. "You're probably right. Just…if there is anything, if you need me, have any problems, my clinic is over at the Senior Center."

Her cheeks flushed pink and she wouldn't meet his gaze. "Yeah. Sure. Thanks, Daniel. And, you know, thanks for the rescue." She turned and hurried away, the rapid click of her heels and impatient jerks on her suitcase indicating just how desperate she was to escape his presence.

He shoved a hand through his hair before he turned to head back to the truck. Could he have been any more pathetic?

So much for having moved on. It'd be better for both of them when Piper left town again.

He frowned. Neither of them might want his help, but how was he supposed to protect Piper *and* his brother?

CHAPTER 4

Daniel. It had to be Daniel to come to her rescue. Again. As always.

Piper cursed beneath her breath and dragged her suitcase over the gravel parking lot the bar shared with the general store, the post office, and the gas station. The suitcase hadn't seemed that big until she'd had to haul it out of an SUV that was tangled in bushes and drag it down the highway.

The girls were waiting at the bar, and honestly, maybe she had head trauma from the accident or something, but there had definitely been a toad, hadn't there?

She could have, maybe should have, let Daniel help her.

The suitcase thunked up the three wood steps to Beckwell Restaurant and Pub, otherwise known as Lou's Place. It looked like a cross between a Victorian bordello and a biker bar, complete with steel door. One step more, and her heel stuck between the gap of two boards on the porch. She tried jerking it free. Nothing.

She slipped her foot out of the shoe and bent over to yank it out. A car honked and teenagers hooted in appreciation for her rear.

The shoe popped free, and Piper almost somersaulted headfirst into the steel door.

She touched trembling, cold fingertips to her forehead and sucked in a shaky breath. Maybe a good concussion would knock some sense into her. What had she been thinking coming home? She'd barely made it back to town and she'd already been in a car accident and humiliated herself in front of her ex.

Her hands shook as she slipped the shoe back onto her foot. Daniel, who yet again had to rescue her and looked impossibly better than she remembered. His skin still had a sun-kissed glow darkened by his First-Nations heritage, which had also gifted him with killer cheekbones and soulful, dark eyes. He made her hotter just saying her *name* than some guys had done with an hour of serious effort.

But he wasn't hers. Not since she'd handed that ring back to him and he'd just stared down at it in his hand, like he didn't recognize what it was.

She swallowed past a thick throat and straightened her shoulders. The girls were waiting, and it wasn't like she had a ride out of here.

She reached for the door, but it opened, and Piper jumped out of the way as an older woman stepped through.

"Oh, I'm—" The words died on the other woman's lips, her hair and spine as steely as the door. Ms. Boniface, the fear of every history student at Beckwell School, who'd always taken particular delight in calling on Piper when she knew a) Piper wasn't paying attention, and b) Piper didn't know the answer. The school catered only to Beckwell students and went all the way to high school, so Piper had been stuck with the woman for thirteen years.

There was no proof, but Piper was also almost certain the woman had always turned a blind eye on the mean nymphs who'd spread the rumors that Piper had slept with every boy in the school.

Piper stuck a pale smile on her lips. Frick. She probably looked like something the cat had dragged home. Being in a car accident wouldn't be an acceptable excuse to Ms. Boniface.

"Hi, Ms. Boniface."

Ms. Boniface straightened in her serviceable Oxfords and offered a tight smile, touching the tiny silver pin depicting shears she'd always worn on her lapel. In Beckwell it was considered rude to ask someone about their pedigree, associated myth, and ancestors. All the families who lived there had lived in fear of the gods and hatred of their kind for too many centuries for that instinct to hide their true selves to disappear in a few short centuries. But gossip spread like wildfire, and there'd always been bets on who was who. Everyone pegged Ms. Boniface as one of the Fates. Probably the mean one who cut the thread and killed people.

"Why, Miss Bane. You've made it back to town, and just in time. How fortunate. I hope nothing…delayed you?"

Something in her look almost suggested she knew about the accident. Or maybe Piper's doubts about coming home. "I wouldn't miss Ginny's wedding."

Ms. Boniface's lips spread into something that would have resembled a smile if piranhas could smile. "Oh, I'm looking forward to it, too," she said with especially creepy relish. "Enjoy your stay, Ms. Bane."

Piper watched the old spider retreat to her faded silver Chevy convertible parked out front, and shivered.

Add Ms. Boniface's name to the list of "to be avoided" during the visit.

She turned back. Okay, better get inside, face the music and dance before the town threw any other unpleasant surprises her way. Piper pushed open the heavy steel door to the bar, giving her eyes a moment to adjust to the dimmer light.

Country-Western music played, a bouncy tune at odds with the few occupants. Two large men hunched at the bar. Other customers gathered in clutches around the tables in mismatched wood chairs.

The large, antique bar against the far wall dominated the room, mirrors and bottles lined up behind it. The bartender, Lou, a big guy who liked plaid, had a beer gut, and more hair on his chin than on his head, restocked the clean glasses.

All conversation ceased and all eyes turned to Piper and her suitcase.

Piper swallowed, and her face heated.

Lou lifted a hand in greeting, then pointed to the left, where her three friends huddled around a table: Ginny Lack, Anna Fray, and Nia Amort.

Piper spotted the girls, and a sudden giddiness flooded through her and added a bounce to her step. She hadn't called enough, should have made the effort to keep in touch with these women who'd been her friends since kindergarten.

She bee-lined toward the table. It was unusual for a town as small as theirs to have all four horsemen clans represented, and even more unusual, the four youngest representatives were the same age. Which had only fueled the rumors that it wasn't coincidence and they would be the four to rise. The fact that the clans could blend with Normals, unlike many other Beckwell residents, also hadn't earned them allies, and had meant they'd been thrown together perpetually at school. Not like any of the other parents wanted their children playing with Death, War, Famine, or Pestilence. As fellow clans, they were immune to one another's abilities, and their relationship had evolved as time wore on. No one else understood what it was like to have everyone constantly watching for a sign they were coming into their abilities. Abilities that would put them on equal footing with the gods, if the stories were to be believed.

Not exactly the kind of thing that earned you friends in high school.

Ginny, Famine clan, was red-headed and the tallest of the four at just under six feet. She spotted Piper first and jumped up from her chair, coming around the table for a hug. "You came!" Her embrace was a warm, soft squeeze, surrounding Piper with the sweet scent of baking, which seemed kind of cruel for a daughter of Famine. Though Ginny was definitely the sweetest of the four, and the most "normal," if that word could be applied to any of them.

"I wouldn't miss your wedding," Piper said, squeezing back and ignoring the twist of guilt at the fact she'd considered not coming. Ginny's hug was almost reason enough to have come home. That, and it was her sacred duty as a best friend to vet the fiancé. He might have also been a Famine clan member, but that didn't mean he was good enough for Ginny.

The two friends pulled back to better assess each other.

"You look even better than you did in high school," Ginny murmured. She scrunched up her face. "Mom found me a new diet, but I won't have lost all the weight I was supposed to before the wedding."

"You're curvy. Guys love that." Piper squeezed Ginny's hand.

Ginny *was* a bit softer around the middle than she'd

been in high school. Plus, she was dressed in Style by Mom, which today meant a hot-pink sweater set that clashed with her hair and white slacks that pulled too tight across her thighs.

Ginny was the only one of the four whose family was considered "upper class" within her clan, which meant more Famine genes via intermarriage within the clan, and thus usually more ability and money. The Lacks had more money than anyone other than Loki, but Ginny didn't seem to have any more ability than Piper. Then again, what would a powerful Famine ability look like? Death to all bread and tomato plants? Still, Ginny's sweet nature more than made up for the frequent failures in her life, like the end of her first marriage two years ago that had brought her home and back into her mother's fashion clutches.

"Stop hogging her," Nia said. She gave Ginny a teasing poke and winked at Piper.

Maybe it was because Nia Amort was from the Death clan, but ever since kindergarten, people in town had been a bit afraid of her. Including Piper. And that was before she'd grown a fetish for black and oversized hoodies. Nia was the only one of the group shorter than Piper, and now the petite woman with caramel skin felt too thin in Piper's arms. It looked like she'd borrowed her overlarge track pants from a man five times her size. Shadows lurked in Nia's eyes where mischief used to twinkle. The only good thing to be said was at least she'd given up the heavy Goth makeup, her straight black hair cut in a short bob that further shadowed her face. Nia had likewise come back to Beckwell two years ago or so. And she was extremely tight-lipped about what had happened to her while she'd been away.

"Hey, Pipe. Glad you're home," Nia whispered in the raspy, sex-kitten voice she'd always hated. "We're going to figure this out and kick some ass. Promise." She squeezed Piper again.

"Um, what?" Piper said.

But Nia stepped aside, leaving Anna in her place.

Anna Fray, War clan, looked Piper up and down.

Piper fought the urge to squirm.

Anna had a creepy knack for delivering the equivalent of a three-hour lecture with five words and a hard look. She still wore her long, thick brown hair back in a braid, and her clothes looked like they came straight out of the *Silver-haired and Senior* catalogue, what with the sage green slacks, cream blouse, and a moth-eaten gray sweater. She'd taken to being town librarian with terrifying zeal, which was good, since she'd never left Beckwell. Not even for a daytrip. But despite her rough edges, she'd always been fiercely protective of their group, and she was probably a genius. She knew more about the history of the horsemen and the clans than anyone else in town, possibly anyone anywhere. It mostly made up for the fact she wasn't great with people.

Anna pulled Piper in for a fierce but stiff hug. "You shouldn't have come," Anna said bluntly, keeping her voice pitched for just Piper's ears.

Piper shook off her friend, hurt rolling through her. "Gee. Thanks for the welcome."

Anna wouldn't let go of her hand. She winced. "That came out wrong, didn't it? I'm glad to see you. But you don't understand what's going on around here. There's—"

"And this round is from the gentleman over there," Lou said, interrupting in a large, rolling voice that matched his salt-and-pepper beard and plaid-clad hugeness.

Two large, freckled men, definitely Quilans from the looks of it, and relatives Daniel didn't associate with, waved and whistled from their table on the other side of the room. They were the usual sort of Fomorian: big, ugly, and mean. One of them even had a tail.

Lou winked, and light caught the twinkle of the stud in his right ear as he set down two beers, a cider for Ginny, and bottled water for Anna.

Piper broke away from Anna and the disquieting intensity and concern in her friend's voice.

Anna refused to even look at the bartender, her face hot pink. She'd always been a bit extra-odd when it came to him, going out of her way to avoid him, and turning red as a tomato the few times she'd run into him. She'd refused to explain her reaction then or ever. Maybe she had a thing for huge, bearded bartenders. Then again, Anna got excessively abnormal around most men. Probably why she was single.

For his part, Lou glanced at Anna and amusement twinkled in his blue eyes. He patted a meaty hand on Piper's shoulder, which made her jump. "Glad to see you back here, Piper. Now, you girls, I run a peaceful establishment. I don't want any trouble." He cast a particularly meaningful look at Anna, who refused to acknowledge him.

The four of them looked innocent, but that was only if you didn't know better. Not that Piper made people sick frequently, but if very upset, she had once or twice caused biting insects to swarm. Ginny had been known to make food spoil in the proximity if she likewise became emotional. Nia communicated with the dead, who seemed to be walking around pretty much everywhere and appeared to Nia as clearly as the living. And if Anna lost her temper, her voice could incite people to violence. Maybe part of why she acted abnormally around guys.

Then again, that's part of why they'd gotten stuck with their nicknames in high school, courtesy of the mean nymphs. Famine, Death, and War. Sometimes known as Frigid, Druggy, and Weirdo.

Piper's nickname had been Pussy. Oh, but if only that had been because she'd owned a lot of cats.

She adjusted the neckline of her blouse to conceal the purple lace bra.

"No worries, booze-man," Nia said, winking at Lou.

Lou shook his head with a smile and lumbered back to the bar.

Piper leaned toward Anna. "What are you talking about I shouldn't have come back? What's going on?" What could be more strange or bizarre than everyday life in Beckwell?

Anna opened her mouth to speak, but Nia, who faced the door to the bar, gave her a poke. They both looked up. Then looked at Piper.

Piper wouldn't have even needed their reactions to know who'd come into the bar. She'd always been aware of him in the room, like a prickling warmth that spread over her skin, a heightened awareness between her legs, and breathless anticipation for when he'd touch her. Piper clutched her cold beer.

"You, uh, going to be okay seeing Daniel?" Nia asked, her gaze over Piper's shoulder.

"Of course," Piper lied.

"Good. Because he's coming over."

Piper's skin tingled, and she resisted the urge to turn. To watch the way Daniel walked over. It wasn't a swagger, but more of a warrior's confident, no-nonsense stride. The breadth of his shoulders swayed with each movement, all the way down to his trim hips and sexy butt. Watching it tempted her to run toward him, grab his shoulders, jump up, and wrap her legs around his waist.

At this junction in their non-relationship, that would be really awkward.

Her skin prickled into high alert, and a boot scraped

behind her. The heat of his body radiated toward her, his body just to her right, his hand grazing the back of the chair.

Which probably put her about eye level with the fly of his khakis.

Heat raced through her, the beer bottle slippery in her grasp. Yeah, not helping with the avoiding-idiocy part. Maybe if she just didn't look at him, he'd go away and she could pretend he didn't still turn her to mush. She focused on staring at the beer bottle in front of her, picking at the red label.

"Ladies," he said, his glorious baritone rolling over her, vibrating through her. "Piper, I'm sorry, but I just wanted to make sure you're all right. I should have insisted you come back to the clinic for further assessment."

"Why? What happened?" Anna said.

"Piper's car went off the road at the barrier."

A gasp from Ginny. "Why didn't you tell us?"

Nia's grumble. "Was that ghost standing in the middle of the road again? Did he cause your accident?"

Daniel's fingers brushed her shoulder, and he knelt down at her side.

Piper gulped down a mouthful of beer. She'd look like even more of an idiot if she didn't acknowledge him soon. She turned to find his face level with hers, concern etched on that gorgeous face, in the deep brown eyes.

He frowned at her, staring into her eyes not in a romantic way, but a doctor way. Thank goodness. "Does your head hurt?" He brushed back hair from her forehead, prickles of awareness lighting up like flares where his fingertips brushed her skin.

"No."

"Any dizziness?"

Only when I stare at you too long. "Nope." *Breathe. Pretend this is all normal. That he doesn't affect you like he does.* "I really am fine. Promise. You checked me out at the scene—" including noticing her bra, she was almost certain, "—and I swear, I'm not going to come after you if something shows up tomorrow. You're a good doctor."

His frown deepened. "What's wrong? What do you think will show up tomorrow?"

"Nothing. I mean, I'm fine. Really." She pulled back from his hand. Otherwise, she'd lean into his touch, when all he was trying to be was good old responsible Daniel.

Her turn to frown. The Saint and the Slut. That's what everyone had always called them, hadn't they?

Daniel straightened. "Of course. I'm sorry. I just—" He cleared his throat, forced a smile. "You know where to find me if you need anything. Ladies." He nodded at the other women, then headed to the bar.

Piper enjoyed the view and had the unusual sensation of envying a pair of cheap khakis and the way they got to cup Daniel's butt.

Nia cleared her throat and gave Piper's arm a light pinch across the table.

Piper turned back, blinked. And met her friends' knowing looks.

"Totally over him, right?" Nia teased, though she kept her voice low.

Piper's face burned.

"He'll be at the wedding. Maybe he'll ask you to dance," Ginny said with a hopeful smile.

The cold sip of beer was not enough to quell the heat rushing through her, or all the stupid thoughts she'd had since seeing Daniel again. But it did give her a few seconds to compose herself before she faced her friends. "You guys know the deal with Daniel. It's over, okay? It has to be."

They didn't look happy about it, but one by one

each of the other women nodded.

"Okay then." Piper straightened in the chair, tucking her feet beneath. "What's the big deal, Anna?"

Anna leaned into the table, and the other three followed suit. She kept her voice low. "There's a group trying to start an apocalypse."

Piper snorted. "Same old, same old."

Anna shook her head. "Not this time." She paused. "Not since you made everyone sick."

The beer turned bitter in Piper's mouth and her hands trembled. Pretty quick it was going to be her who was sick. "What are you talking about?"

"She means that town up in Scotland. Oban maybe? That one where you were bartending," Nia said.

It came back to her then. That short phone conversation with Mom, who'd been going on and on about cousin so-and-so who'd caused a SARS outbreak in Asia, and that other one who'd spread measles at Disneyland. And Piper had opened her big mouth and maybe said people were sick there, too.

"No. It's not true. I mean, I didn't do it. I might have told Mom I did to keep her off my back, but I'm pretty sure it was the pickles. The pickle-juice looked pretty murky." Piper turned from one friend to the next, who all met her gaze evenly. And didn't look convinced. "You believe me, don't you? It's just a misunderstanding. You know how Mom gets. I had to say something. I just…I wanted her to stop with how everyone else was doing a better job at spreading disease than I was, and yeah, so I said the wrong thing. But I swear, it's not true."

Mom had shut-up all right. She'd been incapable of more than excited, garbled syllables, then had accidentally hung up on Piper. She'd never understood Piper's desire to be normal. Probably because she'd been born that way and had chosen to marry into the

Pestilence clan.

Piper tightened her fingers on the cold beer bottle. She couldn't have actually made those people sick. She wouldn't. She hadn't had a slip for years now. Had always maintained her cool around people so her abilities didn't get loose. Kept moving on before she could accidentally make anyone sick through simple association.

"Guys, seriously. It was the pickles. Maybe a few cases of sniffles, but that's normal, right? And so the regulars were gone for a few days. They all knew each other. Maybe they made plans together."

Ginny took one of Piper's hands. "Sweetie, I know this is hard to hear."

Nia plucked the beer out of Piper's other hand, and squeezed Piper's icy fingers. "If it makes you feel better, we've gone from least likely to accomplish anything to most likely to lead the world into apocalypse."

A ringing started in Piper's ears. The room blurred, and she blinked to try to focus on Anna. The voice of reason. The expert on all this nonsense. "It was just the pickles, right? Maybe it's got the rumor mill going, but it's not true. It can't be true." If she gained her powers, if she became *the* Pestilence, she would never be normal.

Because the other girls held Piper's hands, Anna reached for Piper's forearms. "I'm really sorry, but I investigated when I heard. It wasn't the pickles. Everyone got well again as soon as you left town. And the clans are buzzing. The Fates—all of them, in this town and the others around the world—have spoken. The Four will rise. It will begin with the youngest. You." She paused and frowned down at the table for a minute before she looked back up. "And it will be the four of us."

The room blurred in front of Piper and her hand flew to her mouth because this time, she was certain she was about to puke. "No. You're wrong. You have to be wrong. They're all wrong."

Anna patted Piper's arm then leaned down beside her seat and pulled up an enormous heavy brown book so full that the cover no longer lay flat and newspaper clippings stuck out of the pages. "Believe me, I'd hoped so, too." She shot a look at Ginny, who colored. "I didn't think we should invite you for the wedding. I hoped maybe if you didn't return it wouldn't come to pass. But as you have…"

Piper's head spun. She could barely see clearly. She yanked her hands free from the other girls and jumped to her feet. Her chair fell backward with a distant clunk she barely heard. "No. I'm sorry. You're mistaken. You should check again." She was going to be normal. She wasn't going to become the embodiment of disease. The embodiment of everything she'd avoided and never wanted. The one thing that had messed up everything in her life.

The other three stood more slowly, all looking worried.

"Piper, sit down again. Please," Anna said quietly.

Piper shook her head. Couldn't seem to stop shaking it. She backed away. Tripped over her suitcase. Grabbed it. Yes, she'd need that. "No. I'm sorry. I know you know, like, everything Anna, but this time, you're wrong. You have to be. And, you know, I'm, uh…" She backed away, collided with another table. "I'm really tired."

Anna massaged her eyes and then waved to the other women so they stepped toward Piper. "Of course. We can go home—"

"No! I mean…I should go visit Mom and Dad," Piper said, for probably the first time ever. The original plan had been to stay with Anna because Mom and Dad were…well, Mom and Dad. But staying with Anna would probably mean talking about this misunderstanding and looking at the huge ugly book. And gossip. And rumors. And so many things that just weren't true.

"Piper…" Ginny stepped toward Piper.

Anna touched Ginny's shoulder. "Just let her go."

Ginny. Her friend. The wedding. Piper pasted what was probably a manic smile on her face. "Oh, and I'll be there tomorrow, bright and early. Decorating at the school for the engagement party, right? And, you know, by then I'm sure you'll have figured out how this is all just a big mistake, right, Anna? Nia, maybe you can get some ghosts on helping Anna."

Piper didn't see her friends' reactions, and the faces in the rest of the bar were blurry as she sped out, her suitcase bumping behind her.

What they said couldn't be true. Wasn't true. She'd know.

Wouldn't she?

CHAPTER 5

Daniel turned to watch Piper flee the bar, her suitcase thumping down the steps after her, those silly little heels clicking over the wood. First the car accident, now a fight with her friends? Piper's day was going so well, she might be hit by lightning next.

At least she didn't look any worse off for the accident that still had his adrenalin in overdrive. Certainly hadn't dulled the volume of her shouts. Poor Piper. He knew more than anyone how much she hated the few powers she had, how afraid she was of accidentally making someone sick. Of killing someone by association, like her childhood friend, Sandy.

She'd told him as much when she'd handed back the ring. It was part of why she said they could never be together.

Of course, he'd have had to end it himself if she hadn't been brave enough to do it first.

Daniel rubbed a hand through his hair and grimaced.

Well, the upside of Piper's return was that she made Beckwell more interesting. In a town where sprouting horns and spontaneous human combustion weren't unheard of, only Piper made his heart pound, his palms damp, and his libido crazy.

Tightness spread across his chest.

He should have resisted going over to the table and checking on her. Should have trusted she really was fine. And not looked for another excuse to catch a waft of her sweet scent, to feel her energy tap dance along his skin and call to him with a siren call and the lust he'd almost forgotten he could still feel.

Daniel sighed and swiveled back toward the bar. Her friends' news must have caught her like a sucker-punch.

He'd never expected when he'd asked Piper out to gain Anna, Nia, and Ginny as his friends. They might have just been girls back then, outsiders in an insular school, but they'd also been the only people he'd met in Beckwell who didn't give a fig what his so-called powers were. They'd called him on his mistakes, joked with him, and never asked him for favors or help. They'd been the best friends he'd had outside of his brother.

And, unfortunately, when Piper left him, he'd lost those friends, too. It'd been awkward without Piper, and he hadn't wanted to make them feel they had to choose a side. It was a lonely decision. Now Ginny had invited him to the engagement party, demonstrating no ill will. Maybe it hadn't been the women he'd tried to protect when he cut off ties.

He lifted his half-empty glass of milk to his lips. It was so cold and fresh, it was too good to leave behind. And not what you'd expect to find at a bar. But then, Lou's wasn't typical.

Lou had been bartender here for longer than Daniel

could remember. It was Lou who'd called a teenage Daniel when either Mom or Dad needed to be picked up. And it'd been Lou who'd told the other high school boys to shove it when they'd laughed at Daniel for asking for water rather than a beer on his eighteenth birthday.

At the age of eighteen it was a rite of passage in Beckwell to sidle up to the bar and legally order a beer. Daniel had seen enough alcohol and its effects in his lifetime. He didn't need to taste it. Lou got it, and offered not only water, but milk, several fruit juices, even virgin cocktails.

Lou leaned meaty forearms over the bar. "You're going after her, I expect?"

Daniel sighed. Piper had told him she wasn't his responsibility anymore. She was right. "Yep."

"Those four girls could be a problem. They're gaining their abilities, and I'd bet my right thumb they were brought back here intentionally."

"Do you think they have anything to do with this apocalypse plot?"

Lou snorted and began refilling the bowls of shelled peanuts lining the bar. "Involved in it? No. But they're about to rise to become the four horsewomen of the apocalypse, and someone wants to start an apocalypse? Of course, they're connected. What's this about Piper being in an accident?"

Daniel scraped a hand back through his hair, and took a long cooling sip of his milk. "She says the barrier killed her car, but whatever the case, she ended up in the ditch."

The bartender blew out a low whistle that ruffled his bushy beard. "Damn. She's lucky it wasn't worse."

"I know." Daniel rubbed the back of his aching neck. "Someone's going to have to tell Loki the barrier needs looking to. He's the one who built it, isn't he?"

Lou popped one of the peanuts into his mouth and

nodded. "It was supposed to protect the residents."

"That's a laugh. Protect the residents…but still meddle and cause trouble, the kind that will endanger Beckwell a heck of a lot more than any Normals."

His old friend slowly and deliberately closed up the large jar of peanuts, frowning to himself, bushy brows lowered. "You have a beef with Loki?"

"Besides that he's probably in on this apocalypse nonsense that Mal's messed up with? Yeah, I do. What kind of god sees the pain and trouble in this town and does nothing?"

Lou put away the peanuts and wiped down the bar before he answered. "A careful one."

"Yeah, maybe," Daniel said. He didn't have the time and it wasn't worth the headache to argue with his old friend about Loki's uselessness. Lou had been around for a long time. No telling exactly what the bartender's genetic abilities were that made him settle in Beckwell, but he was old. Which meant he probably at least knew Loki.

Daniel set down the empty milk glass. Not his concern. But Mal was.

Long ago, Daniel had become convinced if he was good enough, if he worked hard enough to protect his brother, somehow they could both avoid the destiny everyone pictured for them: one brother killing the other.

His jaw hardened. Not on his watch.

"Are you sure Mal's involved?" Daniel asked Lou quietly.

"I am. And whether Piper realizes it or not, she's gaining her abilities, which makes her a threat to the town…and beyond."

"I'll make sure she's not."

His old friend leaned both beefy arms on the bar and gave Daniel a skeptical look. "While simultaneously looking out for your brother, taking care of your aunt, and running to the beck and call of everyone who scratches their knee?"

Daniel rubbed an eyebrow. If Mal would actually do his job and become the town peace officer, it wouldn't be that way. "Look, I'll do what I have to, what I've always done, okay? Keep your ears sharp and let me know if you hear anything new." He laid a five on the table.

Lou picked the five up and shoved it back into Daniel's shirt pocket.

He rolled his eyes but gave his friend a small smile before he turned and headed after Piper. He'd argue with Lou later about how a bartender only made money if people paid for the drinks. But right now Piper was hurting. She wouldn't want to see Daniel, she wasn't his responsibility, but with the stricken look she'd worn out the door? She needed him, and that had always been enough.

⁊

The suitcase and her heels caught relentlessly in the gravel parking lot, leaving Piper stumbling blindly onward. The back of her throat ached, and she still felt sick to her stomach. Anna had to be wrong.

Even if she had never been wrong before. There was a first time, right?

Piper almost broke her ankle in a pothole on the asphalt, and staggered to the empty four-way stop. Where did she go now? She wanted to run, but with no car plus the promises she'd made to Ginny, how could she? She wouldn't get very far on foot.

From behind her came a peculiar sound.

Plop. Plop. Plop.

She swung a quick look around. Nothing.

Plop. Plop. Plop.

She turned around, and looked again. *Plop.* She looked down, and into the black, gold-speckled eyes of a large brown toad. Who looked suspiciously like the one that had landed on her windshield moments before the accident.

She swung back around, a near hysterical laugh trying to escape past her lips. "Awesome. Now I'm being stalked by a toad."

She trudged through the empty intersection but couldn't resist a bleary glance toward freedom, down past the Cow Palace and her crashed rental. And saw Daniel walking toward her dressed all in black.

She blinked, cleared her eyes. No, not Daniel. His twin brother, Mal. Mal swaggered. He and Daniel were identical: same dark brown hair, high cheekbones, broad shoulders, narrow hips. And yet he'd never been as sexy as Daniel. There was something different about the very essence of them, a kind of sad darkness in Mal never quite disguised by his glib tone and easy charm. Daniel was just…better, in each and every way. And Mal had always known it. Maybe part of why she liked Mal. He understood what it was like to be on the outside, to never be good enough. Plus, he was a shameless flirt.

Mal looked up, saw her, and frowned. "Piper?" He strode more quickly toward her, adjusting the messenger bag on his shoulder.

She swayed where she stood, one heel sinking into the sand. "Hi, Mal." Her voice quavered, and she blew out a breath. She did not need to end the day with the final humiliation of bursting into tears in front of anyone. *Plop, plop.* The toad stopped about a foot away, staring at her.

Mal touched her arm gently, peered down at her, concern in his blue gaze. That was another difference between he and Daniel: eye color. "It looks like you've been having one hell of a day." His mouth curled up in one corner, his voice sympathetic.

She brought a shaky hand to her forehead and

closed her eyes for a second, her smile tight. "Only since I got back here." She frowned slightly at the large glass sphere in his side bag, the water and sparkles catching the light. "Are you headed to visit Aunt June?"

"What?" He jerked the flap of the messenger bag forward to cover the contents more completely and rubbed the back of his neck. "Oh, yeah, sure." Another small frown, and he hunkered down to look her in the eye. His touch on her arm was gentle, worry creasing his forehead. "Do you think maybe you should sit down?"

Now it could be the concussion talking, but it had definitely looked like a super-gaudy snow globe in Mal's bag. Maybe he'd been embarrassed to expose his soft side if it was a gift for Aunt June, but from the look of the thing to Mal's reaction, the whole thing was weird. Even considering all the other weird things that'd happened today.

Her shoulders sagged. She shrugged, let the suitcase fall over onto its belly. She crumbled on top, gaining an uneasy perch.

The toad just stared at her from unblinking black eyes.

"All I wanted to do was come back to town for Ginny's wedding, but now…" Her throat clogged and she massaged her eyes with icy fingertips. "Anna and the others say we're going to become the four horsewomen of the apocalypse. Isn't that just the dumbest thing you've ever heard?" She tried to smile, but her eyes were watery.

Mal crouched next to her and kept his voice soft. "Hell, Beckwell would probably hold a barbeque. 'Come for the ribs, stay for the destruction of humanity. There'll be fireworks.'"

In spite of herself, she shared a small chuckle with him. "Beckwell would totally do that."

"You know it."

"Beckwell: Center of Weirdsville."

"Corner of Buttscratch and Nowheresville."

Her chuckle came out choked, and she pressed trembling fingertips to her lips and blinked rapidly. "They're wrong, right? The girls and I, we're not really going to become *the* Four, are we?" Her voice quaked. "I'm not really going to become *the* Pestilence, am I?" Her gaze found horrifying sympathy in Mal's deep blue eyes. She looked away and pulled her knees closer to her chest, wrapped her arms around herself.

He squeezed her hand. "Not everyone thinks you're going to end the world, and not everyone wants you to— even in Beckwell. But whatever happens, remember that you are kickass, Piper Bane. And if that means you become *the* Pestilence, then I guess it means you'll be a kickass one of those, too."

"But I don't want to be." Her voice was a broken whisper.

He nodded and squeezed her hand once more. He stood, letting his hands drop down to his sides. He shook his head as he glanced off toward the Cow Palace and down the highway for a moment. When he turned back, it was with the more typical flirty smile she remembered. The old Mal-mask in place. "But you'll make the end of the world sexy-as-hell. Who else could do that?"

The smile was too tight to be natural, a shadow flitting through those blue eyes.

She gripped her knees and tried to smile, but the back of her throat ached too badly, and moisture burned her eyes. She looked to the slate sky above and blinked rapidly.

The toad hopped toward her foot, put a little webbed hand on the toe of her shoe, almost as if it were trying to comfort her. Weird little thing. Definitely belonged in Beckwell.

"You're going to be okay," Mal said, voice rough.

He squeezed her shoulder and offered another crooked twist of the lips. "Besides, Daniel's around. And you know he can't seem to resist trying to rescue both of us." He cleared his throat. "Speaking of which, here he comes. Which means I should be going."

She didn't want to be alone right now. Didn't want him to leave, even if his need for a sudden escape made it sound like he and Daniel were in that avoiding-a-fight phase they'd often gone through during high school instead of just discussing things like normal people.

She lifted her gaze to his. "See you at the wedding?"

Mal glanced back and cocked his head to one side, a slight smile on his lips. But there was a downturned edge to it, tension in the pale knuckles that gripped the handle of his shoulder bag. "I get first dance, don't I?" He winked before he slung the messenger bag more completely over his shoulder and headed back through the four-way stop toward the school.

She stared after him, at the swagger and lope of his walk. The loneliness of it.

Heavy footsteps crunched over the gravel and Daniel crouched down beside her, blocking the sun and enveloping her cold fingers in his big warm hands.

"It looks like you might need a ride. Think I could help you out?"

CHAPTER 6

Piper placed her small hand in his, and Daniel was a goner. He pulled her to her feet, then waited as she righted her pink cheetah print suitcase. She followed him to his truck and let him be the hero.

Just like he had been so many years ago when he'd first spotted her walking down the road, late at night, clothes so torn she had to clutch her dress together over her chest. While he'd seen her around school, he'd never even spoken to her before that night. Yet he'd felt the urge to hunt down whoever had done that to her and make them pay.

Maybe she'd known. Maybe that's why she'd never told him who'd hurt her.

She'd never wanted to be his responsibility, even back then.

Piper brushed her silken pale hair from her face, and massaged her temples. "There's a toad following me."

He glanced behind them. Yep, there was a big

brown toad. Huh. Kind of like the toad from the accident scene… Nah. Couldn't be. He turned back and looked ahead, where he'd moved his blue pickup in front of the bar. "Looks like."

They continued on a few more steps, accompanied by the sounds of her clicking steps, the rumble of the suitcase, and the plop of the toad.

"The girls think I'm getting my powers," she said, voice small.

"I know."

His tongue refused to form the words to tell her that her friends weren't the only ones who believed she was becoming The Pestilence.

She narrowed her eyes on him. "Are you following me because you think I'm hurt from the accident? I'm not. And wiping out humanity also isn't on my to-do list, in case you're wondering."

They arrived at his truck, and he reached for the passenger door. In the distance he could just see the glint of her crumpled SUV and tried not to think about what he might have found today. Sal was taking his sweet time before towing away the wreck.

Daniel swallowed before speaking quietly. "My uncle died driving too fast through the barrier." He turned to her, his voice rough. "Today, for a few moments, I thought it had killed you."

It was one thing for her to live thousands of miles away, and quite another to know she wasn't somewhere, anywhere out there. Alive, vibrant, like a part of himself he'd had to cut away, but could never forget.

Piper's face paled, and her lips parted. She turned away, unable to hold his gaze. "I'm so sorry, Daniel. I…I didn't know."

"You've been away a long time. There's lots of things you don't know."

"It's like I don't understand half of what's going on

around here…and at the same time, it's like nothing has changed."

He nodded. That was Beckwell all right.

She sighed and tucked her hair behind her ears again. "Is that toad still following me?"

Daniel glanced back. Even the wildlife was enthralled by her. Not that he could blame them. "Yep. So, what's the plan? Anna's place?"

She grimaced.

"Your folks' then?"

"What choice do I have? I can't leave. Ginny's decorating party is tomorrow. And I can't miss the wedding on Saturday."

Come back to my place. He blinked and pressed his lips together, hard. The idea of her coming home with him was…inappropriate? Ill-advised? Completely unlike him because it was destined to lead to unforgettable sex and a heck of a lot of fun?

He could practically hear Mal's laughter.

"Do you need a ride tomorrow?" He reached for her suitcase.

Their fingertips brushed, shooting sparks of heat through him straight to his dick. He froze for a moment, stunned at the intensity of it, of the image going through his mind of her thighs around his hips while he ground into her in the cab of the truck right here on the side of the road. It stole his breath and made his khakis considerably snugger.

She stared at him a moment, her eyes growing wide and dark. Their fingertips brushed again. Piper swayed toward him.

Daniel forgot his name.

Piper blinked, looked around as though realizing where she was, and jerked away. "Um, sure. If you're available. Otherwise, I'll figure it out." She fiddled with the seatbelt, trying to get it fastened.

He closed the truck door, stalked toward the truck bed, and took longer than necessary to stow the suitcase. Geezus, what was wrong with him?

Mal's amusement crept through their connection. Daniel tried to get ahold of himself before he climbed behind the wheel and swung the door shut.

The cab swirled with the scent of lilac and woman. This woman. The one who'd always reduced him to a babbling idiot, right from that first night he'd picked up a tearful teenager.

This woman was far more dangerous. And it had nothing to do with her being the descendant of Pestilence. Nope. It was because she'd been *his* Piper, and no matter how hard he tried to forget, some things stuck.

Yes, because you're an idiot.

They drove silently toward the acreage area of Beckwell Woods and her parents' place.

You can't be together. Remember how you felt after sex? Supercharged, like you could count every blade of grass with a glance, fight legions. And that's how Mal felt, too. That's how powerful he was.

Which only brought on more images of Piper. Tugging off those tight white jeans. Finding out what she wore beneath. If she still felt as tight and hot as she had.

Daniel swallowed and clenched the wheel.

The silence gelled and hardened between them. His brain and his dick seemed far too capable of inventive imagery.

Piper stroked her throat, and crossed and uncrossed her long, luscious legs about a million times. Finally she broke the silence, her soft voice raspy. "The rumors are false. I didn't make anyone sick in Oban."

He cleared his throat and tried to ignore the distracting erotic images in his head. "Maybe there are signs you've missed."

Surely she wasn't as unaffected as she pretended. She had to remember how good they'd been together. Never more so than in bed.

He drove them around the corner and up in front of her parents' home, a two-story house with bile-yellow vinyl siding. It was habit not to drive up the driveway as per her mom's request. She'd always hated the potential inconvenience of wanting to go somewhere and possibly being blocked in by another car. He'd always hated the idea of a confrontation with her over the topic...especially if he happened to be sneaking Piper home after a late-night make out session. He turned to find Piper staring at him, a bruised look in her eyes.

"You believe the gossip?" she said, hurt in her tone.

At this point, he was fairly proud of his ability to form complete sentences, considering the images in his head.

He forced himself to focus. "Piper, if there's one thing you know about me it's that I never listen to gossip and rumor, especially when it concerns you. If you say you didn't do anything, I believe you. I'm sure things will die down. The wedding isn't until Saturday. You have time to show people and your friends you aren't the same little girl who runs away from her problems."

She yanked her purse on her shoulder and turned away. "Yeah, well. Maybe that is who I am."

"I don't think so. Never have. Isn't it about time you showed the rest of them? I'll pick you up tomorrow."

ⅎ

Daniel's words echoed in Piper's head, and she stared up at the puke-yellow house where she'd grown up, extra ominous in the gathering twilight. During the three years they'd dated, he'd always told her he believed in her.

Well, that made one person in, like, seven billion. How was he still so naive? She *had* run away. Hell, she should have it tattooed on her butt—*Still running.* She didn't stick around, she didn't grow roots, and she still didn't belong in this town.

Even if Daniel did make her heart pick up speed and heat dance through her blood. He just looked at her and she wanted to jump out of her panties.

Only Daniel would be so nice after our history. She grimaced and adjusted her collar. She didn't deserve his kindness.

Daniel and his truck rattled off.

Piper hiked her purse up on her shoulder and gripped the suitcase in her other hand. No more running for today. She started up the steep driveway to the house, which Mom had always objected to people actually using. Yet another of Mom's unreasonable rules and expectations. Piper's shoulders tightened. Which was why she'd planned to stay with Anna.

Anna and her mistake about Piper gaining her abilities. It had to be a mistake.

Piper blew out a breath. *You can do this.*

Plop, plop, plop.

She paused, an uneasy kick jumping in her belly. It hadn't rode with her. It could have been a coincidence. It didn't feel like one. She turned, already suspecting what she'd find.

A toad.

Stalking her.

Awesome-pants. She put her hands on her hips. "You're determined to make this all weirder, huh?"

Fortunately, the toad didn't answer.

The curtain in the large picture window twitched, and a few seconds later, the light came on beside the front door.

"I don't know what your deal is, toad, but don't let

Mom see you." She paused. "But thanks for the backup. I'm not sure I could do this alone."

Plop, plop, plop.

"Hopefully, tomorrow, after a good night's sleep, I'll discover you're a figment of my imagination," she muttered.

The toad was amused.

Not that it smiled. Or said anything. But a feeling slid over her.

She hurried the rest of the way up the driveway, ignoring the webbed-stalker.

There was some awkward conversation with Mom, who was dressed as usual in clothes that were both too young and too tight for her. Dad never turned away from the computer screen, muttering only vague hellos. Then again, he hadn't bothered looking up that day ten years ago when she'd come to tearfully beg him for enough money for a plane ticket after breaking things off with Daniel. He'd handed her the money without ever turning around.

It was with some relief that only an hour and a half later she escaped to the privacy of her childhood bedroom. The setting sun outside the window cast the shadows of trees from outside across the room like bars.

Piper massaged her aching temples again and perched on the edge of the frayed yellow bed quilt. Even this room where she'd grown up didn't feel much more like home than the hotel rooms she spent the rest of her life in. She moved around too frequently to make renting even an apartment feasible. And for a while, the bartending jobs, finding something new that would pay enough money to put a roof over her head, had been a fun way to see the world.

It'd stopped being fun about two years ago.

Mal hadn't denied that he thought she was becoming The Pestilence. Because he didn't know, or because it was true?

Daniel hadn't really denied it, either.

Piper's gaze was unwillingly dragged toward the small pink lace sachet pinned to the wall, faded by sunlight and musty with age, each tiny stitch painstaking. Poor little Sandy Kappa had learned how dangerous choosing Piper as a friend could be. She hadn't lived to regret her mistake.

Ten years ago, one week after Daniel had proposed, Piper had the gossip mill going again. Rumors whirled that she was becoming The Pestilence. After all, she'd had enough ability to kill her childhood friend, Sandy. Some had feared what would happen if she stuck around. If their children would be in danger.

That same week, Piper's period was late. She knew how Daniel felt about kids. And what if her kids weren't strong enough? What if they weren't immune to her? What if just by being their mother, she doomed them to a death sentence?

She bent forward and dropped her head into her hands.

There'd been no doubt after that what she had to do. She'd returned Daniel's ring.

She couldn't have him or the happily ever after she dreamed of back then. And from the looks of it, Beckwell wanted to remind her that for daughters of Pestilence, there were no happy endings.

CHAPTER 7

"Gentlemen. Put down the walker and the cane. Very. Slowly," Daniel demanded.

Was it too much to ask for a quiet evening to visit to his aunt and finish paperwork?

Apparently. The Senior Center might have the only equipped and suitable medical facilities in town for his practice, but the location did come with unique challenges.

Daniel lowered his med bag to the ground and raised his hands before slowly walking toward the two white-haired men in the center of the Beckwell Senior Center's common room. Around them were the singed remains of a love seat, and the pile of ash that had been today's flower bouquet.

Beckwell Senior Center was a large one, because Beckwell seniors not only got curmudgeonly, their genetic gifts meant no one else could handle them. Or wanted them. They also tended to make weapons of mass destruction—the magical variety—out of their mobility devices.

One white-haired man, Mr. Filipov, swore in Russian at the other senior, and waggled his cane ominously. The cane's rubber slip-guard shot sparks into the air.

Mr. Kozel glared at the Russian. Pale wisps were all he had for a beard and hair, and his voice shook as he swore a vicious streak in Ukrainian. He lifted his walker menacingly. A coil of smoke curled up from one of the legs.

A few seniors hid behind furniture but watched and cheered on their favorite. One little old man snored loudly from his wheelchair.

"He said his mother was a what?" A squat old man shouted to his companion next to him under the puzzle table.

"Theesh'll bite 'is ash," another old man shouted, sliding a pair of false teeth toward Mr. Kozel.

"What'er you sidin' with him for? Give him hell, Filipov," a white-bunned granny said. Her voice turned flirtatious. "And I'll give you a ride on my vacuum cleaner." She leaned coquettishly on her walker and blew the Russian a kiss.

Daniel filed that one under "don't know, don't want to know."

More Russian and Ukrainian curses filled the air. A throw pillow went up in a puff of smoke.

Hard to say whether either combatant understood the other, but Daniel had had enough. "I mean *now*, gentlemen," he said, in his best angry doctor voice, the kind that suggested this was the man who was in charge of the meds around here. Particularly the Viagra.

The two old men exchanged a couple more swears, but slowly lowered their weapons/mobility devices. The cane clattered to the ground, and attendants moved in on the men.

"Daniel, sweetie, there you are!" A middle-aged woman in a fuchsia track suit waved, cheerfully walking right into the middle of the war zone.

Daniel leaped forward, sheltering his aunt with his shoulders. "Aunt June! I thought I was coming to your room."

He sent a few terse orders over his shoulder, circling back to scoop up his med bag before leading his oblivious aunt toward her own room, a gentle but firm arm around her narrow shoulders. The perils of running his practice out of the Center blazed front and center today.

"I thought I'd surprise you in your office," she said sweetly, looking up at him from chest-height. The attendants had done a nice job with her hair today. A tidy French braid caught the silver above her ear and swung gently behind her back.

"Yes, well, it certainly was a surprise, wasn't it?" He forced a smile, trying not to picture his aunt turned into a pile of ash like the doomed petunias they walked past. He swallowed hard.

That was close. Too close. What had riled up the two men?

He paid for Aunt June's room here expressly to keep her safe. And because she was too fragile and forgetful to live on her own, though only forty-nine. Medically, after witnessing her brothers' murder-suicide as a teen, she'd been diagnosed with PTSD, paired with mild schizophrenia to account for the delusions. He'd suspected early-onset dementia, except for the fact his aunt's memory was exceptionally sharp when it came to facial recognition and long-term memory recall.

But in a town like this, with his family history, could modern medicine fully explain Aunt June, and the things, sometimes people she claimed to see? Mom had always explained away Aunt June as fey or eccentric, but was that all it was? "Not good with reality" could be a diagnosis for a lot of Beckwellians.

He glanced back to see if he was needed, but the attendants had things well in hand, lifting up seniors who'd taken cover on the floor. Two aids scrambled to pick up the walkers, keys, and teeth strewn about the room. Maria, in Day-Glo orange scrubs, gave him a wave and shooed him off with a smile. He nodded, continuing down the east wing toward Aunt June's room.

The entire facility formed a figure eight, so even those suffering from dementia could eventually make it back to either their room, or into the atrium, which held the common room and restaurant. If a rogue patient passed the nursing center or his office, also located off the central atrium, it was a red flag they were lost. Or casing out the Viagra cabinet.

The Center had been built fifteen years ago with a full doctor's office and exam rooms, but Daniel was the first doctor who'd ever made use of them. Almost like they'd been waiting for him.

Aunt June smiled up at him. Smile lines bracketed her lips and dark brown eyes held an innocence unusual in a woman who'd almost seen five decades. Her Algonquin heritage was evident in the high cheekbones Daniel had inherited, and the warm, bronze tone to her skin. She turned the knob and pushed open her suite.

Daniel smothered a sigh and followed her in. "I thought you were going to lock the door, remember, Aunt June?"

She waved off his concerns. "Oh, please. Who would want my old junk?"

Fortunately, theft wasn't common at the Center, but why tempt a senior citizen with too much time and too much power? Of course, Aunt June would hear none of it. He closed—and locked—the door behind them. His pulse still jumped from the incident outside and how close Aunt June had come to walking into the middle of a fire fight.

Was it still safe here for her? He wasn't home often enough to look after her, even if his house had been suitable. He could rearrange his schedule, but there wasn't another doctor to cover for him.

She led the way into the welcoming bachelor suite warmed by the last ribbons of setting sun that rippled through the wall of windows opposite the door. Sun touched her mauve love seat and chair, and behind that the alcove with her bed and dresser. Framed pictures, a veritable family tree, covered her walls.

Daniel tried not to look too closely at all the sets of male twins. Or remember the stories of which one had killed the other.

Although kitchenettes and larger suites were available, Aunt June had a tendency to forget she'd been cooking and accidentally start fires.

She sat on the love seat, switched on the table lamp to bathe the room in rose-colored light, and patted the spot beside her with a smile.

Daniel returned the smile, and sat beside her, placing the med bag to the side of the love seat. He leaned in to give her a gentle hug, breathing in the scent of the flowery perfume she favored, face powder, and the coconut oil she massaged into her long hair.

Mom, her sister, had always smelled of cigarettes, rye, and medicated ointment. Sometimes it was strange to think the two women were related.

"I saw that nice young Death boy today," Aunt June said, a tiny frown creasing between her eyes as she grabbed a throw pillow to tuck behind her back. "He was here for Mr. Johansson. It was the man's time. But Mr. Death was sweet enough to stop for a tea with me first. He didn't have any, of course, but he was good company for almost a quarter of an hour."

Oh. It was one of those days, was it? Mr. Death was one of her more common delusions. Arguing with her didn't help, and though he believed in many things, he did not believe his aunt had tea and conversations with Death. After all, the only personification of death around here was Piper's friend Nia.

"I'm sorry to hear about Mr. Johansson," he said. The man had been suffering from a number of heart-related ailments for the past two years. "How was Mr. Death today? And what else did you get up to?" He should remember to call the psychiatrist, just to stop by and do a check on some of the residents, particularly Aunt June, to ensure she hadn't slipped further.

"Don't you humor me, Daniel," Aunt June said, a bit of sharpness in her tone. She folded her hands carefully in her lap and looked up at him, brow raised. "I know you think it's BS, but I assure you I know Death quite well." She shrugged. "Life, I've never met. I don't think I much want to, either."

After what she'd been through, watching her brothers die, only to lose her mother less than a year later, and then finally his own mother? Yes, Aunt June was far too acquainted with death, which was maybe why she'd never been much good with life. It made his heart squeeze with the need to protect her, to make sure the rest of her life was as happy as it could be.

He forced a smile before he reached for the med bag. He opened it up and dug under the files and other miscellany: stethoscope, first-aid kit, notebook…ah, there they were. Placing the bag back on the floor, he pulled out a box of chocolate-covered cookies and presented them to his aunt with a flourish. "I did remember to get these for you."

"Oh, sweetie, how wonderful!" Aunt June's smile widened, and she picked at the cellophane until she tore it open and pushed open the lid. She offered Daniel a cookie, then took one herself.

For a moment or two, they ate their cookies in silence, until Aunt June, her tone conspiratorial said, "I heard Piper's back in town."

Daniel choked on his cookie. Gossip traveled faster than light around here. She'd only been back a few hours.

He cleared his throat and resisted the urge to run a hand through his hair. Aunt June would ask what was wrong. "Yeah. I ran into her," he said as casually as humanly possible. His thoughts filled with how good Piper had looked, fresher and curvier than he remembered, the body of a woman now, not a girl. She'd always been a knockout, but now she was way, way out of his league.

"Excellent. Do you think she'll visit? And maybe bring some of her cookies?" Aunt June leaned forward eagerly, as though Piper hadn't been gone ten years without word. "I always loved her cookies."

"Yeah, I always liked her cookies, too," he said roughly.

Aunt June brought him back to reality with a gentle pat on his knee. "I don't care what anyone said. You two were a wonderful couple. Good for each other, I always thought. I liked her from the first time you brought her here. The way you looked at her, that softness in your eyes I've never seen since. She made you...more."

It was suddenly hard to swallow. Daniel pulled at his collar. The first two buttons undone didn't seem like enough. With Piper, he'd *felt* like more. Heck, he'd felt like the whole darned world could open up for them, and they could have whatever they wanted.

He sucked in a breath between his lips, and slowly released it through his nose.

Yeah, Piper melted his brain and logic. No wonder

he could hardly fault Aunt June for her eccentricities. Especially at times like this, when she seemed to see a heck of a lot clearer than anyone else.

"We were good together, but that was a long time ago. We were kids," he said gently, though he wasn't sure whether it was for her benefit, or his.

Aunt June munched on another cookie before she answered. "Well, I liked her, and I hope she visits and brings some of her cookies." She cocked her head to one side. "Do you think your mother will come by tomorrow?"

Even after all this time, all of Aunt June's slips, this slip in particular hit him like a punch to the gut. They'd been gone four years, and he still wondered if he could have prevented it. He should have convinced Mom to leave Dad years before. Heck, Mom and Piper should have left at the same time.

He took one of Aunt June's hands, and massaged it carefully. "I'll be here tomorrow, but Mom and Dad are gone, Aunt June. They've passed."

"Oh." She frowned, touching a hand to her brow. "I remember now. Of course." She lowered her hand and looked up. "So maybe next Tuesday then?"

CHAPTER 8

Dark hugged the corners of his cottage and pooled beneath the spruce trees by the time Daniel stomped up his porch and pushed open the door to his house later that evening. The ladder still rested against the wall, waiting for when he next found a chance to finish resealing the chimney. The two-by-fours propping up the porch roof held for now, but he needed to get to that before winter. In his spare time.

He stepped inside the house and let his shoulders sag like the tiny porch roof. Now that the sun had set, he felt every hour of work the day had brought. He shoved the door closed behind him, flicked the deadbolt, and let the darkness of the house swallow him.

He sighed and toed off his boots, leaving them at the door. He'd stripped the wallpaper in the hall, patched and sanded the walls. Still needed to buy paint. Maybe when the world wasn't ending, and his brother wasn't in on it.

He trudged toward the living room, which was best

viewed in the dark, when it was harder to see the water stains on the pale yellow-and-blue pinstriped wallpaper, or the dirty window with moth-eaten curtains he hadn't gotten around to taking down. Half the window was covered in decade-old newspaper. Once upon a time, this house, long abandoned, had been his and Piper's retreat from the real world, a place where they dreamed together.

Daniel ran a hand through his hair and flopped back onto the sagging plaid sofa across from the sleek black flat screen TV hung on the wall.

Piper had put up the newspaper years ago, with plans to repaint this little place, turn it into their home. She'd looked at the faded wallpaper and seen someone's loving care in the detail, had planned her own touches.

Progress had been slow in the four years he'd been back, but he'd steadily chipped away at decades of neglect. The floors had all been sanded down. He'd fixed any major leaks and done what he could to modernize the electricity and plumbing. It was mostly the cosmetic issues and exterior left. To make it into a home.

To make it into the home she'd pictured.

Daniel clutched the back of his head with both hands and leaned forward, his elbows sheltering his face. He closed his eyes and swallowed hard. *Piper might be back, but she's not mine. She can't be. I have to focus on Mal. I can save him.*

Somehow had to, because Mal no longer looked capable of saving himself. There was the drinking and fighting. Indulging in whatever vice he could find, as if to say everyone had been right all his life: he really was the evil twin. And he was becoming just as Fomorian as Dad had been.

Daniel dropped his arms and stared down into his empty hands. If he wanted to save Mal, he had to choose: Piper or Mal.

It had to be Mal. If Daniel didn't save his brother, no one else would. Mal had never made himself popular or liked around town, and all the progress he'd made building a life for himself outside of Beckwell, the friends he'd made on the force, he'd intentionally cut out of his life after the tragedy.

A sofa spring dug into Daniel's right butt cheek, another into his back. Buying a new sofa definitely needed to move up the to-do list. Ignoring the springs and looking for distraction, he grabbed the remote and flicked on the TV.

Female moans and sighs filled the room. A woman bit her lip, a hand pushed through her blonde hair.

Daniel fumbled for the remote. The buttons wouldn't work.

The woman writhed and twisted against the sheets and the screen, her neck arched as her breath came in shorter, faster gasps.

The woman's full lips parted, and she stared straight at him, her hair such a pale blonde it was almost white, her eyes a striking amber. "Daniel!" Piper gasped in ecstasy from the TV screen.

Daniel's fingers froze on the remote. He couldn't breathe. His dick strained against his khakis. Somehow, finally, he was able to change the channel, away from the image of Piper's desire-blushed expression. He swallowed a few times and stared blindly at the news channel. He could barely make sense of the reporter's words. Tension on Ukrainian-Russian border. Shots fired.

It hadn't been her really, had it? Darn Mal and his porno channel anyway.

He watched the images of blasted buildings and terror-filled civilians along the Russian border a moment longer before he switched back to the other station. He had to know.

The woman still moaned and gasped. But she had brown hair, not blonde. Her eyes, when she opened them, were blue. And her breasts were unnaturally large and stiff.

It wasn't Piper. It didn't look a thing like her. The porno left him cold, while just a brush of Piper's hand had him hard.

"Huh. Is this what you do when no one's watching?" Mal dropped onto the sofa, his presence deepening the shadows of the room. He set the remains of a six-pack beside his feet.

Aww, crud. Heat climbed Daniel's neck. "That was on when I turned on the TV." Terrific. Now he sounded like a defensive sixteen-year-old. He pressed the button to return the images of stricken Ukrainian civilians to the screen. His lips tightened.

Mal chuckled, and pressed an icy beer bottle against Daniel's hand. "Hey, I'm not judging."

Daniel's fingers closed around the beer bottle, and he glanced over at a face identical to his own except for vivid blue eyes and the fifty-dollar haircut. As twins, they should have had the same eyes. But then, there were a lot of should-haves when it came to them. He lifted the beer bottle, and his shoulders loosened moderately. "This is non-alcoholic beer."

"No shit." Mal rolled his eyes like it was a surprise he'd cared enough to buy non-alcoholic beer for his brother, and took a swig from his regular beer. "So, is watching porn something you do a lot, or just on days Piper gets back into town?"

Daniel took a sip. Hopefully, it cooled the heat in his face. "Piper and I were over a long time ago."

Mal snorted, his amusement filtering through the connection they shared. That same connection Daniel had used when they were kids to find Mal when he headed off, escaping the family home.

"She's back now," Mal said.

"She ended things."

"So, maybe you fix them. I've never understood why she picked the ugly brother—" Mal smirked, "—but she was crazy about you." His tone softened, colored with a hint of something Daniel couldn't identify. "You were good together. Better than good."

Don't I know it. With Piper, the world made sense.

Until that night with Mom and Dad. A reminder that even if you pretended you were just like everyone else and could have the same dreams, that didn't make it true.

Daniel stared at the television, his mind skating away from that night, from what he'd known he'd have to do. Part of his mind noted that the news had turned from the tension between Russia and Ukraine to flooding in Pakistan. The two seniors at the center today battling it out. One had been Russian, the other Ukrainian. Had they fought over the news?

He cleared his throat. "Trouble at the Senior Center this afternoon. Aunt June almost got caught in the middle of a fire fight."

Mal froze, his beer suspended midair. He swallowed, jaw clenching and unclenching. Uneasiness slid through their connection. "This afternoon, huh? She okay?" He took a long draw of his beer.

Mom and Aunt June had tried to outrun their curse after their brothers killed each other, so they'd come west. It'd followed them. Then Mom got pregnant. Found out Dad was Fomorian—something he'd neglected to mention. The first born in their maternal family line were always twins. They probably wouldn't have been born at all if it hadn't been for Aunt June, who even with her fragile mental state—or because of it—had convinced Mom not to abort.

Every time Mal had gotten into yet another scrape,

Mom liked to remind him of that. And how she'd wished there'd been a way to abort just one of the twins.

In time, it was like Mal had started to agree. And Daniel had promised himself the family line died with him. No kids. Definitely no twins.

Daniel's shoulders tightened. "You know something about what happened? What might have riled those men up?" Mal didn't get up to his old mischief like he had when they were younger—things like riling up a group of dangerous senior citizens. But something about his reactions suggested he might know something more about what had happened.

His brother stared steadfastly at the television, chugging his beer. "Nope. All I know is Aunt June promised to introduce me to her Mr. Death tomorrow." He popped the cap on another beer.

Daniel bit back the temptation to tell him to slow down. That'd only make him drink faster. And since that child had died and Mal had left the police force four years ago, he'd been drinking more heavily.

From Dad's side, they'd inherited Fomorian genes, and from Mom's side the curse that all the twins in her family always killed each other. From both parents they'd inherited a long history of alcoholism.

The darker side of their Fomorian nature had always come more easily to Mal. An affinity for shadows and bad luck. Never mind the hard drinking, picking fights, and general chaos and troublemaking. But Daniel would be damned before he'd let his younger brother fulfill the dying-young part Quilans were also known for.

"You headed to the bar tonight?"

Mal rolled his shoulders. "I bring you beer, and you give me lectures, huh?"

No, Daniel just refused to be one more set of tragic dead twins, their pictures hanging on Aunt June's wall.

"You should talk to someone. I can give you some names of therapists. Good ones."

Mal groaned. "Oh, hell, no. I'm not drunk enough for this."

"You were the officer on duty, but there wasn't anything else you could have done differently."

"A three-course lecture. Fan-fucking-tastic," Mal said bitterly. "Shit happens, the world just keeps on turning, right? Who cares if some little kid bites it. There are lots more." Bitterness and deep shame soaked through their connection.

Daniel softened his tone. "Mal, the PTSD isn't going to get better if you just ignore it."

"Maybe drunk and disorderly is growing on me. A calling."

Daniel massaged the back of his neck to keep from wrapping his hands around his brother's throat. He'd bring up the topic again later. "You have somewhere to stay?"

Mal had been staying here off and on for the two years he'd been back in town. But two weeks ago he'd stopped coming home, packed up, and taken everything but the TV. That he hadn't taken it was the only reason Daniel figured he'd be back.

"I am actually capable of taking care of myself."

Yes, and also capable of a lot of self-destructive behavior.

Daniel took another sip of beer before he headed into the next verbal minefield. "Lou thinks you're working with those fools who want to end the world."

Mal snorted, polished off beer number two and opened number three. "That's direct."

"Are you?"

"Does it matter?"

"Of course, it matters," Daniel bit out. "Those fools are going to get people hurt. They need to be stopped, not encouraged. You're the town's peace officer. *You* should be the one stopping them." Daniel growled and tried to hold his temper. It was never more of a challenge than around Mal.

Mal snorted and polished off beer number three. If nothing else, Fomorians had to have impressive livers to handle that much alcohol. "I didn't ask for the job."

"You were a good cop."

"No, I wasn't. And besides, the legal system in the regular world is messed up enough. Not sure I could stomach handing anyone over to a tribunal of gods who hand out death sentences like candy."

"This isn't some game, Mal."

"Game?" Mal barked with bitter laughter. "Shit, you don't get it, do you? This is no 'game.' This world *should* end. It's broken. Ugly. People care more about their smart phones than they do about their kids. The color of your skin still determines your worth." His voice dropped. "Can you imagine what humans would do if they knew about us? How well do you think horns or green skin would go over? Fear and hate rule this world. I'm Fomorian, but even I know we can do so much better. Remake it into something...beautiful."

"Do you hear yourself? What about the world we have? How can you think destroying it will make it better?"

Mal shoved a hand back through his hair on an infuriated bark of laughter and climbed to his feet. "I should have known you wouldn't understand."

"Then explain to me. What am I supposed to understand? Why would you get involved with them? Why would you think getting involved with that group will make anything better? It won't. People will die." He reached out to clamp a hand on Mal's shoulder. "I know you don't want that. I know you."

Mal shook off Daniel's hand. "No, you just know

the man you think I should be."

"Whatever you've gotten involved in, back out. We can fix this. Together."

Instead, Mal backed away. He held out his arms, almost able to reach across the small room. "Take a good, hard look, Daniel. I may look like you, but I'm not like you. And it's about damned time both of us accept that. I have. When will you?"

CHAPTER 9

The next morning, Piper hurried down the stairs toward the front door. Her suitcase thumped after her. Daniel had just texted to say he was out front to drive her to the school for the decorating party or whatever it was Anna had planned, and Piper had to escape the yellow miasma of her bedroom and the suffocating atmosphere of the house. And Mom. Mom was working on plans for how Piper could monetize her abilities…such as selling protection packages like some kind of mafia godfather. The very idea made Piper sick to her stomach. She'd taken little Sandy's sachet and tucked it in her pocket, a physical reminder of why she'd never become what Mom wanted, and that was a good thing.

Mom had always thought Piper should figure out a way to get more power, more ability. She'd never understood that Piper would have paid someone to take away what she had.

Piper stepped outside, closed the door, and leaned against it. The sun warmed her face despite the crisp air that chilled her fingers. It was a new day, a new chance. Today, everyone would realize she was just Piper, and if someone was becoming The Pestilence, it wasn't her.

She opened her eyes to find Daniel striding up the steep driveway, wearing another button-down and boring khakis again. Jeans had always looked better on him, but maybe this was what Dr. Daniel looked like. His shoulders and chest still filled out the striped shirt, and yesterday when she'd slid against him, it'd been clear there was nothing but sleek, hard muscle beneath his clothes. The sun brought out the Irish-red highlights in his deep brown hair, and a slow smile broke over his handsome face.

A pang of regret soaked through her. How many times had she waited for him, just like this, right here? When he'd been hers. When they'd been off on some date, off somewhere, anywhere so long as they were together. To kiss. To touch. To lay in the back of his truck bed on sleeping bags and watch the stars together. If she could have, she'd have frozen that moment and stayed in his arms forever.

She fought to swallow down the memories, to remember that nasty little thing called reality.

But then his gaze slid over her, climbing up her bare legs and over the casual cream skirt like a touch. Over her pink silk blouse with the lace peek-a-boo that felt like his hands touching her. Heat spilled through her.

Color climbed his neck as he pulled his gaze away from her chest. He cleared his throat, meeting her eyes. "Sleep well?"

She touched her lips with her tongue. She wasn't drooling, was she?

"Oh, um, yep." Her voice rose on a quaver. Yikes. She definitely should have texted one of the girls to pick her up instead. Far less temptation. Even if today they thought she might become Satan.

He reached for her suitcase, paused, then pointed at it. "Can I get that for you?"

"Okay." *Gee, Piper. You're sounding more brilliant all the time.* She held out the suitcase handle awkwardly.

His fingers grazed hers. Sparks danced between them, like the heady electric heaviness before a summer storm. Their eyes locked.

Piper's tongue traced her lips, and Daniel's eyes narrowed on the movement. She forgot how to breathe. How would it feel to kiss him after all these years? How did grown-up Daniel taste?

When he used to kiss her, her body would go hot and wet almost instantly. Clothes became this horrible invention that kept their skin apart. And when they actually had sex? Holy hell, if having him move inside her wasn't enough, her world exploded after, into hypersensitivity and certainty, where she could hear every heartbeat, feel every breath like her own.

She stepped forward half a step. Her suitcase pressed against her knees, trapped between she and Daniel.

He stared down at her lips. His hand tightened over hers. His breath brushed her face, and he still smelled like toothpaste and soap.

Her eyelashes fluttered. Lust ricocheted through her body like a loose bullet, setting everything it touched on fire. Her insides coiled and tightened in liquid desire. She came up on her toes. His lips hovered over hers. She could feel him, the heat of him, the solid strength of him.

Until he let go of her hand and her suitcase. He took a step away from her. Then another.

He cleared his throat again. "We can't," he said, voice rough.

Piper shook her head and smoothed her skirt with trembling hands. "Of course. We better, uh, get going, right?" Because lordy, he'd already gotten her going too easily. Ten years hadn't cooled a thing. If anything, what burned between them was even hotter.

She started down the driveway, her face on fire, destination his beat-up old blue truck. The same truck they'd laid together in the back and stared at the stars.

A lifetime ago. An eon of nonexistent possibilities ago.

So why couldn't she seem to get it through her head?

❧

Daniel followed Piper down the driveway. A second ago, all he could think about was how good Piper's lips would taste, how she'd fit into his arms. Because he was still a moron who couldn't learn a lesson the first time around, but needed his heart stomped on three or four times just to get the information to his head. And other body parts very interested in reacquainting themselves with Piper.

Piper had switched her shoes for more sensible flats that only emphasized how petite she was.

And vulnerable.

Ten years ago, he'd made the mistake of thinking just because he wasn't always Fomorian meant it wasn't really a part of him. But blood always showed eventually.

"Hey, uh, Piper?"

She turned. "Yes?" Her voice was breathy and expectant. Like she anticipated he'd ask her something else. Like he'd kiss her, or carry her off and make love to her all day.

Desire tightened around his neck and other parts of his anatomy like a vise. He frowned. "Remember that toad from yesterday?"

She blinked, and her face turned bright pink before her gaze slowly tracked down. Toward the large brown toad squatting in the driveway behind her. Following after Piper like a loyal poodle. And looking a lot like the one he'd spotted at the accident yesterday. Coincidence?

Piper's shoulders fell. "You again, huh?"

The toad hopped a step closer.

She frowned at it. "I'm sorry. But I've got enough weird to deal with already. Go find someone else to stalk, okay?" At which point she looked up at Daniel and cringed. As though she just realized she'd been talking to a toad. "It's, uh, nothing," she said in a strangled tone, before she spun and hurried the rest of the way to his truck, hauling on the handle. She finally got it open and climbed inside.

The toad remained where it was, but as he passed, it craned its neck to stare up at him. The fine hairs on the back of Daniel's neck rose as he and the toad exchanged a look. "Sorry, I think you're staying here." Great. Now he was talking to the toad, too.

He left the critter in his dust as he hurried to the truck, putting Piper's suitcase in the back before he climbed behind the wheel and hauled the groaning door closed.

He eyed Piper. "You okay?"

She opened her mouth, paused with a small frown, then turned to him with a tight smile. "No. But I'm going to figure it out. It'll be okay." Her smile warmed somewhat. "You don't need to worry about rescuing me."

Of course he didn't. She was the most incredible woman he'd ever known—and that had been before, when she was really just a girl. She was more than capable of saving herself.

But that didn't mean he didn't want to.

CHAPTER 10

They pulled into the school parking lot and joined the handful of vehicles beside the two story, faded brick, 1950s monstrosity. Piper's stomach churned and she squeezed shaking hands. If she needed to exorcise Beckwell from her psyche, this was definitely the place to do it. From the outside, it looked innocuous enough. But the memories clustered around the doors like ghosts.

No. She could do this. She settled her shoulders and climbed out of the truck. The other cars must have belonged to teachers and staff. According to the itinerary Anna had sent last week, this was just supposed to be mostly just the four of them plus maybe Ginny's parents for some decorating and getting ready for the engagement party later this week.

Anna had probably figured out her mistake by now. They could laugh about it, celebrate starting normal lives.

"I, uh, have a few hours before clinic." Daniel tucked a hand in his pocket. "Mind if I come in? Just for a little while?"

Keep her company as she braved this place again? Definitely.

All she had to do was remember to keep her hands—and her lips—to herself.

"That'd be great." She gave him a smile that was probably too warm for what they were supposed to be to each other now, but oh well.

She walked through the gravel parking lot, Daniel a few steps behind. Next to the entrance, nothing much had changed about the rusted bike rack. Other than the large, brown toad perched on it. Who was becoming all too familiar.

Piper sighed. "Didn't find someone else to stalk, huh?" And how the heck had it gotten here?

The toad cast a baleful glare at Piper with its black eyes. It flashed annoyance, but no answers on whether it flew or something to get to the school before they had.

She paused. Huh. Now she was talking to an empathic toad who seemed to have magical stalking powers. And up until that second, she hadn't seen anything weird about it. She shook her head. Call it the Beckwell effect.

Daniel stopped dead beside her. "That's the same toad, isn't it?"

"Yep. Toad, um, stay." Bringing a toad into the school was probably against the rules. Although, did magical toads have to follow the same rules?

Her slimy stalker carefully shifted to turn its back to her.

Great. Now it was mad at her.

"I don't think I've ever met a magical toad," Daniel mused aloud as he reached for the door and held it open for her.

"Yeah, well, see how much you like it when it starts stalking you." She stepped into the school, the yellowed floor tiles and chipped paint on the walls and lockers not much different than she remembered. Even the bright, elementary school artwork did little to alleviate the beige gloom.

Daniel waved at the secretary as they passed, someone Piper didn't recognize, and she peered into the next-door window that allowed a peek into the energetic room pulsing with knee-high kindergarten kids, splattered with paint and joy.

Ah, kindergarten. The crayon-laden gateway to education hell. Those poor critters in there had no idea yet that they were stuck at Beckwell School until they graduated high school. Probably had no concept of how long that imprisonment would feel.

The children's happy cries stuck with her, bringing her back to when she'd first started here. How she'd met the girls. Anna, so pale and gaunt, a new arrival in town without parents or friends, and taken in by Ginny's family like a charity case. Piper had been terrified of her, but shared the Play-Doh anyway. It was in that room Piper, Anna, Nia, and Ginny had first received the slightly uneasy reactions when people first heard the whispers. They were from the horsemen clans. They might end the world.

What little suckers were trapped in there now? They had no idea what awaited them. How students would watch and laugh at them from behind locker doors. How one trio of mean nymphs and a loser boy could start jealous rumors that a chaste kiss had been more than a kiss. And suddenly Piper's locker was stuffed with scraps of paper, every one bearing the word "slut".

And that had been before Stephen. Before his lies. The lies of his teammates. Lies covering up the terrifying and ugly truth.

Piper wrapped her arms more tightly around herself.

Daniel pushed open the little gym's heavy steel

doors and the combined essence of rubber, old gym equipment, and stinky socks washed over Piper.

She pictured Stephen Howser and his football team doing laps while she, Ginny, and a few of the other cheerleaders watched. What a naive idiot she'd been.

Piper shuddered and slammed the memory door shut on that horrible night, when she'd discovered just how foolish she'd been.

Inside the smaller of the two gyms was a hive of activity. Maybe a dozen tables were scattered around the periphery, each of them swarming with people. Balloons at one table. Some kind of paper flowers being created at another. Another table had huge bowls of some kind of candy, while women worked around it, tying them into little sachets and moving them to another bowl, which then someone scooped up and moved to yet another table.

Who were all these people? And what were they doing here?

Piper searched for her friends. There they were. Over in an isolated corner with their own table.

She turned to Daniel, but before she could say anything, sharp quick steps brought Ms. Boniface and her practical Oxfords in front of them with a crocodile smile for Daniel.

"Excellent. Daniel, we need help moving some tables." A much cooler look for Piper, her almost black eyes shark-like. "Ms. Bane. I trust you've been finding your stay thus far...illuminating."

"Uh, sure?"

Ms. Boniface grabbed Daniel's arm and he looked back somewhat helplessly as she dragged him away.

Piper frowned and bee-lined toward the girls before things got even weirder.

Anna, dressed in muddy colors that almost camouflaged her long brown braid, had her back to the wall and spotted Piper first. She set down the paper she held, but there was no welcoming smile.

Butterflies stirred in Piper's belly. Anna was probably upset because she'd found out she was wrong about Piper becoming The Pestilence. Right?

Nia climbed to her feet from where she was sitting on the floor. Today she wore some kind of black running outfit made for someone twice her size, the hood pulled up and covering her dark hair, hands stuffed deep in her pockets. No smile there, either.

Piper's step slowed somewhat, some twelve feet from her friends.

Ginny wore hot pink sweats about six inches too short for her, and a matching pink T-shirt that said "Bride", her red hair pulled back in a ponytail. She was the last to turn, and when she saw Piper, she bit her lip and ducked her head before she hurried toward Piper and grabbed her arm. "Thank god you came," she whispered, taking her time making it back to the other women. "Anna's still hurt you'd think she'd make a mistake when it came to research, and Nia's calling you a whiny b— Er, she's mad, too. But it's okay. You came, just like I told them you would, and we'll talk about it and it'll be all good, right?"

Yeah…didn't much sound like it. They continued a slow walk back toward the others. "If Anna's pissed, should she be out in public?" Her anger triggered her war clan abilities—already plenty scary even without so-called "true" power.

Although…if she couldn't talk, that also meant she couldn't spout crazy theories, right?

Ginny snorted. "Probably not. So she's not talking. Which isn't making her any happier."

"Awesome-pants." *Not.*

They'd almost reached Anna and Nia. Probably no accident that their table was nowhere near any of the rest—though whether Anna had seen to that or someone else had was hard to say.

"Ginny, who are all these people? I thought this was supposed to be just us."

The redhead sighed and rubbed the back of her neck. "About that… It was supposed to be that way. You know, just time for us to chat and stuff? ? But then, well, Mom wasn't sure we'd be able to get everything done. Like, all eight-hundred wedding favors."

"Eight *hundred* favors? What do you need that many for?"

They'd reached the others, and Nia replied with a snort. "'Cause the whole town is coming. Why else? Ginny getting hitched is now the 'event of the season'."

Anna added her own sniff.

Ginny's face pinked, and she picked up the pieces of paper again. "I was just telling Piper how this became kind of a Beckwell thing instead of a just us thing." She turned back to Piper. "So, that was when Ms. Boniface volunteered the school gym…and maybe to organize everything."

"And take over everything. It's Principal Boniface now, and it hasn't made her any nicer," Nia added. She shrugged and poked one of the papers with disdain and a cold smirk. "Which is why we've been trusted with triple-checking the RSVP list and cutting out the seating place cards. Though arranging the actual seating is waaaaayyy above our talent level."

"I'm sure Mom didn't mean it like that," Ginny said quietly. Though they all knew Mrs. Lack had probably meant it exactly like that. None of them had exactly been Mrs. Lack's favorites, and the woman protected Ginny with a gimlet eye and terrible sense of fashion. Anna had lived with them for almost fifteen years, so occasionally deserved a kind word. Piper and Nia she tolerated because of their respective clans, but they'd never been top of the invite list.

Anna picked up two pairs of scissors with uncut place cards and tried to hand a pair to Nia, who stuffed her hands farther into her pockets. She held the other out to Piper but refused to relinquish them until their gazes met. Anna raised a questioning brow and pursed her lips, her "are you going to be reasonable according to my narrow definition" look.

Piper snatched the scissors and paper out of Anna's hand and avoided her gaze.

"Ginny? Ginny, I need your help over here," Mrs. Lack called, an attractive blonde in a sweater set and slacks. She waved at Ginny from across the room with a small, tight smile. Probably hoping she could extricate Ginny from the four. Pestilence, Death, and War weren't quite appropriate for their little upper class Famine.

Ginny looked pained and chewed her lip, even as she put down the scissors and looked back and forth between her waving mom and the other three women. "I'm really sorry, guys…"

Anna patted her arm.

Piper gave her a forced grin. "Go on. We'll catch up later."

Ginny's answering smile was relieved, and she hurried across the room in a little half-run, half-walk, like she was already in trouble for keeping her mom waiting.

Piper leaned back against the table to face the room, half-heartedly cutting out the place cards and watching the hive of activity across the room. Nia leaned on the left, and Anna lightly elbowed Piper to make room for herself on the right.

"So, is the staggette on Friday still 'our' thing, or has it also become a community event?" Piper asked, trying to keep some of the irritation from her tone. It wasn't Ginny's fault. But she'd come just to see her friends and for the wedding. Not to see the whole damned town.

"Oh, the coup was complete when old Boney-face got involved. Engagement party on Thursday, then the staggette on Friday the night before the wedding," Nia said, then shrugged. "But I set it up with Lou at the bar that even if everyone and their dog decides to show up, we have a little corner to ourselves, so it'll be good."

The memory of what had happened yesterday at the bar and Anna's proclamation about their rising as The Four sent a chill sliding through Piper. She shifted and frowned. They hadn't brought it up, so maybe it was a dead topic? She sure the hell didn't want to talk about it.

"So, how does Ginny's new mister check out? Does he make the grade?"

Nia shrugged. "Dunno."

Anna likewise shrugged, carefully comparing two sets of lists.

Piper lowered her scissors to her lap. "Seriously? You guys, Ginny is a douche magnet. Remember Jimmy?"

Jimmy, her first husband, had been her high school sweetheart, never the brightest bulb in the first place, and a tad controlling. That first year they were married, he didn't get any nicer, and it got worse when he gained a dangerous amount of weight and blamed Ginny for it. After she nursed him through losing the pounds, he'd run off with his dietician. So someone else definitely needed to check out the new guy. The other two knew that. Why wouldn't they have seen to it? Especially Anna? Ginny was practically a sister to her.

Anna paused in her list checking, her lips parting slightly, brow furrowed as she looked at Piper. She and Nia exchanged a look. Anna shrugged.

Nia cocked her head to one side. "Uh, Pipe, didn't Ginny tell you?"

"Tell me what?"

"None of us have met the guy because she hasn't, either. Her folks arranged the marriage. Some richy-rich Famine dude."

"It's a *what?*" Piper practically screeched, gaining attention from the other side of the room.

Anna and Nia hurried to shush her. "An arranged marriage," Anna leaned closer to whisper. "And Ginny is happy with it, so you will be, too, understand?" Two women across the room shouted at each other and pulled each other's hair. Looked like it was at the balloon table. Ms. Boniface and a younger woman escorted the two hair-pullers out of the gym.

Anna snapped her lips closed, before giving Piper a dark look.

Piper didn't give a damn. "Just because it's arranged doesn't mean she shouldn't have at least met him first. They're getting married this week."

Nia toed the gym floor with her battered sneaker. "Oh, believe me. We tried to talk her out of it."

Piper's stomach twisted. She should have been here. Maybe she would have been able to make Ginny see how dumb the idea of an arranged marriage was. Instead, Ginny hadn't even told her.

"She says the guy's some goody-two-shoes working in Africa or something and wouldn't be able to get here until just before the wedding. She's expecting him any day now." Nia shrugged. "In the end, she says since she seems to always go for the wrong guys, maybe someone else can pick Mr. Right." Nia looked up and met Piper's eyes. "He's also Famine clan. Which means when she gains her abilities next, at least he should be safe. Ginny isn't in denial about it. What about you?"

CHAPTER 11

Piper's mouth fell open, her skin tingling. Maybe she'd misheard. "I-I'm sorry?"

"Bet your ass you should be," Nia continued, relentless, voice still pitched low. She crossed her arms over her chest. "While you've been off romancing rock stars, we've been here, dealing with reality."

Clueless, friendly female chatter continued across the room, while Piper's heart rate accelerated. "I told you guys yesterday. It's a misunderstanding. I'm not The Pestilence. It was just to get Mom off my back." Her voice rose in desperation.

Anna came around to Nia's side, and there was sympathy in her blue eyes.

There was fire in Nia's dark gaze while the smaller woman wrapped her arms around her narrow torso. "All of us have been dealing with it. All of us have experienced growth in our abilities." Her voice dropped, became even raspier, and she focused on the scarred gym floor, brow furrowed. "I can barely keep up with the number of ghosts knocking on my door, showing up everywhere I go. Most of them aren't even from around here, but from halfway around the world."

She poked Anna. "Anna's causing fights left right and center, even with the meditation. I've been working library hours because she can barely speak to patrons."

Piper tried to inject some lightness, setting the scissors and paper down, desperate to prove Nia was wrong. "Like Anna was ever very great at conversation to start with."

Nia looked up, but there was no answering smile. "Two grannies almost killed each other over a knitting book last week." Then she nodded toward Ginny, still across the room, seemingly helping with the urgent task of candy sachets. "It's because the clans are so certain that Ginny's folks were able to set up the match for her with a family that'd be way out of their league otherwise."

"But she's shown no new ability yet?"

"She says no."

Piper crossed her arms, uncrossed them, picked at her fingernail. "Okay. So maybe the two of you are getting your abilities. I'm not denying that's possible." She turned to Anna. "And I'm sorry. I know what that means for you." Anna had craved normalcy and a way to dampen or get rid of her abilities even more than Piper. It's what had led to expertise in everything horsemen.

Anna nodded and tugged on her long braid.

"But I swear to you, I didn't do anything in Oban. I haven't made anyone sick. I'm the same as I've always been." Though, there was the weird toad thing. But that had nothing to do with Pestilence power, and more to do with Beckwell. Right? She dug her nail into the fleshy part of her hand, her fingers trembling.

Someone had started coughing, stopping the chatter on the other side of the room. Someone else started to sneeze.

Anna tossed her braid over her shoulders and crossed her arms, lips tight.

Nia groaned and rolled her eyes. "Seriously, Piper. Open your eyes. Anna was on the phone for almost five days straight checking and re-checking sources about what happened in Oban. And she did check on the pickle juice. Apparently, that's a fairly common thing in bars, so she totally covered it. There was no other reason those people got sick—and they did get sick. Just. You."

"Why do you want to ruin Ginny's wedding this way?" She shoved her hair behind her shoulder, her chest tight, body shaking. "I don't want to fight you. But it isn't true. It's never, ever, ever going to be true, no matter how many times you say it." She scratched at her arm. "Look, whatever. Um, tell Ginny I had to go. I'll, uh, see you later."

She spun away but only made it half a step before she collided with a large, hard body. Mal. She frowned, stumbled back.

He caught her arms to steady her. "I'm sorry about this," he said.

She saw something troubled in his deep blue gaze, apologetic even, the second before he dragged her close and mashed his lips to hers.

It wasn't a kind kiss. It wasn't romantic. It was cold and calculated. Mal's hands pinched her arms. Wouldn't let her go. Wouldn't let her back away. His steely grasp didn't care as she struggled against him, tried to bite his lip. Her heartbeat pounded in her ears. He held her immobile. Prisoner. She could have been in the backseat of Stephen Howser's car. His hand beneath her skirt, his lips rough and demanding. Cruel. Black spots danced in her vision.

Someone jerked Mal off of her. Piper gasped in air. Daniel. Daniel shouting at Mal. Their words rumbling nonsense, interrupted as they fell forward in coughs. In choking.

She blinked. The entire gymnasium of people flooded in violent hues of yellow and purple, dotted with black. The room echoing with coughs. With choking. With sickness. She couldn't breathe. Could barely see.

Slim arms linked with hers, a body on either side of her. Anna and Nia. Dragging her out of the gym. Away from all that sickness.

From all she'd caused.

℘

Wanting to smack some sense into his brother was nothing new. Wanting to wallop Mal into the next decade was. Daniel had come in after helping set up tables outside to find Mal holding Piper captive and physically assaulting her with a punishing kiss. The remorse didn't offset the triumph he'd felt from Mal through their connection.

Just like the coughing and tightness in his lungs hadn't prevented Daniel from roaring across the room and ripping his brother off of Piper. He'd taken a swing at Mal even as the coughing and choking reached a crescendo and he could barely stay on his feet.

Nia and Anna rushed Piper out of the room, and he sucked in clear air. The coughing slowed.

"What the hell are you doing?" he growled.

Mal smirked, a pinch of regret shivering through their connection.

Daniel lunged for Mal, knocking him back into a table, the movement skidding the table across the gym floor and sending a cascade of papers fluttering into the air.

Mal climbed to his feet, rolled his shoulders and cracked his knuckles. "I warned you, didn't I? I'm not you."

Red flooded Daniel's vision. "And that was Piper."

They were brothers. Mal had always been Daniel's little brother, playing knights in the woods behind the house. For a while in med school, living together in the city, they'd been friends again. Mal knew more than anyone what Piper had been to Daniel. What her leaving had meant.

And what her coming back meant, too. He'd felt Daniel's reaction. He had to have felt the hope, the temptation, and, yes, the desire beating through Daniel's blood in a way it hadn't for a decade.

Now they circled each other, enemies looking for an opening.

In the back of Daniel's mind he remembered he was the town doctor. He should be seeing to his patients. Making sure everyone was recovering from…whatever that had been.

But he couldn't get past the look of Piper, struggling helplessly against his brother. He'd never told Mal everything about the night he'd met Piper, but there'd never been any doubt: they protected Piper.

They sure the hell didn't hurt her.

"Oh, believe me. I know who that was," Mal said, still circling, but on the defensive, not the attack.

"Stay away from her," Daniel rasped.

"Or what, Danny-boy?" Mal tsked. "Careful. You're acting kind of like a Fomorian."

Daniel slammed Mal harder into the table. The table's metal feet screeched backward against the floor, and the last of the paper slid to the floor. There were gasps behind him, a few surprised cries.

For once in a long time, Daniel didn't care.

"You have a problem, you come to me. You never go after her. These games of yours stop now. I'm not going to let you hurt people."

Mal's expression hardened, and he shoved Daniel back and climbed to his feet. He and Daniel circled each other again, though Mal stopped with the emergency exit doors directly behind him. "These aren't games. Welcome to the new reality. Because things are about to change around Beckwell. And around the world." His voice dropped. "What happens in Beckwell won't stay in Beckwell. It was no coincidence a Russian and Ukrainian rumbled and in the news Russia and Ukraine are at odds. You were right. It was planned." He held out his arms. "This was just a small demonstration. *We* control things now." He pushed the doors open behind him, then very intentionally turned, and walked out.

Daniel was breathing hard, sweaty, and ticked. What was Mal talking about? What happened in Beckwell happened outside in the world?

The whispers and shocked voices around him penetrated, and he knew he was acting like a brainless, muscle-bound Fomorian, like Dad, shoving people around because he was bigger than them.

Piper. He had to find her. Before she left Beckwell.

CHAPTER 12

Anna, Nia, and Piper smashed through the front doors of the school, Piper between them like a limp noodle. As the fresh air hit her face, she staggered away from them. Tears blurred her vision, but she scrubbed them away, bent over, her hands on her thighs as a half-sob, half-cry tore from her throat.

Oh god. She'd made everyone sick. Everyone.

Anna and Nia reached for her, but Piper straightened and jerked away, wobbling like a drunk. She lurched away from them. From their voices trying to comfort her.

She didn't want comfort. What could they say? There was no making this better.

Buzzing filled her ears as she stumbled, half-blind across the school's parking lot. Almost fell down the steep driveway but somehow kept upright.

How many had she made sick? How sick? Any of the kids?

A blue sedan braked, horn blaring as she staggered

through the four-way stop. She had to get out of here. It was Beckwell. That was it. If she got out of here, none of this would be true anymore. She'd be free. She could still be normal.

It started as a tripping walk down the road. Something bumped against her leg, like a cat looking for attention. She looked down out of confusion to find a large skunk. With gold speckled black eyes reminiscent of a stalkerish-brown toad.

As though to confirm her suspicions, the toad/skunk flashed the image of the toad morphing into a skunk into Piper's mind like a really screwed up Internet video. The next image was of a video game screen with "Upgrade!" flashing in red.

Piper shuddered. Turned away. Tucked her arms against her chest. Walked faster. Then jogged. Toward the Cow Palace. Toward the barrier. And beyond that, freedom. Freedom from Beckwell. Freedom from… A chill chased through her, and she couldn't finish the thought.

Ahead of her, the road was crowded with cars. People stood around, stared at thin air, held their hands out into it. The soft click of claws bounced along the road next to her.

She wouldn't look down. The buzz of insects surrounded her. A swarm of wasps flew like a miniature air squadron at her side. Piper turned her jog into a run. It didn't matter what everyone else was doing at the barrier. She knew what she had to do: escape.

Except as she drew closer—about even with where the dead silver hulk of her rental SUV still hugged the tree—the air grew….thicker.

Great. The barrier had found a way to be even creepier.

But if she wanted out of Beckwell, she couldn't stop.

Townspeople gathered around the crumpled hood of an old blue Buick, the growing crowd surrounding an older man and woman, the man cradling his head. "It felt like we hit a cement barricade," the old man muttered. "I just… I thought it was just talk at the bar, those people saying something was different about the barrier."

Townspeople murmured, covered their lips, wrapped their arms around themselves. Fear leached off them like diesel smoke. Some were on their cells, their movements jerky and tense, red, black, and yellow waves roiling around them. Others, ignoring the rising panic of conversation, investigated the barrier themselves, gingerly raising their hands into the air and into the barrier. Many jerked their hands back to cradle them carefully.

Piper swallowed and slowed to a walk once more. The colors surrounding the people had emotions associated. Emotions she could feel. And share. That wasn't right.

The air in front of the Buick didn't look any different. Ahead, she could see the open highway, clear and waiting. She clenched her jaw. Maybe the barrier was extra creepy today, but she couldn't stop like the others. She couldn't stay here. She leaned into the thickening air and kept walking.

The air tingled against her skin and brushed like feathers over her arms. The tiny hairs on her neck jumped. Her belly twisted, but she pressed on. She squeezed her hands, anticipating the usual effect of the barrier. It washed over her like icy pinpricks, intruding, testing her. But the air grew thicker, like she was pushing through soft jelly.

She couldn't stop now. The barrier wasn't that thick, right? If she just kept pushing, she'd get through. She pressed her hands into the gelled air around her, and focused her eyes on the empty highway ahead. Freedom.

Tears pricked at her eyes, her knees softened, but what else was she supposed to do? Accept that she was The Pestilence? Make people sick like she had little Sandy? No.

She pushed harder, her arms now suspended in the thick air. It pressed against her chest, squeezed out her breath.

"Piper. Piper, stop!" Daniel's voice behind her.

She grit her teeth harder, and leaned harder into the thickness. She was almost through. She had to be. Her chest tightened, as though she'd breathed in pudding and her lungs didn't know what to do with it. *Almost there, almost there.*

Suddenly, she couldn't move any farther. She jerked and twisted in the thick air. Her breaths were short pants. She couldn't get enough air. She couldn't move her arms. She couldn't go forward or back. She was going to die, trapped like a bug in an invisible spider web. Harder to breathe. Spots danced in front of her eyes.

The world grayed.

Arms wrapped around her and jerked her out of the solidified air, pulled her against a firm, warm chest. Daniel tucked her head beneath his chin. "I've got you. You're okay. You're okay," he repeated again and again.

Piper sucked air into her lungs, blinking and unable to look away from the highway ahead. Leaves danced and bounced along the asphalt and over the yellow dotted lines. There was no trace of the invisible wall that held them here. Imprisoned.

She turned away from the taunting view of freedom, and rising up on tiptoe, she turned her face into his neck. Inhaled the clean, warm scent of him, that faint hint of spice she'd never been able to identify. Eau de Daniel. Maybe if she hid there in his arms, she'd be safe. Everyone would be safe. From her.

He held her tightly enough it almost hurt, but it was safe.

Would he still hold her if he knew the truth?

"Are you okay? Mal never should have…" His jaw clenched against her hair, and his grip tightened around her for a second.

Piper shuddered and squeezed her eyes shut. Mal was the least of her problems right now.

"I refuse to make people sick. How do I stop this?"

"I don't know, sweetheart. But I think I do know what might have caused your car accident. And that right now, we're all trapped in Beckwell."

CHAPTER 13

Daniel squeezed Piper tight, inhaling the lilac scent of her hair. There was noise from the growing crowd, and the frosty touch of the barrier still coated his skin. His heart pounded, his muscles were tense, and he wanted to keep her safe in his arms forever. He felt like he could move mountains for her.

They'd gone down that road. It was a dead end.

He still couldn't let her go. What would have happened if he hadn't followed her from the school? What if she'd stayed trapped in the barrier? He could barely resist squeezing her tighter.

He clenched his jaw. Damn Mal anyway, for what he'd done to Piper at the school. And for neglecting his job as peace officer. He should have been here, calming these people down.

Which meant, right now, when he least wanted to, because he'd been the one to suggest his brother for the job, and because said brother couldn't be bothered to perform his duties, it fell to Daniel. No one else would do it.

Something bumped against his leg, and his nose wrinkled. That, coupled with the uneasy crowd, meant he couldn't just go caveman and protect Piper. He looked down to find a massive black and white skunk, twining against Piper's legs like a cuddly tabby cat.

The skunk looked up at him and offered a spike-toothed smile.

Daniel opened his mouth but had no words.

Piper glanced down at the skunk and grimaced. She pulled away and smoothed her hands down her skirt. "My stalker toad turned into a stalker skunk." She absently reached down and slid her hands over the bushy tail. With each stroke, her tremble lessened.

And he found himself envying the skunk. He had to let her go. It'd been ten years since he *had* let her go.

Piper hugged her arms around herself and couldn't meet his eyes. "Was anyone hurt at the school?"

He wanted to drag her back into his arms, but couldn't. He crossed his arms. "Everyone recovered as soon as you were gone."

"Good." She nodded, as though answering some question only she knew. Her gaze flickered up to him, then over the crowd, followed by a small frown. She took a step back, her eyes once more finding his. "You should help them."

"Maybe Lou or the mayor—"

She shook her head. "They need *you*, Daniel. They're scared, and they trust you. They need someone strong right now, a natural leader. Tell them it will be okay, and they'll believe you."

He swallowed. "Will you?" The only one he wanted to help right now was her.

Her smile was sad. "I don't need rescuing, remember?" She looked out over the crowd again, her frown deepening.

He turned to face the town. Some fifty people had gathered, and more cars arrived each moment as they received calls from friends and family. Gods only knew if it was like this at the other three roads in and out of Beckwell.

He cleared his throat, and though the sound wasn't loud, people began to turn toward him. They looked up at him from beneath wide-brimmed hats that couldn't conceal inhuman yellow eyes or green-toned skin. Some were almost human in appearance, while others, like the two pale and trembling satyr boys, were anything but. Beckwell was supposed to be their sanctuary, and now it had turned into their prison. They looked to him for answers, and he didn't have any.

It couldn't be coincidence that rumors of a group causing trouble swirled, Mal attacked Piper, and now the barrier had solidified. Especially after what Mal had said back at the school. *What happened in Beckwell, didn't stay in Beckwell.*

Damn it, Mal. How could you do this? These are your family, your neighbors.

It wouldn't be true to say friends.

"What's going on, Daniel?" Mrs. Panne asked, pulling her gray sweater more tightly around herself.

"Tell us we're not trapped, Doc," said someone else. Horns poked through the man's cowboy hat, and he pulled his wife close.

Daniel swallowed. Could Beckwell survive itself? Or would they tear each other apart?

"It's the gods, isn't it? Come to get rid of us at last," someone farther back shouted.

Another favorite fear: that the gods at last had come to wipe out their unpopular descendants and lesser mythic creatures just because they could.

The crowd rose in volume and tension.

He'd studied medicine, not politics for a reason,

darn it.

He raised his arms and cleared his throat. "Okay everyone. Simmer down a minute."

"You can get us all out of here?" Yet another said.

He rubbed the back of his neck. *I wish.* "Let's be clear: we are *not* going to panic." He accompanied this with his best stern look, and holy heck, it better work, because some looked wild-eyed. "We've got this, and we're going to be fine. Groceries arrived yesterday, extra for the wedding, and we have plenty of supplies. I was in the store this morning, and the shelves are full."

Which gave the town maybe three weeks or so of food, and that was a conservative estimate.

What they wouldn't survive was each other. Residents appreciated the country because they needed the extra space and isolation, needed the distance from others because of their explosive powers, short tempers, and often, both.

"*Is* it the gods?" a man called out from near the back of the crowd.

The crowd stirred uneasily. More cars with more residents pulled up.

Something inside stirred. Like his heart rate, like the way he'd felt when he'd torn Mal away from Piper. "You will calm down." His voice carried and boomed through the air, not a shout, but a command.

Startled silence followed. Faces turned to him, pale, expectant, but also hopeful.

Huh. Maybe he was better at this than he thought. He rolled his shoulders, his shirt feeling unusually tight, like it'd shrunk somehow. Or he'd gotten bigger.

"What we need first is a plan," he said.

The audience stared, silent and enraptured.

So did Piper.

∞

Piper stared at Daniel and couldn't look away.

Because Daniel was glowing. Not like he was the picture of health. But emitting light. A faint aura of gold surrounded him, like he stood in front of a spotlight.

It was fascinating in a what-the-hell-is-going-on kind of way. Had she developed a non-disease-related ability? Like seeing Daniel glow was some kind of side-effect of becoming The Pestilence? That'd be nice. Even if it was still creepy.

The soft tickle of the skunk's tail against her hand and the oddly soothing contact was the only thing keeping her calm. Because while Daniel might have been glowing, the townspeople were Technicolor with emotion.

She turned toward them as the diaphanous, vivid shades of emotions feathered over them, shifted and changed like a watercolor painting. The whirling black of fear and bright yellow cowardice had largely faded to turquoise curiosity and orange determination as Daniel mapped out his plan and asked for volunteers to check how far the barrier extended, if there were any weaknesses.

Just like when he'd led the basketball team to victory in school. Or encouraged her on her final exams to get the best grades she'd ever achieved her entire school career.

"Next up, we need to know more about the barrier," Daniel was saying. "Where did it come from? When did it start? Find out the last time anyone left or entered town. What is it? And most of all, how do we get rid of it? Volunteers?"

Hands shot into the air.

She looked out over the gathered townspeople, people she had spent so long running from. For a moment, these people, who were just as scared as her, were beautiful.

She pressed her lips together and tried to ignore the

fluttery feeling in her chest. And they were trapped here. With her.

"Now hold on a minute." Mal's voice rang out over the crowd. "Who decided you should be in charge?"

Piper's hands clenched involuntarily, and her breath sped. The skunk pressed against her legs and sat on her feet, sending soothing feelings through her that didn't do a damned thing.

Daniel paused in assigning volunteers. "Well, since our peace officer doesn't seem to want to do the job, I guess I will." His voice dropped. "You've caused enough trouble for the day, Mal. Go home."

Tension crackled between the two brothers like a live wire: red with anger tinged with purple worry and anxious green. While she couldn't read the emotion on the two men, it seemed to flow between the two of them.

She swallowed. Cloudy black whirled among the crowd. Violent bursts of red, violet, and electric green shot through the crowd, destroying the harmony. The crowd made an alley for Mal.

He strode forward, a dark silhouette, almost more shadow than man. The same reason she'd seen Daniel as glowing?

"But you have so much fun playing the good guy, should I spoil your fun?"

Daniel ground his teeth, his shoulders almost seeming to broaden before her eyes. "This isn't a game."

Mal stopped, less than ten feet from Daniel. "No. It isn't." His face remained serious. He caught sight of Piper, and a tiny flicker passed over his face before he clenched his hands and turned to face the crowd. "You have been given a gift, Beckwell. The gift of power. From today onward, thanks to the barrier, whatever gifts you possess, whatever mysteries lurk in your bloodstream, will make themselves known. You will become what you were truly meant to be. And when you have that power, you will have to choose what you do with it. Keep hiding from the gods and humanity... Or make yourselves known."

Daniel, fists clenched, strode toward Mal's turned back.

Piper faltered after him. Froze. Bit her lip. Was it her place to interfere anymore? Oh god. It was just like high school, those times when sometimes the twins would rumble, and all she could do was get between them, thinking all the while: is this the time they kill each other?

"Daniel. Don't."

He didn't hear her, or didn't care. He grabbed Mal's arm, swung him around with a jerk. "Enough," Daniel's voice was stony. "Enough of this show you're putting on. Enough of the troublemaking. Enough of whatever it is you think you're doing to punish yourself and everyone else around you. These people don't deserve that."

Mal's smile sent shivers down Piper's neck, though he pitched his voice low. "What will you choose, Daniel? Are you going to keep hiding?" He pointed to Piper, though he didn't look at her. "Her hiding days are over."

Daniel stepped between her and Mal, blocking her view of him. He clenched and unclenched his hands at his side. His shoulders heaved. Red and electric green sparked with orange arched between the two brothers.

Piper stepped forward. Pressed her hand against Daniel's back, heat radiating from him like an engine.

His fingers unfurled at his sides. His shoulders settled.

"Mal, stop being such a dink and crawl back into whatever hole you came from," Nia's voice carried over the breeze.

Piper peeked out around Daniel and searched for

her friends.

They weren't hard to find. Everyone had given the three wide berth where they stood, near the back of the crowd.

Ginny waved. Which earned her a glare from Anna.

"Nia Amort, aka Death. Well? What are you going to do then, huh?" Mal taunted.

If Mal hadn't betrayed her and acted so horribly today, Piper would almost have felt sorry for him.

Nia's white teeth flashed, even across the distance, and there was something menacing about her despite the overlarge clothes and the fact she could easily be mistaken for a teenager. "Oh, Mal. Do you really want to meet some of my 'friends'? Because if you even think of touching Piper again, I will introduce you to some of the dead who call Beckwell home. And undead."

Mal mock-saluted Nia. "And you, Anna. Your face is awfully red right now. You must have something you want to say."

Piper swallowed. Anna had a hell of a temper. And she refused to let her abilities hurt people. She'd probably always been more dangerous than Piper, anyway.

Even if Piper had gained her abilities first.

She clenched her teeth to still the tremble in her chin, and clutched clammy hands together.

She stepped forward. "Mal, go away. Leave them alone." Her throat clogged a moment. "You've done enough today already, haven't you?"

Mal flinched. She would have missed it if she hadn't been staring at him, hard, demanding he turn around and face her, but she saw it.

"Okay, Anna. I'll let you off this time." He pointed a finger at Anna like a Vegas showman. "But I want a performance next time, got it?" He started to walk away, back through the crowd, without ever once turning to face her. "Beckwell, I can't wait to see what tomorrow has to bring."

CHAPTER 14

Daniel had a hard time keeping his voice even and the scowl off his face. He focused on the town and not turning to watch Piper wander over to the ditch and take a seat on the grassy slope. It seemed to take an excruciating amount of time to calm everyone down, set up the community hall as their base of operations, and finally—finally!—get them to disperse.

All he wanted to do was hold Piper until the murderous thrum in his blood dissipated. He clenched his jaw. Was that uncontrollable rage what made brother murder brother? Was that the curse?

Or just a reaction to Mal's selfish idiocy?

Finally, it was only he and Piper left near the barrier. And the skunk.

He strode to her side, pausing slightly at the sight of the black and white animal.

As though it read his mind, it turned to gave him another unskunk-like grin.

Piper sat on the upper incline of the grassy ditch ten

to fifteen feet from her crashed SUV Sal had never gotten around to towing away, either because of the barrier's solidification, or the salvager's laziness. The black-and-white furball curled against Piper's thigh. Her legs were pulled up to her chest, arms around her knees, and she stared down the secondary highway, at the leaves tumbling down the asphalt. The wind stirred strands of pale hair, brushing them against her jaw.

He crouched down next to her. "You doing okay?"

"It seems strange we can't see it. The barrier, I mean. Everything looks so…normal. When it's anything but. It's scary and powerful. Maybe deadly."

Why did he get the feeling they weren't just talking about the barrier, but maybe about what'd happened back at the school? She might have meant what was happening to her. Or what had happened with Mal.

He cleared his throat, and pretended he hadn't read anything into her words. "Well, we know it's there, so we can control and avoid it."

She turned, her amber gaze met his, and the world dropped away to only her, like it'd done that first time she met his eyes on that night so long ago. "If I'm becoming The Pestilence, we have to get this barrier down, and I have to learn to control my abilities enough that I don't make what happened back at the school happen to the whole town. Because with the barrier up, there is no escaping. Either for the townspeople, or me."

"Mal as much as claimed responsibility, he and the rest of the apocalypse group." Could he protect his brother and the town? This was looking more complicated than he'd anticipated. Daniel's jaw hardened. "I'm so sorry for what he did to you at the school."

She slid her fingers along his jaw, and Daniel shuddered, clenching his hands against his knees so he didn't grab her.

"It wasn't your fault. And please, promise me, no matter what, don't let me become a reason to fight your brother. To fulfill that horrible curse. I couldn't live with that."

Guilt lay heavy in the pit of his gut. She didn't know he'd attacked Mal already. "Piper…"

"Promise me."

He closed his eyes. "I promise." The gods help him keep it. He stood, then held out a hand to her.

Her small fingers closed in his, and he pulled her up next to him, and couldn't seem to stop his mouth. "Do you want to come home with me?"

She blinked. "Is that a good idea?"

Definitely not. His face warmed. "It's not like anyone will know. Besides, I already have your suitcase in my truck, and we're old friends." They were many things, but they'd never just be "friends". *This isn't about hauling her back to your cave and keeping her to yourself. Let's keep that clear.*

Trouble was, he wanted to haul her back to his place and keep her safe. Beneath him. In bed, until all of this blew over. Actually, in bed, under him, on top of him, against the wall again, and again, and again.

Back to the house that had once almost been theirs.

Which made it an idiotic idea. He couldn't seem to stop wanting her. She was scared and vulnerable. She needed someone she could depend on, not someone who was thinking about getting in her pants. The house was a mess, most of the renovations only partially complete. He opened his mouth to rescind the invitation, to tell her he could take her to the library, Anna's place, anywhere she wanted.

She spoke first, lowering her lashes to hide her eyes before finally looking up at him. "I'd like that. Let's go home, Daniel."

∞

Piper suddenly understood why Daniel had been going on about the house not "being all that big" and "in need of a bit of TLC" on the drive back to his place. They pulled up to the little old house, the headlights revealing the building where it hid in the growing shadow of tall spruce trees.

She slid a sideways glance to watch Daniel tap his fingers on the truck wheel and glower at the house, as if he could magically transform it into something else. Which was silly. It was practically perfect just as it was.

"Why didn't you tell me it was *this* house?" Piper said quietly, her throat thick, not sure what else to say. When had he bought it?

He shrugged, his expression too shadowed to read. "It's seen better days." He coughed. "The renovations haven't gone as quickly as I'd hoped. I didn't want you to be disappointed."

Yes, it had definitely seen better days. But it had always been beautiful to her.

The house in front of them was barely large enough to qualify for the name. Cottage, or maybe shack, would have been a better description. Decades of winters had worn away most of the white paint, leaving the clapboard siding gray and the front porch roof so saggy it didn't look capable of surviving another winter. But someone had propped up and supported the porch with a two-by-four, and there was a ladder leaning against the front, leading up to the roof.

Daniel couldn't have forgotten what this place meant to her, could he?

He climbed out of the truck and came around to open her door for her.

She tried to catch his eyes, but he avoided her gaze. "When you said your place, I guess I kind of assumed you meant your parents' old place." Around here, the same land and homes tended to stay in families for generations, and the Quilans were practically a founding family.

He shook his head before he turned to lift her suitcase out of the back like it weighed nothing. "By the time Mom and Dad died, the creditors got everything and then some." Another shrug of those large shoulders, and he headed for the door. "Besides, not sure I'd have wanted to live there. You know how it was."

His home life had been even worse than hers. At least her parents didn't engage in drunken brawls.

And yet, he'd wanted to live here?

"So you bought this place when you came home?" Piper followed more slowly, taking in the house thick with memories.

He'd brought her to the land for the first time not long after they'd started dating. He'd wanted to show her the small clearing in the woods where he and Mal had played as children, the one place he'd said where they got to be two twins off on an adventure, nothing more, nothing less.

Later, she and Daniel had found the house, had made it theirs. They'd had nothing more than an air mattress and a cooler, but this had been their refuge. Here they could lay together, damp skin against damp skin, and dream of their future together.

Daniel strode up to the house and opened the door without unlocking it. He kicked off his boots on the porch and disappeared inside. She trailed after him, the trees quietly watchful, the house patiently waiting.

What did it mean that he'd made his home here? That he was renovating? Here, in the house where they'd made love for the first time.

The porch squeaked as she stepped onto it, and she trailed her fingertips lightly over the peeling paint on the handrail, the other collapsed and tangled in weeds. Back then, they'd still believed they could make a normal live for themselves. That they could be happy.

That just maybe they weren't defined and trapped by their ancestors and the latent magic that lurked in their blood.

Light blossomed inside and Daniel turned, an imposingly large silhouette within the doorway.

This wasn't the boy on the cusp of manhood she'd left behind. This was a darkly compelling man with secrets of his own. And whatever she'd said about them being adults and friends, as she stepped through the doorway, her fingers and toes tingling, it sure the heck didn't feel as if she was just crashing with an old friend.

"I bought it ten years ago. Before I proposed," he said quietly. "Lou lent me the money."

Her breath caught. Ten years ago. *Before* he'd proposed.

It would have been theirs.

Her eyes prickled and a flutter started in her belly.

He took a step toward her. Stopped. "I'm sorry. I should have warned you before we got here," he said, his voice raspy. "I know what this house meant to you."

What it meant to us. Was that why he'd kept it? She struggled to keep her tone light. "It's nice to see some things, like this place, haven't changed much."

"Oh, they've changed."

She stepped into the small entryway and closed the door behind her. Daniel's features became clear as she stepped into the dim light. Shadows accentuated his strong cheekbones. He didn't step back to give her room. Instead, she basked in the heat of his body. Their toes almost touched, and heat zinged between them.

It was somehow natural to take one more half step toward him, into the heat of his body. She turned her face up to his. His arms came around her, smoothed slowly up and then down her arms.

God, yes. This was where she wanted to be. She

should fight it, it couldn't last, but after a decade, after the horrible revelations of the day, it felt like she'd finally come home. Tonight, she needed that.

Prickles of hot sensation cascaded through every nerve ending. He pulled her close, and she reached up on tippy-toe to grip his shoulders. Their breath mingled before his lips slanted over hers and time slid backward.

Hot damn, but the man could kiss.

Piper twined herself more closely with Daniel as their tongues did the tango. His chest was hot and hard. Muscle jumped beneath her hand. Her fingers found the space between the buttons on his shirt, and slid beneath to encounter smooth, hot skin. Daniel growled his approval into her mouth and grabbed her ass, squeezing. Fire lit a path through her veins, and she pressed Daniel against the wall. All the better to plaster herself all over him.

Daniel let her kiss him for a while, their lips locked, tongues entwined. Suddenly, he swept his hands beneath her ass and lifted her against him. He shoved up her skirt, and wrapped her legs around his waist. He spun them around, now pressing her against the wall. His cock pressed against her core, the thin barrier of her panties riding the ridge of his fly. Lightning shot through her veins. Piper gasped and rocked her head back into the wall.

Frick. They'd barely even touched.

Daniel feathered kisses down her neck, and Piper pulled at the buttons to his shirt. Undid them enough so she could kiss down his neck. Taste the saltiness of his chest and watch the muscle jump.

There was too much fabric between them. Not enough skin touching.

His hand slid under her blouse, and he took her breast into his hand. Her nipples strained against the thin lace of her bra. He continued to move against her, his cock trapped by his khakis, her stupid panties one extra layer between them.

She growled her frustration and reached for his zipper.

The shrill sound of a fire alarm startled her, stilled her fingers.

It rang again, louder this time.

They broke apart, panting.

Piper blinked, and tried to figure out how to see again after the awesome hotness of Daniel's kiss. Cripes, she'd missed him. No one got her as hot—now, or ever—as Daniel could.

Daniel winced as the alarm went off again. He reached into his jean's pocket, pulled out his cell and glanced at it. "Crud. It's an emergency."

Her skin and blood were still on fire, never mind the raging lust in her core, the wet heat demanding some relief in Daniel form. She stepped forward and reached for him again. "Let someone else handle it." She had an emergency of her own.

Daniel stepped out of reach. He stared down at Piper, or more correctly, down her shirt, with a hungry look.

Evidently, he appreciated the peek-a-boo effect of the pink shirt and her bra. Though she'd readily have ripped it and the rest of her clothes off if he'd hurry up and rip off his own.

Daniel rubbed a hand over his face and shook his head. "I'm sorry. Mal is supposed to be the peace officer. They should be calling him."

But Mal is a selfish dick who doesn't want to be useful, she finished in her head.

Daniel's gaze locked on her lips. "I have to get this."

Couldn't someone else wait? She couldn't.

He grimaced. "I'm sorry, Piper." He slid past her

toward the door, and her two-faced body shuddered with desire. Hand on the doorknob, he turned back. "Lock the door and I'll be back as soon as I can. We'll…we need to talk."

The door closed behind him with a click as effective as a bucket of cold water poured over her head. Piper wrapped her arms around herself, desire still shivering through her. She squeezed her eyes shut. Damn it. She hadn't wanted to stop. But maybe it was best that they had? Who knew what amount of exposure to her could be harmful, and the last person she wanted to hurt was Daniel.

Though the fact that Daniel was off to help someone else and she had to come second rankled, too. His generosity had often become the source of frustration when they'd been together. Because she was selfish enough to want him all to herself.

She opened her eyes and clicked the deadbolt locked. Arms still tight around her torso, she wandered farther into the house. Wallpaper peeled in the front room, which held a high tech big screen TV on one side and the ugliest, saggiest plaid sofa she'd ever seen on the other.

The house had slid further into disrepair than when she'd last seen it, but there were signs of new life here and there. The floors had been sanded down to reveal pale wood beneath decades of grime. The main hall's wallpaper had been stripped, taped, and prepped for paint…even if fresh paint didn't yet coat the walls.

So he'd bought this place, left it to molder and rot, but then come home and started to repair it? What did that mean?

A swift knock on the door made her spin and rush back. Maybe he'd changed his mind. Maybe he didn't have a key. She unlocked the deadbolt, and swung open the door. Maybe…

Mal. Standing outside in the shadows, an unrepentant grin on his lips, a leather jacket hugged his shoulders.

Piper tried to slam the door shut.

Mal stuck his foot in the opening and grabbed the door. Pulled it open with so little effort, it was embarrassing. "We need to talk."

CHAPTER 15

A surge of panic scuttled through Piper, and she pushed again on the door. "I have nothing to say to you. Get out." What had Mal been doing? Waiting until Daniel left and she was alone? No ·small guess he was part of why Daniel had wanted her to lock the door. Had he followed them? Shadows lengthened beneath the spruce and there were only night noises from the forest. The nearest neighbors were too far away. They'd never even hear her scream. She struggled to swallow. Before today, she'd never have believed Mal would hurt her. Now…

"Piper—"

"I said go!"

Mal blew out a gusty breath. He let go of the door but didn't move his foot.

She slammed the door into his black biker boot.

"Ow." She couldn't see his face, just the boot. Another grumble this time. "Okay. I probably deserved that."

"Probably? You deserve worse. What you did back

at the barrier? Those people were scared. You didn't have to make it worse. And you didn't have to be such an ass to Daniel. You know you two shouldn't fight. What could happen if it escalated?" She'd never seen Daniel as riled up as he had been today. Would she have been able to stop them if they'd really started fighting?

"And I didn't have to do what I did to you at the school," Mal added quietly.

She leaned on the other side of the door and closed her eyes, the weight of the day crashing down on her shoulders. She'd made all those people sick. She had new abilities like the emotion-color thing developing. She didn't even know what all her abilities were or would be, let alone how to control them. It was practically inevitable she'd hurt people in Beckwell, whether she wanted to or not.

And Mal, someone she'd trusted, practically like a brother, had become her worst nightmare today. How could he look so much like Daniel, and be so very, very different? Maybe that was the mistake she'd made. She'd thought Mal possessed some of Daniel's kindness and generosity.

"Why did you do it?" she whispered.

She'd never told anyone what had happened that night in the car with Stephen. Daniel had found her walking alone down the highway that night, and his offer of a ride had started their relationship. The next day Mal had overheard Stephen's boasts and punched him. It had never been clear how much either brother knew, but they'd made sure one of them was always with her if she was around any of the jocks after that.

It'd been so long, she figured Mal wouldn't answer, when his voice broke through the darkness.

"They—we—needed to know if you really were gaining your abilities. When I met you the day before, even you didn't know." He paused, and his voice roughened. "It was the one way I knew would get to you. I'm sorry."

"Because you attacked me."

"Yeah."

She shifted but didn't relent pushing the door against his foot. Even with the boot, his foot probably hurt by now. And she didn't feel bad about that, either. Well, maybe a little. He had apologized, and from his reaction earlier at the barrier, his inability to meet her eyes, he regretted what he'd done. "Would you do it again?"

A brief pause before his answer. "If I had to, yes."

"Then what kind of apology is that? If that's all you came to say, leave."

He muttered something she couldn't decipher under his breath, then shifted and leaned against the one remaining handrail. "I also wanted to tell you to be careful. You've come home and landed in the middle of things. And...I don't want you to get hurt."

"Even though you're perfectly willing to hurt me yourself."

"And I'm trying to protect you now." There was a growling edge to Mal's voice. "There's a group who want to start an apocalypse. They want to use you and the girls to do it."

"Let me guess: you know all this because you've joined the group, right?" Damn him anyway. When they were kids, Daniel had always been bailing him out of one type of trouble or another, almost like it followed him. But there was also a point when he was just being an idiot. Like now.

"Better I'm part of it so there's an inside man, isn't it?"

She shifted against the door and frowned. "So you're trying to stop them?"

"Not exactly."

She rolled her eyes and grumbled. "You're an idiot."

"Maybe. But they're right about some things. Like using the barrier to incubate everyone's abilities."

Incubate abilities? Piper's heart sped. Was that why she'd suddenly made so many people sick in the school when something that bad had never happened before? Was that why she could suddenly "see" emotion?

Mal continued, oblivious. "Why should we remain relegated to the shadows? Ostracized by the gods because we're not the pretty or popular kinds of mythic creatures? Feared by humans because even if we're mostly human, we're just enough of something else to scare them? Why shouldn't we get to decide what we are and truly be one thing or the other, instead of just somewhere in no man's land?"

Piper yanked the door open. "And what gives you or anyone else the right to decide that?"

He took a step back. Shadows disguised his face, lengthened his cheekbones and made him look more like Daniel.

He'd never be Daniel. Mal had always been junk food, whereas Daniel was a gourmet feast. She frowned. Someone else's feast.

"Someone has to make the first move," Mal said.

She glared at him, feeling something dark rise and bubble inside her. She swallowed it down. "Great moves you've made so far. You attacked me and almost got Daniel to kill you and fulfill the curse. I'm about to become The Pestilence, capable of making everyone sick, and you've trapped me with everyone else— including yourself, I might add—in Beckwell. Freakin' brilliant." She stabbed a finger into her chest. "*I* never asked for any of this. I just wanted to be normal. I don't want more abilities. I don't want more power. Not that you or your cronies care. What's your next move, huh?

Convince everyone to drink the Kool-Aid? Hope you take the first cup."

Mal just stared at her, then tipped his head back and stared at the night sky for a minute, his hand clutching the handrail. Finally, he met her gaze. "I thought maybe you'd understand. But whatever. I tried to explain. I've tried to warn you. I can't make you understand that normal is overrated and that maybe you'd finally be satisfied, finally stop running away from my brother, your friends, and everyone else if you accepted who and what you are. Because I'm just an idiot, right?" He stepped backward down the remaining stairs until he stood on the mossy ground. "Well, I tried. Be careful, Piper." He turned to walk away, then turned back. "And watch out for Daniel for me, will you? He's going to need you. He always has."

CHAPTER 16

Daniel drove toward the Cow Palace, his truck's headlights picking through the darkness. Was it better to thank Ms. Boniface's emergency phone call for saving him from lust? Or curse it for cutting short what could have been one heck of a night?

It'd only been a few hours since the last emergency at the Cow Palace. He shouldn't be the one headed out to maintain law and order. It should have been Mal. But now that his brother and those fools had closed the barrier, it fell even more heavily on his shoulders to make up for Mal's mistakes. Exhaustion weighed on Daniel, always heavier after the sun went down, worse today. He'd attacked his brother. He'd taken charge at the barrier. Was he becoming more Fomorian?

He pulled up to the four-way stop, the taste of Piper and that scorching kiss on his tongue. And his khakis considerably tighter. Geezus. If the phone hadn't rang, he wouldn't have stopped. They couldn't go down that road again.

As soon as he turned the corner, he could see the new crowd gathered out in front of the Cow Palace. This one larger than before, maybe eighty people. The headlights illuminated trucks and quads, even a rancher on horseback. Dozens of anxious faces, ghostly pale.

He'd barely stopped the truck behind a sedan and killed the engine when two slim figures raced toward him out of the night.

He opened the door, and Ms. Boniface reached in and grabbed him. "Daniel! Thank goodness. Quickly."

He grabbed his med bag from the passenger seat, and glanced at the women beside Ms. Boniface. Louise Dole, soccer-mom type, whose son had been around Piper's grade. And a young, pretty brunette, new to town. She worked at the school, but they hadn't met.

So why was she out here?

His footsteps were loud on the asphalt, the crowd eerily silent. They parted like waves and revealed the figure suspended and frozen in the barrier, like a statue of a runner. The man's skin was tinted blue. His eyes bugged. Oh, heck. It was Beckwell's mayor, Ed Blycoomb.

Daniel dove forward in the crowd. "Why didn't anyone pull him out? Stop him?"

"The mayor wouldn't listen to reason," Ms. Boniface said.

"We were afraid of getting stuck ourselves," someone else said.

Daniel shut them out and lunged toward the barrier. He'd survived pulling Piper out, and the mayor didn't look as deep.

The barrier prickled over his skin, then increased in pressure until it was cold pins and needles cascading over him, erasing any lingering lust and every memory of warmth. It squeezed the air from his lungs. He gritted his teeth and pushed forward. His lungs screamed for air, and his muscles tensed.

The atmosphere thickened the closer he got to the mayor. The air was thick and icy, stabbing at his skin, the sensation painful. It was worse than when he'd gone in after Piper. Ed was less than two feet away, his pudgy fingertips stretched toward Daniel. *Come on, a little closer.*

Daniel stretched his arm forward, muscles screaming as he forced his limb farther into the thickness, toward the mayor's fingertips. His muscles tensed. Almost there… Almost…

His breaths came short and fast, his chest too compressed to inhale. His fingertips numbed. His muscles groaned and screamed in protest. Spots danced before his eyes. His pulse raced.

Something snapped, and his muscles seemed to grow and expand. The pressure on his lungs relaxed enough for him to suck in a breath. Focused, grim determination and strength pulsed through him. The skin on his arm darkened and changed hue. He lunged for the mayor's hand, and his metallic bronze fingers closed around Ed's plump wrist.

Daniel gave Ed a hard yank. He and the mayor tumbled out of the barrier and fell onto the asphalt.

Shivers coursed through Daniel, chattered his teeth. Someone wrapped something over him, but he forced stiff limbs to move. Ed. Needed to help Ed.

Ed Blycoomb lay limply on the ground. He wasn't breathing. No heartbeat.

Daniel turned him over and systematically began CPR. One-two-three-four-five. Breath. One-two-three-four-five. Breath. *Come on, you bugger. You're not getting away that easy.*

Distantly, he heard someone call for blankets. Someone else called for hot drinks. A blanket was draped over Daniel's shoulders.

Two cycles, and the mayor's heart started again. Then the man gasped and took his first breath on his own.

Daniel fell back, coming down on his hands and knees. Shivers still wracked his body, like he'd emerged from a mountain stream. Distantly, he was aware of others taking over. Someone said something, maybe him, the words like a distant rumble. They'd take the mayor to the Senior Center. Was it a nurse? Mayor's vitals were good. Daniel was a hero.

He didn't need the hero part.

And he especially didn't need the Fomorian part. Was that what had given him that burst of energy at the end? Changed the color of his skin? He rubbed his arms, relieved to see that though his arms remained icy, they were once more their usual color. That was one problem solved. He shivered and pulled the blanket more firmly over his shoulders. The next problem would be mild hypothermia if he couldn't warm up.

"Everyone," Ms. Boniface's voice rang through the darkness. "You've had your entertainment for the evening. And it should be abundantly clear that for now, we're all staying put. Now stop standing around. Any attempt to force through the barrier is suicidal. Go home, have your dinner, get some sleep. Daniel, we're holding an emergency meeting at the community hall. Considering your brother's latest escapades, it's even more imperative that you attend."

Right now? He was half frozen and worried about what species he was. Not a great time for a meeting. But then, emergencies tended to be that way.

People and vehicles moved. Sounds of retreat grumbled around him, both the people and their vehicles.

Daniel fought to drag himself to his knees. Multiple hands reached to help him up, draped more blankets over his shoulders. Two men reached down a hand for him while others watched tensely. Shivers still wracked his body, and it was galling to know that he'd probably have fallen if not for the two men who supported him.

When he could finally stand on his own, he turned to face those who had supported him. Lou and old Joe. A small handful of other townspeople regarded him seriously, faces pale and worried in the darkness. A woman handed him his med bag.

He nodded and managed to mumble a thanks.

"No, thank *you*," someone said, before they nodded, and the group dissipated into the darkness.

The moment unnerved Daniel and weighed on him as he staggered to his truck. Lou steered him toward the passenger side. "I'll drive," he said gruffly and shut the door.

Daniel closed his eyes, felt the shift of the truck as Lou climbed in and slammed the door, then the rumble of the truck engine.

"What's happening to me?" he mumbled to his old friend. He rubbed a hand over his face.

"You're cold. We need to get you warmed up." There was a pause, and Lou finally answered after the tick of the signal light. "You're not becoming anything you weren't before, Daniel. But you, and everyone else, have just been reminded of what that really is."

❧

An hour and three coffees later, Daniel leaned back in the chair at the Community Hall, feeling almost human again. Exhausted, sure, but the human part seemed exceptionally precious.

Geezus, all he wanted was to go home, climb into bed with Piper, and try to feel warm again.

"Daniel? Daniel, did you hear what Counselor Hecate said? The reports have come back and the barrier encompasses the town like a dome. It extends over all Beckwellian properties. There are no gaps, no escape, though some fools like the mayor had to test it for themselves. Meanwhile, there have been reports of price gouging by the grocer," Ms. Boniface said.

He looked up to find those steel-gray eyes on him. In fact, a quick glance around showed a dozen gazes on him, including the pale face of the red-haired Hecate girl. What was her name again? Erin?

Then there was Ginny's dad, skinny Mr. Lack. Ms. Boniface, of course. That new woman, Daphne, they'd called her. Since when was she part of the town council? Louise Dole, the over-the-hill soccer mom always in a tracksuit. Old Henry, a former mayor. And Lou.

Daniel inhaled slowly. "I take it you want me to talk to Abe." Abe, the grocer, was a good guy. So long as morality didn't get in his way of making a profit.

"No, of course not," Ms. Boniface said.

He raised a brow and glanced around. For once, he didn't have to solve the town's troubles?

"Now, son," old Henry said. Settling his elbows on the table, he steepled his fingers. "You're the town doctor. Not the mayor, and not even officially on this council. It should be your brother sitting here, the town peace officer." The gray-haired farmer cleared his throat, and glanced at the rest of the council.

Daniel leaned back in his chair and crossed his arms over his chest. This had to do with Mal. Usually, they never hesitated to ask for his help.

"We'll handle Abe," Ms. Boniface said, in a way that made one very glad they weren't Abe.

Henry waved her down but kept his steady blue gaze on Daniel. "We need you to handle your brother. And the girls."

Unease rippled through Daniel, unsettling the icy depths inside. His neck prickled. "The girls?"

"Now, Henry, I've told you my Ginny wouldn't cause any trouble," Mr. Lack spoke up, half rising from his chair.

"Oh really?" Erin Hecate said. "*Your* Ginny stopped into the grocery store yesterday, and as soon as she left, Abe found half his bread spoiled. I was there. I saw it."

Daniel's shoulders tensed. "That doesn't sound like something Ginny would do, nor any of the other women, since I assume you mean Piper and her friends. They don't cause mischief, they don't play games, and I assure you they have no intentions of harming anyone in this town."

Louise, the aging soccer mom, snorted. "Intentions are well and good. But that Nia character, she's a menace. Wherever she goes, there are spirits playing havoc with the electrical systems, scaring the livestock, putting people ill at ease."

"That's hardly her fault," Daniel said. So far as he remembered, it'd been the same all through high school. And it had never been something Nia had been happy about.

"And we all know the difficulties Anna Fray causes," Ms. Boniface said. "She should be removed from her position as a threat to the peace. She's causing fist fights in the aisles of the library."

"Surely not intentionally," Lou offered, shooting Daniel an apologetic look.

"Then there is Piper Bane," Ms. Boniface continued, lingering over Piper's name. "She made everyone in that gymnasium and half the school sick today."

"I'm sure she didn't mean what happened," Daphne said, sympathy in her tone.

Mr. Lack finally found the courage to clear his throat and speak, though he focused on a piece of paper in front of him. "I'm sure Piper didn't mean any harm, either. But we never considered what would happen if the girls, er, women gained their abilities. And now we're trapped and isolated in here with them."

Heat, the first he'd felt since Piper's kiss, shot through Daniel. He clenched shaking hands on his thighs beneath the table and straightened. He tried to keep his tone even, a tight smile on his lips. "So it was just fine if they destroyed the world, so long as Beckwell was safe? And Piper certainly did not intend to cause harm, nor does she ever. Besides which, there were no lasting side effects. It was an accident, and it's over."

"How can you be sure there have been no lasting ill-effects? Seems to me you've spent all your time since at her side, not seeing to your patients and the well-being of this town," Ms. Boniface snapped.

Daniel's fingers dug into his thighs. "Just what are you insinuating?"

"Daniel, son, you're being mulish about this," Henry said, warning in his tone.

Why shouldn't I be? Daniel wanted to shout, but the old man didn't deserve that disrespect. He stared at the table so he didn't glare at the old man.

Lou sighed. "Everyone, calm down a minute. Yes, the girls may be a threat, but I agree, it isn't an intentional one." He waited until Daniel met his gaze. "What we do know is that our town peace officer, your brother, is working with a group of people very willing to cause harm to this town, and they've started with that barrier of theirs."

"I move that we finish discussing how Daniel is to deal with those girls and better see to his duties," Ms. Boniface said, her tone sour. "We haven't finished the discussion."

"Oh, we've more than finished it," Lou said, tone firm. He and the school principal exchanged a hard look.

Color bloomed on Ms. Boniface's pale, sunken cheeks, and she sniffed.

Lou turned back to Daniel, his gaze sympathetic. "I

know this can't be easy…"

A muscle in Daniel's jaw twitched.

Henry straightened his crooked spine and cleared his throat again. "You're the town doctor, are you not?"

Daniel's eyes narrowed, and he turned to the former mayor. "I am."

"Then it's your job to keep this town healthy, isn't it?"

His fingers bit into his upper arms. "It is." He didn't like where this was headed. Nor the position it put him in. Possibly worse than pseudo-peace officer who was supposed to stop his own brother.

"Then that makes it your job to oppose Piper, the literal personification of disease and infection. Her and the other women, at least until the barrier comes down," Henry said calmly, logically. "Piper is the biggest threat of the four right now. Her and this group of troublemakers." He nodded toward Lou. "We're hunting them down. And when the time comes, we'll need your help handling your brother, too."

Handle Mal. Did they expect Daniel to fulfill the curse and kill his brother?

Daniel pushed back his chair and stood. "I'll take care of Piper. And yes, I'll protect this town, even if it's from my own brother. But I won't do your dirty work for you." He turned and strode toward the door. This was why Piper hadn't wanted to come back. And for the first time, he really got it.

Annoyed murmurs came from the conference table at the opposite end of the hall. And he didn't want to calm them down this time.

Lou caught him by the elbow just as he reached for the door handle.

"Hey," Lou said, his voice pitched low. "Those people back there are just scared."

"Why do they turn to me?" Daniel's voice was

equally quiet.

"Because this town was founded by Loki, a warrior in his own right. And when things go sideways, when these farmers and ranchers get scared, they want a warrior in charge again. Someone like you. A Fomorian."

"Just what do they think I'm going to do to stop Piper? Or her friends? Or my own brother?"

Lou looked away a minute. "I don't know. Truth is, I don't think they do, either. Most of the people here are generations removed from the badass gods or mythics who used to cause trouble. Suddenly, they're feeling some of that power. And the repercussions. They're scared, and rightfully so. Did you catch the news earlier?"

Daniel shook his head.

Lou's blue gaze was intense. "There was a massive flu outbreak in London. Most of the city doubled over in coughs around supper hour. Hospitals overflowed. Then all of a sudden, poof! It was over. That was around noon here. Sound familiar?"

A chill slid over him, and the hair danced along the back of his neck. Just like what had happened with Piper at the school, when she'd left and the coughing and illness had left with her. Even, it seemed, at the same time of day.

Lou let go of Daniel's arm. "We have every right to be scared. What happens in Beckwell isn't staying in Beckwell anymore."

CHAPTER 17

Piper paced outside in the morning sunshine, her flats sinking into the spongy moss that surrounded Daniel's cottage while she waited for him to get ready. The sun peeked through the heavy spruce cover and illuminated the mossy ground in cheerful splotches.

Should she tell Daniel about Mal's visit? Ugh. That was unlikely to go over well. Ask why he'd bought the cottage? Was she ready for that answer? Okay. Priorities. She needed to figure out more about her abilities and the group of morons Mal was working with. What she needed was a serious chat with her friends.

She glanced over at the skunk, who'd appeared sometime during the night and was curled up in a sunny splotch, watching Piper. "I suppose I should bring you with me."

The skunk cocked its head.

"Well, are you part of all this weirdness or not?"

The skunk sent a mental eye roll and settled down in the moss again.

So that was a yes?

Daniel would be out any minute. She'd surrendered the cottage to him so he had plenty of room to get ready…and so she wasn't tempted to peek at a bare muscled chest and bared flesh. Or tempted to do anything else. Their whole situation was too confusing by half, especially added to everything else. What had Mal meant that Daniel needed her? So she could protect him…or because he needed her in some other way?

He'd gotten in late last night but insisted on heading out early on only a few hours of sleep.

Not that she was feeling especially rested. After a night dreaming about their kiss, interspersed with nightmares about Mal and her developing abilities, she'd been up at the butt-crack of dawn scouring the kitchen and making breakfast. Taking care of Daniel. Playing house.

Her skills had improved substantially from their dating days when she could have burned water, but she'd never cooked for anyone other than Daniel.

She'd never wanted to. Never wanted that kind of intimacy with anyone else.

Oh, crap. That was a dangerous road to wander down. Playing house with Daniel. Falling back into their old patterns.

If he'd kept the cottage intended for them, had he kept the ring? It hadn't been big, a tiny bit of diamond clasped in white gold Celtic design-work. But it had been exactly what she'd wanted, exactly the style she'd have chosen.

Had he ever been tempted to give it or another ring to someone else?

Piper paused and bit her lip. She couldn't ask about that. Shouldn't. And it wasn't like he'd pried into her dating life. Not that there'd been a whole lot of it. And never anything serious. She'd learned her lesson when it came to love. She could never risk staying. She always had to keep moving.

Daniel deserved to be happy, though.

The door slammed, and Piper jumped. Her heart pounded. Were her thoughts written all over her face? Daniel used to always say he could read her worry in the flecks of her eyes.

"Sorry." He bounded down the stairs and strode toward her, muscles flexing beneath the plain button down, those broad shoulders rolling, a little curl in his dark hair where it rested on his forehead.

Warmth and desire unfurled within her. She felt a tad light-headed.

"You ready?" Daniel tossed her the keys.

Umhmm. For you, always. She blinked. Grabbed belatedly for the keys and missed. Her face heated as she scooped them off the ground. "Sorry. Yeah. Uh, let's go." *Smooth, Piper.*

He stood there, those large capable hands loose at his sides. The khaki and the button-down with the gray tie only served to emphasize the trim muscle of his body, the leonine grace as he stepped toward her. His breath ruffled her face. His spicy scent surrounded her. She wanted to rise on tiptoe and press her lips to his. No, she wanted to jump into his arms and lose herself in him. In his safety and his strength, in his faith in her.

Crinkles formed at the corners of his eyes. "I meant are you ready for today? Unless that barrier has vanished overnight, there'll be challenges."

Yeah, like your brother and his crazy group?

"I'll be with the girls most of the day. I need to figure out how to control my abilities. We need to figure out what our next move is." And she owed them a huge apology for not believing them in the first place. Sigh.

Daniel climbed into the truck.

The skunk jumped up and pranced around to Piper's

side and looked from the door to her. She winced. "Not sure he's going to like you riding up front with us. I might not smell you, but pretty sure he does. Maybe in the truck bed?"

The skunk's eyes narrowed. It waggled its tail.

Piper sighed. "Okay." She opened the driver's side door and lifted the skunk onto the seat. Actually, it was lighter than she'd expected. And at least it didn't smell. Probably a sure sign of a magical skunk if ever there was one. That and the fact that it was telepathic and had transformed from a toad.

Daniel looked up and froze in the act of doing up his seatbelt. "The skunk's riding with us?" His nose twitched.

Piper climbed in after the skunk, and hauled on the door until it groaned shut. "I'm sorry, but yes. I need him—"

The skunk projected an image of a pink women's bathroom stall symbol, and flashed annoyance.

"Er, *her* with me when I go see the girls. Maybe they'll know why she appeared."

The skunk scrambled up onto the center console, and then Daniel and the animal exchanged a long, measuring look.

Daniel shifted closer to the door. "Uh, sure." He brushed a hand over his nose. "The Senior Center isn't *that* far."

He cringed when she turned the key twice before the engine finally coughed to life.

She put the truck in reverse and brought it around before she pushed the gas. Too hard the first time and the vehicle lurched. Daniel clutched the armrest. The skunk dug in its claws.

"Sorry." She concentrated on the gas pedal, her hands trembling on the big, unfamiliar wheel as she pulled them out onto the highway.

The weight of yesterday, of all they'd been, all they'd planned to be, everything that cottage represented hung between them. Dammit. She chewed her lip until it ached. If they didn't talk about it, it'd just hang there forever.

She tightened her grip on the wheel as they rattled ever closer to Main Street, but eased her foot off the gas. She needed more time to say her piece.

"I, uh, I've thought of you sometimes," she said. In the least brilliant opening ever.

"I've thought of you, too."

Really? How? She gave herself an internal shake. "What I mean is… I've always wanted you to be happy. You know that, right?"

Daniel settled back in the chair, and looked out the side window. He sighed. "Is this about that kiss?"

Just "that kiss"? More like The Kiss.

"Yes. No. Kind of?" She rolled her shoulders. *Dammit, dammit, dammit.* She was making a mess of this. "Are you seeing anyone?" *Oh, yeah. Much better.* Her shoulders slumped.

Daniel cleared his throat, and massaged the back of his neck. "No. But, I shouldn't have kissed you last night. *We* shouldn't have kissed." He rubbed a hand over his face, and turned toward her. "We can't just pretend nothing happened between us. We were engaged, but you ended it—"

"And I'm so, so sorry."

"And you were right to."

She blinked, and risked a glance his direction, directly meeting his beautiful brown eyes. "I was?"

"Yeah." He didn't look happy about it, just accepting. His words were quiet. "I wish things could have been different, too, Piper. But they aren't."

Piper pulled up to the four-way stop with two other cars, people on foot milling around the store and school.

People whose insides didn't feel cold and hollow. Not that he was wrong.

"I know. I…I'm not good at sticking around," she said.

She chewed her lip. He knew the part about her being afraid of making him sick like she had her childhood friend, Sandy.

She'd never told him about the night spent peeing on pregnancy test sticks. Terrified what that would mean. Daniel would potentially pass on his abilities, a curse he'd always said would end with him and Mal. And Piper? Ha! Some Mom she'd make with her parents' example, never mind the part where she might give her own kid a disease.

"It's not completely your fault," Daniel said. "Casual is probably best for both of us. Safest."

It was her turn at the four-way stop, and she advanced through the intersection. "Right. So we'll just focus on figuring out how to bring down the barrier and keep everyone safe in the meantime."

"Right."

"And since we're clearing the air, I should probably tell you Mal stopped by last night and—"

"Mal stopped by? Why? How long did he stay?"

She winced at Daniel's harsh tone. Probably best to neglect to mention how scared she'd been. She waved her hands, slowing the truck to a crawl. People milled around the library, community center, and Senior's center, some people parking at the library to take their kids into the school. Evidently an apocalyptic barrier was no reason to cancel classes.

"Not long. He came to tell me about some apocalyptic group and their plans. Sounds like they're behind the barrier malfunction. Something about how the barrier will incubate all of our abilities so my friends and I can conveniently end the world for them. And he apologized for what he did at the library." She pulled into a spot in front of the Senior Center.

"He owes you more than an apology for what he did. Though that does explain his guilt last night," Daniel said darkly. He'd been vague about the details when they were together, but it seemed to be one of their twin things to share emotions.

"Point being, I know about them. And I'm going to be careful."

She cut the engine and turned to hold the keys out to Daniel.

Only to find his gaze directly on her, the cab of the truck having seemingly shrunk in the past few seconds. Despite the skunk and console between them, she became hyper-aware of his body, of the gold flecks in his brown eyes, the intensity in his gaze. She swallowed.

His hand enveloped hers. "Promise me. Promise me you'll be careful. Mal is in more trouble than he realizes. The group and their plot could tear not only this town apart, but wreak havoc worldwide. There are also people who believe you might want to hurt them and won't be convinced otherwise. I don't want you in the middle of that. And if something happened to you—" His voice broke off and roughened. "I need you to be careful. I need to know you're safe."

She nodded stupidly. "I'll be careful." Despite everything they'd talked about, their agreement that their engagement ending was all for the best, all she wanted to do was lean across the truck and kiss him.

So much for logic.

"Thank you," Daniel said sincerely. He squeezed her hand in his. Massaged her wrist with his roughened thumb pad. The atmosphere thickened around them.

Her breath sped.

His eyes darkened.

Warmth flooded through her, and she leaned closer

to him.

His gaze went to her mouth. He swallowed, hard. Then ripped his gaze away and gave himself a shake. "I'll, uh, see you later," he said and groped for the door handle.

He jumped out of the truck as though her skunk had threatened to spray.

Piper flopped back against the seat and crossed her arms over her chest. She shared a look with the skunk. "Yeah, yeah. I know, totally pathetic. I'm totally and pathetically in lust with my ex."

CHAPTER 18

Daniel paused in the back entrance to the Senior Center, straightened his shirt, and adjusted his tie. And tried to pretend he hadn't just run away from Piper Bane and those delectable lips for the second time in two days.

She didn't want attachments. She'd never agree to stay in Beckwell—even if they did find a way to bring down the barrier. Besides that, the council meeting had proved just how dangerous it could be here for her.

His body didn't give a damn. He wanted her from her corn silk hair all the way down to her pink toenails. He wanted to lose himself in her body and her scent until he couldn't remember his own name. Or that his ability had streamed through his blood without permission. Or that he was supposed to save this town.

He clenched the door handle and closed his eyes a moment.

He wanted to be with her to forget the man he was supposed to be and remember the man he used to be. When she'd loved him. When he'd still believed in the possibility of his own happy ending.

Ten years ago. A lifetime ago.

He rubbed the back of his neck and strode into the Senior Center.

He emerged from the hallway into the central pavilion. Three tables were reduced to ash. A small fire smoldered on one of the couches.

Two attendants were up on chairs trying to reach the giggling old lady with large leathery wings, who flapped around in circles near the apex of the ceiling. One of the attendants waved, but in a "hi, we're fine" way, not a "dear lord, help us!" way.

At which point Daniel rounded the corner and saw the crowd of Beckwellians swarming his office. They were packed into the glass-fronted waiting room. The line stretched around the corner and down another hall. They had tails. They had horns. One of them was purple.

Daniel gulped. This was what Mal had meant about the barrier incubating abilities? If this kept up, Beckwell would look like the set of the next Tolkien movie by the weekend.

The purple guy spotted Daniel. And told the others.

"Doctor Quilan, I need—"

"Daniel, if you'd just—"

The voices called out to him, canceled out each other.

He smiled. Waved. Forced his feet toward his office instead of in the opposite direction. Many he'd seen regularly, others only once or twice. But all of them looked significantly less human than on previous visits. What were his diagnoses supposed to be? Spontaneous tail eruption? A case of Beckwellitus?

His stomach rolled. How long before he started to show the effects of the barrier and began to look more Fomorian? And if he looked outwardly Fomorian, what exactly would that make him on the inside?

More choruses of voices as he entered the waiting room. People jumped up from their chairs. Where had he been? Why hadn't he been here? How was he going to help them?

He waded through people to the safety of the front desk.

His office assistant, Frizzly, blocked anyone from following with a beefy tattooed arm, but his cheeks were pink and there was panic in his blue eyes. "Glad you're finally here, boss man. They were here when I opened up."

Daniel patted the muscular arm. They borrowed a nurse from the Senior Center on crazy days like this, but otherwise Frizzly was the only staff Daniel had. There were advantages to hiring a former biker. Besides that, Frizzly was very polite on the phone.

"You've done good. Anything I should know first?"

"Actually—" Frizzly's face reddened further.

"Ah, Daniel. I mean, Doctor Quilan," the feminine voice said from behind Frizzly. "Good to see you." It was Daphne Spinner. Didn't she belong at the school somewhere?

Daniel's shoulders tensed, and his hands fisted. Was she wearing one of *his* lab jackets? In *his* office?

Uneasiness flickered through him, his senses warning him of some unseen threat she posed.

"Yeah. That," Frizzly said. He jerked a finger over his shoulder, then lumbered back to the front desk where patients had gathered. "He'll see you all. Now sit down and wait your turn," he thundered.

Which left Daniel glaring at Daphne. She'd played councilwoman last night, doctor today?

She picked up a file from the counter. "Mrs. Merkson? I'll see you now."

A frail woman tottered across the waiting room, blinking through pop-bottle lenses. She peered up at

Daniel. "I think it's my gallbladder, Doctor."

He shot another glare at Daphne but forced his lips into a smile for Mrs. Merkson. "Your gallbladder was removed four years ago," he said gently, patting her arm.

"Oh. Well, then this is a bother." She turned and waggled an enormous, fuzzy raccoon tail springing from the top of her pea-green skirt.

"Right this way, Mrs. Merkson," Daphne said.

"Yes, go on into exam room one. I'll be right there," Daniel said, shooting a glare at Daphne. "Miss Spinner and I need to have a quick discussion."

With the old woman ensconced in the exam room, Daphne's face pink, Daniel jabbed a finger down toward his office at the end of the hall.

She stopped right outside of the doorway, her arms crossed over her chest. And his lab coat. "I would have thought you'd appreciate the help, Doctor."

She was close enough they almost touched. There was that strange warning tingle again, like a red emergency flare. This woman was dangerous.

"A noble sentiment, but this is a medical office."

"And I'm a doctor."

His brows rose. "I thought you worked at the school. Guidance counselor?"

"Which doesn't preclude me having a medical degree." She tossed her head, dark curls cascading over her shoulders and slim, pale neck.

As though she wanted him to be aware of her as a woman. She might as well have been a primed nuke. And she sure the hell couldn't compare to the woman he loved.

He blinked. No. Not love, as in present tense. He *had* loved her. He and Piper had a history.

"Doctor Quilan?" Daphne softened her voice and looked up at him through her lashes. "I'm sorry. I've invaded your space." She touched his arm.

His ability surged against his will, and he jerked away from her. His muscles tensed for attack, heart beating, full battle-ready response. He searched her appearance for any hint of what she was but found only woman. A dangerous woman he wanted nowhere near his patients.

"Thank you, but I have this well under control, and you're not licensed to operate in *my* clinic. Perhaps Ms. Boniface or the town council could better direct your charity." *Get out of my territory.*

Something flared in her eyes, and her expression hardened, though she offered a small, tight smile. "We could have been friends. *Good* friends," she said, her tone and the tongue wetting her lips insinuating something sexual. "I could have helped you. You will regret this."

Now she threatened him? He held out his hand for the file. "I have all the friends I need, thank you. Frizzly, please see Ms. Spinner out. I think she's lost."

Her eyes narrowed to slits, her lips to a narrow line. She slapped the file into his hand and jerked off the lab coat before tossing it on the floor.

Frizzly approached.

She sidestepped him and flipped both the office assistant and Daniel off. She turned, her hand on the clinic door. "You have no idea what you've done." She burst through the doors, sending some of the waiting patients scattering away from her, and flounced out of the atrium.

Daniel tracked her progress until she'd exited the front doors.

"Uh, everything okay?" Frizzly asked.

Daniel frowned, his shoulders hard as rock. He glanced down at the file, twisted and torn in half between dark bronze fingers, the color receding as he stared. He handed his assistant the file. "Tape this together, will you? And that woman's not to come in here again." "Woman" being the best possible term he had so far, albeit inaccurate.

She was a threat. Part of the group of troublemakers? With her threats, the possibility seemed likely.

Frizzly cleared his throat, and he stared down at his large feet. "I shouldn't have let her in here. But her references checked out. And she claimed she just wanted to help with all the patients, that you'd asked her to help."

"And you thought maybe I'd taken your advice and finally hired help and another doctor?"

The man nodded, his thick beard scraping his chest, only a bit shorter than his boss. He finally met Daniel's gaze. "Guess I wasn't thinking as clear as I should." He gestured toward the waiting patients and lowered his voice. "But people are scared. Three already today, injured after trying to break through that dang barrier. One climbed a tree, tried to get out over the barrier, but fell and broke his arm. Another rammed his truck straight into it and got himself a busted leg, bandaged-up head, plus his wife got banged up, and now he has a squashed truck for the effort. The third tried five batteries all tied together, mostly just fried himself."

The big man held up his left hand.

Daniel froze, fought to keep his expression neutral.

Frizzly's fingers had fused until four fingers were only two, the thumb about three times normal size, all gray and rough, stone-like. He frowned at it. "Not sure how long it'll be before the rest of me looks like this, too. Troll blood, you understand. Damned useless for much of anything." He again met Daniel's gaze. "So I get why people are crazy to escape. What're we going to do to help them, Doc?"

Daniel rocked back on his heels and shook his head

before he met his assistant's gaze squarely. "Well, we're going to start by telling them to stay away from that barrier. We're going to reassure them they're not alone, and we're going to figure this out. And we're going to remind them of the kind of people who call this town home, and all the things they're capable of—the least of which is dealing with some unexpected appendages or genetic regressions. Now, get all the rooms full. We've got work to do."

Frizzly nodded, nodded again, scrunching the torn file in his own big hand, and lumbered back toward his desk.

Which left Daniel to head into the first room and first patient. He paused with his hand on the door handle and closed his eyes, his fingers trembling. Who the hell was he to tell other people he had this figured out and that they should have no trouble handling turning into what their ancestors had once been? He didn't want to. And after more than a decade studying medicine, he didn't know how to prevent the change in himself. So how did that make him capable of helping his patients now?

Piper's smile came to mind, the way she'd touch his cheek and reassure him he was being an idiot, the soft warmth in her amber eyes.

Piper, who was terrified of her own abilities, but had headed straight for her friends, determined to learn how to use and control them. Even if it was the one thing she'd never wanted.

Piper, who'd plopped herself right back down in the center of his heart again.

He opened his eyes, firmed his jaw, and squeezed the door handle until the tremor left his hand. For her, he would find a way to perform the miracles necessary to help this town. Even if that meant finding a scientific solution for a magical problem.

He opened the door to the room with a determined smile in place, prepared for battle. "Mrs. Merkson, let's see what we can learn about that tail."

CHAPTER 19

After admiring Daniel's toned butt that filled out those khakis nicely while he escaped to the Senior Center, Piper gave herself a stern lecture on all the reasons her libido should not be in charge. Then she and the skunk hopped out of the truck and headed for the library. It wasn't far, just a short walk down the gravel road that joined the Senior Center, community hall, and library.

Time to talk to the girls—what they'd wanted from the first moment she'd arrived—and figure out a plan to handle all this apocalypse stuff. A plan that, hopefully, didn't include ending the world or hurting anyone.

"They're probably going to be mad," Piper said to the skunk. A bit concerning just how easily she'd taken to talking to the critter. Hopefully because it was magical. And not because she was not-so-slowly losing it.

The skunk waddled beside her and sent the image of she and Daniel kissing, followed by a question, as in: was she going to tell the girls about Daniel and the kiss?

Piper grimaced. "I don't even know what I'd say. So no. Not yet." She adjusted her shirt. "I'll probably start with some groveling for forgiveness because I didn't listen to them, and after that, maybe Anna can hand out the alphabetized binder full of plans she probably has."

This resulted in a small mental chuckle from the skunk at the image of Anna's emergency plan binders.

Piper chuckled back. "Are you in my head all the time?"

The skunk smirked.

"Well, if you're in there, let me know if you make any sense of it, 'kay?" Another glance down, and the skunk still stared at her. "Suppose you need a name. You know, instead of just calling you 'skunk' all the time."

The skunk flashed the image of a regal female in a crown.

"Princess?"

The skunk sniffed and looked away. Again the image of the female in the crown, only this time, it was the image of the queen on the back of a dollar coin.

"Queen? You know, it'd be a lot easier if you could just talk."

Now just the image of the queen plus an E.

"Queenie?"

The skunk bumped affectionately against Piper's leg and sent warmth through their connection. It almost made up for the challenge of communicating.

"Queenie it is."

They'd reached the library, and Piper stepped up onto the porch of the log building and faced the library's double doors. The "open" sign glowed in the front window, and frankly, she'd never even considered Anna wouldn't be here. Anna spent more time at the library than she did at home, and if the world was ending, this was the only place Anna would want to be. She'd said as much whenever Piper asked her why she didn't travel, use her degrees to get a more interesting job. Piper always suspected Anna feared a more interesting job.

Bells tinkled above the door as Piper entered, holding the door open for Queenie. The library was surprisingly large for such a small town, about half the size of a gymnasium, packed full of intimidating rows of bookshelves. Anna had also conceded to the town council and provided a small computer area with eight computers, and one small section of shelves dedicated to movies and music.

The modern concessions to the library didn't begin to compare with the size of the Special Collections and Weirdo Beckwell Stuff Section, which comprised five bookshelves behind the circulation desk. The shelves groaned with scrolls and massive old books full of dangerous knowledge and enough heft to crush a person to death.

Unsurprisingly, with the town in chaos and trapped by the mysterious border, the library was empty.

Except for Anna, who looked up from behind the large oak circulation desk that faced the door. She stood slowly, revealing the most hideous pink, moth-eaten sweater over a rose-print blouse and green slacks. She said nothing, merely raised a questioning brow.

Piper clutched her hands together in front of her. Time to eat some humble-berry pie. "I'm sorry. You were right. You told me the truth at the bar and I...I didn't want to hear it."

Anna's expression softened, and she nodded. "I know. And for what it's worth, I wish I had been wrong."

They shared a moment of quiet. Of the three others, only Anna understood what it was to be terrified of her abilities. And only she hated them at least as much as Piper.

It ended with a pointed look from Anna down at Queenie, who'd stopped at Piper's feet and looked around the library with mild curiosity. "I hope there's a reason you've invited wildlife into my library?"

Piper winced. "I think maybe she's part of my abilities? You were there at the school yesterday and saw what happened. Then at the barrier... I could see emotion as color." Her shoulders slumped. "I'm so afraid I'll make everyone sick in town, and it'll only be the four of us left standing." She looked up. "I didn't make you guys sick yesterday, did I? We always thought we'd be immune to each other, but—"

"And we were correct. Nia, Ginny, and I were unaffected yesterday at the school. It's why we were able to pull you out." Anna ducked, only to pull a huge, ancient-looking book and thump it down on the counter. It looked a whole lot like the one with the newspaper clippings she'd tried to show Piper at the bar that first day.

And no less intimidating. Piper cringed. "Couldn't you just beat me over the head with it for a while or something until I agree with everything you say?"

Anna rolled her eyes and pushed the book toward Piper. "Start reading. You need to bring yourself up to speed on what's going on. I'll call the others. It's time we all have a serious chat. The four of us are probably the best chance this town has."

If that's the case, poor Beckwell.

Piper tried not to drag her feet toward the circulation desk, but sliding the book off, it damn near crushed her. She wasn't quiet about her grumbles as she lugged the thing over to the nearest table.

Anna ignored her, instead quietly murmuring into the phone.

Queenie settled beside Piper's chair, and Piper flipped the cover.

Ugh. It was like a really big scrapbook with photocopied articles pasted inside, Anna's obscenely tiny handwriting offering additional notes. And notes on the notes. It seemed to have some order. "Lost Objects of Myth" comprised a substantial section. Beneath the various articles and photocopied images was Anna's scrawl on pink Post-It notes. *"Found in Beckwell? How? Why? Consequences?"* There was a hideous snow globe some god had imbued with power on a dare—didn't say what power. Huh. Something niggled in the back of her memory, but she was distracted by the photocopied image of the next object, some goddess's mirror, no ability described. A black and white photo of a nasty-looking dagger.

Hopefully, Anna's other binder, the one with all the kickass plans, was still somewhere else. And written in bigger font.

Piper's head ached, and she'd barely flipped begun to read. All those years of library avoidance seemed completely and totally justified.

Finally, she spotted the divisions based on each of the four horsemen, and another section dedicated to the horses themselves.

Piper had to use both hands to open the Pestilence section.

"Sometimes known as 'conquest' or 'victory.' The white horse. Can create new and original disease spontaneously, control and alter existing disease, including disease of the mind and sickness aura. Affinity for swarming insects and animals generally associated with pestilence. Air element, believed to be related to the ability to cause and spread plagues. Original

Pestilence a known empath."

That was it? What the heck was she supposed to do with that information? Piper flipped the next page. It was blank. "Uh, Anna, what happened to the rest of the Pestilence info? Where's the section about how I control any of this crap? Or get rid of it, you know, like give it to some other Pestilence? And why isn't there anything about the barrier?" Anna had wandered away from the front desk. "Anna, help! Seriously, do not leave me alone with the big scary book."

The bell tinkled above the door, catching Piper's attention. "Geez, I'm pissed at you, but even you don't deserve to be punished with the Bigass Book of Boring," Nia said, coming in through the front door. She stuffed her hands in the pockets of her oversized black hoodie, her straight black hair concealed by the hood. She hooked a chair beside Piper with her foot, pulled it out, and slouched down in it.

"I'm not punishing her. She needs to be brought up to speed." Anna reappeared from the rear of the library with four bottles of water. "And that's all there is on Pestilence." She shrugged. "It's not my clan, so they won't share info with me. The barrier isn't an object, and it isn't related to the four of us, so it wasn't something I researched."

Nia leaned forward and reached for one of the bottles. "Just give Piper the Internet-news version. We don't have all century to wait for her to read it."

The door's bell tinkled again. "What are we waiting for Piper to read?" Ginny said, stepping inside, every strand of red hair pulled back into a tight bun. She unbuttoned her ugly, banana-yellow jacket and grinned at Piper. "Hey! Glad you're here and we're all a team again." She took the bottle of water Anna offered and took a seat across the table, then frowned and turned to peer under it. "And, uh, Anna? Why's there a skunk under the table?"

Anna pointed at Piper without looking up, instead drawing the book toward her and flipping to one of the sections near the back. "It's Piper's skunk." Her lips pursed and her brows lowered as she searched for the page she was looking at. "When did it first appear? And do you know if it's had any different incarnations?"

Queenie looked up from where she was at Piper's feet and flashed the image of the toad, then the accident scene and mutual terror as she and Piper hurtled toward the tree.

"*She* started out as a toad. And first showed up the second I hit town. Like, literally. I think—"

A flash of irritation from Queenie, and she waggled her bushy tail menacingly.

"Er, I *thought* she caused the accident."

"*So what did?*" Piper communicated to the skunk.

The skunk flashed the image of shadowy figures, followed by a big question mark.

"Hmm," Anna said.

Ginny peeked under the table again and waggled her fingers at the skunk, albeit a tad nervously. "She's kind of cute. Does she have a name?"

"Queenie."

Queenie got up, and while Ginny froze in terror, rubbed against the tall redhead's leg like a cat before she returned and curled up on Piper's feet.

"Does she have any memory of her life prior to meeting you?" Anna asked.

Piper looked to the skunk and conveyed the question.

The animal cocked its head, again showed the toad, and otherwise big, black nothingness.

"Doesn't seem like it."

"Hmm," Anna said again.

"Okay, so is that a 'hmm, that's really useless,' or like 'hmm, I do believe the world will explode in the next sixty seconds'?" Nia grumbled and leaned back in her chair, her hood concealing most of her face.

Anna finally looked up and met Piper's gaze. "I think—" She frowned and glanced down at the skunk, as though to confirm her words. "I believe she may be your horse."

Nia chortled. "Seriously? Anna, now I *know* you need glasses. That thing is black and white, and less than a foot high. Horse it is not."

The horsewoman of War growled in her throat and assumed the most academic tone she could as she read from the scary-ass book. "'And they shall each be granted a horse. Suitable to the environment, level of ability, and appropriateness of the situation.'"

Piper scowled. "Okay, so I kind of get the environment. Lots of skunks around. Not sure what it says about my ability. But 'appropriateness of situation'? What?"

"Bad smells—miasma—were once associated with disease," Anna said, but even she didn't look certain. She turned to the book again with a frown. "I can't think of why you'd be associated with a skunk—"

"A magical empathic skunk," Piper clarified.

"Yes, that," Anna said, somewhat tightly.

"Maybe you're just a creepy critter magnet," Nia teased.

"Yeah? In that case, I can't wait to see what comes after you," Piper said with a sarcastic smile.

Nia flipped her off.

The two women grinned at each other, and Piper's shoulders relaxed somewhat. Queenie settled more comfortably to nap. The world was screwed up, but right now, back with her friends, it felt a whole lot less scary, and a whole lot more normal.

Ginny cleared her throat hesitantly and spoke softly. "Although horses might have been more common in the days of the first horsemen, they're not exactly an everyday sight nowadays."

Nia snorted. "Yeah, except around here. On, like, every farm. Besides, how 'normal' does it look to walk around with a skunk?"

Ginny flushed and dropped her gaze.

Anna glowered at Nia. "Hush." Then to Ginny. "You were saying?"

Despite being a redhead, Ginny was probably the most timid of the group, and today she seemed determined to prove it. She shifted her shoulders, following a long scar on the tabletop with a fingertip. "I just mean something small, like a toad or a skunk, it would be easier to blend in, right? And Piper, when did it turn into a skunk?"

Piper frowned. "Right after what happened at the school."

"A significant show of power, right?" Ginny looked to the others excitedly. "So, 'appropriate to ability'? The skunk might still turn into a horse. Or maybe something else, the more power and ability Piper gets."

The other three sat back, considering.

Nia was the first to speak. "You know, I think you've really got something there, Gin."

"Yes, you may be right," Anna agreed.

Ginny beamed.

"In which case, I'm hoping for a badass, black unicorn," Nia said.

"I don't think that would blend in," Ginny said with a frown.

Anna sniffed. "Nor is it real. Or appropriate to the environment."

Piper cleared her throat, causing everyone to look at her. "Okay. So say Ginny is right, and Queenie is my 'horse'. Terrific. I still don't know what exactly all that stuff means about my abilities, how I'm going to control or get rid of them so I don't hurt anyone. And has anyone noticed there's a super-solid barrier trapping us all here? If we really are gaining our abilities—and, yes, it's fairly clear I am—how do we protect Beckwell and the rest of the world from us?"

CHAPTER 20

Piper's pronouncement settled a notable pall over the women and silence hung in the library other than Queenie's soft snores. Piper sighed and pushed a hand through her hair. "I'm sorry, guys. I'm just scared."

"Rightfully so. And we do need a plan," Anna said. "We obviously got sidetracked with the unexpected form of your horse. We should be afraid. The potential damage our powers could cause is catastrophic."

"The word you're looking for is 'apocalyptic'," Nia said dryly, which Anna ignored.

"Oh, good. So this is the part where you pull out a different book full of incredibly brilliant plans, right?" Piper said, only half teasing.

Anna's lips twitched, but it didn't evolve into a smile. "Unfortunately, no."

"Damn. I was betting she had one of those, too," Nia grumbled.

The War horsewoman continued without acknowledging Nia. "We know there's a group trying to cause the apocalypse. And in some way, they are likely responsible for what's happened to the barrier trapping us all here and potentially for us coming into our abilities."

"Oh, and Mal's definitely a part of it. He stopped by and said as much." Piper scowled and picked at a scratch on the table. "And tried to apologize for what he'd done."

"The ass. Did you kick him in the nuts? He deserved that and more," Nia said. "If he's part of it, I think it's settled what we should call them. The League of Extraordinary Assholes. Because who but a bunch of assholes would Mal join up with?" She offered a surprisingly gentle smile, which Piper returned.

Even if the girls never knew the details about what had happened that night to Piper, they'd known something had happened. Which had mostly led to high suspicion of every male they came in contact with.

Piper nodded. "Mal also said it meant the barrier would incubate abilities—ours likely included."

"That's unfortunate," Anna murmured, her hands trembling slightly.

"Well, it means the group will undoubtedly have something planned for my wedding. Probably the engagement party, too," Ginny said matter-of-factly.

Piper and the others turned, blinking in surprise, not sure what to say.

Ginny glanced up and offered a half-hearted shrug. "It's hardly much of a secret, is it? Beckwell parties always turn into some kind of fiasco. And now that Mom has turned the whole thing into some kind of community event, it might as well have a red bull's-eye painted on it." She colored under the other women's attention. "What? I mean, I don't even know if there'll be a wedding. If the barrier doesn't come down, my fiancé can't get into town. Maybe I'm wrong and the whole thing's a moot point."

"And you're sure that would be a bad thing? If he doesn't get into town?" Piper asked gently. She couldn't stop thinking about all her conversations and emails with Ginny. And how the topic of almost all of them was Piper. How many times had she remembered to ask what Ginny was up to? Had she asked anything proper about the wedding, the fiancé, the romance?

Ginny flushed burgundy. "They told you, huh? That it's arranged."

"Hey, I'm good with it if you are. I just want to make sure *you* are good with it." Piper reached across the table and squeezed Ginny's hand.

"I really am, yeah," Ginny said with a tiny smile. "He's Famine clan, too, so at least I don't have to worry about affecting him. You know, if I ever get any real ability."

Even back in high school, Death and War were never taken as lightly as Pestilence or Famine. Seriously, what was Ginny ever going to do to anyone? Kill their tomato plants?

Anna cleared her throat. "If that's out of the way, perhaps we can discuss how we're going to move forward. First up, the barrier. Beckwell was founded on a mystical vortex, and as such attracts unusual and powerful beings and objects. I believe a magical object is responsible for recently trapping us. In the front section, I've noted several distinct possibilities."

"Oh, this is the magical garbage dump thing," Nia nodded. "If it's used up, worn out, goes missing, or no one wants it, it ends up here."

Anna's lips thinned to a tight line. "I said it was a mystical. *Vortex.*"

"Sounds like 'garbage dump' to me." Nia leaned back and put her feet on the table. "Which probably means we have Zeus's used condoms, lots of rotting food, and all the other nasty shit people use in spells. Now that makes total sense." Evidently, Nia wanted to get herself killed.

Anna glared at Nia's feet so hotly, they should have been incinerated. "Vortex."

Piper edged her chair away from Nia. Just in case Anna threw a heavy book and missed.

"Zeus probably should have used a condom. Consider how that would have changed history," Ginny mused.

Anna massaged her forehead. "Well, he didn't, did he? And why are we talking about mythological condoms?"

"Because we're scared as hell, and condoms and sex are more fun than magical weirdo-shit. Well, for some of us," Nia conceded, earning another glare from Anna. "Better to think about Zeus's dick than about how somehow we're going to gain the scary-ass powers to become the four horsewomen of the apocalypse, and that we either have to carry out the apocalypse or somehow figure out a way to stop it."

Anna sighed and looked up, her voice low. "The mystical vortex is one issue. The other is that someone should get around to talking to Loki the Liar and see if he'll fix the barrier."

"He's still around? He has to be like a million years old if he's alive. And even if he is, why would toothless old Loki have anything to do with it?" Piper asked, waiting for a laugh from the others at the joke.

There wasn't one.

Just a stern look from Anna. "He's hardly toothless. And because he created the barrier to protect the town when he founded it."

"Uh, yeah. But also at least a hundred and ten percent likely to be part of the League of Assholes," Nia said. "Hot and powerful, or old and shriveled up, why would he help us? Hell, he's probably thrilled with all this chaos. Hello? *Loki*."

"He might help," Anna said quietly.

"Why? Because you asked?" Nia shot back.

Piper searched her memory for anything on Loki because there was clearly some underlying argument here between Nia and Anna that she wasn't getting. She had vague memories of Loki on all those Founders Day picnics they used to have, and even as a kid she'd known he was good-looking. But that'd been years ago. He hardly ventured out in public these days. What involvement would Anna or Nia have with him?

Anna cleared her throat, color climbing her high cheekbones. "So, the barrier needs to be cleared up. Ginny, if you're right and the League will use the events surrounding your wedding, that could give us an opportunity to search the school and see what we can find. Most of the suspect objects I've found seem to have been located there. We should find the object, and then dispense with accordingly."

"You mean break it?" Ginny said softly.

"I mean accordingly. Breaking some of them could have much worse consequences."

"And me? What should I do about my abilities? I don't want to accidentally make anyone sick again like I did at the school. Daniel said they all got better as soon as I left. But if they hadn't..." Oh god. There'd been kindergarten kids there. All those students... Piper shivered.

"Which is where we come to the second part of the plan. You need to learn what your abilities are. And how to suppress them," Anna said.

"Suppress them? Are you freakin' kidding me? That's not going to happen," Nia snorted. "I can 'suppress' all I want, but it isn't going to stop the ghosts from knocking on my doors."

"Are you sure suppression is the wisest idea? Wouldn't it be better if maybe we, you know, learned about our abilities and got really good with them so we could stop the bad guys?" Ginny piped up.

Piper swiveled back and forth between the two of them. Suppression didn't seem like the best plan, because it wasn't as if she'd wanted to make people sick at the school, but it'd happened anyway, hadn't it? Then again, gaining and using their abilities like Ginny said didn't seem much better, either. There'd be no coming back from that.

Queenie sent sleepy but comforting thoughts Piper's way.

Anna leaned back in her chair and crossed her arms, eyes flashing. "Piper? Do you agree with the others? Because the way I see it, if we accept our abilities, we become The Four, and we spread apocalypse."

"I'm not saying we have to end the world," Ginny defended.

"Frankly, at this point I'm not sure exactly what other abilities I'm supposed to gain," Nia said, leaning forward on the edge of her seat. "I see and talk to ghosts. They annoy the hell out of me twenty-four seven, particularly since most of them are pervy degenerates. I can walk the Gray between the living and dead worlds and end up there accidentally in my sleep, which I gotta tell you—super *not* fun. Oh, yeah, and I'm attracting more ghosts all the time—whether I'm actively trying to use my abilities or not, Anna."

Anna's fingers bit into her arms and the color deepened on her face. "Piper? Might as well toss in your opinion."

Piper swallowed. "Well, I don't want to use my abilities, either. And if I had a choice, I don't want to gain them."

Anna leaned closer and almost smiled.

Piper inwardly cringed. "*But*, I didn't want to hurt anyone at the school, either. I've spent all my life trying to suppress my abilities, and it hasn't worked, hasn't helped. Maybe…maybe we do need to learn to use them, even just a bit. Or we figure out how to control them at least. Then maybe we can figure out how to get rid of them from there."

"There's the Piper I remember. Not a complete moron," Nia said. Which was probably supposed to be a compliment.

"How do you propose doing that then, Piper? Nia? Ginny? Any suggestions?" Anna snapped.

Nia crossed her arms and looked away. Ginny wouldn't meet Anna's eyes, just picked at a fingernail. Which left only Piper available to be trapped in Anna's gaze.

Well, Piper was also the only one so far who really knew she was gaining her full abilities. That put her a step ahead of the rest of them. For all that was worth. She cleared her throat. "We can't do it without you, Anna. Who else can I practice with but you or the others? No one knows as much about this as you do. We need you. We need to work together if we're going to get out of this."

She reached across the table, paused, then continued the rest of the way to press her hand to Anna's cold fist that still rested on the giant-ass book of scary. "And I swear to you, if we can find a way for you—for any of us—to not have to be one of The Four anymore, I'll gladly give it to you." She softened her voice. "I don't want this. You know that. I hate this. But I'd hate hurting people more."

Anna seemed to unbend a little. "Maybe you learn to use the ability so you can control and avoid using it?"

"That sounds great," Piper agreed.

"I'd be good with that, too," Nia said.

"I guess so." Ginny sounded the least sure. But maybe that was just because it was Ginny? She couldn't actually want power, could she? Then again, she was from an upper-class clan family, where they usually were born with more ability. Maybe she thought it was her due?

"All right. I can work with that. We'll start practicing as soon as possible. Together, and individually." Anna paused, and slowly blew out a breath. "All of us. I...I'll try, too."

Ginny squeezed Anna's arm, and even Nia gave her an approving nod. Piper offered Anna an encouraging smile.

Anna nodded. "It's agreed then. We all start practicing. But, we also need to talk alternative plans. How we end this if we can't control our abilities, or they start to control us. Our mortality. If we gain our full powers, The Four are said to be as powerful as the gods, which won't earn us any allies. We'll be very strong, but we can still be killed. Are you prepared to die if it means saving Beckwell and the world?"

CHAPTER 21

Piper and Queenie stumbled out from the library, the last rays of sunlight burning through the trees across the road. She and the girls had spent the remains of the day practicing their abilities. Which, without anyone who wasn't immune to their abilities around, had been even harder than expected. She massaged her aching neck. Where would she find Daniel?

Ginny had kept them all fed with the most delicious cupcakes ever—which seemed kind of counter to her famine ability, but whatever. She'd also made one grow a miniscule speck of mold, which was good practice in manifesting and controlling her abilities. Especially when Ginny didn't think she had Famine powers.

Anna practiced her ability to identify lies—there were reams of pages on War abilities in the Big Book of Scary—so she'd gone through the Internet news declaring true or false on all of them. Which seemed half-hearted and not all that challenging in the first place.

Nia held office hours for the dead in the children's section of the library. And complained. A lot.

And Piper? She'd made a list of the colors associated with each emotion, which Anna added to the Big Book of Scary. She'd gotten two hornets to fly in a circle. Probably. Or maybe they just liked flying in circles. And she'd worked on controlling or altering air currents by blowing out and moving around the smoke from a candle. Which hadn't seemed especially helpful.

Her shoulders drooped and she plodded back toward the Senior Center, and hopefully, Daniel. What she'd learned today was hardly enough to uncover, stop, and defeat the League of Extraordinary Assholes. Unless two dizzy hornets and some swirling smoke happened to be among their phobias.

Queenie nipped Piper's heel, and having caught Piper's attention, waved her head toward the Community Hall, a tube-like metal structure with doors at one end of the tube. There sat Daniel's faded blue truck, parked front and center.

Huh. And surrounded by a lot of other vehicles. Piper wandered into the midst of them. At least half the town had to be there.

She pressed her lips into a fine line. Had she and her friends just missed the memo? Or were they not invited?

Well, didn't look like there was a "No Horsewomen Allowed" sign out front.

Piper straightened her shoulders and crunched determinedly through the gravel toward the Community Hall doors. Probably not that surprising she hadn't been invited; she was technically only a guest around here. But what about Anna, Ginny, and Nia? Though they were probably as exhausted as she was. Maybe she should have headed back to the library and gotten them. But she could always just check it out and see what was happening first, couldn't she? Maybe it had to do with something boring.

Queenie conveyed a disbelieving sniff.

The doors were propped open, and she slid inside among the crowd. All the chairs were full, and people crammed the aisles, pressed against the walls, and were five deep in the back of the hall, where Piper stood. The air was heavy with purple worry and the cloying black smoke of fear. People shifted the small amount necessary to make room for her, but their attention was too focused on the front to take any note of her identity.

"Do they have a plan to get rid of the barrier?" A man in a blue baseball cap and lion's tail sticking out through his jeans asked the woman with green skin next to him. "The mayor said it'd be gone in no time."

The woman snorted, gills rippling along the side of her neck. "Like we should believe anything that moron says. He was dumb as toast *before* he got himself stuck in the barrier. Lack of oxygen to the brain probably hasn't helped. We should have someone useful in charge. Like Loki. Or Doc Quilan. He's the only one who seems to be doing anything to help any of us."

Daniel would make a good mayor. Though it would probably mean he spent even more time running around trying to take care of people.

The man nodded, and they both craned to see what was going on at the front of the room. Piper did the same.

"Why isn't Loki fixing this? Where is he?" someone near the front shouted. "Is he dead? Has he abandoned us?"

That got the crowd going. Cries echoed out varying from he'd been dead for years, to of course he'd rescue them, to what did they need him for?

Piper rolled her eyes. It was Nia and Anna all over again. Although no mention of Loki's potential-hotness was mentioned here.

Barely visible, the town council was seated behind a long table and looked nervous. The mayor, Ed Blycoomb in the middle, along with Ms. Boniface, Mr. Lack, Lou, and one of the practically interchangeable Hecate girls.

Daniel stood at the podium in front of them, his hair wild where he'd probably been pushing his hands through it, looking like he hadn't slept in a month. As usual, he was the one doing any real work.

Only Daniel could make exhausted-beyond-reason look hot. He gave the impression he'd been doing something sexier than sleeping. Which was unlikely. Probably just saving lives and being perfect.

Frick. On second thought, that *was* pretty damned sexy. It made him like a superhero without the tights. And seriously? The tights were overrated.

"Loki has been notified of the barrier's malfunction," Ms. Boniface said, leaning over the microphone in the middle of the table.

"Everyone, I know you're frightened. We're trying to figure out what's happening and stop it." Daniel's voice boomed over the sound system. It crackled and went out, smoke rising from the microphone.

"Word is your brother is part of that group of idiots trying to start an apocalypse. Will you stop *him*?" a blonde with bat-wings and a baby in her arms accused.

"Isn't he still sleeping with one of the horsewomen?" an old lady said loudly.

"Maybe it's about time we did something, got ourselves noticed," someone else Piper couldn't see shouted back. "Maybe people should know who and what we are. Why should we keep hiding? We're stronger this way. We should help those apocalypse people. They're shaking things up."

A squat woman in denim and a wide-brimmed hat

stood. "Shaking things up? They're out to end the world."

"Sandra, you're just jealous no one invited you to start any apocalypse," an old man accused the woman, which got some titters of laughter.

The woman wouldn't be dissuaded. "This is no joke, Henry." She pulled off her hat and revealed long, pointed elf ears. "This is what that group is turning us into. Freaks. Monsters."

The audience grew increasingly restless. Red anger and black fear clashed with green righteousness and purple worry.

"Who are you calling a freak?" The man who stood looked like he'd been roughly carved entirely from wood. "*This* is who we are. We might not be pretty or popular enough for the gods' liking, but why should we care?"

"My wife has nymph genes, and she's turned into a tree. What am I supposed to tell my kids?" a man with small pointed horns said.

"Oh yeah? My kid got sick at school yesterday because of that Bane girl," another snapped back. "How are we supposed to keep our families safe from those women?"

Piper flinched and shrank into herself. Maybe coming in here hadn't been such a great idea.

"I said settle down!" Daniel's voice boomed across the hall. No sound system required. He gripped the edge of the podium, his knuckles turning white. His shoulders rippled with more muscle than Piper recalled when she'd checked them out very thoroughly the night before.

He took a deep breath, then another, and seemed to resume something closer to his normal appearance. "What we're not going to do is attack each other," he said very clearly, looking around the room and making pointed eye contact.

His gaze landed on her, lingered a moment, and Piper shivered, heat coiling inside her. Inappropriate heat—the town looked ready to form a lynch mob or light the apocalypse barbeque, maybe both.

Daniel rocked back on his heels and tried to hold the podium more lightly. "Here's what we know: the barrier appears to be dome-like, and no one has been able to get over, under, or through it. And please, don't try to get through it. You will get hurt. I've seen too much of that in my office today as it is. Our food supply is still good." Here he turned and waved a hand toward Mr. Lack, Ginny's dad.

"Despite the circumstances, Mr. Lack has invited everyone and has agreed to still hold Ginny's engagement party in the school yard on Thursday. There will be plenty of food and hopefully a bit of distraction," Daniel continued, and Mr. Lack nodded and smiled.

There were murmurs and comments from the crowd.

Great. Piper sighed and rubbed her arms, chilled. One more reason for the League of Extraordinary Assholes to target the engagement party, just as Ginny predicted. It was Tuesday today. That gave the League two more days to plan their attack. Which meant she and the girls had two days to counter it. Fan-freakin'-tastic, considering how well today had gone.

"What, to kick off the end of the world?" the woman with the pointy ears and bad attitude snarked. "Those women are a problem. A big problem. Look what happened at the school. What will they do next? And are we just going to sit around and wait for them to do something? They're the four horsewomen *of the apocalypse*."

Piper's skin prickled.

"Sandra, that's enough," Daniel said, his voice rough.

"You're biased. How can we trust anything you say?" pointy-eared Sandra said.

"You see someone better around here?" Lou barked. And then pointed a meaty finger directly at Piper.

The audience turned. All those gazes focused on her. The room shifted with smoky black, sparks of purple anxiety. People stood up from their seats, turned to better focus on her.

Piper gulped, her hands damp.

"Why don't you ask one of them yourself." Even with the distance across the room, the intensity of Lou's gaze was unnerving. "Piper Bane, Pestilence clan. What's your next move?"

"Uh..." Oh, crap. Everyone was staring at her. Judging her. Like she was back in high school. She struggled to remember how to breathe. Her stomach roiled.

Someone in the last row of chairs coughed, loudly.

Oh, no. What had she learned today about controlling her ability? Anything?

Lime uncertainty mingled with the smoky black fear above the crowd.

"I, um, *we* don't want to hurt anyone," she managed to stutter.

"Really? And we're supposed to believe that?" The angry woman with pointy ears—Sandra, wasn't it?—pushed through the crowd and barreled toward Piper.

A high-pitched ringing started in Piper's ears, the sound echoing with the laughter and cruelty of the nymphs at school. What had been said both before and after that horrible night. The weight of Lou's gaze still pierced her awareness, and she shied away from meeting it. But where was Daniel? Wasn't he at the podium? She stretched up onto tiptoe but couldn't see past the crowd blocking her in.

Sandra advanced on her, a cruel twist to her lips, bright red staining her round cheeks. "If the apocalypse starts, the four of you will be as strong as gods. You're probably working with Mal and the others. Maybe you're the ones who solidified the barrier. Trapped us all here."

Piper stumbled back. Collided with someone. Her skin grew tight and hot. "No. I-I don't know who they are. Or why they want to end the world. But I don't. I don't want any abilities. If I knew how to stop them, I would."

"Of course, you wouldn't," Sandra scoffed. "Give up all that power? Why would you?"

Piper's vision crystallized as Sandra stopped dead in front of Piper.

Every detail slowed. Piper's heartbeat thudded in her ears, slow and measured. Each breath filled her lungs and lifted her chest.

Sandra's broad, round face blanched. Sweat prickled on her forehead beneath ginger-brown curls. A handful of freckles stood out starkly like drops of blood on pale skin. Brown eyes glanced back and around at those behind her. Brown eyes with light gold specks. A fleck of spit caught at the corner of her lips. The other woman's heart raced. Her blood sped through her veins. Her organs went on working with a gurgle and grind.

Heat coiled and filled Piper until her skin grew hot and tight enough to burst. Something twisted and roared inside, hotter, hotter.

What did the woman, what did any of these people, know about Piper? They preferred their rumors and lies to the truth. The stories they told. Not what it actually felt like, what she wanted.

"Piper, honey. Don't." A steady, firm hand settled on her shoulder, and like a wash of cool air, the heat was forced away, and the roiling settled to nothing but an echo dancing through her blood.

Piper turned, and blinked up at Daniel as though through a thick fog. Coughing filled the room. A woman with curly brown hair had collapsed.

Daniel grabbed her around the shoulders and steered her out of the hall.

CHAPTER 22

Daniel didn't release Piper's shoulders until they were outside the Community Hall and beside his truck. Who knew if there was a lynch mob behind them, but he resisted glancing over his shoulder. Blood pounded through his veins and his clenched hands were bronze-tinted. The town meeting had barreled downhill fast, Beckwellians pitted against each other.

And against Piper. Then she'd gotten scared, and things had gotten a whole lot worse. What if he hadn't stopped her?

He clenched his jaw against the thought and focused on getting Piper out of there and somewhere safe. For her sake and the rest of the town.

"Get in the truck, Piper."

She was shaking, arms wrapped around herself. The skunk pranced nervously at her feet, baring its teeth back at the Community Hall. "I don't think I should," she said, her voice small.

He yanked open the passenger door, and this time

glanced toward the Community Hall. People trickled out. And all of them watched Piper.

"I need you to get in the truck. Now." His voice was hard.

This was his town. He'd sworn to protect it. But that couldn't mean standing by and letting Piper get hurt. Even if right now, she was making it pretty damned hard to keep her safe.

She looked up at him, her lips tightening and brows shooting downward. "You're not listening to me. I think it's a bad idea."

The skunk added a saucy head toss which, under different circumstances, might have been amusing.

He ground his jaw and lowered his face close to Piper's. "You have two seconds until I toss you in the truck bed and drive off. So, if you'd like a more comfortable seat, I suggest you get in the truck. Now," he bit out.

Piper's eyes flared, and she grumbled something to the skunk as she scooped up the animal and tossed it into the cab. Then she scrambled to climb in herself.

He gripped the truck door because this once, he refused to offer her a hand.

Instead, he waited until all body parts were clear, slammed the door shut, and stalked around to his side.

Geezus. He couldn't erase the cold look on Piper's face when she'd confronted Sandra. What the hell had Lou been thinking, calling out Piper like that? Even an idiot knew it wasn't likely to end well, not with everyone coiled tighter than a spring.

Piper was still doing up her seatbelt when he jerked the truck into gear, shot up gravel and pulled out of the parking lot.

"You know what, after the way today's gone, just let me go stay with Anna. I didn't mean to hurt anyone," she said tightly. Her hands shook and she kept rubbing her arms.

"I'm not taking you to Anna's." At this point, he should. But "should" had flown out the door a while back. He couldn't let her out of sight. Because he wanted to protect her. And because it felt like he had to protect his town *from* her.

His hands trembled on the wheel. It was difficult focusing on the road when he wanted to turn and shout at Piper. "You hurt people back there. You made them sick. And the worst of it? I think you wanted to."

"Of course, I didn't," she said, but there was a hint of doubt in her voice. She crossed her arms over her chest while the skunk curled up in her lap.

Of all things ridiculous, he was getting used to the skunk. The darned thing's stench didn't bother him anymore. Much. Though it was like Piper didn't notice it at all.

They rode in silence for a few minutes, through the darkness, the headlights slicing a path down the empty two-lane asphalt.

Piper shattered the quiet, her tone bitter. "What was I supposed to do? Just take whatever abuse the town wants to dish out?"

"They're being unreasonable, they're talking stupid, but no one attacked you. Up until Lou pointed you out, they had no idea you were standing there. They're scared, and with that little stunt, you just made it worse."

She made a growling sound. "I didn't mean to. And doesn't it count that I was scared, too? Knowing that I'm becoming the embodiment of Pestilence isn't exactly a holiday. Frick's sake, Daniel, don't you ever get sick of being the good guy all the time?"

"I'm sorry for what's happening to you, but you're not the only one changing. We're all trapped here. People are hurting themselves trying to get through that damned barrier. The town is threatening to tear itself apart. People are gaining powers and attributes their lines haven't possessed in centuries. And there's that pesky detail of the looming apocalypse!" he roared, almost missing the driveway to his property. He jerked the wheel so hard, the poor old truck took the corner on two wheels.

"I guess I forgot who's sitting beside me. Saint Freakin' Daniel," Piper said bitterly. "The greater good always wins, right? You've got to be the hero."

He slammed on the brakes, jerked the truck into park, and killed the engine. "Excuse me?" He fought a second with his seatbelt to free himself so he could turn and give her the glare she deserved.

"You heard me. Mr. Good Guy. The Saint." She fiddled with her seatbelt to get it undone, finally flouncing back against the seat in defeat. "You have to babysit your brother and the rest of the damned town. I swear, sometimes you don't even see the way they use you. They don't value or appreciate everything you do for them. You're a convenient punching bag. Free target practice."

"Maybe not all of us get to run away."

Piper flinched.

He turned away. Damn it. Low blow.

Her next comment was practically whispered. "Yeah. Guess not. But at least I tried to live my dreams instead of just pretending they don't exist."

He clenched his hands. He couldn't breathe in the closeness of the truck. He wanted to get out and pace, stomp around. Heck, he wanted to hit something really hard, maybe pound it to dust until he wasn't so flipping useless that he hadn't been able to stop the crowd back there. He hadn't been able to protect or stop Piper. He'd been too far away. Too afraid of hurting someone that it'd taken him too long to get through the crowd. Too afraid of becoming the reckless, dangerous Fomorian he'd fought against so damned long.

He shoved open the door, and cool, spruce-scented air rushed in. Piper wasn't wrong. And he wasn't as oblivious as she seemed to think. But that was partially how he served a purpose in the town's ecosystem. He took care of them.

Daniel frowned out through the windshield, squeezing and releasing the steering wheel. Had he become the town babysitter?

The town sucker?

She yanked on her seatbelt again. It still wouldn't release it required a delicate touch.

Piper jerked on the thing, her movements increasingly violent. Her face grew redder and redder, visible in the truck's overhead light. "Stupid, goddamn, freakin' ancient piece-of-shit truck."

It was, for a second or two, amusing. The moment of humor lessened his anger. She'd never been able to operate that seatbelt properly all the years they'd dated. Always in too much of a rush.

The skunk just stared at him. Waiting. For what? He didn't speak skunk, so darned if he knew.

The skunk rolled its eyes, stood, and stalked off Piper's lap. It gave Daniel an indecipherable look before walking over him. It hopped out of the open truck door.

Leaving Piper and Daniel alone.

"Piper? Piper, stop. Here, let me help you." He reached over, and covered her hands with his. Her fingers were dainty beneath his, skin silken. A tiny package that belied the strength of this woman. His breathing quickened while time slowed. He inhaled her sweet scent, and he shifted toward her. Her hair brushed his cheek.

She stilled instantly. The contact of their flesh sent sparks of lust shooting through him. He pressed the seatbelt release and leaned closer.

Piper jerked away. "No. We agreed. We're over this. And I don't need your rescue."

I want to kiss you, not rescue you. And he'd been too afraid to use his ability to rescue her this evening. He pulled back, stung. "You know what? All I wanted to do is help. But I'm pretty tired after helping everyone else all day." He jumped out of the truck and slammed the door. He strode toward the house, shoulders heavy and tense. He left Piper behind, struggling with the darned door, which always stuck, and which she probably wouldn't be able to open on her own, but that wasn't his problem, was it?

The muffled screech coming from the truck's cab made him pause on the stoop.

The driver's side door opened and Piper tumbled out. She scrambled to her feet and threw her small body at the door to slam it shut. She fell against the truck, sliding down it and stumbling a few steps before she found her balance. She straightened and adjusted her blouse, face flaming.

"I didn't want to hurt anyone. I never have. But I can't seem to help it." She yanked her purse up onto her shoulder, turned to him with fire in her gaze, and stalked after him. "You would be on your deathbed and you wouldn't be too tired to help someone. You'd probably offer them the bed."

Or give up rest and food to climb out of bed on two hours of sleep like he'd done this morning? He bit the inside of his cheek and tried to ignore the irritation coiling through him, because he wasn't sure where to direct it. Instead, he stomped up the front stairs. "Yeah, yeah. Saint Daniel. I get it." Bitterness tinged his words and that danged ridiculous nickname. "Sorry, Piper. We all don't get the privilege of deciding when to stay and when to go like you do."

Piper stepped up onto the front steps with him, the

space small, her body brushing his. "Of course, you could decide to leave, you dummy." She put a hand on her hip and cocked her chin up at him. "You choose to stay and play the martyr. Because that's 'the right thing to do', isn't it? And Saint Daniel—"

His hands clenched on the doorknob.

"—always does the right thing, doesn't he?"

"At least I try," he rumbled in a low voice and stepped inside the house.

Green fire flashed in her golden eyes and she cocked her head. "Oh, you do more than try. And it always has to be more than just 'the right thing' doesn't it? You aim to martyr yourself at every turn."

"We're not having this fight." He flicked the light switch. Nothing happened, leaving the room in thick shadows. Moonlight filtered in through the kitchen windows and painted the narrow hallway and his home in silver light.

"Maybe it's about time we did," Piper said, following him inside. She slammed the door and turned the lock.

He turned to her, hands clenched, jaw tight. To find her bathed in moonlight. Which turned her hair to silvery-white, her features porcelain. And brought back all the nights they'd spent here together, so many years ago. Maybe it was exhaustion, but she looked more beautiful than he'd ever seen her.

Even if she didn't seem affected by the moonlight and continued to pursue him with criticism on her tongue. It was such a luscious tongue.

"Fine. You say I run away?" She stopped her advance almost on his toes. "You're right. I do. It's better than being burned or ostracized. I've been there, I've done that, and I won't do it again. It also means I won't hurt anyone, because whether you believe me or not after night, I've never wanted to hurt anyone. I've never wanted anything to do with this insane horsewomen thing in the first place."

"Piper—"

"No. I'm not done." She shook her head, and smoothed a hand through her hair. "I should have said something years ago. I mean, I did. But never seriously. Never like I should have." She leaned closer, which sent her delicious lilac scent whirling up around him like a delectable web. "Daniel, you need to live your life for yourself, not for everyone else, not always doing whatever's right, or martyring yourself for the sake of your brother, or your legacy, or whatever excuse you want to make."

He paused in admiring the low cut of her blouse. "I don't martyr—"

She put her finger over his lips.

The action cut off his words and made him wonder what she'd do if he brought her finger inside his mouth and suckled.

"You were free from this place. You had your med degree." She paused and looked away momentarily, a small frown touching down between her brows. "You could have found someone. Been happy."

He tried to open his mouth.

She pressed her finger down harder, and focused intently on his eyes. "So why are you back here? Why didn't you run when you had the chance? Frick's sake, Daniel, you could have been or done anything you wanted. And you'd have excelled at whatever you chose. You know it, and I know it. So why come back here and let people use you? Why come back here and sacrifice yourself, killing yourself to help people with things, frankly, sometimes they could handle themselves if you gave them a chance to try."

Her face had thinned out with maturity, heightening her cheekbones. The moonlight hid the fact that she'd changed the natural silver-blonde of her hair, the silken strands he'd loved running his fingers through.

But her words trickled through. She made doing the right thing sound like a bad thing.

Yeah, sometimes it sucked. Like coming back here after his parents died, dealing with the estates, the funerals, Aunt June. The old life funneled him back to where he'd been as a kid, and before he knew it, he'd taken the position of town doctor and tied himself down so tight he couldn't have left if he'd tried.

And he hadn't tried. That one time he'd been selfish enough to dream of a life for himself, one outside of Beckwell during med school, that child had died and Mal had lost it. Maybe because he'd been stronger, happier, Mal had been, too, and his bad luck had changed the course of that bullet.

An innocent child might have died because of it.

Piper poked him in the chest and frowned up at him. "Aren't you even going to defend yourself? Tell me you don't have some kind of hero complex and go chasing after trouble just to make yourself handy."

Staring down at Piper helped push the darkness from his mind. He lifted a hand and gave in to temptation to gently weave his hands into her hair and let the silken strands slide between his fingers. He grazed his fingertips over her cheekbones and cupped her jaw.

"No. I have no excuses. I'm not going to defend myself. And yes, for better or worse, I do and always will try to do the right thing. But right now, Piper Bane, all I'm interested in doing is you."

Before he thought better of it, before there was yet another reason why he couldn't, shouldn't, or wouldn't do what he wanted more than anything, Daniel grabbed Piper, lifted her against him, and pressed his lips to hers.

CHAPTER 23

Oh. My. Gawd. The man still knew how to kiss. Piper couldn't remember what she'd been about to say because Daniel's lips were against hers, and there was nothing more important or awesome than that.

His kisses and the feel of his chest beneath her fingers made it clear this wasn't the boy she'd dated. Her touch found rock-hard abs and pecs most other doctors were not hiding beneath their lab coats.

He lifted her, and she wrapped her legs around his waist, all without breaking their kiss. Her skirt bunched up around her thighs, the cool air of the room contrasting with the heat between them. The ridge of his erection rode between her legs, mercilessly just out of reach. He pressed her against the wall and rocked against her, sending sensation firing through her. Firework bursts of pleasure exploded in her mind and made her gasp.

She pulled at his shirt and tore at the buttons, all to get at that smooth, hot skin beneath. Why the hell did he have to wear so much clothing?

Mmm, but his lips moved over hers with such confident finesse. And there was nothing sexier than all those muscles being put to use as he scooped her up and carried her toward the bedroom.

They bumped into the doorway in the dark. They both laughed, maybe because he was as nervous as her. Which was dumb. This was Daniel. She used to know his body better than her own. She leaned forward and bit his lip lightly, eliciting a moan from his throat. That was more like it. She captured his head in her hands, teasing his tongue with hers. She was in charge as she rocked against his erection.

Which got just the reaction she wanted. He growled and tossed her gently onto the bed.

"Where do you think you're going?" She purred and tugged him down on top of her.

Their limbs tangled, his delicious weight pressing her down into the mattress. She kept her legs wrapped around his back, arching against him.

"What's the rush? We have all night," he said, his lips against her neck. His fingers found her breasts and squeezed.

She shivered, but instead of slowing down, tugged harder on his buttons. "What's this shirt made of? Kevlar?"

Why am I in such a hurry? Why can't I slow down for just a minute?

Daniel chuckled and lifted his upper body off hers to slowly unbutton the shirt, revealing sculpted flesh shadowed by the moonlight streaming through the window. He pushed it off his shoulders, muscle rippling in his chest and arms.

"Yum, yes." Piper smoothed her hands up his chest. Heat pooled and sizzled inside of her. She wanted him so damn bad, so much more than when he'd just kissed her. So much more than when they used to do this.

So long ago.

Before he'd been with other women. Who were maybe better than her. Who maybe he'd compare her to…

She forced a deeper smile and slid her hands down to his belt. And then lower.

His gaze grew hooded.

She moved her hand over his erection and gripped it tightly before she jerked open his belt buckle. And just when her temperature and his were soaring, and he definitely had to be thinking she was the best he'd had and ever would have…the stupid button on his fly wouldn't open.

Oh, for frick's sake. Defeated by a simple button. She growled low in her throat.

Daniel smiled and undid the zipper for her.

She reached for the opening, but he caught her hands, brought them to his lips. "It's okay. We're not teenagers anymore. We don't have to rush." He slowly rubbed his knee between her legs, just enough to make her moan and arch against him again.

He bit her neck lightly and kissed it before his whisper. "I want to take my time with you, Piper Bane." He released her hands, his palms caressing down her sides and up again before his fingers disappeared beneath her tank top. He unfastened her bra, and his hands settled on her bare, waiting breasts.

In a quick move, he pushed up the shirt, and ducked his head to her chest, catching her nipple between his lips. He playfully nipped, interrupting her mission to slip her hand inside his fly. And the way he sucked her nipple into his mouth and did something very interesting with his tongue—

"Oh, fuuuck!" she said, arching against his mouth. That was definitely new.

She barely had time to remember her name after he

repeated that new trick with the second breast. And then slid a long finger inside her panties and into her. She squeezed him with her inner muscles and met his gaze as she finally wrapped her fingers around her smooth, firm prize. He pulsed in her hand.

"My turn," she said, while cupping his balls and smoothing her fingers through the moisture gathered at the tip, and rubbing up and down the length of him.

His chuckle ended on a moan, before he found her own little piece of heaven, sending sensation flooding through her even while he added a second finger inside her to join the first. And began to slide slowly in and out.

It took an amazing amount of focus to continue massaging his erection while he— "Ooh. Not too fast. Ohgodohgodohgod—Daniel!"

Piper shattered so completely, so quickly, when she opened her eyes and looked up at Daniel and that cocky grin, it took a second to remember she wasn't still in high school. Best damn climax in a decade.

She smiled at him, even while aftershocks clenched her body. "That...was cheating," she panted, still breathless.

He pretended mock outrage, even while he lifted her hands above her head and pressed them against the headboard, giving her a chance to find the familiar grooves between the headboard spindles. The perfect handholds.

"It definitely was not," he rasped against her neck, his erection pulsing against her thigh. "I'd call it point one to me."

She pressed herself against him in open invitation. Her skirt bunched up around her waist. "First point does not guarantee victory. Never has, never will." Oh, gawd, she'd missed the way sex with Daniel was hot...and fun.

He rained kisses down her neck and slid her panties down her thighs.

Seeing as she definitely approved, she pulled one leg free. Which left her free to rub against him. And gave Daniel one free hand to fondle her breasts.

The other made them both hotter as he slipped his fingertips between her thighs, and drove them both wild, his pulsing hardness against her wetness. Heat and desire spiraled through her. She bit her lip, arching against him again.

The world melted into sensation. Daniel's clever fingers, his hard body. She climaxed against his hand, hard.

"Point two," Daniel whispered in her ear.

She wrapped her legs around him, and in one smooth, probably never-to-be-replicated-again-move, she nudged him toward her opening, then squeezed her thighs around him, surged upward, and sheathed Daniel in her wetness in a lights-flashing-behind-the-eyes moment. She gasped.

Daniel groaned, and thrust harder. His hands covered hers on the headboard.

"Point…one." She cried. Or tried to. Whatever other powers Daniel had, he definitely had control over climaxes. He was really, *really* good at those. Her body already tensed and quivered around him.

"Ah, crud," he said, forcing himself still against her, his face strained.

"Arguing…the point?"

He shuddered, his mouth falling open. He thrust again into her, almost against his will. "No. Condom." He pulled out, and reached for the bedside drawer.

Her body ached without him, but thankfully, the man was fast as he ripped open the packet, rolled on the condom, and returned right where he belonged. Inside her.

"Now, where were we?" he said, sliding into her and lifting her hips so he hit—

"Dan-*iel*!" she cried, the latter part higher than the first, on account of having found nirvana.

"I was about to claim a third and fourth point." He pulsed against nirvana again.

She couldn't answer. Could barely breathe. She clenched sweat-slicked fingers against the bed spindles. She didn't care who won their game. Only the light flashing behind her eyes, the slick glide of their flesh against each other...only that mattered. Only Daniel mattered.

It was maybe a few minutes, a few hours. All pleasure. Daniel's thrusts grew harder. He groaned against her. Their kisses were hard, wet. His body drove into hers, and she rose to welcome him.

He moved harder and faster. She squeezed her thighs around his waist, her muscles screaming, her body tensing. Her body convulsed and exploded. Again.

Daniel followed her half a moment later, collapsing on top of her with a groan.

Piper was boneless. Maybe half dead. Didn't matter. Didn't care. If this was death? Woohoo!

It could have been ten years ago, though even then, she didn't recall it being this good. Seriously, could they have survived that?

Thinking was hard. The only thing she did know? The only place she belonged right now, was here. With Daniel.

CHAPTER 24

Light tickled Piper's face the next morning, making her yawn and stretch beneath the sheet in Daniel's bed. Her lips curled up. Daniel may have ended the night with the high score—nine to four—but from the delicious aches and languid exhaustion that clung to her muscles, she'd definitely been the winner. And not *that* tired, either. Something new zipped and zagged through her bloodstream. Something…excitable. Powerful. And hungry.

Daniel's muscular arm lay possessively across her body, and he pulled her back against his chest more tightly as she shifted, accompanied with a masculine growl. Despite her exhaustion—because come on, last night had been Olympic-level-sexcapades—heat stirred inside her, pooled in her core.

If she'd stayed ten years ago, would this have been life? Instead of all those lonely mornings waking up in hotel rooms, those few minutes trying to remember where she was this time, what if she'd been with Daniel?

She could have woken up beside him each bright morning after every hot night for the past ten years. The two of them together were better than she remembered. Better than she could have imagined. And not just the sex. The way he made her feel. The possibilities he woke inside her.

What if this time she stayed?

She smoothed a hand up his forearm and over his bicep, thick, corded muscle jumping beneath her fingertips. She took inventory of him behind her, every inch of her flesh excruciatingly sensitive to where it connected with his, growing hot and sweat-slicked once more. The feel of his…interest nestled between her butt cheeks hardened into something very intriguing. The beat of his heartbeat and rush of his blood thrummed through his fingertips as they slid along her hip, his heart picking up the pace. Each exhalation of breath stirred hair at the nape of her neck and tingled against her nerves. Blood rushed through his veins, and an electrical charge crackled through his cells with increased neurological activity. Hormones released like a burst of perfume, and a rush of ions through his blood stream caused a metallic tang on her tongue.

Piper froze.

Wait. What?

∾

Daniel nuzzled Piper's neck and slid his hand between her legs, ascending slowly upward. He was throbbing and hard, and though he was very cozy where he was, pressed against Piper's back, cradled in softness, it wasn't where he wanted to be. This would be what, round eight? Heck, who cared. This was Piper. *His* Piper. Her delicious body naked and pressed against his. Warm, wet, and wanting. Exactly where she should be.

Where she should always be.

He tucked his knee between her thighs before he

rolled them both so he ended up on top. This time he wanted to watch the expression in her eyes as he entered her, wanted to have her legs around his waist, wanted to savor the flush of orgasm as it played over her face.

Only, she was frowning as he turned her over, and her eyes widened as they faced him. A shiver slid through her legs on either side of his hips. And the flush of desire faded from her face.

"What's wrong?" he asked, desire leaching away, leaving a chill stinging his skin. Round eight crashed out through the window and into the clouds.

"I was going to ask you the same." She rose up on her elbows, one arm over her breasts. The other hand she reached out, paused, then slid up his jaw line.

He shuddered and closed his eyes, pressing himself into her touch. He bit back a groan. "Mmm... What?" Round eight flew back in and sent desire rushing through his veins again. He cupped her breast and massaged the nipple with his thumb, playing by feel rather than sight.

"Uh, Daniel?"

"Umhmm?" Thank the gods she'd never changed anything about her body other than her hair. Her breasts weren't huge, but perfect for his hands. And oh, so sensitive, the nipples cresting against his palm.

"Your skin is...bronze."

"Uh-huh." Which breast would he start with this time? He'd tried to be gentle, so hopefully she wasn't sore after last night. He nipped gently at a nipple before sucking it into his mouth while his hand quested somewhere wetter, hotter, and very welcoming.

"Oooh, wow!" She grabbed his hand between her legs. "Wait."

He froze, his eyes snapped open, and his gaze found hers.

She grimaced and blinked. The flush was back in

her skin, but she looked rattled. "Daniel…your eyes are black. Like, really black. And your skin is metallic bronze. Not normal."

Almost against his will, his gaze slid down her body. To his hand, still cupped around her perfect ivory breast. The fingers—he wiggled them—no, *his* fingers indeed an almost metallic hue of bronze, darker than any tan or that of his First Nations ancestors. The color it had changed to when he'd pulled the mayor out of the barrier.

He yanked his hand off of Piper's body, a chill chasing over his skin. "Did I hurt you? Are you okay?"

"I'm fine. It's going to be okay. Really." She reached for his face again.

He scrambled off the bed. Away from Piper. Was she telling the truth? Could he have hurt her and forgotten? He stumbled toward the old dresser with its mirror. Oh gods. His whole body was that color. Like he'd been cast in metal. A lot of metal. He wasn't usually that big. All his muscles were bigger, more defined, like he'd suddenly pumped a lot of iron. And steroids. He leaned closer. And his eyes… His throat squeezed. The irises had stretched and elongated until they filled almost his whole eye, a deep brown color so dark it was practically black.

Fomorian black. Like Dad's when he'd had too much to drink and went on a rampage. A hunk of icy cold settled in his gut. No. He couldn't, he wouldn't become that.

Cloth shuffled on the bed, and Piper padded toward him slowly, hand outstretched. Like approaching a wild animal. "Daniel? We can figure this out together. Please, come back to bed."

He jerked away before she touched him, started grabbing clothes randomly, tugging them onto his body. Underwear. Jeans.

"I can't."

Fear burned away into certainty. Fury. This wasn't accidental. He'd slept with Piper before and yeah, he'd felt more powerful, but he'd never morphed into anything. This was all since the barrier had solidified. All since the group with their apocalyptic dreams and dangerous power trip had decided to make everyone into something they weren't. He yanked a shirt over his head, the sleeves tearing as he pushed his arms through. He swallowed a growl. Enough of reacting to whatever they did. Enough of chasing after their pranks and idiocy. Enough of all this BS.

"Where are you going?" Piper grabbed at her clothes, hopping on one foot as she tried to pull on a pair of panties. "Just give me a second. I'll come—"

He turned and grasped both of her arms, steadying her. "You're not coming. It's too dangerous."

Her eyes darkened to honey-brown and narrowed. She pulled away from him. "I'm the freaking embodiment of Pestilence, Daniel. Pretty sure I'm one of the most dangerous creatures in town."

"No. You're not. You're maybe just becoming that. And…and maybe I can change that. Maybe I can stop all of this." He clenched his jaw against anything else, any promises he might not be able to keep. "Stay here. Stay safe. I'll deal with this." He couldn't resist the hard kiss to her lips that she met for every thrust, every gasp.

She was breathless as he pulled away, her lips dark and lush. "Let me get dressed. You're not going alone. We need to talk this through."

"No," he said, and headed for the door.

"Dammit, Daniel! Where do you think you're going?" she shouted after him.

"To find Mal."

CHAPTER 25

Daniel hit the gas harder on the old truck than he usually would and headed into town beneath the early morning sun that flickered through the surrounding trees. He clenched his hands on the wheel to still their tremor, the grip sweat-slicked. He had to find Mal. Get answers.

And what was happening to him? Maybe Mal knew how to stop it. Or reverse it. If they brought down the barrier, would he turn back to normal?

Did this have anything to do with having slept with Piper?

Her shouts, the obvious hurt on her face clung like cobwebs in his mind, and he had to try to brush them away. To focus. He didn't know exactly where Mal was, so he had to focus on their connection, let it lead him to Mal like it had when they were kids.

He reached the empty four-way stop, too early yet for teachers at the school or patrons at the gas station, bar, or grocery. He closed his eyes a moment, pushed past the semi-panic raging through his brain, and looked for his brother. Looked for the emotions that weren't his own...

Sleepy surprise. Elation. Fear.

Daniel opened his eyes and turned left, toward the Cow Palace.

Most of the gates were closed, since it was off-season, so Daniel stopped the truck beyond them and walked into the agricultural grounds toward the large fuchsia barn.

Mal burst out of the door on the right. Froze as he caught sight of Daniel. Stared.

Daniel did some staring of his own.

They approached each other slowly, warily, circling like adversaries.

Mal's skin had changed to a blue-gray ash color, and like Daniel, he was significantly larger and more muscular than usual. His black button-down had popped the seams at the shoulders and along the arms, the dark gray khakis snug. Mal's eyes had turned deep sapphire, the irises elongated, inhuman.

"What's happening to us?" Daniel rasped.

"I think that's pretty obvious," Mal said, unease sliding through his connection.

"You did this?"

"No." Mal pointed toward the nearby barrier, Piper's silver rental still trapped just within its clutches, no one brave enough to retrieve or move it. "It's the barrier. I warned you. Everyone is becoming stronger, latent abilities and genetics emerging."

Daniel jaw ached. "How could you do this? People are terrified. This isn't who they are."

Mal crossed his arms and cocked an eyebrow. "Aren't who they are? This is *exactly* who they—and *we*—really are, even if most of the time you can't see it."

The horrified expressions on his patients' faces yesterday flickered through Daniel's mind. Frizzly's hand, half-turned to rock. Piper last night, the target of the town council. His hand this morning, the metallic inhuman quality of it against Piper's skin.

He flexed his fingers and ground his teeth. "We're turning into monsters, Mal. This isn't who I am. And this person you're pretending to be? That isn't you, either. You were happy being an officer, happier than I've ever seen you. That is who you're meant to be."

Mal looked down, the muscle in his jaw working, his hands balled into fists. Regret and grief rolled through him. "You're wrong."

Daniel took two steps closer but stopped a stride away, breathing hard through his nose. His hands twitched for violence, but he couldn't. This was his brother. This was his chance. Their chance. "If you go through with this, the council will hunt you down. You'll be turned over to the gods. But I know you're a good man. Tell me who they are. Help me stop this. Help me protect our town."

Mal's inhuman sapphire gaze flicked up, his head still lowered, shoulders hunched. "Help you to slay the monsters?" His voice was low and dark. "Monsters like me? Like Dad?"

Like they'd done when they were children, playing at knights who slayed monsters. Daniel could hardly swallow. They'd even had a motto: "Brothers at arms, brothers forever, we protect the world, and we protect each other." Damn. Daniel could almost hear their childish voices chanting the pledge like a prayer. A promise.

A promise he was desperately trying to keep now. If Mal would let him.

"It's not too late. We have to stop the others," he insisted. Pleaded.

"It was too late a long time ago. When you learned to be ashamed of me. And when you realized I'd turned out just like Dad."

Hurt rolled through Mal. How could he believe that?

"You're angry with me, so you attack our town? You turn us into this?" Daniel held out his hands. The hands of a monster.

"What, was Piper a bit put off this morning to find out what she'd slept with?" Mal taunted.

Fury uncoiled like a smoky, smoldering serpent inside Daniel's chest and tightened around his muscles, squeezed his jaw. He lowered his head. "Leave Piper out of this."

"Piper has always been right in the middle of this."

Something snapped in Daniel, the internal boil bubbling out of the pot. His hands fisted. He roared and lunged at Mal.

Daniel barreled into Mal's midsection. His twin was ready for him, stumbling back a few steps. He drove an elbow between Daniel's shoulder blades.

Red blurred Daniel's vision. His blood pounded through his veins and urged him to attack. Urged him to kill. He avoided Mal's jab to the jaw, twisting away and scrambling to his feet. Mal was trained in defense, certainly the more experienced fighter.

Daniel was more pissed off. And more determined to win. When his twin came at him again, he grabbed Mal, and using the momentum of the attack, swung and threw him.

Mal twisted and hit the dust shoulder first. Hit hard.

Before he had time to get up, Daniel went after him. Would have reached him if someone hadn't grabbed his arm and jerked him back.

"What the hell are you two doing?" Lou growled. The beefy bartender inserted himself between the brothers, his bushy beard quivering, sun glinting off his bald head.

Mal found his feet, and they circled each other again.

Lou held his arms out and stayed between the brothers, moving as they moved. "If I had a hose, I'd turn it on you two idiots about now," Lou shouted. "Daniel. Snap out of it. Do you really want to kill your brother in a rage? That'd be true Fomorian fashion."

Daniel jerked as though he'd been struck as Lou's words penetrated. He tried to blink away the red haze clouding his vision. It was less, but just making eye contact with his twin made him snarl. Honest to gods animal snarl.

He stumbled back.

Lou grunted his approval, and risked a look in Mal's direction. He reached in his pocket and tossed a set of keys toward Mal. "You, go back to my place. Cool down and try to get your head out of your ass." He jabbed a finger in Daniel's direction. "You, come with me."

“

Piper fumed and continued her march along the highway toward town. The suitcase bumped her heels and Queenie scampered along at her side. Daniel had raced off in a panic, refused to hear reason or even talk about what had happened, and there was no damned way she was going to sit around and wait for him to come back.

After the meeting at the Community Hall and what had happened this morning, there was no time to waste. She needed to see the girls, and they needed to actually control their abilities, not just screw around. Plus, they had to find the idiotic League of Extraordinary Assholes.

"Can you believe him?" she said to Queenie. "Okay, so it was probably kind of scary waking up looking different like he did. I get that. But he's not the only one involved around here. I mean, that's what he said last night, right? I was being selfish and wasn't thinking about what everyone else was going through? But that makes it okay if he does it?"

Queenie projected a calm pond and soothing nature music.

Piper scowled at her. "I will not calm down." She ground her teeth. "Yesterday, I get. I messed up at the Community Hall. Maybe I screwed up sleeping with Daniel." She kicked a path in the rocks, her insides roiling. She'd done it again. Accidentally hurt people. Proved everyone who was scared of her right. Made the pro-apocalypse bunch believe the end was nigh. "No maybe about it. He'll never forgive me if I helped turn him into that, made him more Fomorian."

The skunk bumped against Piper's leg and projected comfort.

"What's going to happen to all of us? Is it inevitable that we start the apocalypse?"

The skunk looked away. She sent the first image of four mounted riders headed off toward a city on fire. Then she sent a second image of smoke and smoldering ruin. But beyond the ruin was a glowing brightness, like a sunrise. Hope? Queenie sent a mental shrug. She wasn't sure what to make of the images, either.

The rumble of a vehicle along the asphalt made Piper step off the shoulder and onto the scrub grass beside the ditch.

The car crunched slowly toward Piper, and the window hummed. "Piper? Piper Bane, it *is* you, isn't it?" a female voice called.

Piper braced herself, and watched the blue Honda Civic roll to a stop. "I'm Piper."

At first glance, the woman was a decade or so past middle-aged and a few pounds over plump in a pink and white track suit, her curly brown hair pulled back in a ponytail.

A second glance superimposed emotion-color over the woman. Mauves and cheerful yellow. No tinge of black oily fear.

And then, something else tugged at Piper's awareness. Like a slowly awakening cat, the essence of…something, blinked open awareness and peered at her with mild curiosity, wondering if Piper had come to pester it.

The woman laughed, a bubbly, cheerful-with-an-edge sound, and broke Piper's connection to that other awareness. "Oh, of course. I'm Louise. I know your mom. And my youngest was in your graduating class. Randy Dole?"

Piper's memory groped around and produced the image of a skinny kid with curly hair like this woman, glasses, ram horns. A bit of a nerd, but sweet. "Oh. Randy. Sure." Her shoulders tightened. It probably wouldn't go over well if she asked where the woman fit into the pro or anti-apocalypse spectrum.

Louise put the car in park and opened the door. "Why don't I give you a ride? I'm headed to the school anyway."

Queenie projected a flashing orange caution sign.

Piper rubbed her neck and glanced down the road. The library wasn't that far. Maybe a fifteen-minute walk. And what was that other thing she'd felt, that other essence superimposed over Louise? "Um…"

Louise smiled. She popped the trunk. "Oh, honey. I'm on your side. Promise."

Yeah, not exactly comforting considering the talk at the Community Hall. Did that make Louise a potential member of the League?

Piper chewed her lip. But that essence…that was something new. And if she didn't learn to understand and use her abilities, how could she and the others defeat the League? How would she avoid hurting more people accidentally? "Okay. I guess. I'm headed for the library." Worst-case scenario, she could send the woman into a coughing fit, right?

Queenie nipped at Piper's heels. Projected the flashing orange caution sign again with spiking concern.

Piper put her suitcase in the truck, climbed into the passenger seat, and reached for Queenie. *"I've got this. It's okay,"* she communicated to the skunk.

The animal reluctantly let Piper pick her up. She closed the door, and Louise Dole put the car in drive.

Okay. It was a short drive. *Time to focus.* Piper let her awareness of the other woman's emotions blossom in the car, hovering like gases over the woman. Next came awareness of Louise's health and vital signs, the somewhat sluggish beating of her heart, the rush of her breath in her lungs. It was like she was covered in a fine film of sludge that dulled her, made her kidneys struggle, her breaths fast and shallow, her entire body in overdrive but getting nowhere.

Finally, beneath all that was the other...being. Sludgy-yellow, the essence had no definite physical form, but in Piper's mind appeared to splatter the other woman's body like mud. Lightly coated her arms and legs. More densely caked her torso, upper chest, and head, thick as armor.

Then it, whatever it was, turned its attention to Piper.

An icy lump landed in Piper's stomach.

"Do I have something on my face?" Louise said.

Piper's face heated and she blinked. "Oh. No. I'm sorry."

The other woman chattered about her son and his young family.

Which left Piper free to focus again on the sludgy-yellow thing.

It wasn't *on* Louise Dole. It was *in* her. Disease.

Piper's senses zipped forward too quickly for her to control, following the path of the sludgy substance. She passed through bloodstreams and into organs, deeper into cells. The entity slurped and lurched like an angry giant, both attracted to and afraid of Piper.

Queenie's awareness bumped Piper's lightly, like they stood together facing the thing. Queenie bared her teeth and batted a paw.

The sludge bowed its head. In deference. Then without words, more in feelings, it regaled Piper with its battles, its invasive strategy, its plans. Then raised its head in defiance. Dared Piper to do something.

Piper blinked, and she withdrew awareness of inside the body to outside it. To sitting in the car, the sight of the four-way stop still some distance away outside the windshield. Louise continued to chatter on, but Piper barely heard her.

Instead, her gaze slowly traveled up from Louise's hands on the wheel, spotted with sludge, to her face, almost unrecognizable until Piper blinked the image away.

Louise was sick. With a terminal illness. And Piper could not only see it, she'd communicated with it.

The older woman pulled the car into the parking lot beside the library and turned with a smile. A very knowing smile that sent chills sliding through Piper. "I don't have a lot of time left. I know that, just as I imagine you do now. But with what I do have, I'm determined to make this world a better one for my Randy and his little ones. We know you and your friends will try to stop us. You won't be able to. Far better if you help us bring about the apocalypse this world so desperately needs. That way, you might survive it, too."

CHAPTER 26

Piper could barely stagger out of the car fast enough and grab her suitcase. Had Louise Dole as much as admitted she was part of the League of Extraordinary Assholes? Plus threatened Piper's life.

Louise Dole, conversely, seemed in no particular hurry and gave a friendly little wave. "Tell the others we say hi," she called before driving away.

Piper gulped.

Queenie nipped her ankle.

"Ow. Yes, fine. You were right." She and the skunk headed for the library door. Another shiver rippled through her. Was Louise right? Were Piper and her friends doomed to fail? Maybe it was just smack talk.

Hadn't really seemed that way.

The library's double-doors were locked, the "Closed" sign clearly posted in the window. Piper knocked hard on the door, and a few moments later Anna opened it. Dark semi-circles underlined the war horsewoman's eyes, and her braid was half-undone, dark hair scruffy.

Piper's brows rose, and she momentarily forgot Louise Dole. "Wow, you look worse than I feel." Which was something, considering Anna regularly seemed to shop the Wannabe-Cat-Lady section of the Internet. She was proof such a thing existed.

"Gee, thanks," Anna said, exhaustion outweighing sarcasm in her tone. She stepped aside to let Piper, the suitcase, and Queenie inside before locking the door again. A sleeping bag peeked out from behind the checkout counter.

"You're sleeping here?" Piper said.

Anna shrugged, rubbing her arms up and down with her hands, as though trying to ward off a chill. "Someone has to figure out what's going on and how to stop it. The library has better wifi. At least *that* wasn't blocked by the barrier." She shuffled toward the rear of the library and the coffee pot.

Piper followed after her and took the coffee pot from Anna's hands. "We've got a new problem, too. Call the others. Pretty sure I just met a member of the League of Extraordinary Assholes—Louise Dole—who basically threatened me to join them or die in their apocalypse. Last night at the community meeting the townspeople were starting to look like extras in a fantasy movie." She frowned. "Plus, Daniel kind of changed color and was acting like an ass, but not sure that's apocalyptic." Funny. It'd seemed that way when she left his place.

He was okay, wasn't he?

"Coffee. I can't think without adequate caffeine." Anna rubbed a hand over her face, muttering, and headed toward the circulation desk and the phone.

"Why'd Daniel Do-Right change colors?" Nia said, stepping out from between a set of bookshelves.

Piper jumped and almost smashed the coffee pot

over Nia's head. "What are you doing here? Don't tell me you're camping out, too."

Nia eyed the coffee pot, then shrugged and ambled toward the front of the library. "Hell no. There are way too many ghosts and not enough wards. I was trying to catch up on a backlog of the dead, you know, thin them out." She pointed to the small cupboard above the sink. "Coffee's in there. There's a second pot, too. We're going to need it. And make it strong. Thick enough to hold a spoon, preferably."

"Strong, but not disgusting," Anna piped up from the front.

Nia rolled her eyes and mouthed "thick".

Piper rushed to make coffee and started the second pot, mugs clattering together as she hurried them to the long conference table at the front of the library, then hurried back to grab the first pot of finished coffee. Not that she needed any. This morning's events had more than woken her up.

Someone knocked on the door and Anna stared regretfully into her coffee mug before setting it on the table. She shuffled over to answer the door.

Neither she nor Nia looked to be in any particular hurry. Weren't they even worried about Louise Dole?

Piper took a seat at the long conference table, and Queenie settled at her feet. "Drink up. We need to start planning."

Should she call Daniel? Check to make sure he was okay?

Yeah, well, he hadn't exactly wanted to talk it over this morning. Would he have changed his mind by now?

"First, you tell us about Daniel Do-Right," Nia said, curled around her mug, sitting cross-legged on the chair.

Ginny slipped inside, dressed more like Nia in a dark blue hoodie pulled over her bright red hair and dark-colored yoga pants. She pushed the hood back, her cheeks flushed. "What'd I miss?" She scrambled over to the chair next to Piper and perched on the edge of the seat.

Anna smothered a yawn before sinking into her chair and caressing her coffee cup. "Piper met one of the League members. And Daniel changed colors." She lifted the cup to her lips, blowing gently, and peeked over the rim. "I'm guessing because you and Daniel didn't keep things strictly platonic?"

Ginny's eyes widened, and she leaned forward. "Is it true? Are you two back together?" There was no concealing the unabashed joy and excitement in her voice.

Piper grimaced, even as her cheeks warmed. "Of course not. It was just…a mistake."

"You know, I screw up all the time, but it's pretty rare any of those end up with me falling into bed with a hottie," Nia said with a smirk.

"Nor would I expect my bedmate to change color," Anna said. "What color did he change? Could he be ill?"

"You guys!" Piper snapped, wishing she could ignore the heat in her face. "I met a member of the League. She basically threatened to kill me—*us*. Last night there was this creepy community meeting where everyone was flipping out and the town is ready to implode, mostly because everyone is getting their abilities and then some thanks to the barrier. And all *you* want to talk about is my love life, or lack thereof?"

"But none of that is new to us," Anna said baldly. "Well, the community meeting maybe, but the rest…I have new information, too. Like about how not only is the barrier incubating our abilities, it seems to be mirroring what happens in Beckwell into the outside world. However, right now, we care more about you. So, just tell us what color Daniel turned, and then we'll move on." She returned to her coffee.

Piper looked to Ginny for sympathy, who colored but just shrugged. There was no sense looking to Nia for anything other than a smug look.

"Kind of a bronze color. Like a statue maybe?" Piper tucked some hair behind her ears, her fingers trembling as this morning rushed back to her. "Everything was, uh, fine until I noticed he seemed bigger than usual. And a different color. And then that his eyes were black, without a pupil. Which wasn't great, but I mean, we've been through bad before, and this is Beckwell, right?"

"But…" Ginny prompted, leaning across the table.

"But when I tried to suggest we talk about it, he freaked out and ran off. Stranding me, by the way, which is why I accepted a ride and got threatened."

"Is he okay?" Anna asked.

Piper blew out a breath. "I think so. I hope so. If anything, he seemed stronger than usual, so at least I didn't make him sick." Her stomach roiled. Oh, now there was an awful thought: he wasn't sick now, but what if she *had* made him sick? How could she live with that?

Comforting feelings from Queenie who, as usual, was being "useful" by sleeping through most of the conversation.

"Are you okay?" Nia said, making Piper's gaze snap to the smaller woman, to search for hidden sarcasm. There was none.

Piper's throat thickened. "Yes. No. Maybe? I don't know. Everything about us being together is complicated. Dangerous. Despite all the ways we've hurt each other, all the ways we'll inevitably hurt each other again, it doesn't seem to change much. Especially not how I feel." She shifted her shoulders. "It makes my going away almost logical."

Ginny reached across the table and squeezed

Piper's hand, the redhead's eyes bright with moisture. She'd always been a sucker for romance and had believed in true love since the days she'd enacted it with doll weddings. Also possibly why she'd ended up in the mess that was her first marriage. "You two were just so perfect for each other."

"Complete opposites that just…worked," Nia said quietly. She cleared her throat. "But we get it. We know why it can't work. And whatever you need, you know we're on it. Even if we have to tie you down so you can't go jump Daniel Do-Right's bones."

In spite of herself, Piper chuckled. "I'll let you know if that's necessary." She straightened in her chair. "Now. Onto how we stop the League of Extraordinary Assholes."

Anna refilled her coffee, and with the coffeepot empty, stood to take it back to other end of the library. "Ladies, fill her in until I get back."

"So, Dad took my suggestion and invited the whole town to the engagement party tomorrow at the school," Ginny said.

Piper's mouth fell open. "You *planned* that?"

Ginny colored and shifted in her seat. "Well, we talked about how if the League wanted to make some statement or attack, they'd probably attack the engagement party and the wedding anyway, right? So, I thought, better the engagement party—and make it an easy target for them to attend. That way we draw them out rather than have to chase after them."

"Ginny, that was very strategic planning. Well done," Anna said, returning with the other coffee pot and settling back into her chair. "Nia, report?"

Piper could only turn to Nia obediently. Wow. Guess being part of the War clan made Anna practically a general, 'cause she was handling all of this like a pro. Piper's shoulders relaxed, and warmth suffused her limbs. God, she'd missed these three. Why hadn't she come home sooner?

Nia held up a finger and finished her cup of coffee, then signaled for Anna to pour more before she started. "Okay, so I've had my ghosties out looking for trouble and any sign of the League of Extraordinary Assholes. Unfortunately, it looks like they haven't posted obvious signs like 'Bad Guy HQ Here', but listening in on a lot of conversations, consensus seems like we might be looking at the Fates as good targets for who's involved."

"Which means Louise Dole is presumably one of them," Anna murmured.

"She did use the royal 'we' when she told me to say hi to you guys," Piper agreed.

"So, by my count," Nia continued, "that means the League includes the Fates—one of whom must be Louise Dole—plus Mal, and Loki."

"Allegedly Loki," Anna said.

"Oh, he's involved," Nia countered. "Question is: do we know anything else about them? If there are more? The ghosties don't have names. At least, not yet. They're mostly just dropping in and spying, and haven't happened upon a League meeting, either. Though the Fates being involved could explain why the four of us have gotten stuck rising as The Four."

"I know Louise Dole has some kind of terminal illness," Piper said, and became the focus of the other three's questioning looks. She shrugged, and pretended she was more comfortable with what she was becoming than she was. "It's supposed to be one of my abilities, right? To communicate with diseases? Well, I communicated. And it's bad. Plus, she outright said she didn't have much time left." She frowned. "Though she also seemed to think ending the world would make it better for her kids and grandkids, which makes zero sense."

"A rabbit hole," Anna said. "We need to focus on finding out who they are and stopping them." She paused. "With everyone else's abilities in town clearly growing with the barrier, ours are, too. Barring a miracle that would allow us to get rid of them and someone else to rise, the only option I can see is for us to learn to harness and control our abilities."

"What if someone else did inherit them?" Ginny asked for the rest of them.

"When one rises as part of The Four, they gain all the powers of their clan. Everyone else becomes…normal," Anna said.

There was a moment of silence from the three, which Piper took to be mourning and maybe some last ditch prayers. Or at least, she whispered some fast prayers.

There was at least one good thing she'd gained from coming back here: the reminder of how freaking good it felt to have someone—three someones—who truly understood the craziness of being part of the apocalypse clans.

"So," Anna said, rising and heading for the circulation desk, "we need to all practice. Piper, I want you to keep working with the candle and the little windmill in the children's section."

Piper jumped up to go find the windmill, and scooped up the potted plant on one of the low shelves. She plopped it down in front of Ginny. "Kill it."

"Er, it's plastic," Ginny said.

"Excuses, excuses," Nia tsked.

Anna released a gusty sigh and hefted a box. She lugged it to the table and lowered it with a thud that made the big-ass Book of Scary look dainty. She pulled out a small tray of seedlings and a loaf of bread and pushed those toward Ginny. "Famine can alter and manipulate the earth, as well as spoil food. See what you can do with these." She gave Piper a sideways look. "These are real."

Next, she pulled out a jar with what looked like pantyhose on the top, about six to ten moths fluttering around inside, and a second jar with water. These she pushed in front of Nia. "You've got plenty of experience with spirits. But Death also has dominion over water. The insects…I want you to test your necrokinesis—the ability to kill with a touch." She paused. "And then I want you to see if you can bring them back again."

Nia stiffened and clutched the arms of her chair. "That's necromancy. You know how I feel about that. After Dad—"

"It doesn't have to be necromancy. I think you might be able to…take back death. But start slow. See what you can do," Anna said gently.

That darned box of hers still wasn't empty. Next came another candle, this one a big, chunky pillar candle, followed by a set of matches. Finally, she pulled out the remaining three large mason jars, two of which were covered in pillowcases, and a huge pickle jar, the kind they used at bars for pickled eggs.

"Pestilence has dominion over air currents, so I want you to practice manipulating those using the candle." She pushed one of the smaller jars toward Piper, again covered with a stocking, this one duct-taped on. And full of some very angry looking wasps.

Piper leaned away from the table. Even Queenie climbed to her feet, and peered upward. "Uh, can't I just stick with the candle?" And no wonder Anna looked tired. She must have been out all night bug hunting.

"Pestilence also has an affinity with swarming insects. They can't hurt you in there. But I think they can hear you."

"So you've cooked up a whole batch of fun for the rest of us. You'd better be doing a lot more than just looking for lies on the Internet," Nia said, a harder edge in her voice than usual, probably because of any hint of necromancy, something rumor had it her dad had gotten into. Before it killed him.

"Well, War can control fire. Hence my candle." Anna unscrewed the lid on the pickle jar before she carefully removed the two mason jars from their respective pillowcases. Revealing soil and swarming ants in both. One jar of red ants, one jar of black. She blew her bangs out of her eyes, her face pale, and stared resolutely at the scrambling insects. "But first I'm going to start a miniature war. And then I'm going to try to control it."

CHAPTER 27

Lou stomped ahead of Daniel toward the bar, which made it feel all the more like he'd been called down to the principal's office.

Better thinking of potential humiliation if anyone drove past this early in the morning and saw them, him especially with the bronze skin, then to consider the truth. If Lou hadn't stopped him, he'd have tried to kill his brother. Just like the curse had always claimed. Just like Daniel had always promised he'd never do.

He closed his eyes a moment and stuffed his hands in his pockets, the sound of fabric tearing. There went the back of his shirt. Well, damn.

The beefy bartender unlocked the bar and held the door open for Daniel. His moustache and beard twitched. "First clothes. Then we talk."

There wasn't much choice but to follow Lou through the bar into one of the small back rooms. From the desk piled with papers and ledgers, it looked like the office. It was relatively tidy, including the curious bookshelf loaded down with heavy leather volumes that didn't look like drink recipes or ledgers. But seeing as the lettering was some kind of runic writing, Daniel couldn't be sure. Funny. In all the years they'd been friends, he'd never been back here.

The bartender rustled around in the metal cabinet that took up most of the other wall, closed the door, and stomped toward Daniel. He pressed a package of unused men's briefs, a pair of black leather pants, black biker boots, and a white T-shirt at Daniel. "Get changed. Meet me out front."

Daniel stared down at the pile of clothes a moment and spoke just before Lou closed the door. "Why were you out by the Cow Palace anyway?"

"I'm fat. I need exercise. I was out walking when I heard you two, and I knew I couldn't just leave you there." His friend's voice roughened. "Neither of you could have lived with what might have happened."

"Thank you," Daniel said, voice thick.

Lou grunted and pulled the door closed.

Daniel dressed quickly, the leather pants an entirely new experience. He frowned, jumping to get the pants up his legs. All the clothing fit better than his own had, but there wasn't any plaid in sight, and why would the bartender have clothes that weren't his size? He glanced around the office, spotting an expensive man's green silk shirt, a unique pale sage green, on a hanger hanging just tucked inside the metallic cabinet, peeking out of the partially open door.

Maybe Lou had a male lover? Wasn't the kind of thing you could ask.

He pulled on the biker boots before he headed for the front of the bar. He probably looked more like his brother than himself. He felt...conspicuous. Fortunately, the front of the bar was empty, the open sign still turned off in the front.

Lou had already poured a glass of milk and had it on a coaster in front of one of the stools. He gave Daniel a quick up and down before sniffing his approval, then pointed at the stool. "Sit. Drink."

Daniel hunkered down at the bar. His stomach twisted. His heart was still beating too fast, his blood pumping. "I almost killed my brother."

Another grunt. "Drink first. Then we chat."

He looked up. Lou had never been this pushy about drinking.

The bartender crossed his big arms and waited.

Daniel rubbed the back of his neck then picked up the cold glass of milk. He grimaced at the sight of those metallic-bronze fingers. But the milk was crisp and cold. He took a long swallow and wished his thoughts would stop circling toward panic mode. He paused and set the glass down.

"All of it," Lou said.

He picked up the glass and continued to swallow the cold milk. And his heart rate slowed. His blood didn't rush through his ears anymore. He lowered the glass. Stilled. His hands were back to their normal color. He looked up at Lou for answers.

Lou tilted his head and exhaled noisily through his nose. "Simple explanation: the milk calms you down. You turn back to normal, human-looking. Longer explanation, because I'm sure you'll insist. Fomorians operate on a fight-or-flight response."

He paused and brought out a bottle of milk, pouring Daniel another glass. "Fomorians become battle-ready physiologically, not with any kind of armor. Their muscle mass increases, skin becomes tougher, more durable, and they acquire other fight-ready attributes, like claws, horns, wings, that sort of thing. They thrive on adrenalin, which usually tires fighters out more quickly. It just drives them on to fight harder and longer.

When they don't need to fight anymore, they don't need the fierce appearance, either."

The big man poured himself a glass of juice. "They take a beating and keep on going. And I've heard it's possible for them to have a very long lifespan, but they're also prone to a lot of things that tend to get them killed young. But that doesn't seem to matter since they propagate and breed like rabbits. Even their sperm seem to be mean-ass fighters."

Daniel's throat was almost too thick to speak, and he clutched the edge of the bar. "How do you know so much about them? How long?" *Why haven't you ever told me before?*

His friend let out a gusty sigh. "I knew your father and his brothers over the years. I've known others like him. Like you."

"I am *not* my father," Daniel choked out.

This got a snort, and Lou came around the bar and took a seat on one of the stools next to Daniel. "Of course not. But we are all our fathers in some ways, whether we want to be or not." His blue gaze was unnervingly piercing as he pinned Daniel with it. "It's what we do with those abilities that matters."

"I'm trying to do the right thing. I don't want to hurt my brother, but I have to find the people responsible for the barrier and bring it down. I had one of them, a woman named Daphne, basically come to the office and threaten me. But I don't know where to find them, who the rest of them are, or how to stop them." His voice dropped. "Mal won't back down, and I don't know how to save him from himself."

The bartender finally broke the stare. "You could start by remembering you're not the only person in town with a desire and the means to stop them. And you're also going to remember that while the bronze-colored skin might be strange and there are downsides to being

Fomorian, there are also advantages."

Daniel's next sip of milk barely went down. But he had to buy time to get his thoughts in order, figure out what to ask, what he needed to know.

What he was ready to know.

Lou patiently sipped at his fruit juice, waiting.

"Did you know I'd always become…this?"

"Son, you are the same man you were yesterday. I mean, sure, the color's a little different, and I'm curious what triggered it all, but you are still you."

"I don't feel the same."

"Well, now, does that have anything to do with becoming a true Fomorian, or with Piper Bane being back in town?"

Daniel took another pull on his milk, then considered the wet rings left on the bar by the glass as he turned the glass in a slow circle. He offered a half-hearted shrug. Lou knew him too well. "Piper still gets under my skin, no matter how many times I tell myself I need to keep my distance. But last night…I screwed up."

"And you slept together." It wasn't a question.

Daniel nodded.

"Did you use protection?"

"Geezus, Lou."

"I'm serious. Did you use protection? For people like us, I mean. Not for humans. Either that, or at least doubled and tripled human protection for both of you."

He shifted on the seat. Well, damn. "Um, not this time."

Lou sighed and glowered at a point on the ceiling for a second. "That's going to be a problem."

"Problem?" All ability to think or speak fell out of Daniel's head for a moment, and if he hadn't been sitting, he'd probably have fallen. For a second or two, until his brain forced him to inhale, he forgot how to breathe. Problems were not a good thing when it came to the expected behavior of contraceptives.

His friend turned to him with a glare. "Are you a parrot now? Yeah, a problem, with the way you and Piper feel about kids, unless that's changed recently. Because otherwise there's a damn good chance—no, a pretty near certainty, that you've gotten Piper pregnant."

CHAPTER 28

Piper rolled aching shoulders and blinked blurry eyes a few hours later in the library. Turned out wasps, even if they would reluctantly start circling counter-clockwise in formation as she wanted, were assholes. After they'd listened for a while, they then spent the next five minutes stinging the nylon holding them in the jar.

She could convince some bugs to listen to her, and maybe half the time get the air currents and smoke to move as directed. What good was any of it? It wasn't enough to stop the League of Extraordinary Assholes. The barrier was still up, turning the townspeople into really twisted fairytale creatures. The engagement party was tomorrow. Piper and the others weren't ready.

Nia, sunken into her hoodie, only her dark eyes flashing, slammed her jar of dead moths down on the table in front of Anna, making Piper jump. "There. I killed them. Happy?"

Anna, who'd been focusing intently on her pickle-jar coliseum where she'd pitted her ants, threw her hands in the air and stood, shoving her chair back. "I almost had them that time. Thank you. Very helpful as ever, Nia."

"Whatever. I'm done. I'm going home," Nia said, more withdrawn than usual. She shuffled toward the door.

Piper didn't need to see Nia's emotions—since she couldn't see those in the other three, just in other Beckwellians—but it was easy to tell Nia was hurting. "Nia, wait. Maybe—"

"No." Nia turned, fully facing Piper.

Piper gasped. It looked like someone had gone overboard with the smoky-eye on Nia's usually caramel complexion. Instead, her eyes were surrounded by a deep pewter mask that seemed to hover above her face.

She swung around and slipped out the door, letting it bang shut behind her.

Ginny cleared her throat and gently set her tray of seedlings on the table. They'd grown to five times their original size, while stray red curls escaped from Ginny's bun. She winced at the plants and set the bag of black and moldy bread down beside it. "The bread I'm good with. The plants...not quite sure this was what we were going for. And I, uh, I have to go, too. My parents are expecting me home for dinner."

"You're twenty-eight, and you've still got a curfew?" Anna said, her voice sharp, her dark brown braid half unraveled. She looked up, and there was an eerie red glow to her eyes.

"Anna—" Piper began.

"No. It's okay. She's right," Ginny said, pulling her jacket tightly around herself and smoothing the buttons, her voice small. "I know I need to work on my boundaries. But right now, I can't afford a place of my own, I don't want to cause a fight before the wedding, so it's just easier if I go." She headed for the door.

Anna grumbled to herself, rubbing her forehead. "I'm sorry, Ginny. I shouldn't have said that."

Ginny rubbed her arm. "Yeah, well, it's true, isn't it? I'll see you tomorrow. We'll try some more." Then she, too, walked out the front door, quietly closing it behind her.

Anna slammed her fists on the conference table, rattling the jars of insects and knocking over the pickle jar where Anna's last warrior ants had just killed each other. "Dammit!"

Piper gulped.

The other woman sank down onto her knees beside the table. Her long braid swung as she leaned forward and covered her face in her hands. A crumpled, broken version of herself, she made a low, keening sound, barely audible.

Piper's mouth went dry and she bit the inside of her cheek. She'd never seen Anna like this. Ever. Even after she'd accidentally caused a fist fight in their kindergarten class and had to spend the rest of the month doing her schoolwork in a room by herself, she hadn't cried. In high school, people would clear the hall when she walked past, she hadn't flinched.

Queenie nudged Piper's calve. Then batted it for good measure and flashed the image of Anna smiling, of Anna's big-ass Book of Scary.

"Anna?" Piper stood and approached slowly, coming down to her knees beside their tireless, warrior librarian. She reached toward Anna's back, hesitated, then placed her hand between the other woman's shoulders.

Anna flinched. "I've failed, haven't I?" she whispered, her voice muffled by her hands.

So, Piper hadn't been the only one wondering how their lessons would help in the long run. Of course, that wasn't what Anna needed to hear. "How can you have failed? The world hasn't ended yet. That has to be something, right?" The poor attempt at humor came out flat, but Anna spoke before Piper could try again.

"I've failed all of you. I haven't protected you. The barrier is still up. Loki might have built it, but with him as part of the League, he definitely won't help us get rid of it. I have you training insects instead of out in the town because I'm too scared to practice on real people." Her voice shrank even further. "Because I'm too afraid to leave this town. Because I'm terrified of what will happen if I'm around normal people." She smoothed her fingers down the length of her long braid and stared at the floor. "The same reason I avoid real relationships. Even with all of you."

Piper shifted and frowned down at the gray industrial carpet. "Look who you're talking to, Anna. Me. Queen of running away and avoiding people." It was hard to swallow and own up to everything, but Anna needed to hear it. And Piper needed to say it. She looked up. "I haven't been a good friend. I haven't even stayed in touch as much as I should have—sometimes even as much as I'd have liked too. Because…because I was scared. As though somehow, just by talking to you all…"

Anna lifted her head, and now her dark blue eyes were red-rimmed rather than red-hued. "You'd be like us, right? Potentially doomed to end the world, ride forth into the apocalypse."

Piper could only nod, throat too thick for words.

The other woman offered a bleak smile. "When you left Beckwell ten years ago, it wasn't just Daniel you dumped."

The back of Piper's throat burned, and the contents of her stomach sloshed.

"And I was so damned envious of you. That you'd escaped. That maybe, somehow, you'd find a way to be normal in a way I never will."

"Anna—"

She raised a hand. "Let me finish. Please. Most people, men and women, either don't like me, or they're scared of me. Sometimes both. You were one of my best friends. You were one of only three people in this world who cared if I showed up for school. If I was sick. If I was dead. You trusted my advice, and I trusted yours, and then suddenly, you were gone." She picked at a fingernail. "And I know we've never been as close as you and Ginny. But for your sake, maybe for our sake, I hoped you didn't come back. Even though I missed you. Even your comments about my wardrobe. Though not your disrespect for the library."

The two women shared a tiny smile.

Anna had often been in the background, a third but constant presence who shadowed Ginny. But she'd always been there, even if she didn't always participate out loud.

Piper leaned forward and squeezed Anna's hands. "Anna, I'm so sorry. You were my friend. You *are* my friend. At least, I hope so. If you still want my friendship."

Anna squeezed back. "Always. Now more than ever. I can't do this alone. I can't become this...*thing* I'm supposed to be. That we're supposed to be. I've spent years trying to find a way to avoid it, but nothing I've found helps. And now I've chased away Nia by forcing her to confront her horror of necromancy. And I've made Ginny feel bad, the closest thing to family I have." Her voice broke. "None of my research tells me how to destroy this barrier. None of my books tell me how we can stop the League. Nothing I know tells me how to keep the four of us safe, and you from getting hurt."

Well, damn. No big book of plans stashed

somewhere then, huh?

"On the upside, we're hardly made of glass. We're figuring out our abilities, and we know at least some of the League members. And we are immune to each other, so even if we accidentally destroy the world, or the League does it, we'll probably still have each other. That's something, right?" Another pathetic attempt at humor.

"Hardly." Anna frowned into her lap. "We don't affect each other, but immune isn't precisely accurate." She hesitated, twisting her hands together. "Take the War clan for example. They have a history of dying early, and usually violently. From my research, I've found it's quite common for War clan members to be killed by those they've angered or infected with their abilities. And they kill each other. Especially if they marry."

Piper could barely swallow. Anna had arrived as a young child and become a ward in Ginny's household, but she'd never spoken about her own childhood. "Is that what happened? To your parents?"

Anna nodded, a frown creasing her forehead.

Piper didn't know what to say. Or if she should say anything.

"They fought a lot. I remember that about them. More as I grew older. I've been thinking these days it may have been because I'd learned to speak."

Oh, gawd. Piper felt ill. She'd thought the powers of Pestilence were bad?

Anna pressed her lips together and shook her head. "Anyway, they died, and Loki the liar brought me here. I thought I'd found somewhere safe to live. Where I wouldn't hurt anyone. But that doesn't seem to be true. Nor would I even consider marrying or bringing another child like me into this world. I thought you always felt the same."

Uh, yeah. And she'd never caused her parents to maybe kill each other. "Of course. No kids. It's one of the few things Daniel and I always agreed on." Piper shrugged and continued morosely. "Not that it matters now."

"And because the two of you having sex might have made him change color," Anna added, which earned her a glare. She grimaced. "I'm sorry. Just thinking aloud." She paused. "You still care about him, don't you?"

"Yeah. Pretty stupid, huh?" More than cared. Cared too much with that four letter word she sure the heck wouldn't use. "You'd think ten years would be long enough to get over him, wouldn't you?"

"Maybe. If you'd never really loved him before. Or if either of you were ready to move on. The same reasons you ended the engagement remain. They're even stronger, in fact, now that you're coming into your abilities. What we are? It makes the difficult possibilities of a relationship next to impossible for us." Anna sighed and climbed to her feet, stretching her back.

Gee, there was some optimistic advice. Piper stood, Queenie circling her ankles.

"I better start narrowing down the magical objects we should look for tomorrow at the school, during the engagement party." She glanced at her jars. "And maybe practice with my ants some more."

"I could help. With the research, not the ants." Though the ants sounded less horrifically boring.

Anna turned, and put both hands on Piper's shoulders, her expression gentle. "You should go find Daniel."

Piper blinked. "What?"

"I've made a lot of mistakes today. But this isn't one of them. You need to find him."

"I could make him sick."

"Perhaps. Though you never made him sick before,

and even now, any of the illnesses you've caused you've also stopped."

"No, someone dragging me away stopped them," Piper said morosely. She shook her head. "I don't get it. We need to stop the apocalypse. This is hardly the time for me to be more worried about my love life than, oh, I don't know—the fate of the world?"

"Well, from a strategic standpoint, Daniel is very influential. He could make people listen when they just ignore us. He could be very helpful tomorrow. Especially when it comes to a distraction while we search for the magical object. I doubt the League will just leave it unprotected."

"That's true, I suppose."

"But from a friend's standpoint: Piper, the world might be ending. Wouldn't you like to get as much time with the man you love as you can?"

CHAPTER 29

Piper stepped out of the library and pulled her jacket more tightly around herself to ward off the evening chill, the sky pink-hued with another Beckwell sunset. Queenie padded quietly beside her. Time was almost up. Tomorrow was the engagement party, and ready or not, she and the others had to make their first real move.

She tightened her grip on the handle of her suitcase, since here she went again, schlepping the bag all over town. Was this foolish? Wanting a little comfort and one more night with Daniel? Or would it turn into the same mess it'd been this morning?

She fiddled with the button on her jacket and stared down at the cracks in the narrow sidewalk. Anna had called Daniel, and it sounded like he'd rushed right over from wherever he'd been, texting to say he was out in the parking lot. At which point Anna had practically thrown Piper, along with her skunk and her suitcase, out the library door and told Piper to make the most of it.

She stepped carefully over a troop of ants. Had it

only been last night they'd been together? This morning the fiasco with him turning bronze. Then the thing with Louise Dole. Where did that leave them now?

She rounded the corner of the library, her gaze drawn up.

And there he was. He leaned against his battered blue truck, arms crossed, waiting for her like he had so many years before. A snug white T-shirt showed every movement of his muscles when he straightened and saw her, and… Oh my. Were those leather pants? What was he wearing under those leather pants?

Piper's breath quickened and her hand dampened against her suitcase handle.

On the upside, he was back to normal Daniel color, that warm sun-kissed glow a bit darker with his Algonquin heritage, the same chocolate-brown eyes when she got close enough to see them. Her fingers tingled with the need to touch him.

Daniel didn't swagger or exert his masculinity and sex appeal the way Mal did. It wasn't who he was. He didn't care if every woman in the room wanted him, or that he could have anyone at the barest crook of his finger. Because for him, there was always only one woman that mattered.

She shivered, a tingle of awareness sliding through her, awakening a hypersensitivity that deepened the pink of the sky, the faint breeze tugging at her hair and caressing her cheek. She was drawn toward him, as she'd always been.

Because right now, those dark brown eyes were locked on her, and as his gaze licked over her, it was clear the one woman he wanted was her.

She squeezed the suitcase handle tighter and stopped, less than a foot away, breathless and giddy like she was still a teenager, and he was still her older boyfriend, come to watch the stars and make-out in the back of his truck. She stroked a hand down her throat. *This* truck.

He stared at her like a starved man. His hands clenched briefly, then released as his eyes finally met hers. "It would probably be a better idea if you stayed with Anna," he said, his voice rough.

"Maybe. But, I just want to spend the night with you." It was all she'd ever wanted. Her heartbeat pounded in her ears and her knees were soft as jelly.

He pressed his lips together and broke his gaze away to stare down at her suitcase. "I wasn't sure you'd want to see me. After this morning."

"I thought you wouldn't want to see me." Her voice came out small, vulnerable. She had to force herself to look him in the eye. "I wish you hadn't run away. That you'd talked to me." Every nerve ending jangled and sang, begged her to get closer to him. But how could she? Because of last night, he'd woken up changed, more like the thing he'd never wanted to be. Because of her.

He looked away, shoved his hands in his pockets. "I didn't understand what was happening, let alone know what to say. Other than I looked like a monster." His voice rasped, and he turned only his dark eyes to her. "I couldn't risk hurting you."

She couldn't resist the short step forward to cup his jaw with her hand. The prickle of whiskers tickled her palm and sent hot shivers cascading through her. "Don't be a dummy. You'd never hurt me. I'm certain of it."

He frowned, and wouldn't meet her eyes. He held her hand against him for a minute, then gently pushed it down. "That makes one of us," he said gruffly, and reached for her suitcase.

She stood there a second, squeezing her hands together, staring at the ground. Was this a mistake? Maybe she should head back to the library.

Daniel didn't look at her as he carefully lifted her suitcase into the back. His movements were deliberate, his dark eyes troubled, and it was like he couldn't quite meet her gaze.

He'd spent so long fighting what he was. Maybe longer than she had. He was always so busy rescuing everyone else. And now that Mal had joined the League, it left no one for Daniel to turn to.

Who would save him?

She scooped up Queenie and carried the animal around to the passenger side door he'd left open for them. She set the skunk down first before she climbed in and hauled the door closed.

Her palms were damp, and she played out scenarios in her head for what would happen when they got back to the cottage. Too many of them were R-rated. Which wasn't allowed.

Then again, maybe Anna was right. Time could be more limited than they realized. The engagement party was tomorrow. The bachelorette party the following day. Who knew what could happen.

Daniel climbed into the truck and closed the door. The narrow space seemed to compress around the two of them, making her achingly aware of the breadth of his shoulders. The strength in his capable hands and those long fingers as he reached for the keys he'd left in the ignition, but stopped, instead resting both hands on top of the steering wheel, fingers dangling over it.

He exhaled, avoiding eye contact. "If we go back to the cottage, we can't...there can't be any... We can't have sex." He cleared his throat and turned toward her, his gaze desperate, voice raspy. "What if you're wrong? What if you're not safe around me?"

Piper leaned closer and placed a hand on his forearm, muscles jumping beneath her fingertips. "No matter what you look like, no matter what else you may be, I have no doubt that I am safer with you than anyone else in this world."

The troubled expression on his face made it clear he wasn't convinced.

So maybe that was how she could help. She just needed to find a way to prove to Daniel his being Fomorian didn't make him a danger to her.

He turned the keys in the ignition and pulled out of the parking lot. Piper kept her hand on his arm as he drove home. *Home.* She squeezed her eyes shut, heart buoyant, heat radiating through her. She was finally going home. Even if it couldn't be forever.

෴

Daniel clutched the steering wheel of the old truck and tried to focus on the road and stopping at the four-way instead of Piper's fingers lightly resting on his arm. Or the electrical current buzzing between them, desire purring in his blood. He was taking Piper home with him for the night, and it was all too easy to pretend they could have a happy ending, that they could be together.

There could never be another night together. His throat thickened. They couldn't even sleep together, a final good-bye.

He stole a glance in her direction, at the serenity in her expression, the last rays of sun making a pink halo with her pale hair.

He turned away, squeezed the wheel again. There were so many things he should be saying, should tell her. What he knew about the group targeting Beckwell and intent on apocalypse. What had happened this morning. What had happened with Mal.

How she might be pregnant.

He frowned out at the road ahead, the trees making a golden tunnel of the narrow highway ahead. There was no way to even know yet if she was pregnant, let alone figure out how he was supposed to tell her that.

Medically, he couldn't test until at least five days after sex. Hell, Lou could be wrong.

Or it could have happened after round one last night. Because he hadn't known they should have been using super-condoms.

How could he have been so irresponsible? No way would he risk it again. No sex. No risk of activating the Fomorian side with increased adrenalin. No risk of impregnating Piper. No risk of twins like he and Mal, always the firstborn.

No sex. On his last night with Piper. Because this time, they'd have to say good-bye forever.

He turned into his driveway, the truck rolling and bouncing over the uneven grassy driveway. Toward his house. The house he'd always intended for her.

The yard was softly lit with the remains of the sunset, a green fairy glen. A sanctuary. The cottage waited there in the gathering twilight, a warm light glowing inside, welcoming them home. Piper's lilac scent surrounded him, tugged her toward him, plucked at his desire.

He climbed abruptly out of the truck and closed the door. Before he gave in to his desire to pull her into his arms. Before he got lost in her amber gaze, the lush softness of her lips.

He squeezed his eyes closed and gripped the side panel of the truck bed until the cold metal dug into his palms. She wasn't his. He would never see her walk down the aisle toward him. She would never be the mother of his children. She'd never wanted children any more than he had. They'd always agreed they never wanted to pass on their curses. She'd always been terrified she'd make him or their kids sick.

If she were pregnant, it would probably be twins.

Jaw clenched, he grabbed the suitcase, jerked it out of the truck bed, and stalked around the side of the truck.

He pulled open the door.

She reached for the door handle at the same time and tumbled out toward him.

He dropped the suitcase, caught her against his chest, her hands catching his shoulders. Her breasts crushed against him, her thighs aligned with his. His breath escaped, and desire roared in to fill the vacant space.

"Think I finally figured out that seatbelt," she said, her voice breathy.

"You just need to be gentle," he rasped. Gods, could he ever be gentle enough with her? With their children? Or was that uglier side of him just waiting to get out like it had for Dad?

"Daniel? Talk to me." She stroked a hand down his jaw, and he shuddered with need.

He leaned into her touch and inhaled her scent. *Tell me you're not wearing any panties and we can go inside and I can lose myself in you all night.*

Need and possessiveness, raw and animal, pushed through him.

Daniel cleared his throat, tried to push it down. He tried to force himself to let her go, to step away.

It was like his hands had a mind of their own, instead sliding up the soft denim covering her arms, found a lock of silken hair and curled it around his finger, tugged her closer. "I don't know if I can do this. If I can let you go," he said, voice rough.

She stroked his shoulders, clutched his biceps. "I know what you mean." She let her hand drop, grabbing her suitcase in one hand, and his hand in the other. "Come on. Let's go inside."

Yeah, because inside, closer to his bed—*their* bed—would make it all that much easier. He closed his eyes a moment and swallowed a groan.

He let her lead him, docile as a pup, opening his

eyes as she stopped to help the skunk out of the truck, then pushed the truck door closed.

Even as Piper took his hand again, he found his gaze captured by the skunk's dark eyes. The challenge there, almost as though it asked him if he was up to tonight. Finally, it nodded, then waddled off and disappeared under the porch.

He frowned. What if…what if there was some way he could prove to Piper she'd been wrong? Maybe he could prove it would be safe for her to be a mother.

She led him up the porch, their bodies almost pressed together in the small space as he unlocked the door. He closed and locked the door behind them, unbuckling and removing the borrowed biker boots in the narrow hall.

He looked up to find her watching him, her small shoes neatly set beside his inside the door. Like they belonged there. The hall light behind her made her seem to glow, illuminating her pale hair, and she held out her hand, a small smile on her lips.

Once more he placed his hand in hers.

She walked backward, leading him into his bedroom.

He froze in the doorway. The sheets on the bed were still tangled from last night. The echo of her screams of ecstasy seemed to linger in the air. Dents marked both pillows where they'd lain.

Where he'd woken this morning to find himself a monster.

He shook his head, tried to back away. "Piper, we can't…"

She refused to relinquish his fingers, instead stepping closer, her hand sliding up his arm, wrapping around his torso. "No sex. I promise." She looked up at him through the shadow of her pale lashes, her lips plump and moist. "But that doesn't have to mean no touching. Let me take care of you, Daniel. Please."

It was the almost breathless please that did him in. Let her lead him into the bedroom, and sit heavily on the edge of the bed.

While Piper slid her hands down his arms. Over his thighs. And knelt on the floor between his knees.

He almost swallowed his tongue, while his mind made quick work of picturing her taking him into her mouth, her lips wrapping around his hard cock. His mouth opened, but no words came out. He grabbed her hands, stopping their movement. Could he actually ask her *not* to give him a blowjob?

That was a hard no. Hard being the operative word about now.

She cocked her head, a wicked smile tickling her lips. She raised her eyebrows, and did a slow and intentional inspection between his legs.

When she took his hand and sucked one of his fingers into the wet heat of her mouth, he couldn't stop the low groan. He forced his grip to remain gentle on her hands. "Sweetheart, you're killing me here."

She bit her lip, considering the visible swell in the leather pants again. "We did agree no sex. And taking you in my mouth is technically a form of sex. So...not allowed?"

If she got him off, what if it turned him bronze again?

Oh, flipping hell, about now, that was seeming like a not-bad trade-off.

No, very bad trade-off. He growled to himself, eyes squeezed shut, the intensity of his erection painful, the need for Piper thrumming through his blood like a marching band. He shook his head, because he couldn't say the words.

"Because we can't have intercourse...or because you're afraid of, well, changing color again?"

Purple was likely the color he'd be changing any second.

"Both," he ground out. "My heart rate goes too high, adrenalin kicks in, I go bronze." Because that was easier than saying he turned extra-Fomorian.

"Hmm," she said.

Which of course made him picture all the things she could be considering.

All of which made Mal's porno channel look pretty dull.

"What if I could keep your heart rate low enough and control the adrenalin?"

He opened his eyes, looked down at her.

She was still staring at his erection, but turned to meet his gaze. "If I did that, could we…?" A nod toward his groin.

He blinked. "Is that even possible?"

Her smile widened, and she tugged gently at her hands. "Anything is possible. Besides, shouldn't I practice using my abilities?"

He let her hands go, unable to take his eyes off her. "We shouldn't."

"We're not going to do anything risky. I see a hint of bronze, I'll deal with it." She chuckled. "I had been intending a nice massage, but maybe we'll start with this, hmm?" Her expression grew serious, and she slid her hands up his thighs again, cupped his balls and squeezed his dick gently, then released.

"I want to prove to you you're not a danger to me. I want to take care of you the way you've always taken care of me." She reached for the zipper on the leather pants.

He couldn't seem to help himself from leaning back, undoing the button, and making it easier for her to unzip the pants. Fold them back from the bulge in his tighty-whities.

She didn't wait, but pulled the underwear's elastic low, taking his balls in one hand and wrapping her fingers around his dick.

He groaned, pulsing upward into her grasp. His pulse pounded beneath the squeeze of her fingertips. He checked his hand. No bronze. Yet. He reached for her. "What if you—"

She released his balls and caught his hand. "It's okay, Daniel. I've got this." She lowered those delectable lips to the head of his penis. "Let me take care of you." She took him into the wet heat of her mouth.

And he forgot all about all the things he was supposed to tell her.

CHAPTER 30

Piper knew she was alone before she opened her eyes the next morning, the usual cold feeling of being alone having stolen the comfort and peace she'd had last night with Daniel. Somehow, she wasn't overly surprised. And maybe it was just as well. That way there was no temptation this morning. Plus, they could avoid that awkward talk where they both agreed it didn't really matter how they felt about each other. There was no future for the two of them together.

She stared up at the crack running along the ceiling, sunshine through the trees outside painting fairy lights across the dingy paint. As though the world outside were magical, and fairytales could come true.

Last night she'd kept her word. Not a hint of bronze. She'd been able to monitor and regulate Daniel's heart rate and the rise of adrenalin, which she'd come to think of as the color-changing part. She'd been able to take care of him, give him the pleasure and care he always gave to her.

And yet, it didn't seem like it'd been enough, did it? Afterward, he'd done up his pants and curled up with her, then pretended he was asleep, even though she'd known he wasn't. She'd felt too good in his arms to call him on it, to cause the inevitable fight in the short time they had together. At least he hadn't said thank you or something equally awful to cheapen the moment.

At least she'd been able to resist saying those three little words and humiliating herself further.

He was still gone. She was alone.

She climbed out of bed, her T-shirt wrinkled from sleeping in it, jeans uncomfortable, the sheets clinging to her. She pulled her hair over one shoulder and massaged her forehead. Last night would make it even harder to leave Daniel. But she had to. Didn't she? She'd make him sick. Or she'd turn him into something he hated. Both were equally horrible.

Aches suffused her body inside and out as she padded across the room to her suitcase. And the white note waiting on top, her name in Daniel's bold scrawl.

She knelt down beside it, opened it with trembling fingers.

> *Breakfast waiting in the kitchen.*
> *Sorry I'm not there to share it with you.*
> *There's something I have to do. See you*
> *at the engagement party. Be safe.*
> *—D.*

Piper sighed a moment, searching for deeper meaning in the few words. Was that all he'd meant to say?

How would she leave him if he'd said more?

A headache formed behind her temples, and she had that sinking feeling in her belly. But there wasn't time for any of that. She unzipped her suitcase and starting poking through, looking for suitable armor.

ॐ

Daniel jerked his head up off his desk, his forehead stuck to some paperwork. Crud. He must have fallen asleep. Well, on the upside, he wasn't bronze.

He pulled the paper from his forehead and piled the paperwork carefully before he closed it in a folder, then tucked it into the bottom drawer. And locked it away.

He stretched, the restricted movement reminding him he still wore the tight white T-shirt and the leather pants. When he'd left Piper still sleeping this morning, they were the only clothes that fit.

It'd been torture to leave Piper, yet at the same time, how could he stay there with her, not telling her the whole truth? She'd kept him from turning Fomorian last night, just like she'd promised. Given him pleasure he couldn't return, because he needed her to control that part of him. He couldn't seem to.

He grimaced and combed through his hair with his unsteady fingers. So what had he done? He'd taken the coward's way out. He'd pretended he was asleep. Hadn't said all the things he should have, hadn't told her all the things she needed to know.

If he started talking, it would have been too easy to tell her he loved her.

Which might give her false hope. They still couldn't be together. Not with what he was.

He glanced at his watch. Crud, it was almost noon. He scrambled up from his desk, glanced again at his unusual attire. Then shrugged. The people he'd met on the way to and at the Senior Center seemed to think the leather was an improvement over the khaki anyway.

He searched through the papers covering his desk until he finally found the photocopy he'd misplaced. He leaned back in his chair, the paper rattling. He could show this to Piper, and maybe it would make a difference.

Maybe this medical report would change her mind about her future. Maybe this would give her some different options, like having a family.

Or keeping her baby. His baby. Their baby.

Without him.

He looked down at the paper. Even if that meant she'd be better off anywhere but in Beckwell. The Beckwell he'd seen lately was the Beckwell Piper had run away from. The fear, the slights. She didn't deserve that.

She deserved the truth. He had to tell her. All of it.

He had to help get that barrier down, so Piper would be free.

It didn't look like there was any going back from what he was becoming. And he couldn't do that to her.

He loved her too much to do that to her.

Which meant he had to end things.

Either way, he had to talk to Piper. And quick. Before she heard any of it from someone else.

CHAPTER 31

"Well, this is about as bad as I expected," Piper said quietly to Nia, her pink silk cocktail dress rustling. About as close to armor as her suitcase held to get ready for this party. She, Anna, Nia, and Queenie had arrived at Ginny's engagement party early, but the schoolyard already bustled. So much for getting there and scoping things out before it started. And oddly, no one had asked why she'd brought a skunk. Then again, no one said much about hosting an engagement party when there was no fiancé present, so maybe anything went today.

The yard had been trimmed and tidied, tables and chairs set up against the school for the buffet later. Black-clad servers, who looked to be recruits from the upper grades, carried trays of drinks and appetizers around.

"I dunno. Looks a bit like a Renaissance Fair to me. You know, the kind where no one bothers with the historically appropriate stuff and it's all just horns and wings and weirdness." Nia sipped from her plastic cup.

She'd dressed up for the occasion. Which meant black jogging pants and a printed tux T-shirt worn beneath an actual suit jacket. Two sizes too big, of course.

There *were* a lot more horns and wings and weirdness amongst the guests. Only these weren't costumes. Three days after the barrier had solidified, and most Beckwellians were looking a lot less human, and a lot more other. Whereas some, like the woman by the swing set, tried to disguise her newly purple-tinted skin with a heavy—and unsuccessful—application of foundation, others had torn holes in their clothes to free tails and horns. They stood around with their plastic drink glasses, most dressed formally enough for a wedding, watching each other, waiting for the real event to begin. Almost as though they knew something was about to happen.

Well, it was a Beckwell party. Mayhem and chaos were practically as expected as beer and potato chips.

Queenie made a grumbling-whimpering sound, projecting her unease.

"You and me both," Piper conveyed back, trying not to stare at the other guests.

"Try to look like you're enjoying the party, ladies. We don't know who's watching us, waiting for us to make a mistake," Anna said, dressed in a floor-length, floral monstrosity. She took a sip of her pink drink, made a face, and then slyly poured the remainder of it into the grass. It must have included alcohol, a no-no in Anna's books.

Her reminder just made Piper grip her plastic glass until it crinkled between her fingers. No sign of Mal or Louise Dole. But what about the other members of the League they hadn't identified?

And did Anna mean to worry about just the League of Extraordinary Assholes? Maybe she'd included the rest of the Beckwellians who cut a wide berth around the three women, casting furtive looks their way before scurrying away. But a few waved, offered tentative smiles to Piper, Nia, and Anna. The engagement party was a battlefield, and Beckwellians were slowly choosing sides. With the horsewomen in No Man's Land.

"So you think the magical object causing the barrier is inside the school?" Piper whispered to Anna.

Anna barely nodded. "Objects. There must be something making what happens in Beckwell mirror itself in the outside world. Hopefully it's in there, too. The school's side doors will be unlocked so the catering volunteers can access the kitchen. We wait until Ginny and her parents move toward the buffet table. Hopefully most of the crowd will follow. At least, that's the schedule Ginny's mom told her about."

Ginny stood in a painfully yellow dress next to her parents, welcoming guests near the fence that allowed entry into the schoolyard. Anna should have been over there welcoming guests, too. She'd grown up in the house with Ginny, but Ginny had been the only one to ever fully welcome her. To Mr. and Mrs. Lack, it seemed like Anna was a worthy charity case, but not family. It didn't seem to bother Anna, but it'd always set Piper's teeth on edge.

Today was *not* the day to lose control of her emotions and accidentally make anyone sick. She tucked her hand into a pocket of her dress, where the small sachet little Sandy had painstakingly stitched lay. *I won't make anyone sick. I won't make anyone sick.*

"Is there any word yet on the fiancé?" she asked Anna, who seemed to be in more constant contact with Ginny. When she'd been much younger, it'd made her jealous. Until she'd come to understand Ginny was Anna's touchstone. And possibly needed Ginny more than anyone else could.

Anna didn't stop scanning the growing crowd when she replied. "Word is he's still on his way here. Though not sure it makes much difference if we can't get the barrier down."

"And even with all of this going on, Ginny's still determined to marry him?"

The war horsewoman flicked a dark eyebrow quickly upward. "I'd think if anyone understood the increased importance in seizing and making the most of whatever time we have left for happiness, it would be you. Especially after last night."

"Did you jump Daniel Do-Right again, Pipe?" Nia tsked and sidled closer. "I did offer to tie-you down so you'd avoid that. Did he change color again?"

Piper's face heated. "We didn't sleep together. Er, well, we did. Just…no sex." Not technically anyway. And it might have been the most incredible night she'd ever had with him. Did it really have to be the last?

"Seriously? No sex. Are *you* sick?" Nia asked.

"That's our cue. Let's go," Anna said, leading the charge in that horrible flower thing. It didn't even deserve the title of dress.

Piper gave her head a shake before she and Queenie followed the other two toward the school's side entrance. Seriously, at a time like this, why did she still care what Anna wore?

Queenie replied with an image of the four women laughing and joking among each other. On a day when they weren't out to stop bad guys.

Piper nodded and agreed. *Because it's a tiny scrap of normal in a sea of chaos.*

Nia stopped outside the entrance, closed her eyes, and slowly let her shoulders sink back, her short straight black hair brushing her shoulder blades. A dark, smoky gray cloak seemed to rise around her, and that shifting pewter mask darkening her eyes.

Piper gulped. "What's she doing? Is she okay?"

Anna's dark brows came together, and she grimaced. "She's calling the dead. And creating our distraction. Ginny's going to help by spoiling some of the food, then make a fuss over it, pretending someone else tried to ruin her day or something. You and I need to get inside and find those objects." The librarian *cum* army general held open the heavy steel door into the school. "Come on."

Clearly, the other three were on some kind of super-planning text-loop or something Piper wasn't. Piper followed after Anna. Or maybe after yesterday Anna had called the others this morning and apologized. Still, there was a tiny pang to realize she hadn't been included. Until, of course, one considered she hadn't turned on her cell since she'd gotten back to town until this morning to call Anna for a ride. Plus, last night she'd been with Daniel. Even if Anna had called, she wouldn't have answered. Huh. Probably just as well she wasn't part of the super-loop then.

The smell of industrial cleaner, sweaty sneakers, and crayons tickled Piper's nose as she and Anna entered one of the lower halls of the school. Anna strode forward with confidence, as though it was just another building, whereas Piper found herself slowed by memories of events and people with almost every step they took. This place had comprised a significant portion of her life in Beckwell. Not necessarily a great portion, but a big one.

"There are two main trophy cabinets I think should be our first targets," Anna said, her voice pitched low. "If we don't find what we're looking for there, we move onto the smaller cabinets. Principal Boniface's office, the staff lounge, and the science labs seem likely, since they wouldn't want the objects accidentally broken by the younger kids."

"No, but I guess leaving dangerous magical objects laying around where those same kids might find them is just fine, huh?" She rubbed chilled arms, the hair standing on end.

Anna snorted. "Yes, well, safety of Beckwell's citizens clearly isn't high on the League's priority list. I'll take downstairs, you take upstairs?"

Piper had barely nodded before Anna strode off, her long skirt tangling in her legs, brunette braid swishing. She was close to one of the staircases that led upstairs to the senior classes, and the extra bonus was that there was also less territory to cover, which meant hopefully she could get out of this place ASAP.

The senior high floor of the school hadn't changed enough in ten years, and the black outline of the school mascot, the Beckwell Basilisk, looked like it hissed out at her from the scarred painting on the wall. She avoided looking it in the eye like she had since the first time she'd seen it.

Queenie shuddered and scampered ahead.

Piper snorted. "I hear you." Probably no accident that a twined snake also happened to be Loki's ancient symbol. Sounded just like him to symbolically scribble his name all over the town.

She tried to shake off the memories and unease and hurried toward the first large trophy cabinet between two of the closed classroom doors. Queenie peered into the lower shelves, standing on her hind legs to get a better look.

There were framed pictures of the championship teams. She leaned toward the glass with a soft gasp. Like the photo of Daniel's basketball team, the only Beckwell team to legitimately win a trophy after they'd traveled down to the US to face off against one of the few other magical towns. Daniel was the tallest in the back row, a small smile on his handsome face, the black and white photo not that different than how he looked now. Other than less muscular.

Most of the other trophies were between squads, and the occasional challenge against Buttercreek, the neighboring town of normals. Though it was pretty hard to set up a match when Beckwell wasn't technically even supposed to exist.

Piper leaned closer, studying the cabinet's contents more closely. Here and there were odd objects she'd never really noticed before but looked like they'd always been there. A battered pan flute. A set of tiny stone figures all clustered together. Pieces of horn, feathers, and bone. It looked a lot like some kind of reliquary back in the corner. Piper straightened. Lots of magical objects, but which one might be responsible for the barrier? Dammit. She needed a pocket version of Anna's big-ass Book of Scary references.

"Any clue?" she asked Queenie.

The skunk returned a metaphorical shrug.

The next cabinet was likewise a curious combination of school memorabilia and bizarre magical cast-offs. A couple of scary-looking daggers that, even if they were tucked up high and behind other objects definitely shouldn't be around where kids could get them. Rings, a couple of amulets. Ew. Was that a tooth? She was just starting to think her searching for a specific magical object in a cabinet full of them was pretty useless when she raised her eyes to the top shelf. The hair rose on the back of her neck.

Queenie hissed.

There, hiding behind a badminton trophy on the top glass shelf, was one really ugly snow globe. A snow globe a whole lot like the one Mal had in his bag the day Piper arrived. And quite possibly the day the barrier had solidified and possibly caused her accident.

This case had a set of sliding glass doors. She

tugged on the handle. Nuts. Locked. If she had to break the glass, that'd cause a lot of noise, and someone might hear. In frustration, she jiggled the door harder.

The right bottom corner lifted.

Piper bit her lip and slid her fingers along the side of the glass door until she had a reasonable grip.

Queenie scrambled backward, pressing herself against the far wall with a whimper.

"Thanks for the help," Piper murmured. Hopefully it didn't fall. She focused on the ugly snow globe. It was worth the risk. She tightened her fingers and lifted.

The right corner lifted off the track, but the left didn't budge. Piper's muscles screamed at the weight of the glass, and she muttered a few choice swears, her fingers slipping. She wiggled the door, sweat greasing her palms. The door started to go. Oh, crap. It was going to fall. She was going to lose it—

The left corner popped free. The door was free of the bottom frame.

Crap, was it heavy. Piper readjusted her grip, straddling the door and using her legs to help lift. She was able to slowly wiggle it free of the frame and the lock mechanism that held it in place. Finally, she leaned the door against the opposite wall, placed her hands on her hips, and let out a sigh of relief. She rose up on tiptoe to push the badminton trophy out of the way, and then, barely able to reach it with her fingertips, she was able to coax the snow globe toward the edge of the shelf and finally grasp it just before gravity got a bit too helpful. Anna had said they needed to be careful with the objects.

Piper glanced back at the now-open cabinet, all that presumably magic stuff just laying out in the open. Someone would discover it soon and close it up before anyone else got in there, wouldn't they? She eyed the door. Because she was pretty sure she couldn't convince it back onto the track.

Queenie grumbled and padded over to bat at Piper's ankle, hurrying her up and out of there.

Yeah, she was right. Piper headed back down the hall toward the next staircase where she could find Anna, cradling the snow globe in her arms. She sent one glance back at the still-open cabinet, nibbled her lip. Then she and Queenie padded down the staircase to the main floor of the school, emerging near the front entrance and office. No sign of Anna.

Where was she?

The front doors were a direct way out but were way too exposed when so many people here for the party were parked there, and the snow globe was too big to conceal. Plus, they could be locked; there might even be a potential alarm. Better to exit the way she'd come, out the side door, and try to sneak away that way.

Piper and the skunk turned back down the main hall of the school toward the side entrance. There were the two other trophy cabinets. Still no Anna. She readjusted the snow globe, tiny skunk feet of uneasiness tickling the hair on the back of her neck. Queenie made that whimpering sound again. The two of them sped their progress down the hall, back toward the doors they'd come in from. Piper peeked in through the windows on the classroom doors. Where had Anna gone?

And how long could she risk staying in the school? She could smell food as she neared the school's kitchens. Which meant she could run into someone at any minute. And if it was the wrong someone, how did she explain what she was doing inside, or the snow globe?

She made a dash for the doors. Pushed against them until they opened, and then froze when she heard voices outside, right near the door.

A masculine sigh. "Look, I'd love to chat, but I

can't right now. I have to find Piper."

She jolted. That was Daniel, a thread of impatient urgency in his tone. She bit her lip. But he was talking to someone else. While Daniel might not stop her, the someone else might.

Queenie pressed against her ankles, trying to press her nose through the partially opened doors. Piper flagged the animal backward.

"This is important, too," a second, gruffer masculine voice replied. Maybe Lou? He and Daniel had always been close. "Rumor I'm hearing is that Piper went back to your place last night."

"I hardly see what business that is of anyone else's," Daniel said, voice cold.

"You know damned well why that's of concern," the other man growled back, his voice pitched low. "It's bad enough how panicked people are getting around here. They need to know they can trust you. Not that you're possibly conspiring to start the apocalypse with one of The Four."

"Piper and the other women are *not* part of that group of idiots."

Piper glowed at Daniel's vehement denial. She'd always been able to depend on him to defend her. Looked like some things didn't change.

"That may be, but you know how it looks." There was a pause. "And after yesterday? I thought you'd be smart enough to keep it in your pants."

Her face burned. Did Lou mean when Daniel had changed colors? Oh god. Did that mean everyone knew they'd slept together?

Daniel said nothing.

Lou made an impatient sound, and huffed out a breath. "Look, we both know how much that woman meant to you. But we also both know it never would have worked out. She brings out the Fomorian in you.

And if she hadn't broken it off, you told me you would have had to. None of that has changed."

"She's already pregnant. How much worse can it get?" Daniel said.

Piper covered her lips with a shaking hand to hold in any sound. Her lungs squeezed. Which part was worse? That he'd told Lou? That he believed she brought out the Fomorian in him, the part of himself he loathed? Or the fact that he'd have broken it off with her if she hadn't, and he'd let her carry the guilt of that alone all these years?

And what the hell did he mean she was already pregnant? They'd been together once. It couldn't be possible. Could it?

Heat jetted through her veins, spun and coiled through her at lightning speed. Smog-green power whirled inside her, headier than a bottle of fine scotch, burning from her fingers all the way to her toes. It whispered of power. And vengeance.

A hand touched Piper's shoulder. She spun, catching the scream in her throat as she came face-to-face with Anna's serious blue eyes and confused expression.

Anna opened her mouth.

Piper shook her head and gestured wildly toward a nearby classroom. Anything to get away from that door. From the humiliation of being discovered there. Or of hearing what Daniel had said. He hadn't denied any of it. Instead, he'd added the ludicrous claim she was pregnant. Something neither of them had ever wanted.

She and Anna ducked into the nearest dark classroom.

Her ability still swirled, tightened, and located the rhythmic pulse of blood through two other nearby bodies. The beats of their hearts, quick inhales of their breaths. Saw every inhalation as a way in. Every pore yet another entrance.

There was a surprised squawk in the dimly lit room. Desks shifted as bodies bumped into them. Fabric shifted. Muttered complaints.

Anna flicked on the light switch.

Queenie made a low growl, her claws clicking as she bounced lightly on her paws, her bushy tail twitching menacingly.

Piper's eyes took a second to adjust. The woman was vaguely familiar, an older version of a nameless high school classmate. A second longer for her eyes to recognize the half-naked and shirtless beer-bellied man, fly unzipped, in front of her. Less blond hair than he'd had. And it took him less time to recognize her.

A slow smile spread across the blond man's face, and he stepped forward, casually pulling a shirt back on over his head.

Piper shuffled backward, a bitter taste rising in the back of her throat.

"Well, if it isn't Pussy Bane," Stephen Howser said and stepped toward her.

Everything tightened into one crystalline target, right between his eyes. She could imagine the boils growing on his face, the way he would suffer. But inside her. Contained. For now.

She didn't know, didn't care what happened after she groped for the door, shoved it open. Anything to get away. To escape. There were twin masculine and feminine cries of distress inside. Queenie's smug satisfaction.

Piper was halfway down the hall by the time Anna hauled her around by grabbing her arm, the War horsewoman's power a thrashing red fire.

"Piper, what's going on?" Anna grabbed both of Piper's shaking arms in her own. She leaned close. "You don't look well. We should get you back to the library."

The library. Ha! As though there was anywhere she'd feel safe, anywhere she'd be well.

Home was with Daniel. And that'd just gone up in a mushroom cloud.

She wanted to laugh hysterically until she cried and distantly recognized she was too close to the edge. She shoved the snow globe at Anna. "Here. Mal had this the day I arrived. I think he did whatever it was to the barrier."

Anna took the snow globe, hugging it against her, but didn't let go of Piper's other arm, concern in those dark blue eyes, her lips a compressed line. "Let's get the others. We can get out of here. Just the four of us."

"Out of here?" Piper half-laughed, half-sobbed. "Where should we go, Anna? Where will it make any difference? Here, halfway around the world, we're still the same. We're still dangerous." She snatched the snow globe out of Anna's arm. "But here, by all means. Run. See where it gets you."

Piper raised the snow globe above her head.

Anna lunged forward.

Piper swung downward and released. Gravity did the rest, the snow globe seeming to turn in endless slow circles toward the tiled floor. Anna's hands too slow. Too clumsy.

Glass shattered and water splashed onto Piper's legs, onto the lockers lining the hall.

Thunder rattled the school, and the ground shook.

CHAPTER 32

"Run!" Anna shouted. The floor rolled beneath their feet.

Piper scooped up Queenie. The ground shook beneath her feet again. Lockers rattled and quaked. Doors opened along the hallway. Piper ran for the exit at the end of the hall, Anna at her side.

Anna said they were still mortal, and of all the places to die, Piper refused to be pancaked by the Beckwell school when it collapsed. She kicked off her heels for more speed.

She burst out of the doors she'd come in, Anna right behind.

Piper sucked in fresh air. The ground still heaved, but less so now. A few panicked out-of-towners shouted and clutched each other, showing they'd obviously never been to a Beckwell party before. Most Beckwellians rode out the last few trembles, some literally taking a seat on the ground until it stopped shaking.

There was Ginny near the buffet table, black waves

of power rolling off of her.

And Nia, still with her smoky cloak and pewter mask. Both women turned toward Anna and Piper as though called. Stared, motionless.

Someone pointed a trembling finger upward.

Piper's gaze followed. Lights flashed and flickered in the sky, like a screen fighting for a transmission signal.

The flashing stopped. No more light other than the sun and clear blue autumn skies shone above. The ground stopped shaking.

They'd done it. The barrier was down. She could leave.

"Remember the part where I said we'd deal with the objects accordingly?" Anna said. She put her hands on her knees and struggled to catch her breath. "*That* was *not* accordingly."

Piper set a squirming Queenie down on the ground, her insides numb, even her ability sinking back down to wherever it went when it wasn't urging her to make people sick. She probably should have been proud of herself for not attacking Stephen, accidentally or otherwise. Yet all she felt was open and raw, Daniel's words like needles piercing her flesh.

Warm hands on her arms drew her into his arms. Squeezed her against his body that smelled of spicy, sexy man. Of home. "Thank the gods you're okay," he said, his voice muffled against her hair.

Piper gasped for breath. Her eyes burned.

"I've been looking all over for you. What happened? Did you two cause that?"

She said nothing.

Once, he'd said he'd never hurt her. Once, she'd have believed him.

And then she found the strength to set her hands against his chest. And shove. As hard as she could, as hard as she'd ever shoved, with all the pain, all the hurt he'd caused, her very ability and all that she was, all that she would become behind her.

Daniel stumbled back, beautiful brown eyes wide, still dressed in those sexy leather pants and white T-shirt. Still mouth-watering. Still so damned deceitful.

He took a step toward her.

"Don't." She held out a quavering hand, refusing to meet his eyes.

Daniel froze. "What's wrong?"

∞

Piper wouldn't look at him. She stood there, trembling and cold. But she'd pushed him away. She'd never pushed him away. Even on the day she'd ended their engagement, she'd let him hold her while she cried.

Her skunk hissed at him from near Piper's feet, head down, that black and white tail up, teeth barred.

A chill spread through him. He had to fix this. Whatever this was.

"Piper, please. Talk to me," he said, quietly but firmly.

She looked up, and the coldness in those beautiful amber eyes clenched his heart with icy fingers. "Why? You seem to prefer keeping things from me. Telling other people about them."

A wind whipped up just around them, making Piper's pale hair dance but never tossing it into her face. Anna, Nia, and Ginny stepped into place, flanking Piper, and palpable energy gathered in the air, made the hair on his arms and neck come alive.

He swallowed. Things could get very bad, very fast.

Oh, crud. The pregnancy.

Party guests gathered around, some asking for his attention, others eager to see the next part of the show. He grit his teeth. This wasn't how he'd wanted to do this. This wasn't what she deserved.

"I don't keep things from you. I never have." He kept his voice even.

Best not to do anything to make this worse. Especially by pissing off her friends, who didn't look especially happy as it was. Anna had a fierce hardness to her, a steely tint to her blue eyes. Nia's eyes were peculiarly shadowed by a metallic mask, almost black even in the daylight. Ginny had a wild jungle-woman look to her, the way her red hair cascaded over her shoulders, the iridescent gleam to her green eyes.

While Piper…Piper stood straight and bold before him, the wind whirling her hair around her head like a halo, a flush staining her otherwise pale cheeks, perhaps more lush and beautiful than he'd ever seen. Powerful.

And supremely pissed off.

He fished around in his pocket, holding his other hand out to show he meant no harm, because it was unlikely to keep them at bay. Damn these ridiculous pants anyway. Finally he found the piece of paper he was looking for.

"This morning I had to leave to look for this. I wasn't trying to keep it from you." He held it out, the paper flapping in the supernatural wind.

The wind caught it and carried it directly to Piper's waiting hand. She frowned at it. Looked up at him and waved the paper. "What is this?"

"It's a certificate of death." He softened his voice. "For your friend Sandy. The little girl who died when you were both kids." One of the reasons she'd said she'd never have children. Never risk making them or any other child ill.

Piper's face drained of color, and her hands trembled.

"I know there are a lot of medical terms, but it says that she died of complications following childhood leukemia. Something she'd been born with, Piper. It had nothing to do with you."

She glared at the paper again, then back up at him. "What does this have to do with anything? With the secrets you've kept from me?"

Didn't she get it? "It means you didn't make her sick by being around her. You could have a normal life. A family. A child."

She stiffened. "You know better than anyone how I feel about having children," she rasped. The other three women moved closer to her.

Daniel's muscles jumped and his neck tightened. He licked his lips. Started a step toward Piper.

The wind shoved him backward. He felt it, that growing strength, heightened energy in his limbs.

Dammit, he would not become that now, in front of her. He squeezed his hands into fists, clenched his jaw until he could look upward and force a normal tone into his voice.

The palpable pain in Piper's expression, the hurt in her eyes despite the power radiating through her made him ache.

It wasn't supposed to be like this. He closed his eyes, and fisted his hands. Tried to ignore all the other people watching. Even the skunk and the other girls. Until he saw only Piper, spoke only to her. "I think you might be pregnant," he said quietly.

He opened his eyes to watch Piper. To gauge her reaction.

She didn't flinch. If anything, her expression grew colder, the wind around her more fierce. She shook her head. "Why would you say something like that?" She crossed her arms. "We used protection. Besides, you couldn't know, no matter if you have your medical degree or magical abilities to help you. It's too early. It's days before you can..." She flushed, her gaze flickering over their audience. Her voice dropped. "Why would you try to humiliate me with these lies?"

It was instinct to try to take a step toward her, to pull her into his arms.

The skunk growled, and the three woman raised their hands to hip height. He froze again, swallowing a frustrated growl himself. He couldn't just let her go.

"Because of what I am, it means…" He shoved a hand through his hair with a humorless chuckle. "It means even my sperm is a tough SOB, which means there's a higher chance of pregnancy."

Her face flamed. "It's not like this was the first time."

He cleared his throat. "But I wasn't like this before."

No matter what happened, he wanted to be part of his baby's—or babies'—life. Even if they were twins, even if they were cursed like he and Mal, he would make sure every day that they knew how loved and wanted they were.

But Piper's expression hardened. "And I suppose that's my fault, too?"

"Of course it isn't." Even if he had changed after they'd been together.

She scoffed. "I *heard* you," she said, equal parts accusation and hurt in her voice.

His insides twisted. "Piper, I can explain—"

"Why bother? I heard you talking to Lou." She nodded a head toward where the big man stood near the corner of the school. "I heard everything. About the so-called pregnancy, which evidently Lou knew about before me. And how you hate that I make you more Fomorian." Her voice cracked. "And how you would have ended our engagement a decade ago even if I hadn't. Why? Was I never really good enough for you? Is that it?"

It felt like he was on slippery rocks, and rapidly

losing ground. "The pregnancy thing is…complicated. You don't make me more Fomorian."

"And the engagement?" Her voice was almost a whisper. The wind settled around her, dropping her hair. "For ten years I've lived with the guilt of handing back your ring and the possible future we could have had. And all this time, it didn't have to be my fault? Why force me to do your dirty work?"

"At that point, I thought we could still be happy. And then you ended it. And then you were gone. It was after that when I discovered how wrong I was, how dangerous I'd have been to you. When could I have told you?"

"In an email, a text, a letter, carrier pigeon? Any of the five days I've been back home?" Her voice rose. She stabbed a finger at her chest. "It almost *killed* me to have to tell you that day. To tell you I couldn't be with you ever again."

"I know. I was there," he said, a hint of anger in his tone. Anger to cover the growing fear and panic building inside him. "We agreed it was for the best that it happened. That we still couldn't…still can't be together."

Piper's shoulders sagged. "So why in any of those conversations didn't you tell me? What did I do wrong? Were you just dating down like everyone believed at the time? Was it because of Mal?"

He scrubbed a hand over his face, guilt burning a hole through him. There was no way he could say this that wouldn't hurt her. Which was why he'd never told her. "It was over. You did nothing wrong. If anything I was dating above myself. We just…couldn't be together."

"Tell me the truth finally. Please," she said, her voice so small it tore at his heart.

He glared down at the ground, clenching and

unclenching his hands. "Because I refused to become my dad. Or to let Mal turn into him. And being with you…made us stronger."

"Made you more Fomorian. And you hate that more than you can ever love me," she said quietly, drawing his gaze. "Thank you for finally telling me the truth, Daniel. And good-bye."

She turned, and walked quietly out of the schoolyard.

"Piper, wait!"

The three other horsewomen stepped in front of him.

"I think you've done enough," Nia said, that unnerving black mask of hers making her eyes glitter darkly.

"Go have a drink, and you can walk home the long way," Ginny said, the iridescence to her green gaze unsettling.

Anna, her blue gaze holding the gleam of blue steel, smiled coldly.

He gulped.

"Come on, people. Show's over. Barrier's down. Go have a drink, eat some food, and celebrate," Nia said loudly, breaking up the crowd, her metallic mask fading like a shadow in the sun.

With the distraction, he turned to follow Piper and found Anna once more blocking his way, standing loosely on the balls of her feet, hands at her sides. And looking like she was hoping for a fight.

Exactly what happened if the War horsewoman got into a brawl?

He could just see Piper on the edge of the parking lot, a small forlorn figure, shoulders slumped, alone. He'd let her get away before. Could he let her do it again?

Could he let her and their children go? Gods, she'd

be even more frightened when she realized the babies would probably be twins.

Heavy footsteps crunched toward Daniel.

Daniel watched Piper reach the edge of the hill, almost out of view, her blonde hair rippling in the wind. A paper fluttered in the breeze, and he lost sight of her. The weight of the world and his guilt collapsed onto his shoulders.

"You look like a man who could use a drink," a cultured male voice said from beside Daniel. "Come, let's rejoin the party. You're the town doctor, aren't you? I think it's time we met. I'm Loki."

CHAPTER 33

Piper tiptoed across the spiky-sharp gravel of the parking lot. The asphalt road was smooth and warm against her bare feet. Soothing.

The rest of her felt so cold, so empty. Aching and hollowed out.

Queenie bounded along beside her down the driveway.

"Know somewhere I can hide until the world ends?"

The skunk projected comfort, but also confusion. She projected the image of the girls. Daniel. Unease skittered through their connection.

Piper snorted. "I can't go back there." Parties were definitely less fun when everyone had witnessed her humiliation. And she definitely didn't want to hear more of Daniel's excuses.

She approached the empty four-way stop. Not like there'd be anyone to drive through it. They were all at the party. She turned to look down the highway toward freedom, past the Cow Palace and her SUV, still laying abandoned at the side of the road.

The skunk projected increased urgency. The image of the school. The girls.

"I'll just go try to move the car. I know I can't run away. Where would I go?" There was no outrunning what she was. What she was becoming.

She frowned down the open highway, leaves skittering across the surface in the soft autumn breeze.

If she'd been normal, would she have had the same effect on Daniel? Could he have loved her then?

"Gah! What does it matter? I'm not normal, am I?" She snorted. "I'm talking to a skunk. Pretty clear proof there."

The skunk flashed momentary irritation but increased urgency to go back to the school and the other women. She nipped at Piper's ankles.

"Ow. Stop. That hurts. No, I told you, I'm not going back there. We'll see them later, okay? I just... I need time right now." Time to consider why this time she couldn't, shouldn't run away. The barrier was wide open now.

The skunk went for Piper's ankles again.

She jumped out of the way of those sharp little teeth. "I said stop it."

This time the animal flashed an orange caution sign. Then the image of a baby.

Piper swallowed and wrapped her arms around her stomach and kept walking. "We don't even know if that's true."

So what if Daniel was right and she hadn't caused Sandy's illness when she was a child. She was gaining the powers of Pestilence. Maybe she'd make the baby sick in the womb. Or after it was born. The baby could be part Pestilence, part Fomorian, all trouble.

Queenie showed the baby. A pause. Then the

crystal image of two babies, one fair-haired, the other dark-haired. Fraternal twins. Then the caution sign again. The image of the women. The library. The school.

"You're giving me a headache. Stop, please." Piper rubbed her forehead. She'd hurt so badly when she'd overheard Daniel talking to Lou, then seeing Stephen? She shuddered. And then Daniel's confessions? It was like she'd used up her emotions, leaving her just…empty.

What did she know about children, or alleged children? Even if she didn't make the kid sick, she knew nothing about being a good parent. To Mom, kids were a fashion accessory and status symbol. To Dad, an obligation.

My child would know they were so much more. I'd hug and kiss them all I could. And they would never, ever, doubt how much I loved them.

Queenie jumped into Piper's path, bounced on her front paws and bared her teeth.

Piper stepped around her. "I doubt you can actually hurt me. And I'm in no mood for it. Please, Queenie. Stop."

They were almost even with the Cow Palace, and as she approached the abandoned SUV, she didn't get that strange flutter in her belly like she usually did when she approached the barrier. No thickening air.

It was probably why no one had moved the vehicle since the accident. Well, that and they'd been more worried about everyone turning into different creatures, the barrier trapping them all, and the possibility of a coming apocalypse. She hadn't really given it any thought herself until now. But with the barrier down, maybe she could get it going, drive it out of the ditch at a low spot. She'd have a vehicle then.

To drive where? The library maybe. She couldn't go back to the cottage. Didn't want to go to Mom and

Dad's. Which left Nia and Anna. And without a job soon, funds would dry up quick.

Money was also pretty important to support a child—child*ren* if Queenie was to be believed, if the whole idea of being pregnant was to be believed. A quiver of fear rolled through her.

Queenie scampered in front of Piper, lowered her head and raised her tail. She flung fear and terror at Piper. A whole "get back" kind of package deal that made Piper stumble back a few steps. Then once more the image of the library. The other women.

"I just want to get to the car. Is that too much to ask? We're not going anywhere."

The skunk projected the emotions of the terrified toad as it had plopped into existence on Piper's windshield, about to be driven into a tree.

"And I won't drive into anything. Honestly, I'm usually a pretty safe driver." Safe enough to be a mom?

Or a single mother.

The weight of holding back an avalanche weighed on her, a boulder of despair starting a long downward fall through her.

She turned to stare down the empty highway. Gusts stirred white clouds in a bright blue sky, and sent golden poplar leaves dancing along the black asphalt.

The barrier was down. She was free.

If she left Beckwell, maybe the League of Extraordinary Assholes would have to find another Pestilence to rise to power. Maybe she could still be normal. Maybe she really could run far enough, fast enough to escape all this. Or there was always the possibility of an isolated mountaintop with great wifi so she didn't have to worry about hurting anyone.

So long as the babies were immune.

She swallowed and clenched her hands. If the babies were Fomorian, they could be cursed like Daniel and Mal.

She barely heard the soft chirruping sound in time and jumped back. And found a large, green grasshopper, almost three inches in length directly in her path, its essence black and green.

"Hello," it said in her head, the sound faint and scratchy, like the phone connection was bad.

Piper blinked. She knew whom this grasshopper belonged to.

She leaned down and held out her flat hand.

The grasshopper cocked its head, then scuttled onto her palm. It's little feet tickled her palm and yeah, totally made her feel all squidgy with a definite desire to throw the thing in the opposite direction. She swallowed down the faint revulsion and picked it up, since there was no throwing away a friend's horse.

Queenie nipped frantically at Piper's ankles.

Piper barely noticed. Instead, she stared ahead at the empty highway.

Life was freaking hard. Going it alone only made it harder. She'd been alone ten years now. But maybe in Beckwell she could make a place for herself. Maybe she could be accepted. The citizens weren't perfect, but it wasn't like she was, either. Today she, Anna and the others had made a difference. They hadn't exposed and stopped the League of Extraordinary Assholes, but they'd brought down the barrier. Surely that meant something.

Maybe this could be a safe place for her. And the babies.

Queenie projected white-hot terror. Then nothing.

Piper spun. The skunk lay limp in the road, a red dart sticking out from her side.

And Piper stared down the barrel of a rifle. At the end of which stood Mal.

CHAPTER 34

Daniel forced himself to turn away from watching Piper's retreat and to face the man who'd introduced himself as Loki. His hands clenched into fists at his side, but he forced them to relax. This was his chance to get answers.

The god looked younger than Daniel had expected, maybe about the same age, though, of course, appearances were deceiving. He was muscular and broad, eyes an intense dark blue, a hint of dark stubble on his jaw, hair blond-brown. Despite the custom-cut suit and silk shirt he wore like a model, there was the edge of a warrior about the man.

They'd been left alone near the side of the school while the rest of the guests had wandered back toward the buffet tables. Either by chance or intent, it was hard to say, but it left Daniel alone with the town founder. And one of the members of the group trying to end the world. Who'd recruited Mal. Turned he and his brother more Fomorian. Who was willing to cause chaos and hurt people.

"You have a lot of gall showing up like this," Daniel said, feeling the power slide through his veins, the warrior side of himself that wanted to fight. He focused on keeping his breathing even. If it was adrenalin that activated his Fomorian abilities, maybe staying calm could control them.

Loki's lips curled up in something between a smile and a taunt. He put his hands on his hips, the dark blue sports coat pulling open to reveal the silk shirt. The green silk shirt.

Daniel stared at it a second, his mind working out the puzzle.

Loki's words and smug smile distracted him. "It is my town still, is it not?"

It was getting harder to stay calm.

"Then take care of it. And its people. Piper says the barrier is down, but its malfunction has already caused a lot of harm. Altered us."

"Oh, it functioned just as planned."

Daniel's hands curled into fists. The fight unfurled inside him.

Loki's smile grew.

But then that damned green silk shirt caught his attention again. Why? A man could wear whatever he wanted. But it was a unique color.

Just like the one he'd seen in Lou's back office.

His gaze narrowed and focused on the god's blue eyes. In a different face, certainly. But the same blue eyes. Lou's eyes. Someone he'd trusted. Someone he'd called friend.

Daniel sucked in air. His shoulders and chest rose and fell faster. The trickster. The cheat. The liar. His hands clenched at his sides. His muscles grew and tensed.

Loki, the man who had masqueraded as Daniel's

friend, took in Daniel's fisted hands, flicked a look over his expression. He slowly raised his hands to waist height and took a step back. "Ah. Look. I can explain."

"You can *explain*?" Daniel said, his voice dangerously low.

"You go around, expecting everyone to be as saintly as you, my friend, and that's a dangerous expectation. And a hard one to live up to. But give me a chance to explain."

"I. Am. Not. Your. Friend," Daniel bit out. His chest rose and fell. He clenched and unclenched his hands, fury and betrayal riding him hard. The warrior side slid over him, altered his muscles, his skin. "You've lied to me. For years. I trusted you. I confided in you."

"You trusted me because you thought I was Lou, but I'm the same person." Loki glanced over his shoulder toward the party and reached for Daniel's arm. He lowered his voice. "This isn't a conversation to have here."

Daniel stepped back and his fists came up, deep bronze staining the skin. "This conversation is over. Geezus, what other lies have you told me? The town is suffering because of you. We were trapped because of you. What game are you playing? No. You know what? I don't care." He turned and stalked out of the schoolyard. Everything he knew about the group trying to start the apocalypse, he knew from Loki. Everything about Mal's mischief. Loki.

Oh gods…the pregnancy. Piper. Was that a lie, too?

"Daniel, if you come back to the bar—"

"No. I'm not playing your games anymore."

Did he have a right to grovel for Piper's forgiveness? All he seemed to do was bring her pain. Maybe this time she'd run and she wouldn't come back. Maybe this time, she'd be happy.

"You're not thinking clearly," Loki said, his voice

tight and low.

Daniel gave Loki a one-fingered wave. "For once, my thoughts are fucking crystal clear."

CHAPTER 35

Daniel strode out of the schoolyard, leaving the engagement party and Loki behind.

He didn't know where he was headed. Lou had been his closest friend. The only person who'd never asked for anything. Instead, he'd given Daniel good advice, helped him look out for Mal and the town. Heck, he'd helped pay to outfit the clinic at the Senior Center, paid off some of Daniel's student loans, even co-signed for the mortgage on Daniel's property.

And it'd all been a trick. A lie. Because that's who Loki was—look at any history book or book of myths. Loki was a villain. He was supposed to be involved in this plot of world annihilation. A bad guy.

Wasn't he?

At the empty four-way stop, Daniel glanced down the road toward the Cow Palace. There was no sign of Piper's bright pink dress. The silver rental car was still there. But if the barrier was down, she could have left by now.

Everything ached. If he went after her, maybe he could explain.

Yeah, that'd go well. He'd possibly impregnated her. It was probably only a matter of time before he hurt her, even more than he had today. He already said the wrong thing at every turn. He was Fomorian, more so than he'd thought. And, he had to look after Mal. Aunt June. He was the town doctor in a town of magical misfits who, like it or not, needed him.

So this time, Piper would leave and take not only a piece of his heart, but with the child, she'd take part of his soul.

And he'd let her.

He had to, didn't he? She'd never stay here. She'd always hated Beckwell. And he couldn't offer her anything to make the town more palatable, nor leave it behind. He may have avoided drinking, but maybe he'd turned into his father anyway. He wouldn't trap Piper in an unwanted marriage like Dad had trapped Mom.

Daniel's leaden feet carried him toward the Senior Center.

He and Mal had been able to live outside Beckwell before, but that was before the barrier had made them more Fomorian, where an argument could make he and his brother stand out for all the wrong reasons. Besides, Mal didn't want help. He seemed decided on self-destructive behavior, becoming the worst of what everyone had always believed of him.

Daniel pulled open the door to the Senior Center, his shoulders heavy, insides hollow. The atrium was conspicuously quiet, only two small piles of ashes, but no senior citizens flew high today. Maybe they'd attended the engagement party. Maybe it was snack time.

No one called for his attention. Only one white-haired, blue-skinned man shuffled past with his walker, offering only a passing, blurry smile. There was no line outside the darkened office. Frizzly had closed up shop.

No one needed him. Which left Daniel free to stride toward Aunt June's suite. The hallways remained noticeably quiet. A doorway opened near him, and he barely had time to notice the wizened face before the eyes widened and the door slammed shut again.

Uneasiness tap-danced along the back of his neck, and the iciness of his ability slid into his veins in preparation. For what, he wasn't sure.

Another door opened, and Aunt June stepped out as though she'd been waiting for him.

"Daniel!" Aunt June cried. She was dressed in a denim dress and red cowboy boots, and linked arms with him. "You've just missed Mal. He was here and had a chat with Mr. Death. I'm so glad you came by."

"Of course." He ignored the twinge of guilt that he'd come for advice, not just for the pleasure of a visit. And that he'd entertained the idea of running away with his brother. What would happen to her? Especially with her delusions.

She placed a cool hand on his face and brought him back to reality. Her face creased in concern. "What's wrong, dear? You don't look well. Perhaps you should see a doctor."

He took her hand off his face, and forced a smile for her. "I am a doctor, Aunt June," he said gently.

She rolled her eyes and led him back toward her room. "You may be a doctor, but you can hardly diagnose yourself and prescribe care, can you? Come. It looks like you need a cookie."

He didn't have time for a cookie. He sure the heck didn't deserve one. But he wanted one.

She closed the door to her suite after him and waved toward the sofa while she padded around and retrieved cookies, a glass from a shelf, and cold milk from the mini-fridge near her bed.

Daniel rubbed a hand over his gritty eyes. The mauve loveseat dipped as Aunt June joined him and pressed the glass of cold milk into his hands.

He took a sip, but it wasn't as fresh as it could be. And worse, it reminded him of Loki. Which reminded him of the baby. Which reminded him of Piper, walking alone and broken down the highway. Carrying his baby away.

Mom might have been happier somewhere else. If she hadn't married into the Quilan family and all that entailed. Maybe things could have turned out better for Mal, too.

He lowered the glass to his lap and stared down at it. "Have you ever thought of what would have happened if Mom hadn't married Dad? If Dad hadn't tricked her and gotten her pregnant?" Supposedly by accident, just like Daniel had gotten Piper pregnant. "Mom used to say she shouldn't have had us. Maybe she shouldn't have."

Maybe Piper wouldn't hurt so much if he'd never been born. Maybe Mom and Dad would still be alive, and probably a lot happier without each other.

"Don't be silly, Daniel," Aunt June said and squeezed his forearm.

He glanced up toward her.

"I wouldn't have my darling nephews then, and where would I be?"

Possibly not in a seniors' home, but with your sister. Maybe you'd have been able to a lead a more normal life. "Things might have been easier. For a lot of people."

"Maybe. But when I think of your uncles—"

"Please. Don't." Daniel cut off his aunt and massaged his forehead. He loved her like crazy, but he couldn't listen to another uncle story right now. "I know they were great guys, right? In the end, all anyone remembers about them is their curse and how they died."

Aunt June smacked his forearm.

Daniel twisted toward her, his eyes widening.

Her lips pursed, and two high spots of color stood out on her pale cheekbones. There was a snap to her voice he didn't remember ever hearing before. "Now, you listen to me, Daniel Quilan. Those two idiots got into a fight and ended up dead. Their *own* idiocy killed them and stole my brothers away. Not fate. Not some curse. What I hate most and what burns me up is that I remember how much those two loved each other something fierce. Just like you and Malcolm."

He couldn't have said anything even if he could remember he possessed a tongue. She'd never told that side of the story. Or at least, he'd never heard it.

She rummaged through papers on the side table, finally emerging with a small photo that she handed to Daniel.

He stared down into the two innocent, smiling faces of two dark-haired little boys, twins, one blue-eyed, one brown-eyed, though in this picture they were too far away, up in that ramshackle fort they'd built on the property he now owned. They both wore paper eye-patches and waved cardboard swords.

"You were about six there, I believe. I was the queen you were determined to rescue," she chuckled.

It was the week after Dad had sat them down and told them the truth. About what they were. Mom had been sure to add the part that they were cursed to kill each other. His throat thickened, and the photo trembled in his hand.

"I don't know how to save him this time," he said, voice rough.

"Oh, my dear. It's never been about you saving him, or him saving you. Silly men with such silly notions. It's just about love." She pointed at the two little boys. "These dear fellows knew that. They would do anything for one another. Get in a fight over a missing toy, but then forget and go play again the next day."

"We're not children anymore."

"Indeed not. Which is why I don't understand the two of you, acting more foolishly than any six-year-old. You protect your brother, he protects you, and you remember he is always your brother. That's that."

Aunt June patted his leg, her expression and tone soft. "Now, drink your milk, have a cookie, and tell me about you and Piper. When are you going to ask that girl to marry you again? Your parents may have made mistakes, but following their hearts wasn't one of them."

He almost choked. "Mom might still be alive if she'd left him."

"Alive, maybe. Miserable, certainly." Her expression warmed with memory. "They were as happy as newlyweds that last night they headed out." She met his eyes. "Neither of them were perfect, but they loved each other. I hope you understand that. But we were talking about you and Piper."

He did what he was told, chugging down the milk and cookie. Because Aunt June wasn't going to like what he had to say.

Milk and two cookies gone, he had no choice. She waited, a patient half-smile on her face.

Daniel could hardly meet her gaze. "Piper and I…aren't together anymore," he mumbled.

"You broke up again?"

Had they ever really been back together to break up?

Gods, it felt like they'd never really been apart. Like the ten-year gap had been a pause, an uncomfortable hiccough that hadn't changed his feelings for her. If anything, the time had only made his emotions stronger.

"Yeah, something like that," he said.

Aunt June scoffed and shook her head, lips again pursed. "Now why did you go and do a stupid thing like breaking up with Piper?"

He rubbed the back of his very warm neck. "It's complicated."

"Because she's a powerful woman you love but seem too afraid to make your own?"

"Aunt June, I'm becoming *more* Fomorian. Because I was…um, with Piper."

Oh, crud. The day had found a way to get worse. His face and neck burned. He was discussing his sex life with his aunt.

"Daniel, you're a fully grown man. I certainly hope you've had sex by this point. It's one of the greatest pleasures of this life."

He couldn't look her in the eyes. "If I'm with Piper, I'll become more Fomorian. I might not be me anymore."

"And a bus might hit you tomorrow. Well, probably not a bus out here. Probably a pickup truck. Possibly a tractor." Aunt June grabbed his face. She forced him to look at her, his face squished like he was a little kid. "My point is that you don't know when my friend Mr. Death will come visiting. None of us do. So what's wrong with you? Stop worrying about the what-ifs and go fix things with Piper, you hear me?"

He nodded.

Aunt June nodded back and finally released his face. "Good. And when you do, ask her to make some of those cookies, won't you?"

He stood, not sure what he should do. Go find Mal first? Or do what Aunt June suggested. She could be right. Maybe he and Piper should take that chance, no matter how short a time they had together. Maybe it wouldn't be a long life, but they'd experienced so much in just the five days she'd been back. In five days, it was like they'd squeezed in an entire lifetime.

Aunt June looked up and wagged her finger at him. "And you be nice to your brother. Remember what I said: you're brothers, no matter what. He's a good boy at heart. He just…makes crappy decisions. Other than the flavors of cookies he brings. He's very good with cookies."

Daniel bussed Aunt June's face with a kiss, and she beamed at him.

"I'll be nice to Mal. He is my brother. No matter what crappy decisions he makes."

"I'm glad you said that." Aunt June stood and fished in her pocket, then the other pocket, until she emerged with a handful of papers, and sorted through them. "Now, it's here somewhere. I wasn't sure if I should give it to you. I didn't mean to read it, but when I was looking for a phone number, I opened it up."

She flipped through a few different scraps of paper, finally opened one, and handed it to him. "Here we are. Your mother, myself, and Mr. Death decided it was the right thing to tell you. Not that I think Mal would do anything to Piper, but, well, crappy decisions, what did I tell you?"

He snatched the paper out of her hand and read it. Blood pounded in his ears. The note was terrifyingly brief and to the point.

I have Piper. Meet me at the party
tomorrow if you want to see her alive.
—M.

CHAPTER 36

Daniel ran from the Senior Center to the library. He covered the distance in under a minute. His chest heaved, sweat gathered on his brow, and the leather pants were cooking him alive. The sun had set, but light still burned inside the library.

He banged on the door. Waiting, he looked down and plucked at the tight white T-shirt and the ridiculous leather pants. He looked like an idiot. Must have given Loki quite the laugh.

He had no idea what welcome he'd get from the girls, but he had to try. There was no one else he could trust, and he couldn't go into this alone. Not when it was Piper's safety at stake.

He raised his hand to bang again, when the door cracked open.

Three faces peered out at him. All three of the horsewomen.

Nia blew out a bubble of pink gum, then popped it and sucked it with a slurp. "What do you want, Daniel

Do-Right? 'Cause after that shit you pulled with Piper at the party, you're not exactly my favorite person. I'm thinking of siccing a whole frickin' army of ghosts on your ass. All the perverted ones."

"I never wanted to hurt Piper. I still don't," he said, directing his reply to Nia but knowing all three judged him. The hair on the back of his arms lifted, and chills passed over his skin.

The wind rose, and a wave of anger, hurt, and fear washed over him. *Damn you, Daniel. You were supposed to be one of the good ones.* Ginny glowered, her face almost as red as her hair. "You made Piper cry. And you messed up my engagement party."

And the absence of her fiancé hadn't done that? He gritted his teeth, clenched his hands, and forced himself to try to be patient. He deserved this gauntlet, and if he wanted their help, he probably had no choice but to run it. "Piper and I had a misunderstanding."

"No, *you've* had a misunderstanding," Anna said, and something glowed red and hot behind her blue gaze for a moment. "Piper is our friend, now we can't find her, and it's your fault. And you are very mistaken if you think the four horsewomen take hurting one of their own lightly."

Finally, the opening he'd been hoping for. "Which is why I need your help. My brother has Piper, and I'm going to rescue her."

Ginny gasped. Nia ground her teeth. Only Anna seemed unsurprised. None of them were moving fast enough.

"Well?" he said.

"Do you know where they are?" Anna asked.

"No, but—"

"Do you know if he's taken her to the League?"

"No, but—"

"Do you have a plan?"

Daniel squeezed his hands into fists after being cut off so many times. "No. But we can't just sit around, waiting for the party tomorrow. I have to rescue Piper. I have to stop Mal. Now."

Anna stepped back and opened the door. "And we will. But the barrier is down. There's a line-up of people coming and going. Mal could have Piper anywhere between here and Buttercreek. The League will know we're coming, and I guarantee you'll be one of their targets. What we need first is a battle plan."

❧

The moon peered in through the barn's window, and Piper squirmed against the ropes binding her wrists in front of her. "You are such a dick. You didn't have to shoot my skunk." She glared at Mal, who texted furiously on the other side of the loft. She had to get out of there and tell the people in her life how important they were. And then stop the apocalypse. Or, you know, whichever came first.

"I shot the stinkball with a dart, not a bullet," he muttered.

Piper's insides squeezed. She again pictured the skunk, a limp pile of fur in the middle of the road. Oh, gawd, she had to be okay. What if someone tried driving out of town and drove over her?

"Queenie, are you okay? Can you hear me?"

The skunk had claimed to read her mind before. Hopefully they didn't have to be in close proximity for it to work. But they'd never been very far apart since she'd first showed up.

She had to restrict her squirming on the planked floor so she didn't accidentally squish the grasshopper in her pocket.

Her hand grazed her stomach. There was still the pregnancy-issue to worry about. Mal had jostled her a bit. Surely that wouldn't hurt the baby. Not that she had any clue whether it would or not.

I don't actually want a baby, do I?

No. And yet…the idea had taken root. And the idea of the baby being gone—or maybe never having existed—her belly knotted.

Mal shoved his phone in his pocket with a frown, poured something from the thermos next to him, and rose to cross the loft floor. The shadows lengthened and thickened around him like a cloak. "I told you, I'm sorry about the gun. And the ropes. And the cold floor. But this is a kidnapping, sweetheart, not a date." His voice was rough, the joke flat. He crouched down beside her and checked her wrists for chaffing, his own hands shaking. Seemingly satisfied, he pressed a warm mug into her bound hands. "Noodle soup. Come on, it'll fill you up and keep you warm."

"If you're so concerned about my welfare, why did you kidnap me, you jackass?" Care which had started the moment he'd gently tied on the blindfold and lifted her into the truck. Which continued with the sleeping bag he'd curled around her, while he sat on the cold loft floor.

He returned to his place on the opposite wall, pulled his denim jacket more closely around himself. The shadows clung to him, deepening the hollows beneath his cheekbones as he crossed his legs at the ankles and closed his eyes. "Get some rest."

She sipped at the chicken noodle soup thoughtfully and watched him pretend to sleep. There were a lot of barns around the area that had lofts. Hard to say where she was, especially with the barrier down. Maybe Nia's ghosts had been following Mal still. Maybe her friends were on their way to rescue her.

There was a slick gray rolling suitcase on the other end of the barren loft, the top closed but unzipped.

"You know, as far as bad guy hideouts go, this is

kind of…sad," she goaded him. She wrapped her cold fingers around the soup. Her legs and most of the rest of her was relatively toasty inside the sleeping bag.

Mal pulled the jacket around him more, shadows darkening around him. He kept his eyes closed. "It's not a hideout, so moot point."

So he was living here. Surely there somewhere better for him to stay after he'd left Daniel's cottage.

It still hurt to think about Daniel. But the urgency of the kidnapping brought things into some perspective. Even if he didn't love her enough for them to be together, it was Daniel. He'd still come for her.

"Mal, this is stupid. Even for you."

Her insides gelled and chilled. Maybe this was some new plan to steal her abilities. She struggled to swallow. Would Mal hurt her, like he had at the school? He'd seemed to regret it before, but that was before he'd kidnapped her.

Mal didn't open his eyes, but a frown flickered over his handsome face, his dark hair slicked back. "It probably is stupid. But I haven't been left with much choice."

"You always have a choice." She tried to shuffle closer, almost spilling the soup. "Let me go. Come back with me to the library. You can tell me and the others everything you know about the League. We can stop them, Mal. I really think we can. With your help."

Mal opened his eyes, the irises elongated and deep blue, no pupil visible. Shadows seemed to gather around him. "It's too late. I'm sorry, Piper. I had to choose. And I've made my choice."

"Oh god, Mal. You can't hurt him." She felt ill, the chicken soup sour on her tongue. If they fought, brother against brother, who would survive?

Daniel would never hurt his brother. She set the cup down and pushed it away. "You're brothers. Daniel would do anything to protect you. He loves you."

Mal closed his eyes, wrapped the coat around him again, and turned away. The darkness grew so thick, he all but disappeared, his voice coming out of the black. "I'm doing what I have to do. Daniel's not the only one who'll do whatever's necessary."

CHAPTER 37

"Seriously, Mal. You're a shoo-in for the Worst Kidnapper in History award," Piper griped from behind the blindfold, since sarcasm was a comforting contrast to the scared-stupid queasiness in her belly. Somehow, she was supposed to stop Mal and save Daniel. Plus, there was still that detail of the League of Assholes and their plans.

A full night of restless sleep in the barn loft, and she still didn't have a plan. She rocked forward as the truck stopped and Mal killed the engine.

She had to do whatever was necessary to save Daniel. And the babies. Even if that meant embracing the powers of Pestilence.

The truck door beside her creaked open. "I'll keep your performance review in mind if I ever decide to kidnap someone else," Mal said dryly.

He helped her out of the truck and then lifted her against his chest to carry her across gravel that crunched beneath his boots. Gallant, since she didn't have shoes. It was one more thoughtful gesture on his part that made it harder to be pissed at him. That, and even with the blindfold, she could read the oily black fear and puke-green anxiety pulsing through him.

"Ugh, that reeks."

"What does?" She turned her head, though, of course, the one thing Mal got right about the kidnapping business was the total-blackout blindfold.

His chest muscles flexed against her side. "Someone parked some nasty old Porta-A-Potty sucker truck here. And believe me, we're damn lucky it's not a hot summer day. Seriously, don't you smell it?"

Uh, no. She even sniffed the air. That was…weird. A strange awareness tingled through her though, and a half-formed thought niggled in the back of her mind.

She'd never smelled Queenie, either.

"You know, for a former cop, you sure do break a lot of laws," she said, stalling. "How many years is it for kidnapping someone at gun point?"

He grunted. "Minimum four to seven years." A pause. "But if you break the law in Beckwell, you're not tried by the Canadian courts. You're sent to face a tribunal of gods and other deities. I've never heard of anyone who's come back."

"Wow. I, uh, didn't know that."

"You do now."

"Then why would you risk that? It's not too late. Mal, I know inside you're not actually a bad guy. Let's go to the library—"

"Don't confuse me with my brother," he said, voice hard. "I've made my choice. I told you. Now, let's establish some ground rules. Keep the sarcasm to a minimum. Be polite. Don't get us incinerated. Got that?"

Her heart sped, and any thought of the truck evaporated. "I-incinerated?" she squeaked.

What was her play? Try to make Mal sick? Was it

Queenie outside who'd turned into something else, or did Piper just have a really poor sense of smell?

Her palms dampened. Then again, this was her chance to find out more about the League and their plot. She'd been able to see Louise's disease. Would she be able to see or sense anything else that might help to identify the others?

But what was she supposed to do with the information? Unfortunately, telepathic communication with the other women wasn't one of her abilities.

Frick. Being a hero was complicated.

Mal used a free arm to open another door, then set her down barefoot on a cool, smooth floor.

Piper's nose wrinkled at the smell of dirty gym socks, peanut butter sandwiches, and crayons. Nothing wrong with her sense of smell, despite not being able to smell the weird port-a-john. "Seriously. The *school?* This place is worse than death."

"What did I say about sarcasm?" He gave her shoulder a light pinch and led her down the hall. From the increasing stench of dirty socks, they were headed for the gym.

Sure enough, she recognized the squeak of the gym door when Mal opened it. Crap. Why couldn't Mal have sucked as much with the blindfold as he did with the kidnapping?

The grasshopper wriggled in her pocket, reminding her of the new trick she'd learned yesterday with her abilities and Louise Dole. One that might not require eyes to see. She sucked in an unsteady breath, and let her power pool up from her belly and through her veins, clouds of Pestilence swirling within, potent and rich. Deadly. At the same time, she focused on just the one ability so she didn't make anyone sick. At least, not yet.

"I've done what you asked. Here she is," Mal said loudly, his voice echoing in the gym. He stopped suddenly.

Piper stumbled, her toe catching on the narrow plank boards. Only Mal's quick reflexes prevented her face-plant. She snorted softly. Damn him anyway. Most people wouldn't have noticed, or might have let her fall. Mal was more like Daniel than he let on.

Eyes closed, she took another deep breath, and tried to use her new trick to "see" the room.

Mal appeared first next to her, a red-orange color. He was in perfect health, despite the streaks of black fear and more prevalent puke-green anxiety.

She reached out with her new ability, the sensation like stretching out incredibly long fingers that grew as she needed. Her grasp extended outward while she stood perfectly still.

Two other heartbeats. No. Three? Four? One was very distinct, strong and powerful, that body full of vigor and power, more than she'd ever encountered. They pulsed like a lighthouse with similar wattage. It had to be Loki. Piper cringed away.

The other three heartbeats strangely beat in time with each other. A steady, pulsing rhythm. Nia had theorized the Fates were involved, so was that why they were so attuned with each other?

She focused more deeply. Found a mild hesitation in one of the heartbeats. The body caked in sludgy disease that was concentrated on the head and torso. Louise Dole.

Piper pulled back into herself and swayed, dizzy and disoriented with the sensation. She was back to staring into the black blindfold. Holy crap, that was weird. But she'd seen them. She'd seen the League. All four of them. Five if you counted Mal.

"You okay?" Mal grabbed her arm and kept his voice pitched low. "Cool it. If I'm crappy kidnapper, you're a crappy victim. You're not supposed to get yourself in more trouble. Let me take care of you."

"Are you quite done, Ms. Bane? I didn't want to interrupt your analysis." A rich, cultured male voice said from in front of her, the tone amused. "I doubt I need to introduce us. Your friends have dubbed us the League of Assholes—pardon me. It's the League of Extraordinary Assholes, isn't it?"

Well, crap. Somehow he knew Nia's nickname for them. Was that one Loki?

There was a rapid whispered discussion up front, too far away to make out.

He knew Nia had named the League, which meant he could have heard a lot more.

Gulp. Anything about his being toothless and pathetic?

She might have some power. But she was barely learning to use it. He was Loki. A freakin' *god*. She wasn't even playing the same sport, let alone in the same league. Ugh. Damn Mal for getting them all into this mess.

Loki sighed up front. "I'm fairly certain I know the answer to this, but I've been directed to ask whether you will join our little soirée and help us bring about the end of the world." His voice deepened. "The Four are *much* more powerful than I believe you realize."

She didn't know how to take the emphasis on the much. Crap. *Did* Loki read minds? Because it sounded like he knew she'd been thinking just how powerless she was.

Mal elbowed her again. "Answer before we get zapped into dust."

Ohmigod. Definitely should have researched Loki's powers before deciding to face him down.

"Zapping you into dust is not on this afternoon's schedule," Loki said dryly. "Of course, if you don't join us, my associates prefer we dispose of you so you don't disrupt our plans."

Well, damn. He *could* read minds. Piper cleared her throat, her mouth dry as toast. "Uh, sorry. But I kind of like the world how it is. Un-destroyed and all."

Loki sighed, and it was obvious from his lowered voice he wasn't speaking to her. "You see? I told you. I'm still not convinced we need The Four. Death or War are more than adequate. And I believe I have the means to persuade them."

More rapid and whispered discussion. Louise and the other two. The other voices sounded female, but too muffled to identify.

Mal cleared his throat. "I brought her here, as agreed. Which means now it's time for you to make good your end of the bargain."

"I hardly think you're in a position to negotiate, Malcolm," Loki warned. "When we asked you to bring her to us before, you refused. Said she'd turned us down, as though that were the end of the discussion."

Their *end of the deal*? Sounded like Mal had made some kind of bargain. She'd assumed before he was after Daniel. Now, she wasn't so sure.

Her head ached. None of this looked like it left her in a good place.

Well, if she was probably going to die anyway… "Why do you want to end the world? And why do you want or need my help? Or any of the horsewomen for that matter?" Piper asked. "I mean, sir—Mr. Loki, you're *way* more powerful. I'm guessing it was you who trapped the whole town."

Loki sniffed in disgust. "Hardly. My barrier has protected this town for over a century. But it was sacrificed for the greater good. To make you and the others stronger. It might have taken a B-movie prop that some idiot god imbued with power in the 20s—all on a dare and for a lark, because why else do the gods do anything? But what's done is done. You all have your power. And we have our chess pieces."

"My friends and I, the people of this town. We're not chess pieces."

Mal elbowed her to shut her up.

She elbowed him back.

"I forget, sometimes, how young you all are. Too young to realize we're all chess pieces in someone's game," Loki said quietly. "And you, Piper, are clearly not a student of history. Or you would realize as we do that this Age of Man must come to an inevitable end. As it has before, as it will again. We merely seek to end the suffering swiftly. And while there is still some world and some little life worth salvaging."

Loki's tone darkened. "You and your sisters carry apocalypse and hopelessness to the hearts of men. They won't be able to escape you. An outside attack might rally humans together to survive. But they can't escape The Four. You bring disease into their bodies and minds that medicine can neither prevent nor cure. Famine steals the ability to ever feel satisfied again. Death walks the earth, making the certainty of life versus death a gray line. And War turns all men against each other, brother against brother, husband against wife."

Piper could barely swallow. Huh. Pretty sure Anna didn't have that exact description in her Book of Scary. And it'd never been a part of the family lore. Probably 'cause knowing that kind of crap would drive you whacko. Suicidal or sociopathic. "Oh. I mean, thanks for clearing that up."

"Damn," Mal whispered beneath his breath.

But why was Loki telling her all this?

"Because you need to know it also gives you the ability to change the story," Loki said in her head.

Piper sucked in a breath.

Out loud, Loki chuckled. "You're very welcome.

Think on it, Piper. If you joined with your sisters, The Four could end humanity so swiftly, there would be little time for suffering. Join with us. Help us bring on the next beautiful and glorious Age that will be free of the ugliness and rot diseasing this one."

Thick, smoky panic clogged Piper's brain, the kind that made her want to curl up beneath a table and breathe into a paper bag. End humanity swiftly?

Daniel's face flashed through her mind. Then Queenie. The girls. Her hand brushed her belly.

Nope. No running away. No hiding. Heroes didn't do that.

"And if I don't?" she said timidly.

"Then you, like the rest of humanity, will not live to enjoy the next Age. Start the plague at the bachelorette party this evening that will spread to the rest of the world and hasten the apocalypse. What happens in Beckwell will be reflected through the world." He paused. "Or we will be forced to initiate our own attack. Daniel will be the first to die. You'll live just long enough to witness his death."

Piper's hands shook and she felt dizzy.

"No," Mal rumbled. Piper didn't need to see him to feel a ripple of power next to her. Maybe that muscles expanding, going Fomorian thing Daniel did? "You promised me a way to save Daniel. Hurting him was never part of the plan."

There were annoyed whispers up front again.

Loki sounded tired. "I'm sorry, Malcolm. It appears I've been outvoted. Though, if it's any comfort, there never was a way for us to break the curse between you and your brother. You were deceived, not robbed."

The god's voice held a note of resignation. "Do with your day as you will. Just so long as neither of you leave this room. You will be notified by text when you are permitted to leave this room and move to the bachelorette party at the bar across the street. If you do not show up, Daniel will die. If you try to contact Daniel or your friends—and I *will* know—Daniel will die. If you take too long... Well, I think it's fairly clear what the consequences are, isn't it?" He sighed. "A shame apocalypses are such nasty business, really. But whatever has a beginning must too have an end."

A heavy, quick masculine stride brushed past her. It moved the air and disturbed strands of her hair. More footsteps from multiple people scurried on the other side of the room, before a distant gym door opened, and closed.

"Shit." Mal sounded pissed.

Good for him. She wanted to puke. She'd messed up and not listened to Queenie, and it put Daniel in danger. She'd said she was willing to embrace the powers of Pestilence to save him, but did that mean she was willing to start a world-ending plague?

"Well, I certainly hope you're happy," she snapped at Mal.

He didn't reply.

Piper sighed. "Can you please take my blindfold off?"

Mal removed it.

Piper blinked and took in the dim, empty gymnasium.

If she didn't agree to help the League, what was their next move? Besides killing her. Or Daniel. Gulp. Her hand found her belly.

Mal rubbed an eyebrow and glared at the ground. His movements were jerky, unsettled, his shoulders hunched.

"We have to stop this, Mal," she said.

He scowled, his eyes that strange, elongated Fomorian form again. His skin had a faintly blue-gray hue, like stage makeup that had either been partially wiped off, or only partially applied. He turned to her, speaking through his teeth with forced restraint. "What do you suggest?"

"Well, Daniel is always running around saving everyone else. Especially us."

Mal snorted his agreement. Or at least, that's probably what it meant.

"And neither of us is completely without power. Before you turned into an idiot, you were a cop. That means saving people and stopping bad guys was kind of your specialty, wasn't it?"

He crossed his arms and leaned back. But he wasn't disagreeing.

Piper's mouth tasted of dust and she forged ahead before she thought better of it and listened to the voices in her head that questioned what she knew about saving anyone or playing the hero. "So maybe this time, we figure out how to save him. We figure out how to be the heroes."

CHAPTER 38

Shortly before sunset that night, Daniel stepped into Lou's Place for the bachelorette party and to find Mal. Tonight it was time to stop the League and save Piper. Music pulsed through the floor into his feet, lights flashed, interrupted occasionally by the strobe light that distorted the crowd. His gaze immediately shot toward the battered wood bar, hunting for the man who'd once been his friend. He had no idea what he'd have done if Lou stood there. Demanded the truth? Hell, he'd just have preferred to find out Lou wasn't really Loki. That his friend hadn't betrayed him.

Someone pushed him. "You should be ashamed of yourself."

He turned to find an older woman in her eighties, who gave him another push, her head around chest height.

She looked up. Squinted at him, and blinked. "Doctor. I-I'm sorry."

"Perfectly all right, Mrs. Decklan," he murmured

and continued on his way through the room. Actually, better than all right. Confirmation part of the plan might work: people might confuse him for his brother, thanks to a wardrobe adjustment, and a new cut and style from Nia. He glanced toward the bar again.

No Lou. Instead, it was a pair of young satyrs working the bar. The tables and chairs had all been moved against the wall and stacked, making the place more spacious than he'd have believed. There must have been over a hundred people inside, which meant despite the steady stream of cars coming and going through the barrier, not everyone had decided it'd be a better night to stay home.

"Congrats, Ginny!" was scrawled on bright pink paper hanging over the length of the bar. Someone had taped a second piece of paper near the bottom corner: "Second Time's the Charm."

He snorted. For Ginny's sake, he hoped so. Hopefully, the fiancé in question showed up soon.

Though maybe the sign could also hold true for he and Piper. All day he'd wondered if maybe this time, they had a chance. He was stronger, so maybe Piper couldn't make him ill. Maybe together they could figure out a way to make this work. And she'd seemed almost happy back home. Before he'd screwed everything up.

"Dude, that thing with the barrier was totally sick. Now I don't have to go to Regina to visit mom's cousins," said a kid who jumped in front of Daniel with his two buddies, their faces soft and hairless, bobbing Adam's apples, and probably barely legal for the bar, if that. He proudly pointed out the very large and noticeable ram's horns that protruded from his forehead and would not be easily hidden, his grin toothy. One of the friends was pea green and picked at the leaves sprouting from his elbows. The last kid offered a spike-toothed smile.

"Er, thank you," Daniel said. The kid either didn't know he and Mal were twins. Or didn't care.

Daniel nodded at the boys and continued to work his way into the room.

Space was tight, with a lot of thirsty patrons. It'd been torture not hunting down his brother and Piper over night, but despite his searches, he couldn't sense Mal this time. Loki must have been hiding him. After "Lou" had interrupted the fight at the Cow Palace, he'd given Mal his keys. Maybe Mal had been staying with Loki all this time, wherever that was.

He shook off the thought and instead used his height to stare out above the crowd, searching for any hint of Piper's fair hair or his brother's tall form. No sign of either yet.

There was Anna near the bar, keeping watch, also taller than most of the crowd. There was something shiny and metallic blue in her dark hair that caught the dance lights, and she nodded. She'd keep watch from the rear.

Ginny was also pretty easy to spot, with her height, the red hair, and the silver plastic tiara perched in her hair that glinted in the lights. She'd taken the far right and had a good view of the front and back entrances.

Nia, likely dressed in typical black and incredibly petite, either blended so completely into the crowd that he couldn't spot her, or she'd gone around back to round up more of her ghosts to help keep watch on the exterior of the bar.

Daniel squeezed his hands into fists and sidled past yet another group of chatting people who'd decided to just stop in the middle of the floor.

Maybe it was his Fomorian side talking, but about now he thought it was better to smash heads together and punch his way through a plan until he had Piper back in his arms. It'd been agonizing to listen to Anna's reasoning that the bar was locked down tighter than the Senior Center pharmacy, and unless they knew where Piper and Mal had gone, they had no choice but to wait until the bachelorette party. It gave them longer to come up with a plan, practice, and get themselves in order.

Sure. A good idea. Except for the waiting around while Piper was in danger somewhere. That, he hated.

Yet here they were.

Still no sign of Piper.

The plan was outwardly simple. Find Piper. He'd find Mal. Find Loki, and use him to find the rest of the League and shut them down. He'd go down the middle, dressed similarly to Mal, and maybe it would throw whoever was watching. Anna would come from the rear, Nia kept watch on the entrances and exits with ghost-assistance, and Ginny played lookout.

Daniel squinted as the strobe light turned his way. The barrier had been busy. Some Beckwellians getting out while they could. Still others coming in for the wedding, minus the groom so far. The rest were a combination of the curious, the apocalyptic-hopefuls, and the stupid.

Things could have been different if he and Piper had avoided each other as planned until the wedding was over. If they hadn't had five days together.

Five days to realize how much they still cared about each other.

He rolled his shoulders, the leather jacket foreign and heavy, the ridiculous T-shirt Nia and Ginny had insisted he wear almost as tight as the white one had been. At least the jeans were comfortable, though they belonged to Mal. No saying how long Nia had been stalking his brother, but she'd also stolen a pair of jeans and leather jacket early on with the idea that if Daniel dressed like Mal, it might make things more confusing for their enemies. The blue T-shirt with the red, white, and blue shield on the front was Nia's. She'd grinned like a Cheshire cat when she'd handed it over.

Well, it was comfortable, too. Comfort to go into battle. Strange how comfortable he was with the concept. And if he really needed to be battle-ready, he might quickly grow out of the shirt and jacket. The jeans at least seemed to have been cut big. Must have been too big for Mal normally.

Yet today, *he* was battle-ready. He had no choice but to help fight the League. And to confront his brother. There was a chance neither of them would make it out alive.

Someone grabbed his arm with sharp nails. "You were told—"

He looked down. Found the brown-haired woman, Daphne, from the school, the town council, and yesterday at the office. His eyes narrowed.

She dropped her grip on his arm, widened her eyes. "Whoops. My mistake." She leaned close. "Glad you're here for the show, big guy." Then turned and slid effortlessly into the crowd, her height and coloring making it seem like she'd vanished.

Damn it. She probably was a member of the League, and he'd just let her go. He took a step after her.

And someone else grabbed his bicep.

He turned with a glare. And found himself nose to nose with his brother. He jerked Mal close. "Where's Piper?"

"She's fine." He took in the jeans and jackets, his hint of a smile turning his lips. "Clever. My jacket and jeans, you look enough like me. Though you need a better haircut." He cocked a brow. "Not sure why you're so pissed about Piper. You were going to let her leave Beckwell again."

Fire burned through Daniel, his heartbeat flared. "I was trying to protect her. And I didn't know the barrier was down."

"I think you were too gutless to make her stay. Too afraid to get your heart hurt again," Mal said, voice low.

Daniel reached for Mal again with a snarl.

Mal sidestepped away. "Be careful, and get ready. Things are about to get ugly." He jerked his head toward the right side of the bar. "She's over there. Go grovel. And make sure you take care of her this time. She's one of the good ones." He pulled away from Daniel and seemed to melt into the crowd, despite his height.

Daniel's gaze skimmed the crowd and bumped into Piper's across the room. Right where Mal said she'd be. She still wore the pink dress from the engagement party. Her hair hung loose and wild around her shoulders. And she padded barefoot through the bar.

Beautiful. *Mine*, a quiet voice whispered through his thoughts.

CHAPTER 39

"There he is," Piper whispered when she spotted Daniel across the crowded bar. A text had come into Mal's phone just as promised, and they'd crossed the road from the school to Lou's Place, the feeling of watchful eyes making Piper's skin crawl.

Mal had squeezed her arm, told her to remember the plan, then blended into the crowd. He hadn't seen their faces, either, so while he had guesses who they might be, he'd be League hunting half-blind. He'd also said he'd handle any threat to Daniel, but had refused to offer any details. All he'd asked for was a distraction, and it needed to look like she and Mal were following directions to save Daniel.

Which meant Piper had to make everyone sick.

As though she'd called his name, Daniel looked up, and they made eye contact. He strode toward her.

She squeezed her hands at her sides. The plan she and Mal had come up with seemed really stupid about now. There were so many people here. Not the whole town, but maybe a hundred or so? Celebrating and drinking hard. Clueless.

Piper's chest ached and her hands were icy. All these people had no idea what was about to happen. That even if they thought the danger had passed with the engagement party and the barrier coming down, the real danger had yet to come.

Especially now that she and Mal had arrived.

Mal thought being Fomorian made he and Daniel stronger, that they'd been less affected when she accidentally made everyone ill at the school during decorating. But he hadn't been certain. Could she intentionally make everyone—including Daniel—sick? It was the one thing she'd tried to avoid all her life. The whole reason she'd broken their engagement.

She squeezed little Sandy's sachet in the pocket of her wrinkled dress. Coming home had given her a different perspective of Beckwell. No, these people weren't perfect. Neither was she. But here, she was able to be herself more than anywhere else. This wasn't high school anymore.

The music was loud, pulsing through her feet. Though, with all the tables and stuff moved, the bar was almost as big as the half-gym. Not a lot of room to maneuver. But that meant not a lot of room for the League members to hide either, right? No sign of Loki or Louise, and no one obviously watching her. And surely the League would be watching.

She met Daniel's eyes again as he closed the distance between them, and a swarm of butterflies whirled inside her stomach. The only reason she could see him was that he stood taller than almost everyone else. She glanced to her side. Other than Mal, who even with the same height, seemed to have melted into crowd.

She found Daniel again as he sidled between two gyrating dancers, his hand gentle but firm against one of their backs. He'd hurt her with both his omissions and truths. He hadn't been able to deny that he hated his Fomorian side more than he could love her.

And yet…last night when she'd thought Mal threatened Daniel, she knew she'd jump in front of him to save him. If he was close enough, maybe she could protect him.

She was only a few feet away from Daniel, his gaze intent on her. Piper's insides curled and heated.

Finally, no more khaki. And he'd lost the leather pants, too. Daniel wore designer jeans that looked like they'd been made for him. Beneath the worn brown leather jacket his T-shirt was baby blue, printed with the dark blue, red, and white Captain America shield. But even sexy Chris Evans hadn't made it look as good, not with the way Daniel filled out the shirt as it strained over his muscles. The jacket hugged his broad shoulders and made her want to jump on him. Oh, yum. Her insides melted, and she squeezed her thighs together.

Seriously, get a grip. Which did nothing to reduce the desire and relief spinning through her. They were still alive, and she wanted to celebrate that fact with Daniel ASAP.

Daniel locked eyes with her. He sidestepped and politely smiled but dismissed the people who got in his way, who tried to stop and say hi.

Oh god, she wanted him. Which was completely inappropriate considering the mayhem she had to start soon. All the things that still stood between them. But, oh my, yum.

Someone stepped into her mouthwatering view of Daniel and backed into her.

The man turned toward her, and whatever he'd been about to say vanished as his mouth hung open. He gave his head a shake, eyes still wide. "Pussy Bane," he wheezed.

Piper froze. Her gaze traveled up from the small paunch not hidden by the long-sleeved dress shirt and tie, nor by the charcoal sports jacket.

Stephen Howser's ice blue eyes traveled over her in a way that made her want to block her chest with her hands. As he leered down her dress, all she could think of was how it'd felt to be under him. How powerless and small she'd felt while he pulled the switchblade, cut her bra straps and panties. He stumbled closer.

The familiar panic streamed through her. Her vision narrowed to a fuzzy pinhole focused on his face. Her breath rasped. Her body shook. She couldn't blink, couldn't look away.

The voice in her head demanded she run like she had yesterday, to put as much distance between them as possible.

She hadn't been this close to him since that night in the back of his car. The night he'd tried to rape her. And she'd unleashed disease and swarms of insects on him. She let them fight for her when she couldn't fight back herself. At the time, she hadn't understood how she called the insects in the first place. All she'd wanted to do was get his weight off of her, his hands out from between her thighs. Before that, he'd been the perfect guy. When he'd asked her out, she'd been on cloud twenty-four. She'd wanted to give him her virginity.

He'd wanted to steal it.

"Oh god," he muttered, covering his crotch.

Bile burned Piper's throat. She couldn't find her tongue to make some sharp remark.

She stumbled back a step. Chills chased up and down her arms. This was why she hadn't wanted to come back to Beckwell. To feel that small again. That powerless. What had she been thinking, that she could be a hero? She couldn't stand up for herself, let alone the League. Never mind a literal *god*.

"You and I need to have a discussion about how you treat a lady." Daniel's voice rumbled over Stephen's. He clamped a hand down on Stephen's shoulder.

Stephen jumped and paled beneath his orangey-fake tan.

Piper's vision widened to include the pale faces of the witnesses to the altercation, the revulsion on their face. Not for her. For Stephen.

The nausea faded. Her skin warmed.

She wasn't that teenager she had been. She'd traveled the world. And then she'd come home and truly learned about her abilities. Maybe even started to accept them.

She could make people ill, read and understand illness, control air currents and swarming insects. She was one of The Four.

"He's the one who hurt you, isn't he?" Daniel said softly. "Piper, honey, look at me. It's all right."

She hadn't wanted to tell Daniel the truth that night when he'd picked her up, limping down the side of the road. She'd never even told the girls the whole truth. She'd been terrified of what she'd done to Stephen. Worse, after he announced his conquest all over the school, and with other boys chiming in they'd had sex with her, too, she'd been terrified no one would believe her. Because of what Stephen had done, it'd been months before she'd let Daniel touch her.

"He is," she said, her voice distant even to her own ears.

"I saw her that night," Daniel said to Stephen, his voice a low growl. "Her tears. The cuts and bruises."

"She attacked me! She's the real monster. She made my penis and balls swell up. The doctors couldn't even diagnose what I had, and with the wasp and ant bites? It was months before I could pee properly, let alone get any."

"You're saying the attack was unprovoked?" Daniel's tone held a hard edge of warning.

Stephen shook his head rapidly, and his hands still shielded his crotch. "O-okay. Maybe I-I wasn't as nice as I could have been. And I swear, if I'd known you'd be here, either of you, I wouldn't have come."

There were gasps and a few chuckles from the crowd around them. Electric-green indignation and red anger rolled through the crowd.

Just like that, the monster from her nightmares was transformed into a pathetic worm.

"Daniel, I can handle this," Piper said.

Daniel raised a brow.

She smiled, but it was a little one and it cooled quickly, her adrenalin spiking, her abilities sitting just beneath her skin but waiting for her command as she took a step forward and got in Stephen's face.

"You were a bully and a coward that night. I never had sex with you or anyone else before then. You needed to hurt someone like me to feel big yourself." She leaned closer, her head barely chin level on Stephen.

He lurched back.

"You tried to rape me." There were a few surprised gasps, but Piper ignored them. "And I fought back the only way I could. With my abilities, when my arms weren't strong enough and I was too afraid. I didn't say anything then, but I'm not scared of you anymore. And if you ever *think* of hurting another woman, I will hunt you down and give your testicles so many diseases you'll wish I'd just hacked them off."

Stephen had turned green.

"Do you understand?"

He replied with rapid nodding.

Well, damn. She'd wanted to punch him, but it would make her the bad guy if she did that. "Good.

Then, um, you can go."

Stephen scuttled off like the dung beetle he was.

Daniel slid his fingertips down her forearm, sending chills of a different variety dancing through her. "You are incredible," he whispered into her ear, and she shivered again. "I've missed you. And I am so, so sorry."

She took two steps toward Daniel, and he opened his arms so she could fall against his chest. She put her lips next to his ear to whisper, "The League wants me to start a plague, and if they don't, they're going to kill you. Loki and Louise Dole are members, but I don't know the other two. Mal is on our side now, but I'll be damned if I'll let you sacrifice yourself to save Mal, or vice versa. Because the one thing I know is that I love you, Daniel Quilan. Bronze, purple, Fomorian, human, I love you. All we have to do now is stop the League and save the world. After that, if we stay here, if we go, I don't care. Just so long as I'm with you."

He cupped her face with his hand. "That's what you want? For me to go with you?"

She broke into a watery smile. "Of course, you dummy. I love you!"

He leaned forward, and touched his nose to hers. Would have been better if it'd been his lips, but there'd be time for that. "And I love y—" His voice broke off. He blinked, and his eyes went blank. And then Daniel wrapped his hands around Piper's throat.

CHAPTER 40

Daniel's fingers squeezed off the air in Piper's throat. She gasped for breath. And understanding. He couldn't be strangling her. Her hands grabbed at his wrists. Nails dug into his forearms. The blank expression in his dark eyes didn't change.

He'd been possessed or something. Daniel wouldn't do this.

For a second, it was like she was back in the back seat of Stephen Howser's car, his body on hers, one hand on her throat while the other clawed at her clothes, groped her body.

The pressure on her throat increased. Her lungs burned. She clawed at Daniel's arms. Struggled to kick him. Break free.

Black spots danced in front of her eyes.

This was not Stephen. Daniel wouldn't hurt her. Never.

She pictured him rising above her when he made love to her. His gentle smile. The careful way he always touched her.

His fingers were like steel on her flesh.

She kicked his shins. Tried to dig her fingernails into his skin. Her fingers slipped and slid against his hands and arms. So useless. Too slow.

Just behind Daniel's right shoulder someone moved toward her. Blurry. Rescue?

A man. Green silk button-down. Black jeans. Perfect masculine face. Brown-blond hair.

Loki.

"You have a choice to make, Piper," he said. "I did warn you about alerting Daniel to the plan."

Her fingers fumbled against Daniel's forearms. It was harder to lift her limbs. Her eyesight blotted with blood spots.

Her vision faded entirely, her last view of Daniel, the only man she'd ever loved, staring blindly ahead as he tightened his killing grip around her throat.

The baby.

Her ability roared through her like a typhoid tornado. Rich and yellow-green hued, powerful. It waited at her fingertips for a thought. But didn't lash out without her.

Attack Loki? He'd be immune.

Daniel wasn't.

Strength leached out of her. She used the last thought to drive her ability like a spore-laden spear into Daniel's chest. Light exploded through her mind.

Time paused. A moment. Minutes. There was light, there was dark. And then Piper sucked in air. Once. Twice. Again. Thank God. Her throat burned with fire, but she could breathe. Could fill her lungs again. The grasshopper wriggled in her pocket, sending blurred thoughts and questions Piper didn't understand.

The moments before rushed through her. Piper opened her eyes, sat up, and searched for Daniel.

Hands reached for her, tried to help her. The emotions were fond pink and purple anxiety tinged. People blocked her view as she searched. She waved them away. And then spotted the large pair of black boots. Soles up, body prone on the floor. The rest of the room faded away. All she could see was Daniel on the floor, garishly spotlighted in the darkened room.

She couldn't walk, so she crawled. Dragged her protesting and aching body across the floor to Daniel.

He coughed, black blood splattering his shirt. Blood gushed from his nose, blackish-red in color. He shuddered, face shiny, large blue-black nodules on either side of his neck the size of baseballs.

Piper choked back a sob that made her throat hurt even more. She reached Daniel's side. *Oh God.* I *did this.*

He raised a shaky hand toward her. His fingers were black. He reached toward her, tried again to wrap his hands around her throat. His hands clenched into fists.

Piper covered his black fingers with her own, but had to stay far enough away that he couldn't reach her.

He snarled and broke into a coughing fit that wracked his body and fell back onto his back on the floor.

She tried to tell him it was okay, that she knew he hadn't done it. No words would come out past her swollen throat. Tears pinched her eyes. *I'm so sorry. I never wanted to do this. Not to you,* she wanted to say. All she could do was take his hands, his fingers stiff in hers as she pressed a kiss to the blackened flesh.

She felt more than saw the other horsewomen come to her side. The raging red of Anna's energy. Smoky gray of Nia's Death. Black and pungent for Ginny. They surrounded her. Held her.

Anna put her hand on Piper's shoulder. Ginny knelt at Piper's side. Nia stood behind Piper, her muscles taut, her small body and dark energy anticipating a fight.

One of the party guests took off his sports coat, folded it up, and with the help of someone else, lifted Daniel's shoulders and helped put it under his head. The guests were pink and orange tinted. Orange for determined. One of them met Piper's eyes briefly before he broke the stare, his face coloring. Another used a shawl to cover Daniel's shaking body. He made mumbled, incoherent sounds. He coughed again, and his body shook so hard, Piper lost her grip on his hand.

And then someone else started to cough. And another.

It was spreading. The disease she'd given Daniel was spreading.

She reached for her abilities again. Felt the edges of the disease, looked it in its butt-ugly face. It was so powerful, so angry.

Daniel's eyes closed. He sagged against the floor.

How strong was he? Could he survive this?

"Mal, where are you, dammit. I need your help."

How could she stop this?

❧

Daniel's vision blurred. He grunted, sank further onto the floor.

He lived in a red-hot world of violence and anger, irrational demands to punish Piper for whispered sins. He ground his teeth against the whispers. His head was on fire, his throat felt like he'd swallowed acid, and his brain was like a popsicle in July.

Until it began to fade, as though he sank through the floor of the bar. Away from the heat and pain. Down through a psychedelic elevator shaft that zipped him elsewhere.

Just as quickly as it had begun, Daniel hit the ground hard enough to knock the air out of his lungs. He opened his eyes.

The world had faded to grays. He climbed to his feet. Fog swirled around his ankles and floated through the air. He stood in a flickering, indistinct image of a decomposing room, sometimes a forest, sometimes a field. His hand glowed softly, like he'd been painted with phosphorescence. Bronze and muscular. He moved, and huge leathery wings swished behind him.

Where was she? Those voices told him to hunt her.

"Daniel? Where are you?" Mal's voice.

Daniel swung his head, finally spotted Mal.

His brother stepped out of the misty gray, his skin blue-gray with large curled ram's horns on his forehead, his eyes elongated and blue-black. Massive leathery-black wings unfurled with a snap from his shoulders, and a cloak of shadows coiled and swirled around him with each step.

Daniel growled. The voices whispered all the things his brother had done. Showed him images of Mal and Piper together. The images were gut-twisting, sinew tensing ugly. He curled back his lip, lowered his head, and prepared to charge.

"I should have known this wouldn't be easy," Mal muttered.

Daniel crashed into Mal with a roar and all the force of a semi.

Mal let the momentum carry them upward and back, using his wings like a sail. They hit the ground, and he locked a leg behind Daniel's knee and twisted, bringing Daniel down onto the ground.

Daniel's fist connected with Mal's jaw. Mal grappled to control Daniel's arms.

The older, bronze-colored brother growled and snarled, tried to sink his teeth into Mal's shoulders.

Mal flipped him over, pinned his arms and body to the ground with his knees. "Now," he barked.

Daniel thrashed and growled. Fury and blood thirst

rolled through him. He'd kill Mal for this. He'd get back and finish off Piper, Loki, everyone who had ever wronged him. He grunted and twisted, tried to free his hands, get his brother off him.

Mal was as immovable as a mountain.

A cultured voice, soft and almost lisping, cut through. "Are you sure about this? It isn't reversible, and we don't know the end result—"

"I said now!" Mal shouted, and flattened himself over Daniel's back.

Daniel tried to throw his brother off, to avoid the final blow.

"Will you stay still? I'm trying to prove for once that you don't have to be ashamed of me. You don't always have to protect me," Mal said. He gasped, his grip loosening slightly.

Daniel grunted at the cold pain of the blade sliding through his chest, tried to move. Mal held him still.

"Just a minute now. This is the tricky bit..." the other, unknown male muttered.

The blade seemed to heat, then just as suddenly turn to ice.

"Just a bit more... Done."

Antarctic ice floes slid through Daniel's veins. Slipped over his mind and cooled the rage. He gasped as the blade painlessly slid from him.

And Mal slumped against his back.

Daniel blinked. He'd been in the bar with Piper. She'd told him she loved him. He needed to tell her about Lou being Loki. And the plan with her friends.

Mal.

He pulled himself out from under his brother, heart pounding. Mal's dark wings drooped—wings? Daniel shook it off to figure out later. His twin's body was limp and heavy. Geezus. His throat compressed. Had he killed his brother?

He turned Mal onto his side, and Mal's deep blue eyes, still Fomorian, flickered open. His lips twisted upward. "Did…it work?" he gasped. Only, he wasn't talking to Daniel. But to someone behind him.

Daniel turned and found a slim male figure with a narrow black moustache, dressed in an old-fashioned black tux standing in the swirling gray fog. And holding a very large, very sharp-looking scythe in front of him.

The man lowered the scythe to lean on, pulled a slim cigarette from his pocket, and lit it. "I believe so, yes. Daniel Quilan, are you now in possession of full control of your mind?"

"What?" Daniel turned back to Mal, his brother's eyes growing dim. He gave Mal a shake. "Where are we? What have you done? What worked?"

Mal seemed to gather his energy enough to grab Daniel by both arms, pull himself closer. "What I had to. Now go back. Save Piper. Make babies. *Live.*" He sucked in another rattling breath, closed his eyes, and opened them with great effort. "For both of us," he whispered. His hands slid from Daniel's forearms. He sagged. His breath grew faint, each one smaller and more labored than the last.

Daniel ripped open his brother's shirt. Looked for wounds. Signs of blood. Signs of any injury. "What's happened? Is he bleeding?"

"No, just dying," the slim man said, casually walking over to peer over Daniel's shoulder. "Too late for any of your medicine now, I'm afraid. This is the Gray. The place between living and death. Nasty little place, and not somewhere I care to linger." He turned to stroll away. "Honestly, I'm not sure tea and cookies is truly worth this messiness."

Daniel grabbed the man's arm. The movement knocked the cigarette from the man's hand, and Daniel dragged him close. "Tell me how to save him," he said through gritted teeth.

Black pooled in the man's eyes, covering every hint of white, pupil, or iris. "He made the deal. He gave himself in agreement that I would protect you, do whatever was necessary. In this case, I've found a B-class charm and imbedded it in your brain so no one else may control or alter your mind."

He jerked free of Daniel's grip using greater strength than someone so slim should have possessed, then dusted off the sleeve of his black evening coat. "You were attempting to strangle your ladylove in the mortal world, by the way."

As the man said it, the horrific images slid through Daniel's mind like a dream. His hands around Piper's throat, the awful rage filling him, and the desire to kill. Nausea raced through him, and his gut tightened.

He squeezed his hands into fists, looked back to Mal. Each breath was so shallow now, it barely moved his chest. "I don't know what he offered you, what deal he made. But please. How do I save my brother?"

"I told you. *You* don't," the man said, plucking another cigarette from his case before cupping his hands to light it and take a deep draw. He glanced at Mal. "It's almost done now as it is." His eyes, mostly human-like again, even if he was clearly anything but, turned to Daniel. "Besides, you don't even believe in me."

Daniel's mind clicked frantically over everything he knew about the man. Anything the man had said. *Tea and cookies.* Aunt June. His eyes widened. It hadn't been a delusion. "Mr. Death."

The man's lips twitched, he raised a brow, and took another draw on the cigarette. "She did say you were sharp."

He'd promised Aunt June to protect Mal. Had made that same vow to his brother decades ago. "What did he offer you? I'll give the same in trade."

"You offer too quickly. Especially when you've no idea what you offer." He tapped the ash from his cigarette and considered Daniel. "No, I can't take both of you. The powers that be—" he gestured upward, "—would not be pleased. There would undoubtedly be paperwork. Besides, I thought you loved the woman, the one who will be Pestilence. Rumor is, she's expecting twins."

Daniel's mouth dried. His fingers twitched at his side. Piper. He'd hurt her. Both now and before. And if she really was expecting their child—their children, could he abandon her?

But that same Piper had stood up to Stephen Howser. Had her friends to support and help her. She could survive without him.

He couldn't ask for a better mother for his children.

Mal's breath rattled out. He didn't inhale.

Daniel grabbed his twin's hand. Checked for a pulse. Leaned over him. Checked for breath. Anything.

Mr. Death turned on his heel, leaning his scythe against the shoulder of his evening coat, and began to walk away, into the gray mist.

"A bargain. What can I give you?" Daniel rasped, letting his head drop as he knelt over his brother's body. Cursed to kill each other since birth. He'd killed his own brother, his own blood. *Mal, I'm so sorry.* "Anything."

Quick footsteps made their way back. "Are you sure about that?"

Daniel climbed to his feet, towering over Mr. Death. "Yes."

The other man cocked his head back, and flicked away the stub of his cigarette. "He will be as you are. Will gain identical life force to yours, a mirror-image— less paperwork that way."

"Whatever you want. I agree."

"Good. Because I want your humanity."

Daniel frowned. He must have misunderstood. "What?"

"Your human side. I want that. 'Anything,' you said. Is that not on the table?" Mr. Death glanced at Mal. "And do decide soon. The body's cooling, and there are…complications if life returns too late. Besides, around here, something else might take residence first."

His humanity. He'd never thought of it as a separate thing. Daniel paced, massaging the stiffness in his neck, jaw clenched. It would mean Mal would come back Fomorian. And so would Daniel.

Like Dad.

And Piper was pregnant.

"Tick tock, Mr. Quilan. Time may move more quickly here than in the mortal realm, but I do have appointments to keep."

Did Fomorian have to mean like Dad? Lou hadn't thought so. Though Lou had also been Loki.

Piper didn't think so. She'd even been able to control how Fomorian he became. She'd said she loved him. No matter what color, what species. Just like she'd love their children. Something he really wanted to see.

And he couldn't live with himself if he let his brother die here.

He turned to Mr. Death. "Agreed. Mal lives, and you take my humanity."

CHAPTER 41

"Piper Bane. You've started the job. Now I expect you to finish it," Loki said, his accented voice ringing out across the bar from where he stood next to the front door, the sound audible even over the spreading coughs of everyone else. Many had collapsed.

The disease had leaped from Daniel onto every available host, like a hungry shark smelling blood, though she'd only infected him a few short moments ago.

Piper's shoulders stiffened. Daniel had just mumbled Mal's name, but no sign of Mal anywhere. Damn him anyway. Had he decided to just abandon her for one of his own plans? He was supposed to be saving Daniel.

"Piper, most of them aren't going to be able to survive much longer," Nia said, urgency in her voice. She dropped down beside Daniel. "We'll keep him safe. Do what we can." Unspoken was the promise she could help guide Daniel's spirit to the light if he died.

"He's stronger than the rest. Please, Piper. Make Loki stop this," Ginny said, likewise kneeling beside Daniel.

Piper ran her gaze and senses over Daniel. He was very ill, but as the others suggested, in much better shape than any of the others. His heart rate was still relatively regular, breathing labored, but stable.

It only took a glance around the rest of the room to see greater severity. There was coughing and fever. Boils and rashes. Faces turned almost purple with suffering, gasping for air. Others heaved the contents of their stomachs, in the fetal position on the floor, too weak for anything else. Some leaned against the walls. Some were too still. All were dying.

Wait. Over there, near the corner. "It's Louise Dole! Over near the bar."

"On it," Anna said and started to head in that direction.

"I am waiting. And I am not a patient man," Loki snapped.

Piper moved slowly, deliberately, as she leaned forward and pressed a kiss to Daniel's swollen, dry lips. Then, she slowly climbed to her feet, letting her senses creep out. Her abilities bristled like a yellow-green halo around her. They sent strength to her muscles, speed to her thoughts, healed the pain in her neck from Daniel's fingers. An unnatural breeze shot up around her, tussled her hair. The disease was a yellow-green monster.

Her yellow-green monster.

She squeezed her hands, then reached into her pocket, buying time. Out came the grasshopper, who chirruped and padded around on tickly feet over her palm. Piper met Ginny's widening gaze.

The large green bug hopped out of Piper's hand and settled on the top of Ginny's head, settling down in a bed of shining red curls.

The Famine horsewoman's mouth opened.

Piper touched Ginny's hand. Smiled gently.

Anna said they weren't immortal. But they were strong. And she was supposed to have dominion over disease.

So perhaps that meant if she could create disease, she could also eradicate it.

It's time. I can do this.

Piper rose to her feet, squeezed Sandy's sachet in her pocket for a moment, and took a deep breath. Then she turned to look Loki in the eye.

The slick bastard wore a blue silk shirt and black jeans. His blond hair, those icy blue eyes…he probably thought he was slick shit. He could read minds. He'd controlled Daniel's mind. There was no other reason why Daniel would have hurt her.

"You did this," she said, her voice low and rumbling. She raised her hands, and winds picked up outside. Swirled around the bar, banging the walls, tearing at the shingles.

Loki crossed his arms. "*You* infected him. What will you do now?"

Illness flowed around the room like a living, hungry thing, looking for a host to devour.

"End this," Piper said.

Loki smiled.

She flung back her head, stretched her hands out at her sides, and let ability flow through her. Green and yellow, thick and viscous like oil, striped with black, the ability soaked through her. She let it mingle and coil with her bloodstream, fill her until she could feel the heartbeat of every person in the room, knew the progression of every illness, every infection. She knew the names to call each and every disease of the mind and body, and how to call them down.

Then the scratching started. The flutter of countless

wings. The rumble of thunder outside. Swarms of wasps and bees and armies of ants slid in through the cracks in the ceiling tiles, from under the doors, from through the ventilation system. They converged on Loki. Climbed his legs. Attached themselves to his arms.

A furious engine roared. The image of a white stallion flashed through Piper's mind. Moments later, the front steel door and part of the wall crashed down, and in drove an ugly three-quarter ton, snot-green truck with the words "Suck it" written on the sides of the doors in dark green. "Queenie" was written in gold across the top of the windshield. A large metal holding tank took up half the truck bed, hooked with a yellow hose that oozed out black and green disgustingness.

There was no driver in the driver's seat, but it headed directly for Loki.

He might have had time to turn. Might have been able to see it beyond the swarm of insects. He might have raised his hands the second before the hood of the truck smashed into him. He disappeared beneath the truck that bounced over him. Reversed, then ran over him again.

The hideous truck known as Queenie prickled with pride and glee.

The truck's brakes squealed, and it came to a stop beside Piper. The raspy, half-angry and defiant words from P!nk's "Cuz I Can" blasted out of the radio.

Piper stroked the truck door. Power, green-yellow, similar but not identical to Piper's own, flowed up her arm, strengthened her even more. Queenie's essence, even now that she was a heavy-duty, kind of gross truck, still felt the same. *"You really are a kickass horse."*

The truck flashed a headlight at her, like a wink. Queenie sent the visual and the warmth of a hug toward Piper. The image of the truck shimmered, shrank, and compressed in on itself. Until only a snooty looking little skunk stood in its place and pranced to Piper's side. She excitedly projected the image of a toad, turning into a skunk, turning into a truck, and then reversing the procedure at a dizzying rate.

But where the truck had been? There was no Loki. Only a small red smear on the floor to indicate he had been hurt. He'd vanished.

The coughing in the room had almost stopped. The disease had mutated into a purple-yellow beast, jumping from person to person like an insatiable flee, the whole of the beast masking the room in thick, mucous-like illness.

And at the center of it, Daniel. Still prone on the floor. His heartbeat jumping, he sucked in a breath, shuddered out another.

"Time to fix this, Queenie."

All the doubt that had haunted her for so long screamed in Piper's head at an ear-shattering volume. She closed her eyes and shut them out. Lowered her hand so it brushed against Queenie's bushy tail.

She found the illness. Called to the thing. It turned with suspicion, eyed her warily. "Come on, dominion," she muttered. And called the disease to her. A firm, hard command.

The disease growled and snarled, tried to pull away even as it started to sweep toward her in a wild wind that cleared the air in the bar, sucked the disease from people's lungs.

Piper gasped, the rush of strength she'd so shortly enjoyed dissipated. Whereas disease flowed out of her with ease, reversing the process was like pulling on a mammoth grizzly's leash to rein it in.

She set her feet, fisted her hands, and pulled harder. Pulled it back inside her, made the outward disease rejoin with her ability. It kicked and screamed. Her lungs burned. Her muscles wanted to give out.

Queenie nestled more tightly against Piper's leg, teeth set in a snarl, her essence mingling with Piper's. Power jolted through Piper like an electrical wire as Queenie joined the fight.

She met the disease rampaging through Daniel and the gymnasium head-on as it pulled against its leash, against her command. It turned, like a monstrous beast in the dark, and dove at her, hungry maw open.

Her knees trembled. She couldn't hold out much longer. Her breath came in short bursts, and black spots danced before her eyes. She fell to her knees. Couldn't let go of that leash. She had to stop this. She would stop this.

Even if it killed her.

A hand squeezed her shoulder, and light, pure and clean as sunlight, flowed through the connection. It was raw and wild, like a childhood summer. Like first love. Despite the impossibility of it, she could smell the spiciness of him. Knew without any doubt who wrapped his arms around her, pressed her back against his chest. Daniel.

The red, black, and gray energies of the girls supported her, twined with hers. Kept her upright even as she could barely keep her eyes open, her fingers slipping on the leash, the beast still furious. Though there was less of it. The air in the room grew clearer. Bodies dragged clean air into their lungs.

Her head swam. Her vision blinked in and out. Stopping the disease was a hell of a lot harder than starting it. But it was *her* disease, and *she* would stop it. She wouldn't let the League use it or her to end the world.

Even if she might not be around to enjoy it.

Piper opened her arms, and welcomed the angry beast. Let it slam into her so hard, she fell back against Daniel.

It struggled and tore through her, attacked her lungs, screamed and clawed at her insides. She couldn't seem to inhale.

Piper's body went limp. Her last awareness was of the final energy that poured over the disease within her, stilled its rampage. Something new and fresh and green. Pure and yet unformed. *Twin* energies.

The breath left her lips. The world turned black.

℘

Piper collapsed against him, muscles completely slack, skin blue-tinted. She wasn't breathing.

Daniel turned her over, as gently and as quickly as he could. No pulse. She'd gone into cardiac arrest.

"Someone get the defibrillator from the Senior Center. Fast," he ordered, and someone raced off.

Don't do this, Piper. Don't you dare try to leave me again.

Panic roared through him, but years of medical training controlled his muscles, led him through the steps of CPR. Locate the edge of her rib cage, align his hands on her sternum, and begin compressions. One, two, three, four... Fifteen compressions, then two breaths, his lips over hers.

Her lips felt cold.

He couldn't think of that.

Again. Compressions. Breath. Four cycles of CPR. No pulse. No breathing.

"Come on, Piper. You can do this. Come on, honey."

Again. Another cycle.

Daniel was dimly aware of others around him. People getting up, moving around. He'd recovered faster than others, had been healed almost as soon as Mr. Death had returned he and Mal. He'd tried to help Piper, but it hadn't been enough. She'd destroyed the disease, but it may have destroyed her.

The three other women surrounded Piper, though out of his way. The skunk pressed her head to Piper's hand.

Onto cycle sixteen of CPR. Still no response. "Where's that defibrillator?"

Keep going. He had to keep going. Her heart would start on this cycle. She wouldn't leave him. Couldn't.

"Here it is!" someone shouted, scrambling forward with the small machine.

"Get it ready. Follow the directions. I'll continue with CPR. Come on, honey. Wake up for me. Get that heart beating. You said you loved me. Well, I have a lot of things I need to say to you. And I'm not saying them unless you wake up."

The skunk wriggled under his arm. In his way.

"Get it out of here," he snarled, beginning another cycle of CPR.

Anna reached for the animal.

The skunk opened its mouth and chomped onto Piper's hand.

Piper gasped and opened her eyes. "Ow."

He froze before another compression. Fumbled for her pulse with shaking fingers. Pulse perfectly regular, breathing fine. Color returned to her face.

He checked all her vitals twice more, just to be sure, his hands shaking more with each time.

She turned toward him and grabbed his hand before he could check her pulse again.

"Daniel, you're bronze again. And your eyes are doing that black-brown Fomorian thing. The wings are kind of cool, though."

He could hardly swallow, his tongue thick, throat clogged. All he wanted to do was drag her into his arms, but what if he'd missed something? She'd been in cardiac arrest. She'd single-handedly just ended a plague, for the gods' sake. He tried again to check her vitals.

She swatted him away. "Help me sit up, will you?"

He pulled her up, and wrapped her in his arms, pressed his nose into her hair, that lilac scent curling around him. "Thank the gods."

"Are you okay? The disease… Daniel, I'm so sorry. Loki did something, and I didn't know how else to stop you—"

"It's fine. I'm fine." He pulled back enough to see her face, tucked her hair behind her ears, and searched her neck for bruises. There were none. "I'm so sorry, honey. It's…a long story, but he'll never be able to do that to me again. And I swear to you, I will never, ever hurt you again."

He cleared his throat. "But this…" He leaned back so she could see what he'd become, what he'd traded for Mal's life. "This is what I am. I'm not human. I'm Fomorian. And I still love you with every cell, every molecule of my being. Just like I did ten years ago. Just like I always will. I'll just never be stupid enough to let you get away again."

"And I love you, Daniel Quilan. Unicorn, human, Fomorian, I'll always love you."

He pulled her toward him for a kiss.

But instead found a furry, rather smelly black and white coat. He lurched back, and the damned skunk gave him a spike-toothed grin.

Piper giggled. "Queenie, that's rude." Which was followed by her wrapping her arms around the beast and cuddling it like a teddy bear. "I was so worried about you, too. Yes, I know. I'll listen to you next time. Promise."

Well, it had saved Piper's life, whatever it'd done when it bit her. And now that he was Fomorian, at least it didn't stink as much.

Anna cleared her throat, reminding him it wasn't

only the skunk who was their audience. "I hate to be the bearer of bad news, but Louise Dole wasn't among those who recovered and left the bar."

"My ghosties say two cloaked figures dragged her out during all the chaos," Nia confirmed.

Piper looked up, eyes wide. "Was she healed first?"

Nia consulted with what looked like thin air, then turned back, her dark eyes grim. "It doesn't look like it, no."

"But she couldn't have been that sick, could she?" Ginny said, stroking an enormous green grasshopper who perched on her hand.

Piper met Daniel's eyes, and he hated what he had to tell her. "Even if she's not that sick, it means Loki and the others have what they wanted: their patient zero to start a plague."

CHAPTER 42

"I feel so stupid," Piper said, her shoulders sagging as she and Daniel emerged from the jagged hole in the front of Lou's Place about half an hour later. She stared up at the full harvest moon with a scowl. "I came here determined not to make anyone sick. And despite everything I learned, all my training, the plans… I may have still accidentally caused a pandemic. It's almost like none of it mattered."

People milled around outside the bar, telling their stories, passing out hot chocolate and coffee from thermoses. There was what looked like a bonfire in the middle of the four-way stop, and folks toasted marshmallows and hotdogs.

"They all think it's over. That they're safe. They don't know we don't know where the League is—we don't even know who all of them are." She stared down at her feet.

Daniel stopped and turned her toward him, gently lifted her chin until her gaze met his. His skin was still bronzy, the horns and wings a bit disconcerting, but it was still Daniel's gentle gaze waiting there for her. His love.

"Piper, you almost gave your *life* to save these people, to stop that plague. Together we can figure out a cure for the disease—I might have some medical experience." He raised a teasing brow.

She gave him a flat look.

"But no one even knew Pestilence was capable of destroying and curing disease—but *you* figured it out. You faced down a god, and you lived to tell about it. You are the most incredible woman—" He glanced down at his hands and fluffed his wings, his smile crooked. "Make that the most incredible being I have ever met, and that I will ever meet."

"Guess you're not planning on going out much after this, huh?" she said, face warm.

"If I get to stay curled up somewhere for eternity with you, I can live with that." His expression turned troubled. "But before anything else, I have to tell you…" There was a long pause. "I traded my humanity for Mal's life."

"Um…what?"

He blew out a breath. "It means I'm Fomorian. Not half Fomorian. But—" He held his arms out at his sides, extended his wings. "I'm this. Not bronze all the time, maybe, when I calm down enough. But it will always be there, a part of me waiting to come out. I'm stronger, tougher, and meaner than almost any other creature out there. I'm not quite sure what that will mean in the long run. Who that makes me." His shoulders and wings sagged, and his voice rasped. He raised a fingertip toward her throat, but didn't touch her. "I hurt you. If I ever did something like that again…"

She swallowed hard, and slid her hands up his forearms to his biceps, the muscle bulging, granite beneath silken, warm skin. "You would never hurt me. Loki made you do that."

"My family is cursed. I've grown up knowing only stories of all the uncles I will never know because they killed each other. As Mal and I were destined to do." His voice became hardly audible. "As Mal and I did. I have a darkness inside me that terrifies me. Especially if you ever saw that side."

She cupped his jaw and tried hard not to show how much she wanted to cry for him, telling her all these things he'd never dared tell her before. "I'm hardly perfect. I'm Pestilence. I'm one of the four horsewomen of the apocalypse, and yes, this time maybe we almost won, but I think this war is only just beginning. I make people sick by being around anyone outside the horsemen clans. I used to run away from too many of my problems. And the people I cared about. Oh, and did I mention I have a pet skunk?"

His lips curled into a small smile, but fear still haunted his warm brown gaze. "I didn't break off our engagement ten years ago. I let you do it. I didn't tell you I agreed or that I should have done the same, because I was afraid I wasn't strong enough to have done what you did. I...I witnessed what my father became." He swallowed, his voice barely more than a whisper. "He beat my mother almost senseless one night. I found them like that, him in tears. He didn't even remember why he'd attacked her. Other than because of what he was. What I am."

She chose her words carefully, because saying "he'd probably been drinking" was too facetious. She'd only met the senior Quilan a few times, but even those times he'd been falling-down drunk. Chances were pretty good that'd been the case the night he attacked Daniel's mom. Like the rest of the Quilan relatives, there was a violent side.

One Daniel didn't seem to have. Or if he did, he had it under control.

Piper pressed more closely against him, her breasts brushing his chest and bringing every nerve ending to life with sizzling efficiency. "Daniel, you are not your father. Nor will you ever be. You are you. A healer. A good, kind man who always gives more than he takes. The man I've spent ten years trying to outrun, trying to forget. The only man I'll ever love."

His arms tightened around her. "I love you, Piper Bane. Are you sure? Even with the wings and horns?"

She grinned. "Even if you had a tail." She leaned forward for a kiss.

Daniel pulled back. Took away his warmth and heat.

"Wha—"

And dropped to one knee.

There were gasps and oohs from the gathered crowd.

Piper didn't even see them. All she saw was Daniel pull out his wallet and extract a ring. The Celtic knot with a tiny heart diamond. Her ring. Her hands started to shake.

"I have carried this for ten years. Every night it sits beside my bed while I dreamed of ways I could put it back on your finger, ways we might be together. Because the truth is, I have only been half a man until the day you crashed back into town, Piper Bane. And brought back my heart, my soul, and who I really am."

He reached for her hand and stroked up her fingers even as his gaze never met hers. She felt the steady rhythm of his heart calm, the roar of his blood calm. The bronze color receded from his skin, the horns disappeared beneath his brow bone, even the wings faded until they were a black tattoo, a tip of feathers just barely visible on the side of his strong neck.

"I am far from perfect," he said. "I'm not even human. But I promise to love you every day of our lives, no matter how long or how short those may be. I will fight at your side, or guard your back, whatever and whenever you need." His voice thickened. "And I promise no one will ever love you, or our children, more. Piper, will you marry me?"

He slid the ring onto Piper's finger.

It was still a perfect fit.

Piper dropped down onto her knees and intertwined her fingers with his. "If you allow me to make my promises. I promise to never run from you again, because I know I am stronger with you beside me. I promise to face my fears and any battles that come because I know you're at my side, and there's no battle we can't win together." Moisture burned her eyes. "I promise to love you all this life and be waiting for you in the next." Her hands grazed her flat belly. "And I promise I will love our children so fiercely, so completely, they will never care nor fear what they are, beyond incredibly loved."

Daniel wrapped his arms around her, cocooned her in his warmth, angled his lips, and brought his mouth to hers.

She pressed herself more completely against him. Her breasts compressed against the warm, hard wall of his chest, their hips aligned. A perfect fit. Hard to soft, every angle a complement to every curve. Exactly where she was meant to be.

His tongue swept her mouth, and she dueled with him. Heat rose between them, along with his erection pressing against her, spiraling more heat, more insistent desire along every nerve, demanding release.

They were both breathing hard by the time they pulled back. At first Piper thought it was the rush of her blood in her head. Until she realized it was clapping and cheering of all the Beckwellians who'd witnessed their very public appreciation of each other. She pressed her hot face into his shoulder but couldn't suppress the grin.

"I take it that's a yes," he murmured, the rumble of his voice vibrating through her.

She pulled back to see him, and ridiculously, her eyes burned, the sound of the crowd receding as they moved off to give the couple some privacy. "Of course, it's a yes. It's always been a yes, since that first day you rescued me from the side of the road. I love you."

"And I love you." He slid his hand down her side, pressed it against her belly. "You think we'll be able to handle parenthood?"

Piper cocked her head and pretended to think about it. "Well, whatever they are—boys, girls, Fomorian, or Pestilence—our twins are powerful. It's probably not always going to be easy." She glanced around. "But I think we've found a pretty good place to raise them. To teach them to accept what they are. To love what they are."

"You make it sound easy," he said, rubbing a hand through his dark hair, those beautiful brown eyes full of love for her.

"Oh, come on. If her groom ever shows up, we still have Ginny's wedding to survive tomorrow. A Beckwellian *and* a horsewomen event. Compared to that? Parenthood is probably a piece of cake."

Daniel chuckled, rising to his feet and holding out a hand to pull her up beside him, tugging her body once more flush against his. "You make a good point."

She lifted herself up on tiptoe, and he lowered his head so her lips were even with his. "Besides, we're in it together. We'll be okay."

His lips brushed hers. Once, twice, his touch set fire burning through her all over again. "We don't have to be at the wedding too early, do we?" He settled his mouth over hers for a breath-stealing, firework show of a kiss before he pulled back with a rumble of impatience.

"I'm sure Ginny would understand if we're a teensy late," Piper murmured, already picturing all the things they could do in the hours before the wedding.

Daniel glanced over her shoulder, and growled, perhaps seeing his truck and the rest of the vehicles crowded in by people. Instead, he tugged her toward the road, in the direction of his cottage.

"Come on, I'll race you," he said, and took off running for the house.

Piper laughed, kicked off her shoes, and raced after Daniel.

Who the hell needed normal? She was Pestilence, pregnant, and about to marry the sexiest Fomorian she'd ever met. Finally, she'd found exactly where she belonged.

A SNEAK PEEK AT FAMINE

Ginny Lack's life could be described as a really bad reality show. Tomorrow's episode would be titled *Marrying the Man of Her Parents' Dreams*. Which was much less scary then the second episode: *Don't Screw Up and End the World*. Because right about now, she was balancing on the tightrope of insanity, keeping secrets from everyone, and there'd be no one willing to catch her if she fell.

Which was why, instead of getting a manicure or something relaxing the night before her wedding, she was jogging across the gravel of her parents' backyard as subtly as one could while carrying a two-foot stepladder. The wind rustling through the autumn leaves and plastic wedding bells strewn around the yard in no way concealed the crunch of her footsteps from the back door of her parents' place to the guesthouse.

"I don't see how this is necessary." Roger the grasshopper communicated telepathically from her hair, his back-alley Cockney accent rattled and high-pitched.

The little green guy clutched several strands and held on for dear life because of the wind and said running. It was a bit more of a lope at this point.

Her slipper came loose and skidded off. No time to go back. She might be spotted. That new yard light Dad had installed was far too bright. *Frosting!*

With the amount of sins she'd racked up all her life, swearing had to go, and the pseudo-swear almost had as much bite as the real thing.

But not nearly as much bite as the gravel on her bare feet. Of course, she couldn't have been born into one of the other horsemen clans, one that didn't shrivel every blade of grass within shouting distance. Nope, she'd been born into the Famine clan, who made weed killer look plant-friendly. Because sneaking across a soft and plushy lawn would have been waaayyy too easy.

She grit her teeth and loped on, the light of the guesthouse a warm beacon.

Yes, she was getting hitched tomorrow, and this time she'd get it right. That whole messing-everything-up phase? Done with. Ruining this marriage like she had her first? Not going to happen. Hopefully. As soon as she got through tomorrow's ceremony. And married a man she'd never actually met.

Oh dear lord, she was starting to hyperventilate again. Cue the boob sweat and flashy lights before her eyes. She leaned on the ladder a moment, wheezing.

"You humans. So overdramatic about the whole sex-thing," Roger suggested unhelpfully. Thank gods she was the only one who could hear him. *"Let's go back to your room. Get some rest. See the bloke tomorrow. He's cute? Marry him, shag, it's all good. You have more important things to worry about."* He—or rather it—was another problem. Her symbolic horse, and a sign she was really becoming the horsewoman of Famine.

Long story.

One she couldn't focus on at the moment if she didn't want to be seen.

Back to running across the extra-sharp gravel. And hopefully not passing out. She squeezed the stepladder and considered the bright windows, trying to keep the crunch of her footsteps to a minimum.

Front window would be too obvious. She'd try the kitchen window and see if she could get a peek, just one tiny peek, of her fiancé. Who, like her, had agreed to the marriage sight-unseen. Well, kind of not. There had been photos in the dossier, but because this time she was determined to let her brain be in charge rather than her foolish heart, she'd made Mom throw his out. Besides, originally, they were supposed to have gotten to know each other before the wedding. But then the League of Extraordinary Assholes had tried to take over Beckwell in their bid to end the world and no one had been able to travel in or out of the town limits.

Then a magical plague had crashed her bachelorette party earlier tonight. It'd been a rough week. Suddenly, it was too late to back out of the wedding. The whole romance of the arranged-marriage thing dried up the minute she'd watched her best friend, Piper, and the man of Piper's dreams valiantly battle for their love and lives before pledging their hearts to each other.

While she was off to marry a stranger. *Voluntarily*.

Sometimes, it was like she had the intellect of a half-baked muffin under her unruly red curls.

She slowed her step for a sneakier, quieter walk around the side of the guesthouse. Hopefully the windows weren't open so her fiancé and his family didn't hear her panting from the run.

Oh yeah. That was the trouble with this side of the house. Some idiot had planted rose bushes all along the side, and by some miracle, her family's combined

Famine powers hadn't killed them. Not these vindictive things. They didn't bloom, but boy were they efficient in thorn production.

Ginny swallowed a sigh and opened her step stool. Ugh. There was no way to avoid all those thorns. Still, braving a few scratches was a small price if it meant she caught a glimpse of her husband-to-be. The lights were still on in the guesthouse, so he must still be awake too, right? Yeah, okay, she could have just knocked on the door like a normal person, but the whole magical plague thing had taken all intelligible conversation right out of her. Tonight's plague drama and general grossness had ruined any chance of charm. Better to see if she could sneak a peek.

All the screw-ups in the past twenty-eight years had led to this moment. Modern women in this society didn't let their parents choose their husbands. But the way she seemed to choose men? Better anyone *but* her. She'd tried to choose her new Famine partner so objectively, she'd even refused to look at his photo or name, in case it biased her.

So what was so wrong with him that he'd agreed to an arranged marriage?

The stepladder and the rose bushes did not make friends. In fact, the rose bushes seemed determined to knock over and possibly devour the ladder as she stuffed it in among the plants, the faint light glowing from the kitchen window still well above her head. Five feet eleven came in handy—not that she usually snooped through windows—but this wasn't one of those times.

The ladder roughly propped in the rose bushes, Ginny eyed the dimly lit climb, then sucked in a breath and stepped on. The little ladder wobbled, thorns clawed at her legs, and she grabbed at the guesthouse wall for support. Up one step. Two. *Cupcakes!* Even on the second step, her nose was barely above the bottom of the sill. She'd have to climb to the top step—which wasn't safe on level ground, let alone when the ladder was throwing down with rose bushes.

Soft footsteps crunched in the gravel.

Ginny froze.

The footsteps had been pretty quiet. Inhumanly quiet. She didn't feel her brother's characteristic chill, yet reached out to him telepathically anyway. *"This one's for us, Thomas. Leave me alone right now."* He had a tendency to materialize at the most inconvenient times.

She blew out a shaky breath, braced herself on the house, and climbed up onto the top step. The ladder trembled, but held. Her plan was simple. Woo her husband. Get him to help her learn about her Famine abilities. And absolutely, under no circumstance, get tripped up by love. She needed to gain her abilities and help save the world. Love couldn't get in the way of that.

Now, if she could just get a peek at him...

More soft footsteps, too quiet for a normal person. But not too quiet for a ghost.

"Not now, Thomas," she said telepathically again.

"Um, Ginny..." the grasshopper tried, the politest he'd been yet.

"Please, bug—" she communicated back.

"It's Roger."

Sugarplums. She clenched her teeth. *"Please,* Roger. *Some horse of the apocalypse you are. You have to ride ME. I will deal with the whole becoming Famine weirdness later. Right now, I just want to see what my fiancé looks like and would appreciate one minute without anyone asking any questions, offering any commentary, or otherwise presuming to know what I want. Please."*

The insect settled down in her hair with a "humph."

Ginny peered into the window.

The guesthouse was an open floor plan, with the kitchen connecting into the modest living room. A lamp burned bright in the corner.

An older man stood near the far window wearing a navy sports coat over his broad shoulders and cravat—seriously, a *cravat*? Ginny flushed at the feel of her yoga pants and tank top but focused back on the gentleman. Cravat-man stood near the sideboard pouring amber liquid over ice in three tumblers. His sun-bronzed skin highlighted the silver in his blond hair, and, squinting, she could just make out the faint creases around his eyes. Nope, he was too old. He wasn't her groom. Probably the father.

Everything about him said just how much higher his family stood in the Famine clan ranks, which meant they should have had more paranormal ability, too.

Ginny bit her lip. Surely that meant her fiancé would understand how it felt, growing up with all that pressure like she had. He could be the ally she was hoping for. The one who could help her gain and control the rest of her abilities.

Of course, that didn't mean he'd take it well if she confessed her ability to assess a person's character through touch and the associated taste they evoked. Telling anyone you tasted people and that everyone had a distinct flavor just sounded wrong.

Cravat-man said something as he carried two drinks back toward the sofa and his companion, but Ginny couldn't hear the words. Probably something very cultured in that British voice. He handed one of the drinks to the woman who had her back to Ginny. Also blonde, though more of a washed-out ash blonde. Pearls, dressed in something pale green and probably expensive.

Holy cupcakes. These people could have been James Bond's parents. If, you know, their tragic dying hadn't turned him into, well, James Bond. They were so. Darned. Perfect. Could she possibly become part of this family?

The grasshopper stood and tugged on a few of her hairs, then circled the top of her head. Those little feet in her damp hair gave her the heebie-jeebies. Still, it kept its mouth shut. Which, from the near nonstop litany of observations, droll repartee, and general criticism of everything since the moment she'd met the thing four hours and thirty-three minutes ago, was something of a miracle.

The father took a seat beside the mother.

Then someone interesting stepped into the picture.

Ginny's breath shuddered, and she leaned closer, the ladder creaking.

Almost as tall as the father. Fairly broad across the shoulders. Blond, too, though slightly less tanned—that was good, less chance of skin cancer and all. His jaw was strong, and he said something undoubtedly witty as he crossed the room, his lips twisting slightly in an almost-smile before he reached the sideboard and his drink. He threw that one back, and then the boy poured himself another.

Er, not boy. Man. Quite possibly her fiancé.

Ginny's knees and feet hurt from standing on the narrow stepladder, and she shifted slightly. The ladder rocked. She froze, hands braced against the house again.

The faintest sound of disturbed gravel, so light, maybe she'd imagined it.

She searched the window again for a glimpse at the boy-man.

He wore a crisp pullover suitable for afternoon polo and stood chatting with his parents, one hand casually in his pocket while he held the drink with the other. He could have been at some event with the British Royals.

He was good-looking. Very handsome. Just...quite

possibly not old enough to legally drink in some countries. Twenty maybe. Perhaps a few years older if he was cursed with one of those baby faces.

Ginny made a face, and lifted her foot to ease the ache in her right knee. That made her practically a cradle—

The stepladder lunged left.

The roses and the ground gave out from under her. The ladder toppled.

Oh frost—

She didn't have time to complete the almost-swear. Ginny went down in a messy tangle of yoga pants, stepladder, and rose bush.

Someone caught her before she hit the ground.

She bit back a muffled scream.

Someone muscular and tall, who triggered her ability. The mouth-watering taste of dark chocolate, toasted coconut, and just a kiss of sea salt burst on her tongue.

Someone who most definitely was not her dead brother Thomas.

Someone who had witnessed her spying on her fiancé's family.

Oh, *cupcake*. If that was James Bond's family inside, looked like she'd just found 007 himself.

Right about now, she probably shouldn't wish she'd just been captured by a homicidal stalker. Hoping someone else had planned to spy through the windows and she'd just gotten there first was not what she should have wanted. Then again, she'd never wanted what she was supposed to.

He let her down slowly, and her body slid against his, evidence that he might trigger the taste of chocolate, but he'd clearly never imbibed in his life. Nope, not in the past two lives. He was lean, rock-hard muscle. Broad in the shoulders, narrow in the waist.

Her toes found the gravel. He still stood at least four inches taller than her, maybe more since anything more than two seemed like quite a bit. She patted his forearms in some bemusement, muscle and vein twitching beneath her touch, the skin lightly haired.

She couldn't find her tongue. Really didn't want to look up and find his face. Because if he wasn't as attractive as the rest of him, well, that would be disappointing. If he was as attractive as the rest of him…far better to dissolve in a pile of shame into the gravel.

"You all right?" he said, his voice deep. And, *holy gingerbread*, with an accent like that, it was clear why James Bond always got the girl. Or at least into her panties.

Besides mortified beyond belief? "I'm fine." Because that's the kind of thing you're supposed to say. "Thank you for saving me." Good manners were a must for any daughter of Famine. At least, Mom always said so.

"Do you always peer through windows at night?"

Only when I'm about to marry the stranger inside. "No. This, uh, this is a first for me." She tried to sound breezy and humorous, but instead she probably sounded more like a strangled duck.

"Um hmm." There was an edge of amusement tickling the sound. "Likely to become a habit, do you think?"

"No. I, uh, think I'm cured of it. Especially when rosebushes are involved."

His chuckle wrapped around her in the darkness, caressed her in places it had no business being, and made her want to make him laugh again.

She hadn't felt that way in…she didn't know when. If ever. Even her first husband had never made her ache so much that she wanted an excuse to press herself against him, feel the chuckle ripple through his body and through her.

And so, she made the mistake of looking. At a narrow face with killer bone structure evident even in the dim light, the shadows and his stubble further highlighting the sharpness of his cheekbones, a lean nose, and intense eyes.

Nope. Not a disappointment. That face perfectly matched the super-body. If he hadn't acted or modeled, he'd made one or two women swoon in his lifetime.

"Are you here for the wedding tomorrow?" he asked.

"Uh, yes?" If he wasn't her groom, she had no business thinking about aches and ripples and swooning.

More amusement again. "You're not sure if you're here for the wedding?"

"I'm not quite sure how to answer," she said truthfully. Was he or wasn't he? He could have been part of the groom's family. Ugh. After meeting him, any idea of arranged marriage seemed even worse. Good reason why she couldn't admit she was the bride.

Yet…what if it was him? What if the man-boy in the guesthouse wasn't her fiancé?

Not so great that he'd caught her spying on his family.

There went those tingles chasing up and down her, circling in her middle like sugar-drunk butterflies.

What if she got to marry James Bond?

"Eye on the prize, little sister. We want to ascend as Famine. Not get your heart broken again." Thomas's voice whispered through her, and a chill chased over her skin, startling goose bumps up and down her arms.

Well, *frosting*. Trust her dead twin to kill the mood.

Must Love Famine – Book 2

Available April 2018

ABOUT THE AUTHOR

Shelly Chalmers' first favorite book was Cinderella, so once she could form letters, naturally she turned to romance where everyone "loved" each other—though mostly because she didn't yet know how to spell "like."

A 2014 Golden Heart® finalist, she has a bachelor's degree in English and French, and has never lost her love of romances and their happily-ever-afters. Her stories run the gamut from Regency shifters to space opera. All include a touch of magic, a sense of humor, and a dab of geek. She makes her home in Western Canada, where when not reading, writing, crafting, or hunting unusual treasures and teapots, she wrangles a husband, two daughters, and two nutball cats.

She loves hearing from readers and chatting! You can find her at:

Website: shellychalmers.com
Email: shellychalmers@scchalmers.com
Twitter: @scchalmers
Facebook:
https://www.facebook.com/ShellyC.Chalmers

Check out her Facebook readers group: The Brazen Librarians. Here you can chat books, have some fun, and get the inside scoop on works in progress.

Plus, if you'd like to be the first to know about Shelly's new releases, giveaways, and other goings-on, sign up for her newsletter, and get Five Magical Things in your inbox once a month. shellychalmers.com